GOD AND MONSTERS

R.M. GAYLER

God and Monsters

Copyright ©2025 Randy M. Gayler

This is a work of fiction. Names, characters, places, and incidents are either the product of the author's imagination or are used fictitiously, and any resemblance to actual persons, living or dead, business establishments, events, or locales, is entirely coincidental.

All rights reserved. No part of this book may be used or reproduced in any manner whatsoever without written permission of the author or RAVG Publishing, except in the case of brief quotations embodied in critical articles or reviews.

Contact information: randy.gayler@gmail.com

ISBN-13: 978-0-9864352-8-7 (Paperback Edition)
ISBN-13: 978-0-9864352-9-4 (eBook Edition)

Cover Design by Melissa Williams Design

Interior Typesetting and Layout by Melissa Williams Design

ALSO BY R.M. GAYLER

Download Incomplete

The Neon God

The Neon Prince

GOD

AND

MONSTERS

To B.J.

Mother, mentor, a beautiful soul

CHAPTER ONE

IN HIS WORLD OF GOD and monsters, Patient #173 was certain of only two things; he had been imprisoned by one and forsaken by the other.

A high-pitched scream echoed down the long wide corridor. Maybe the young girl he had seen two cycles ago. He closed his eyes and pictured her strapped to a metal gurney wheeled down the viewing corridor.

She screamed again. He hurried to the thick plexiglass wall and pressed his cheek to see up the long corridor. The hairless, naked girl struggled against the polymer straps as she screamed and spat at the two faceless orderlies. The few times he'd seen her, she tried to acknowledge him with a glance, or a nod, a hint of a sad smile the last time she passed by. Her sky-blue eyes empty, soulless like his own, condemned to the monster's cruel torture.

He stepped back. Except now her swollen breasts and the basketball growing inside her belly said she was pregnant and ready to pop if he had to guess. She was a prisoner no different than him, a human guinea pig for the Techna-Clone Corporation's medical researchers. He pressed his other cheek against the cool plastic and watched her disappear down the corridor lined with sheets of thick plastic identical to his own. Empty cells.

What would the monsters do with the baby? Was the baby destined to live a miserable childhood like his own? Had God forsaken even the youngest children?

He stepped back and checked his ghostly reflection in the clear glass. He pulled his shoulders back to flex his formidable chest then tightened his rippled abdominal muscles, grinning at the definition. Blossoming from a skinny teenager into a muscular young man within the last three months, he was virile, a mutant. And a ticking time bomb.

Sitting at a tiny workstation in the corner, he heaved a sigh. The unborn baby gnawed at him as he continued reading the headlines on a generic info website. The banner said the day was May 1st, the year a blank box and kept secret. People continued to abuse, maim, slaughter, and make war with each other. He tapped the mouse pad to continue to page two. The provincial government of North America was in financial trouble, again, overspending trillions of dollars to combat the ever-changing landscape of a planet decimated by per-petual plagues or deadly new pathogens. The impoverished major-ity continued to struggle for survival and the wealthy continued to receive massive tax breaks for valiant efforts at raping the environ-ment.

"You deserve what you get. You vote the same corrupt idiots into office, and you'll keep getting—"

The scream echoed again, fading into a slow, guttural moan. What kind of imprisonment would the girl endure with the birth of a baby? Would they help her with the pain? Or would the sleezy male orderlies continue playing sick games?

He stood and backhanded the soft screen with his fist. The plastic flip-flopped on its stiff rubber attachment, then righted itself. An impression of his knuckles marred the solid blue screen. He stopped his fist from throwing a second blow. He had endured their torture on countless occasions, even managing to steal one of their electric prods to beat an orderly with a passion that had suspended time. The bloodied faceless monster had been rescued by three cyborgs rushing into his cell, but the orderly's sarcastic words were never heard again.

They did what they wanted. To whomever they wanted, when-ever they wanted. The heartless monsters didn't even have the guts to show their faces.

The girl's scream sounded again, weak, and sad. He cocked his ear at the wail of a newborn baby.

Massaging his hand still stinging from the punch, he traced the sixteen sharp angles of his oblong cell with his eyes, hoping to distract his growing anger. The room was a white oil slick, void of color. The plastic desk and chair matched the walls, the plastic toilet, and plastic bed frame, and linens, and blanket, and the white gloss of the epoxy floor. Everything matched, even his own alabaster skin.

You'll die here. They'll inject you with something you can't fight off. Then you'll die writhing like a white maggot on a white floor.

He stood and paced the length of his cell. Ten paces, thirty feet. Five paces wide. Good-sized room for a convict, except he wasn't a criminal. He pressed his nose against the inch-thick clear Plexiglas separating his cell from the hallway. The workday had begun.

Dreary monsters passed back and forth as they traversed their own private freeway. Mechanized and biological. A dome-shaped bot rolled on rubber white wheels. An oblong shelf on articulated legs stepped meticulously slow to transported small vials of liquid fitted across its spine. Hairless retrievers with dull grey eyes pulled carts of refrigerated vials marked with biohazard symbols. Human cyborgs walked the sidelines watching, spying for their masters, like soldier ants guarding the movement of a colony.

He narrowed his eyes at a female cyborg. A failed military experiment, or a death row convict, or maybe a volunteer, a human implanted with nanobots and supplanted with mechanical limbs, its torso sheathed in white Kevlar grafted onto her skin. Enhancements in return for life. But to live a life of what? Outfitted with pincers for hands, her black eyes served as optical cameras to inform demented human operators. Living, breathing surrogates for the monsters who conceived them.

He sneezed and wiped his nose with the back of his hand. A short man-bot outside the glass partition turned his head and aimed a black-glass eye at him. He feigned a sneeze, then another and another until he was on his knees. He dropped and rolled onto his side, clutching his stomach with pain, studying the cyborgs' reaction. His ruse ruffled neither muscle nor cybernetics. The freeway bustling with machines, and monsters rolled on.

He rolled across the cold floor and pressed his bare buttocks against the cool Plexiglas.

——*Study this.*

The length of time he lay there was lost, minutes—hours, time was irrelevant in his prison. He thought of the girl again. His fingers stroked her chubby cheek, traced the outline of her cute pug nose as he imagined her as a simple farm girl, the youngest of five sisters, but she wanted to be cool, a plain Jane wanting to be desired by the star quarterback, or maybe the class president. Or so he fantasized. Regardless, she would remain the most beautiful creature that existed in his world, on the planet, a fantasy he found each night where they held hands, kissed for hours on the banks of the Big Lost River, made love as the plops of monster fish rising to a summer hatch rippled the water, or maybe they held hands and walked through an endless field of alfalfa warmed by a summer sun he might never feel.

His life was a freak show, he was the freak, and he was undeserving of love.

He rolled over and commenced a set of pushups, exhaling one breath with each lift as he focused his eyes on the blemish of a tiny bubble rising from the floor's flawless coating. He concentrated on subsets of five repetitions each. At eighty-five, he dropped to the floor, winded and spent. He listened to his heavy breathing as his heartbeat drummed into the white floor. His resolve flared.

Their success will bring my freedom.

He sneezed again, but this time he allowed a wad of snot to drop from his nostril and drip over his lips. "I heal myself with everything I say and do. I heal myself with everything I say and do."

The monsters like when I say that.

He stood up and sat down at the table and adjusted the battered computer screen with practiced precision. He tapped the mouse pad to enlarge a tab and picked up reading a Wiki-page chronologically listing the events of an unknown era. Mars Colonization War officially ended, medical advancements to stem plague resistance, years of economic recession, and another pandemic caused by the omicron variant of the Gaian Flu with Arkoff Pharma saving billions of lives. Communication with the Mars Colony lost.

He estimated with fifteen years of non-stop research of anything the data streams and Wiki-pages offered, his knowledge might warrant a Nobel Prize as a historian versed in the musings of count-less authors, intimate strategies of an untold era's politicians, an unrecognized expert in the advances, or impediments, to human evo-lution. Given trousers, a shirt, and a pair of shoes, he was convinced he could teach a postgraduate program at any university.

He tapped on a tab explaining the origins of Gaian Flu II, a virulent strain of a genetically modified virus that had killed more humans than all wars combined. Nothing comparable to that strain had ever manifested itself again, thanks to cutting-edge research by Arkoff Pharma.

Research sure. More like "drain the antibodies from my body and claim victory."

He used his finger to swipe the cursor over to a red X at the top and tapped. The wonderful things he could accomplish with a keyboard to send and receive messages, communicate with scholars, and foremost, maybe discover if others like him existed outside this prison. He sighed. Information was a one-way dead-end, and he was a nobody, a forgotten child who longed to see the simple splendor of the sun.

He slumped onto the bed and curled into a fetal position. He ran his hand over his scalp and scratched a week's worth of stiff stubble. Grooming day tomorrow. The attendants might be especially tired from their escapades with the pregnant girl down the hall. Maybe they would be a little sloppy. Maybe tomorrow was the day. His birthday had to be soon. Maybe his escape could be an early gift.

Hairless from the weekly shaving of his body hair, he usually complied with their grooming regimens, occasionally spicing up the monotony by springing quick as a cat to choke the neck of an orderly or maybe thrust a knee into the groin of a cyborg, anything to break up the endless cycle of boredom.

The latest strategy found his fists pummeling the mirrored face-plate of a monster's contamination suit, and three months ago he almost succeeded, cracking open the welded seals to sneer victory at a horrified face struggling to keep imminent death from entering his airways. The monster's eyes both perplexed and enraged him, a set of frightened eyes, hollow and soulless, seared into his memory. An ugly reminder that a forgotten God wasn't responsible for his lot.

God didn't exist, at least not on the info web, not in the minds of cyborgs, not in the hearts of the orderlies. The mere mention of God, or Buddha, or Muhammad called for banishment, or at best, reprogramming. The forbidden concept continued to seep into Patient #173, calloused by years of hopeless existence yet yearning for the tiniest drop of water.

He clasped his hands to rest his chin on outstretched thumbs, as if praying, and let his thoughts drift to last night's dream. Naked on a rock jetty, surrounded by dense willows lining the banks of an emerald river, he made a cast with a long staff of bamboo that felt right in his hand. A clumsily constructed insect pattern tied to the end of his line landed with a splash into a deep pool teeming with fish.

He groaned and jumped up to pace the room. The river was false, so was the bait, but the dream wasn't—it couldn't be, and never would be. If the dreams stopped . . . then he would find a way to end his own life.

He recited a butchered version of the Lord's Prayer he had deciphered from bits and pieces of relentless searches. He felt stupid with the silly futile words. And yet . . . a glimmer of hope always accompanied the words.

Patient #173 fell asleep. The dream returned, of a man emerging from a brushy riverbank on the opposite side of the wide river. With a neatly trimmed beard, and long, shiny brown hair flowing out beneath a wide-brimmed fedora, a tattered fishing vest loaded with spools of tippet, worn-out fishing flies hooked to a swath of cotton, a pair of scissors dangling from a lanyard around his neck. His father waved for him to cross the turbid river, yelling, "C'mon, son, let's go! We've got work to do!"

He stared aimlessly at fake toast, runny eggs, and real oatmeal while deep in thought. The double yolks born of GMO chickens stared back. A dream of his father had never dominated his thoughts after waking. The images always faded, along with the exhilarating thrill of running and jumping into the emerald water just to meet a stranger.

He sniffed. His nasal passages were clear, and the sneezing had stopped. Whatever virus they had infected him with was eliminated. A double dose of luck. A successful cure, and a grooming day. Both required to be completed within the same day. He heard the fisherman's exuberant voice call out from the eternal distance, as if summoning him off the riverbank of a fading memory.

"Let's go!"

He stood and practiced a slow methodical dance of tai chi, letting his mind drift to calculate the multitude of precise movements that would transpire in a procedure room where he would be strapped down and drained of three pints blood. He pictured the future in his mind, felt the monster's slick polymer suits brush his legs, felt their weak grips on his arms as they shaved his groin. Two orderlies for the draining, three for the grooming, but the transfer point often turned into a disjointed pissing contest for control between the faceless dolts.

And an opportunity.

The dream voice echoed, *"Let's go!"*

He stiffened his posture and faced a blank wall as a door-sized portion depressed four inches and slid open. He offered a slight bow to the crowd beyond the doorway.

Two men in biocontainment suits stepped in. Three cyborgs followed, a defensive front of mechanized linebackers. The group blocked what lay beyond. A lot of muscle for a single man, as if he was a criminal supervillain.

Only two monsters this time. Not the usual three. Somebody called in sick.

"Let's go, kid," the man nearest the door said.

The words reverberated. He lifted a smirk to his face. He stepped forward, his palms held out in surrender. He considered a quick knife punch to the man's throat, then spinning and thrusting an elbow into the other man's temple. Simple. In theory.

With unfettered access to the vast info web, he had memorized multitudes of self-defense disciplines, taekwondo, karate, and Brazilian jujitsu. Each fighting style came naturally, as if he was meant to master each art form, though rare was the opportunity to practice the arts he drilled during the darkest hours of the night.

Each discipline emphasized patience.

The grooming room reeked of synthetic bleach. Sterile sky-blue walls, a sink cultured from synthetic polymers, a black table-top readied with instruments and sundries, and a burnished metal cabinet, each a welcome contrast to his ugly white cell.

He sat and reclined, stretched out his arms and legs. One of the men squirted a cold clear gel on his chest, arms, and legs and spread it with fingers sheathed in thick rubber gloves. The other man followed with a rough scraping of his skin using a straight-edged razor.

"What did you do to the girl?" he asked. "And that baby. Shave her pits like you do mine?"

"Quiet now, boy. Let's get in and get out without any trouble," the monster said.

He clenched his teeth at the dismissal but resisted balling his hands. He curled his toes into clubs. *Patience.*

"What happened to her?" he continued. "Why was she screaming?"

The man's hand stopped as the razor quivered above his thigh. Not a tremble of fear but the vibration was unmistakable, the orderly was chuckling.

Patient #173 tightened his jaw. He ran his fingers over the smooth skin, like anyone might after a fresh shave. His fingers collected the gooey remnants of the clear shaving gel. He began to knead the gunk in each hand, slowly, squishing it in and out of his fingers, gathering more as the blade ran across his skin to bulldoze more gel into nooks and folds. His nervous fingers slowly changing the sticky mass into a loose paste.

Control yourself.

"Getting drained today, slick," the monster said, as if talking to a dog. No response required, just a simple fact. "Makes thirty-three you've fought off. That last one was a nasty little bugger, a rare strain of Ebola. A diamond dictator in New Kenya will pay a fortune for those antibodies. A couple more cures and management will put you out to stud. You know, make more little cure factories for planet Earth." The man laughed.

Thirty-three of the planets most virulent and deadly pathogens had been injected into his body, many leaving him writhing on the cold floor, bleeding from his nostrils or mouth or eyes, close to death. And death would have been preferable. The mechanism supercharging his immune system had remained a mystery.

"Where's the girl? What'd you do to the baby?" he asked again.

"None of your concern," the monster said.

He twitched his leg as the man ran the razor down the side of his calf. The razor bit. A small drop of blood mixed with the slick goo.

"Watch it, douchebag," he said. "You cut me!" He reached down to his injured calf with one hand as his other hand found a large dollop of oil in the crook of his knee.

The orderly squeezed his thigh hard, pinching the nerve with practiced perfection, then continued the grooming. Blood would ooze when the time was right. He continued kneading the slime, spreading it onto his fingers, appreciating freshly shaved areas with his hands to pick up more goo. His hands remained in plain sight, as if empty.

Don't blow your chance now. Patience.

The monster paused the razor and said, "You're not hurt, son. Getting a little sensitive in your old age. Let's get this over with, and you'll get those chocolate bars you like so much."

Chocolate bars. A treat in exchange for three pints of his blood. Woof, woof.

He relaxed and let his fingers massage the oil into a paste too thick to drop from between his fingers. He feigned being cut at the armpit, then the genitals, gathering the clear gel until his hands balled, reinforced with the semi-solid goo.

The monsters finished shaving his scalp and motioned for him to stand. He looked at the door. The blood-draining orderlies would be waiting on the other side.

And maybe freedom.

He craned his neck and stretched, bones and ligaments cracking with anticipation. He had nothing to lose. Failure meant the grooming would continue, the draining would continue, until he was injected with a microscopic bug his immune system was unable to fight off. Punishment for an escape attempt was irrelevant.

The disjointed memory of his dream returned. The fisherman's soothing voice imploring him to cross the river. Except the fisherman was nothing more than an apparel model in a wrinkled sports catalogue given to him by an orderly, to appease him and quiet his constant barrage of questions about a world he had never experienced.

Because you've got work to do, the fisherman repeated in his head.

"C'mon dipshit. We don't have all day." The orderly's impatience, muffled by his face shield, was crystal clear.

"Let's do it," Patient #173 said.

The men prodded him to the door but offered no towels to clean himself. He stretched his shoulders back and eased his eyelids shut then smiled imperceptibly, playing the next moments of his life like a vid.

The monsters' posturing would start immediately. Escorting him to the exit, their complaining, bitching, and whining were predictable, but his docile nature would placate the silly matter. Patient #173 would be greeted by two others dressed identical to the groomers. Except the one on his left would be a bulldog of a woman. Monsters were monsters, equal among the sexes.

Then let the pissing match begin.

The door swooshed open. He darted into the center of the mix.

"What's with you, Rick? Wipe him down like you're supposed to. My sampling room is spotless, and I intend to keep it—" She lowered her head and aimed her mirrored faceplate at the tiny spot of blood clotted on his calf. "Son of a . . ."

He jerked his arms backwards, twisted his forearms, and broke free from the loose grips on his wrists. His hands came up and slapped nasty muck on faceplates, smearing the substance to distort their vision. He kicked out with his right leg, and his foot cracked the short woman square in the helmet. She crumpled.

Her partner came at him as he was halfway into a spinning back-kick, aiming his heel into the crook of the man's neck. The slick goo proved an accelerant for years of imprisoned rage. Anger and adrenaline fueled his fists as he pummeled faceplates. Rigid plastic shattered. Seams tore open. He dug his sticky hands inside helmets and roared at the horrified faces inside. His spittle and breath hit each with a viral deathblow.

He bolted down the hallway, ready for a cyborg to emerge from a room or around a corner. The oily goo hindered his speed on the slick floor. He ignored an opening with its curtain of air whooshing with his passing. He passed an airlock protecting the draining room he had seen countless times. He passed a door leading to an exercise yard he was forbidden to visit. He passed dozens of empty cells identical to his own, then slid to a stop in a triangular alcove offering a choice of three doors. Two wrong choices in two previous years; only one remained. Only one could lead to the building's entrance—and freedom.

The scream of a newborn baby echoing from the maze of corridors turned his head. The imprisoned child screamed for freedom. Shouted for him to return and take it with him. The hiccupping scream pierced his heart, the choice to return twisting its barbs. He would certainly be stung by a cyborg's prod and returned to the cage.

He made a hollow promise to return.

He pushed on the panic bar of a steel door and triggered an alarm. A swoosh of warm air from the negative pressure airflow blew over his head, and he ran. The light of the sun muted by thick gray clouds penetrated tiny clerestory windows and steered him down the hallway and through doors marked as emergency exits until emptying into a reception area with an expansive glass storefront. Bright red biohazard symbols marked the panes of glass on each side of the front door. The identical symbols warned of hazards, coming, or going. The irony made him smirk.

Patient #173 pushed the door open and stepped onto a wet concrete stoop. His chafed skin tingled in the cold moist air. He closed his eyes, and his nostrils flared with a multitude of strange aromas. Damp soil, sage and ozone, a spring rain shower, the aroma of the placenta of his rebirth. The sun hidden behind a layer of potent grey thunderheads warmed his skin.

He ran naked to a gravel parking lot sparse with a smattering of vehicles encircled by a metal alloy fence topped with coils of electrified black razor wire. Beyond the fence, an expanse of sagebrush drifted to the horizon in every direction. He closed his eyes, and walked with his nose tilted up to the sky, the brisk wind offering a cavalcade of earthy aromas. The overload of sensory input sent shudders into his chest.

"Let's go" The premonition of the old fisherman watching him from behind the veil of clouds jarred him from his fugue.

He counted five vehicles parked beneath a light pole swaying in the gusts of warm wind. Acres of parking, more open space than he had seen in his lifetime, and yet the monsters chose to huddle their vehicles like a herd requiring protection. Colored movement fluttered between the cars, a cloud of white smoke whisked away by a stiff gust, the faint chuckle of man, a flash of neon orange.

He jogged across the compacted gravel towards the cars, hunched over, then circled to keep the vehicles as a shield. Sharp pebbles stabbed and punctured the soft soles of his feet, the pain oddly comforting.

Above a vehicle's white rooftop, a whip of orange hair fluttered in the wind. A girl giggled then spoke with a graveled voice aimed at a disheveled, unshaven man. The man took a long suck of an ugly brown cigarette then dropped it to grind into the gravel.

Patient #173 sprang atop the hood of a car, a flash of naked white lightning, and let his heel connect with the man's skull. The man dropped, his face landing next to the smoldering cigarette butt.

His assault played just like he had watched on vids, exactly like the military training videos, identical to the moves he envisioned every night. He reached and squeezed the girl's throat in his hand. Thin wisps of smoke trickled from her nostrils. Her hands grabbed his wrist.

"Which one is yours?" he said.

"Fucking lunatic. What'd you do to Terry—"

He tightened his grip to cut off her voice. "Point to your car, and you'll live another hour."

He scanned the gray sky for surveillance drones then bored his eyes into her brown pupils and eyelids coated with smoky black mascara. Her tear fell onto a cheek caked in thick makeup. *They know not what they do.* The thought of mercy enraged him, and he bit his bottom lip.

The Fisherman's voice.

The girl pointed, and he checked her aim then pulled her by the neck to a rusty white Arkoff Motors mini bug. The cool breeze raised goose bumps on his skin, and splashes of rainwater dripped on his feet as he opened the door. The sensation surprised him. He shoved the girl into the passenger seat, then crowded her over to the driver's seat.

"Drive."

The girl fumbled with her ignition fob and words that tickled a faint, distant memory. He stared out a windshield spotted with dirty rain, towards ugly plumes of dust and smoke billowing from a mountain range of massive spikes of granite, the peaks disappearing into clouds of grey. A hundred miles east stood the White Cloud Mountains, and maybe home.

They know exactly what they do. They treat their world as they do themselves.

His own thoughts betrayed him as the car rolled through a wide-open gate and accelerated down a lonely asphalt road to abandon the last remnants of Patient #173.

"Where . . . Why are . . . Which way?" the girl said.

He closed his eyes and thought of the map he had memorized for this precise moment. The vehicle's synthetic tires sanded the rough asphalt as it accelerated on a rollercoaster highway cut through a vast landscape of blue-tinged sagebrush. He searched his memories about the monsters who had imprisoned him.

Perhaps Mother Earth had tired of the monsters chewing on her skin or polluting her lungs, and as if in response, she produced a cluster of children born near the farming community of Arco, Idaho. Mutants. Born with DNA altered from the radioactivity leaking from twenty-three unprotected nuclear reactors stored like a scrap heap of rusty cars at the bankrupt Idaho National Laboratory. A cluster of children discovered, and kidnapped, and imprisoned by the Arkoff Industries Pharmaceutical Corporation to be concealed in the isolation of central Idaho. A facility once bustling with prisoners, guards, and doctors, and monsters. Until he was the last prisoner remaining.

"Arco. Go to Arco."

The nervous girl pulled and twisted her hair. "No way are you getting through the Moon, freak."

He shook his head as the plume of destruction appeared to grow in volume with each passing minute. "Get me to the Moon and you're done. I'm sure you'll get a reward when you warn them. Enjoy every penny."

She said nothing.

He studied the smooth white skin of his legs, a sharp contrast to the dusty black fabric of the seat. He turned to face the girl. She looked his age, her vibrant orange hair matching the color of an internet cartoon he once fancied as a young child.

"You know what I am, right?" he stated. Of course, she did. They all did. A harbinger of death escaping from prison. "Get me to the Moon, Ariel, and you're free."

She gave him a lingering side-eye.

Ariel knew the Moon, local slang for Craters of the Moon National Monument before the land was sold to Arkoff Industries to be used as a dumping ground for failed medical experiments. The ocean of petrified lava remained a bleak reminder of ancient volcanic eruptions. An area he had visited through web-based drone footage and the vids of concerned healthcare workers. Desolate, mineral deficient, and sitting atop a radioactive river flowing beneath a stagnant bed of lava tubes. The Moon waited as a sunbaked purgatory.

"They'll find you. Even those lepers won't hide you." She eyed his naked white body from toe to head. "Drones are probably following us right now."

"Maybe," he said. But probably not. The gusty winds were too stiff for the winged propellers to overcome. However, a satellite high in orbit might be. "What's your name?"

Her face remained blank. She tightened both hands on the steering wheel as the car weaved around an increasing number of rain-filled potholes blistering the asphalt.

"Your name will be Ariel. You're a mermaid trapped on dry land. You're looking for your prince among the toads. Or was that your Prince Charming I laid out back there?" He chuckled.

The billowing plume of dust, and smoke, and poison mushrooming above the White Cloud Mountains magnified with a twitch of sunlight penetrating the thick cloud cover. He swallowed hard. The bleak desolate landscape was home. If there ever had been a home. His mother was certainly dead. The memory of a baby sister taken from home was faint, yet still echoed. She had been undoubtedly used for experimental medical research like him, and she was most likely dead.

"We've got work to do." He banged his head with his palm, hoping the memory of the dream might flee. And yet the bearded fisherman called him to swim across the rivers cold turquoise water.

He searched the back seat for something to cover himself, then thought better of it. *They did this. Let them see what they have created.*

"Where do you live? Burley, maybe Shoshone?" he said.

She said nothing, and he knew she wouldn't. Her clenched jaw signaled her anger, her twitchy finger tapping the steering wheel signaled fear, and darting, nervous eyes said she wondered if the stories she had heard about him were true.

"Pretty sure I was born in Arco, a house right behind an old gas station with a green dinosaur. I used to sneak out to visit the old, wrinkled lady selling rock candy inside the store. She'd just wave me on in, like I was one of her own kids, let me take two or three pieces. But if she didn't know you, she'd watch you like a hawk, wait for the slightest wrong move, then she'd pounce and scream at you, make you empty your pockets. Poor tourist kids never had a chance." His mouth was suddenly dry, and he winced to swallow the faded memory.

Miles of grass and sagebrush passed in silence as the giant plume of smoke and dust grew in volume. The girl lit a SynCig cigarette with a fob swinging from the rearview mirror. She sneered a challenge at him.

They know exactly what they do, he thought.

Topping a hill at the end of a long blind curve, he spotted a carnival of half-hidden tarpaulins flapping above the crevices of blackish lava rock. Craters of the Moon. The expanse of rusted lava undulated as a rocky ocean of lichen-covered crests and dark, forbidding troughs. A gnarly, solitary ponderosa pine stood sentinel near a large billboard warning travelers of biohazards ahead. The car slowed. He kept his eyes trained on the highway swarming with people dressed like nomads, clothed head to toe in thin charcoal-grey fabric.

"They'll swamp the car," Ariel said. "I'll never get back."

"Pull over," he said.

The car braked to a quick stop on the highway shoulder. He considered the girl, her hair, her harlot's face, her ample cleavage, and her place in his world of God and monsters. A kiss, a spray of spittle from a cough, even a simple sneeze aimed towards her face would free her soul from the torment of a failed world.

Let the monster have her day first.

He opened the door, and the sudden rush of cold air chilled his razor-burned skin. He stepped onto the asphalt and shut the door with deliberate ease. The car whirred forward, made a quick U-turn, then fell silent behind him.

Moonies watched him as he waited, appraising his nakedness, and the oddity of his white, unblemished physique. The Moonies

turned away, to barter trinkets, drink from metal canteens, light cig-arettes, and chase away small children, ignoring him as if he didn't exist. He extracted a wooden surveyor's stake driven into the gravel shoulder; a marker to plot a course of destruction into the White Cloud Mountains. The warped piece of wood was rough, weath-ered. A faded orange ribbon still fluttered on its tip, but the four-foot length felt perfect in his hand.

A sword, much like a toy he had played with as a child.

He veered off the road, down an embankment onto a worn path coursing through shallow ravines of porous volcanic stone littered with food wrappers and hydration packets. The sharp pain in his feet was welcome as he stepped over pointed fragments of lava. He aimed for a rainbow of tents a hundred yards away. He leaped across the deep crevice of a side channel before noticing a small bundle of grey cloth at the craggy dead end. The bundle shifted almost impercepti-bly. He watched a child's small hand emerge stealthily from the cloth. He coughed for his presence to be known.

"Jeez, idiot, can't you see I was hunt—" The Moonie boy jumped up then fell back at the sight of a naked, hairless, white, and curious man.

"Hunting what? Nothing out here but gophers and snakes."

A girl's voice from behind. "And a snake would've been a welcome meal."

The little boy scrabbled up the rocky embankment and disap-peared. A waifish girl stepped forward, her face half-hidden by the grey hood she held tight around her face. A bundle strapped to her chest wiggled then emitted a squeak. "My brother will bring my father and others, so whatever you need to do, you'd better hurry."

He was confused by her words. Do to her, or do for her? She stiff-ened as he stepped close. "Let me see your face," he said.

She pulled her scarf aside enough to reveal half her face, a soiled cheek, full lips, and an emerald eye as beautiful as any he'd seen on the computer screen. She looked no older than twelve or thir-teen. He dropped the wood stake and grabbed her head between his hands, then pulled the cloth down onto her neck to reveal her whole face. Her other eye was a dull grey, lifeless. A chocolate black lesion spread from her cheek down onto her neck. More lesions scabbed beneath the thinning blonde hair on her scalp.

He bared his teeth. Her eyes grew wide, and she recoiled. He held tight.

The monster's handiwork.

He kissed her hard, pushing his tongue and spit into her mouth. *I heal myself with everything I say and do. And I heal you!*

She screamed and he released her. She stumbled backwards, falling back against the sloped ravine. A baby cried out.

"Is that a baby? What's wrong with it? I can—" He stepped back as three robed hulks filled the ravine, each brandishing long metal rods. He sidestepped to avoid a javelin of steel thrown by the figure on his right. His adrenaline surged, fueling ancient instincts to resurface. He pressed his lips tight then attacked.

The men were clumsy in their robes, predictable with their weapons, and easily put on their backs by precise kicks and strikes. He stood over the man who had hurled the spear, then raised one of the metal rods to impale him through the heart.

"No!" the girl shouted. "They were just protecting me."

He looked at the girl and let his muscles relax. Her grey eye had already begun to soften its sick color. "The baby. I want to see it."

She stepped back. Her eyes darted from the men, up to the road then back at him.

"Please. I've never seen one. I won't hurt it," he said.

She clutched the child close to her chest. Her face softened as she looked at its face. Her grey eye twitched. Confusion and maternal instincts kept her eyes narrowed as she carefully pulled open the swath. She smiled and cooed. Love radiated from her soul as she gazed down at her baby, then she offered him the baby.

His skin chilled, and he swallowed dry grit. He dropped the metal rod.

Flawless soft skin, eyes the color of a Pacific coral reef, innocent and beautiful. Bright inquisitive eyes stared at him. Virgin eyes that weakened his legs. His taut, powerful arms relaxed, and yet felt supreme with the bundle he held. A tear fell down his cheek as his heart filled with love and purpose. He wanted to hold the child tight to his own breast. He wanted to flee with the child. He wished for all the goodness remaining in his world of monsters to find the child.

And he knew what must be done.

He offered the baby back to the girl. "What plagued you is gone.

Give the . . . Give my gift to the child on his first birthday. My kiss will keep you safe from any virus or disease, and the child, and you can offer it to whoever else you think might deserve it."

The defeated men had risen but kept their distance. The girl's father picked up his steel spear, a four-foot piece of sharpened concrete rebar, one end wrapped in frayed duct tape.

The father approached with a limp and pushed his face close. He smelled of campfire, his face mottled with melanomas, his teeth coated with fresh blood. "What do you want? Your kind always brings trouble."

"My kind?" he said.

"From the labs. Others like you, making their way to that cesspool some still call Arco. Praise the Lord you'll be the last."

The girl moved close to her father, comforting the baby with a smile. Rays of sunlight broke free of the blanket of dark clouds blowing east. Shadows appeared, only to disappear as the chaotic sky streamed like a turbid river. The blossoming brightness illuminated the ugly basalt with the shadow of a woman burdened with child, and of a man aided with a staff suited for a shepherd.

Ancient memories stirred.

His will to be done. His direction to be obeyed. The Fisherman.

Patient #173 realized he was the last of the Arco children to escape, but maybe the first to know the truth. He would find the other children like him. The sun broke free of the carpet of clouds to warm his face and shoulders, and he bathed in the brilliance of pure light unfelt for years, eons, an eternity. He lifted his face to revel in the radiance. He opened his eyes and stared into the burning wisdom of the sun. His retina's burned then healed, burned, and healed again. Behind the brilliant orb a shimmering world opened, a dimension without description, of everlasting joy, of immense beauty, of timeless peace. Home.

He sensed the Fisherman smile down as the blinding truth soaked into his skin and soul.

"They'll be coming after you. They always do," the man said.

Patient #173 blinked, and his ancient consciousness ceded to the present. He searched the blue sky before his eyes settled on a formation of silver jets trailing behind the mask of clouds. The arrowhead formation of machinery spewed exhaust to expand into contrails in the cold thin air. He squinted at the pointed configuration as the warmth continued to reinvigorate his bleached skin.

"It's an angel," the boy said as he peeked out from behind his father's robe.

He looked at the boy then lifted his chin to signal the boy to continue.

"They always fly over us, but . . ." The hint of enthusiasm in the boy's voice faded. "One's gonna land here and help us. It's gonna. Someday."

"Fighter jets escorting some CEO, more like it," the father said, regret shuttering his eyes before squeezing the boy's shoulder. "Maybe an angel, but he's gotta help others first."

From the mouths of innocents are whispered truths.

His rebirth finished, his mission clear, his path was his own. He would start his search for the others in Arco. And maybe his own destiny.

"They'll be coming after you, boy," the man warned.

Patient #173 moved to within handshake range and motioned to the father for his metal staff. Their eyes locked. The man's eyes narrowed, then he consented as if struck by sudden recognition. He handed over the metal rod.

Patient #173 turned to walk up the ravine. The pain of sharp rock stabbing his soft soles disappeared. He thought of the family behind him, and how shadows had revealed their humanity with utter simplicity. He knew his own Father. Why he was reborn.

He had battled Satan in Heaven, defeated him and his minions, and threw him down onto this land, only for the beast to rise again. He was born for battle, born to defend His realm, born to wield a sword for the Fisherman.

"Son?" the man yelled from behind him.

He turned. The girl pushed back her hood. Her diseased eye sparkled. Flecks of gold penetrated the grey cataract. The chocolate facial melanoma had paled.

"These children want to know your name, for the campfire stories," the man said.

He lifted the steel rod, a comfortable but useless sword compared to the weapon carried inside his blood and spittle. He pointed the staff at the sun, then at a young boy staring at him with wide, expectant eyes. He considered many answers. In the land of the Fisherman, he would carry only one name.

"My Father calls me Michael."

CHAPTER TWO

CYDNEY ARKOFF THOUGHT HER TRUE reality could not exist in the dark pine forest, the passing of time barely discernable within the thin blades of morning sunshine piercing the medieval forest canopy. A light mist hugged the ground. Cyd sidestepped around a hefty boulder to leap effortlessly over a jumble of deadfall, then sprinted across a spongey bog of grass. She could run through the forest forever. If only it could remain so.

The narrow trail was fraught with puddles of muddy rainwater, gnarly elbows of aspen roots sought to falter her gait, and sharp stones sought to pierce a warning into her Kevlar running shoes. She danced around a root ball then increased her brisk pace.

Exhaling two quick puffs of air, Cyd's breathing synchronized with her footfalls. Her lungs began to burn as each suck of air followed an identical rhythm. Living life as if tomorrow would never come, her lungs screamed at having to pay the price today. Her breathing rhythm unraveled again, and she removed the bud from her ear. The "Won't Get Fooled Again" mash was righteous, but the old-school lyrics shrieking for teenage revolution rattled her breathing. She twitched her jaw to shuffle through the selection of ancient rock, old rap songs, and the latest techno beats.

She sucked in two quick breaths as the trail narrowed into a series of sharp switchbacks ascending a steep hill dense with ponderosa and

Doug fir. She pushed the earbud back in her ear and jutted her lower jaw, a motion no more than a blink. The music streamed "Where the Streets Have No Name." A perfect song. Great buildup, easy rhythm. She changed her mind and muted the music by another twitch of her jaw. The climb ahead demanded concentration and precise breathing.

Her thoughts returned to her father, his domineering, his manipulation of her young life, and his insistence on isolating her in the remoteness of Yellowstone Park. She was sixteen after all, old enough to have her own apartment, and friends, find a job, and start a life free from a controlling parent.

She'd march into his office and demand a hover-drone to fly her to New York. No. Down to Los Angeles, the City of Angels and Hollywood. She would get a job as an actress, land a few commercials to start, for sure, everybody had to pay their dues first. She was pretty enough, and the Arkoff name would get her foot in more than a few doors. An email sent by Daddy Dearest and doors would blow wide open. He had to agree, or she would threaten to expose her secret, threaten to embarrass him publicly by revealing an Arkoff family flaw. The great Samuel Arkoff would not stand for his daughter's face being plastered over the gossip websites.

She slowed her pace at a crack of deadfall on her right. Shadows danced behind the mist and sunlight. She pulled the speaker from inside her ear and let it hang from a fiber-optic wire jacked into a port beneath her earlobe. She reduced her speed to a hurried hike and watched shadows darken then disappear as if something ran alongside her. Her speed slowed again, but her heart continued to race.

Wolves! Stalking me like a helpless deer!

Jurgens lied when he reported no wolves, cougars, or grizzlies for at least a four-mile radius from home. The Lodge's facility manager had completely lost it. He was so screwed up by his own drug concoctions that his brain finally shriveled into mushy oatmeal. 3Bz—his precise combination of heroin, cocaine, and fentanyl—was heavenly but deadly. Maybe Daddy and Jurgens conspired to have her killed in a tragic wildlife accident, put an end to her constant haranguing.

Cyd stopped and pulled the bud from her other ear. The forest came alive. A rodent shuffled in the underbrush. The shadow of a bird flittered through the dark canopy. A twig snapped.

She turned in a slow circle, lost in the domain of nature's noisemakers. Music always accompanied her while running, and now she regretted her ignorance. She swallowed a lump of dry gritty spit and began a deliberate walk backwards. A root grabbed her heel, and she stumbled. She caught her balance but felt helpless, exposed like a wounded deer. Her eyes darted from the dense brush to the dirt trail then over to an outcropping of ugly black basalt. Lava rock.

After all, you do live atop the world's biggest volcano, Jurgens liked to remind her.

Cyd crouched, her eyes searching the dense underbrush for a reason the forest had suddenly gone silent. Something was watching her. She could feel the eyes on her. A grizzly, or maybe a black bear. She eased her footfalls backwards, stepping blindly. Waiting for the rush of fur and teeth to spring out of the brush. Her mouth hung open as her breathing stopped. She turned her neck to stare at a big Canadian grey wolf watching her with curious, intelligent eyes. The beast rose up on all four legs, tufts of a thick winter coat still hanging on its muscled flanks.

A lone wolf meant a pack was near, at least ten or more, probably searching for breakfast. Cyd took a step backwards, mesmerized by the hefty size of the beast. Easily two-hundred pounds and a face that radiated intelligence as it beheld easy prey half its size.

Her heartrate refused to slow. Turn and burn. She wouldn't make it a quarter mile before being overtaken, and the Lodge was at least two miles away. She took two steps backwards, her feet cooled as muddy water wicked through the fabric of her dirty sneakers. Shadows of the wolf pack danced eagerly behind the mist, growing nearer with each heartbeat. The pack was surrounding her, prepping for the kill.

Cyd continued her retreat, her eyes searched for a branch or even a rock to use as a weapon. Her Camelback half-filled with water felt like dead weight. She pulled her sweat-soaked ball cap off her head and flipped it onto a pine sapling in a feeble attempt to distract the wolf. She continued backwards as the wolf simply watched.

The wolf shifted it gaze to something up the path, squinted, and lowered its profile into a predatory crouch. Cyd resisted an over-whelming urge to turn and sprint, and instead, followed the wolf's gaze.

Hiding in a stand of deadfall ten yards to her left, a set of glossy eyes stared at her. The cougar's tan hide melded flawlessly into the jumble of wood and spring brush. A flick of its tail confirmed its presence.

Jesus!

A bolt of pain stabbed into her head. The mythical name banned and prohibited, it proved to be an inexplicable source for excruciating pain. Cyd winced as her fingers rubbed her temple, her eyes torn between apex predators. She continued her retreat with deliberate steps.

Three thousand square miles of Yellowstone Park all to herself, and both wolves and cougars invade her private backyard on the same morning. Impossible. Maybe Jurgens forgot to mention a grizzly would soon join the impromptu party. Jurgens would pay for this. If the hungriest of the beasts didn't rip her apart first.

A hundred yards. Get a hundred yards away from the wolf, and she might turn her back and run like Hell. The wolf pack might toy with her before making the kill. The mountain lion would overtake her like a newborn fawn. The apex predators stared at each other then each turned to watch Cyd.

Her right foot slipped on a patch of mud, and she fell backwards into thick pine straw. Her blind hand crawled through the cold mush and sticky pine needles, searching for a weapon.

The cougar yawned then looked up into the canopy as if distracted by a bird. Cyd eased into a crouch and crawled backwards down the dirt path. Weak. Helpless. Like a common prey animal asking to be devoured.

She jumped to her feet. She was dead meat either way. Cougar or wolf. She turned and sprinted back down the path, leaping over a small rock escarpment she had negotiated with care just minutes ago. Cyd ran and refused to look back. Down the muddy trail, over roots and patches of dirty snow, stepping on her own footprints, sure each step was her last before a heavy weight would bludgeon her backside, sharp claws tearing into her skin, sharp teeth clamping down on her neck with the animal's putrid breath sucking the life from her.

And she would die. Death never frightened her, but where would her soul go? And death was always far away, years, a whole lifetime. Jurgens, or Zac the zookeeper, and even her own father talked as if death was a simple refuse pit. People live, people die, then back to the worms. She had never felt that way. People were like snowflakes, unique, each born with a purpose. Some saved lives, others provided care for the sick, some helped to save the dwindling populations of wild animals remaining on the planet.

A whirring buzz filled the air as Cyd sprinted, her lungs burned like never before, and she cursed her own use of the 3Bz. She promised herself to never touch the powder again. She promised to take the exam and achieve her high school diploma. She promised to learn the Arkoff family business like her father demanded.

Adrenaline and fear fueled a speed she hadn't known existed. A buzzing filled her ears, like an angry hornet's nest. She cursed a set of steep switchbacks that either predator might leap over in two bounds. She heard her name shouted from above as if God called down to her. Her feet pounded on a wooden footbridge spanning a swollen creek the maintenance crew had built just for her three summers ago. She ran as her name repeated above her like an annoying mantra.

"Cyd. Cyd." The volume intensified. "Cyd, hold up!"

A shoe-sized dragonfly dropped into her view and hovered, keeping pace with her sprint. The four wings flittered independently to create the insect-like buzzing, two bulbs of mini-cameras as eyes and the drone's simulation of a dragonfly was complete. Digitized by the tiny speaker system, Cyd recognized Jurgens' voice.

She slowed, then stopped to grab her knees and gasp for air. A second drone dropped from the treetops to hover near her face.

"The predators won't hurt you. They're ours. They're surrogates."

Cyd curled her hands into balls as she swallowed dry spit. Beads of sweat ran down her temples and tickled her hot cheeks. She avoided an urge to grab the flittering carrier drone by its six articulated legs and slam it into the ground.

"What the hell are you talking about?" Cyd snapped.

She suspected Jurgens conducted secret experiments behind the locked doors of the zoo's medical clinic. The wolf and the cougar did look familiar. She had fed them often, along with a multitude of foxes, bison, coyotes, porcupines, squirrels, and rodents indigenous to the park. She should have known. Daddy didn't pay to safeguard the animals from a nonexistent sense of altruism. He was ruthless. He was arrogant. He kept them alive to make money, maybe worse.

"Ours?" Cyd said. "From the cages?"

"It's Rondo and Sheba. You didn't recognize them?"

Recognize them? Like she would stop in the middle of the dark forest and check for identifying marks on big predators eyeing her like she was Cyd McCheeseburger. She spat again. Jurgens was an idiot, a certifiable, drug-addicted computer geek with the common sense of an emotionally stunted sociopath.

"Cyd, do you recognize them now?" Jurgens said. The little drone buzzed closer to her face. "The collar on Sheba, we put it on her yesterday afternoon. You and Zac helped me."

Cyd groaned and shook her head. Yesterday afternoon was a blur, as most afternoons tended to be. The 3Bz warped her memory but required her muscles and body to stay busy. The old days had called it tweaking, or speed-balling, until the 3Bz portion of synthetic blue tar heroin kicked in. Then the euphoria was pure, heavenly bliss.

"I remember," she lied. "You didn't say they were gonna roam the park."

The lime-green drone lifted high above her head and turned in circles. Jurgens was a child. The drone dropped. "Do you want me to connect your earbuds to Sheba? Just to feel comfortable."

The animals hadn't moved. Sheba crouched, motionless in the deadfall, an apex mannequin. Rondo stood supreme, though his attention often shifted to the faint yelps of a wolf pack roaming the surrounding hills.

The workout squashed, she walked down a wooden board-walk past the quiet remains of a dormant Old Faithful. 3Bz waited at home, hidden beneath her mattress, waited with mind-numbing ecstasy. And so did Jurgens. And Daddy Dearest. And an interminable loneliness all the drugs or zoo animals couldn't cure.

She started down the trail. "What about the wolf pack? You control them too?" Her question reeked of sarcasm. She sighed.

The drone paused its flight. "You're right, Cyd. Perhaps you should keep running."

———

SAMUEL ARKOFF JUMPED UP FROM the padded office recliner. "I could have killed her, Jurgens. Pounced on her and ripped her throat out." He pulled a thin monofilament fiber-optic thread free from the tiny port implanted below his left ear and dropped it on his desk. "That was fucking incredible. The power, the strength living inside that wolf. Hell, the olfactory senses alone would knock an ordinary man senseless. Get the bugs out of the auditory link. I want the full experience next time."

Jurgens swiped at a holographic touch screen in front of his face, throwing data files into folders. "Yes, sir. I wasn't sure you could handle the sensory overload. And manage the experience effectively. Obviously, I was wrong. Again."

"Again." Samuel studied his own holographic screens, knifing his hand through holo-mail images, deleting links to incoming files, continuing the business interrupted by Jurgens arrival and the remarkable offer to link consciousness with Rondo. Jurgens was a crackhead, a junkie twisted into a 3Bz pretzel, and the most brilliant consciousness theorist money could buy. "Get me into that beast again, Jurgens. I belong with him."

"I need to assimilate the data from this experience first. Then I can make the auditory link. And we need to capture him again. I had hoped you might have piggybacked him back into the enclosure."

A holographic screen popped up into Samuel's peripheral vision. The stern face of a young Air Force captain filled a backdrop of blue sky. He nodded for the officer to proceed with his official report. Time conveyed in O-hundreds and locations described in longitude and latitudes in relation to the equator, the current parameters of a killer satellite orbiting three hundred forty-five miles above the planet. Military people were blunt killers, born without finesse or panache, idiots destined to only take orders. But necessary.

"Thank you so much, Captain. Keep up the stellar work." He blinked twice and closed the screen. "Michael has finally joined the game."

"We could monitor him with the new dragonflies." Jurgens said. "The AI guidance system I programmed would make it virtually—"

Samuel gripped Jurgens by the neck. "High tech and computers. Nothing we do will prevent the finality." He squeezed hard. "All that happens now has been written. All that happens after the inevitable confrontation will be dictated by me."

Jurgens winced but rubbed his hands together as if he was a child

anticipating a reward. A skinny rail of bones, thin hair, thin skin, a body emaciated by years of drug use, but Jurgens maintained a mind equal to an alien superintelligence. "Would you like to ride in Sheba next time, sir?"

"Absolutely. But then I'm not really a cat person. Let's get into Rondo again first. I think we might have finally done it."

Cydney banged her way into his office. Her grey sweatshirt dark with sweat, her cheeks red and her brow furrowed. Her short platinum-blond hair matted with sweat. The epitome of an Amazon warrior—tall, athletic, a teenager blossoming into a woman, just as Samuel had predicted. She was chained tight to his world. Only her death would set her free, but she too served a purpose, as all God's creatures did.

Samuel offered his open hands in an apology. "Cyd, I watched you for miles. Protecting you. Jurgens finally found the right frequency to connect us, but then—"

"Fuck you! Fuck Jurgens. I've had enough of this place. I'm leaving."

She sounded serious this time, and she might succeed, if he allowed it. But Michael was now roaming the world, and he would soon ignite a chain of events unparalleled in history. The Archangel was young, and strong, and the exact opposite of Samuel's body that had aged for millennia and saddled with an extra seventy pounds on a shrinking six-foot frame.

He clicked his tongue. God had put his knight in play, onto a chessboard Samuel controlled. Cyd would remain his ace in the hole. Now that Jurgens had refined the technology to transcend species then, well, a different game had evolved. A game Samuel would master and one that would leave God dumbfounded.

"What is it, dear? What have I done to upset you so much? I thought you liked your animals, your friends, the forest," Samuel said. He stepped closer to embrace her.

"I want to roam, Daddy, but not here. I want to go to Hollywood, make movies, and live a normal life."

Samuel slumped his shoulders in defeat then dropped into his desk chair, tilted his head, and shook it in a slow deliberate manner. Nicotine. He would add a measure of nicotine to the 3Bz.

"Let's go get some breakfast, and you tell me your plan, dear. I understand Hollywood is swimming with sharks and leaches. And you'd be isolated there too—no friends, no family," Samuel said. Her eyes wavered, darted to Jurgens,' then back down to meet his. "Do you think you're prepared for that?"

He had her. Guile ruled the world, and he oozed enough to warp every civilization that had existed on the planet. Romans were overcome by their own arrogance. The French doomed by pride. The brutal Nazi regime had been mere months from becoming his crowning achievement.

Cydney's hands trembled. She avoided his eyes. He looked at her neck and the artery pulsing with hot angry blood. He imagined Rondo sinking its large canines into that soft flesh. He would smell the copper, taste the blood, lick her soul into his mouth.

She wasn't going anywhere.

"Jurgens, get the hover jet prepped and fueled, and ready to rumble. If our Cydney wants to be a Hollywood movie star, then who are we to delay destiny?" Samuel said.

Maybe one of the zookeepers could spell out the 3Bz unavailability situation in Los Angeles for his adopted daughter. The bison keeper, Zac, would be perfect for the job. After all, she was sixteen now, as she liked to remind him every fucking morning.

"Cyd, let's have some breakfast. What movie roles are you considering? I have some nice connections that may open a few doors for you."

"I was thinking of getting on a sit-com first . . . then . . . I'm not sure . . . but an apartment in Malibu would only cost a few hundred thousand a week, so . . ."

"Exactly what I was thinking. Let's get you into the mix with the Malibu crowd," Samuel said.

In a few hours, the only thing his little angel would desire was another hit of 3Bz. He held Cydney's hand as he led her out of the office, down the musty hallway alive with the scent of pine, and into the great room of Old Faithful Inn in Yellowstone Park. Two female servants no older than Cydney scurried out of the kitchen entrance to begin their duties. Samuel's stomach growled, perhaps a side effect of his joining consciousness with Rondo. The air in the three-story room was heavenly with bacon, eggs, and cranberry scones. Everything lightly spiced with the acrid stench of 3Bz fermenting down in the basement.

Samuel pulled out a chair for Cydney to sit. He looked up at lacquered wood beams and weathered antlers dressing the high-pitched ceiling. An expansive and labor-intensive work of art like a quaint American knockoff of the Sistine Chapel.

He swallowed hard.

Michael was free.

Let the game begin.

CHAPTER THREE

LIKE CHEERLESS, SMOKY WRAITHS, HUNDREDS of Moonies lingered on the pitted and buckled two-lane highway, their dirty grey robes flapping in the brisk wind. With mottled faces absconded behind veils of fabric, the Moonies parted before Michael as he followed the broken white line of the highway. Soiled and diseased faces, sad eyes, suspicious eyes, hopelessness, and despair clothed in black melanomas. Modern-day lepers. Men, and women, and children discarded into the trash heap of the Moon's bleak wasteland.

He pointed the sharp rebar at any brave soul who looked at him as if he were an easy target. Michael kept a brisk pace as the warm wind wicked sweat off his heated white skin. He scanned the sky for drones then stopped at a gang of seven spreading wide across the asphalt, blocking his path. Their intentions were unmistakable. Moonies crowding the road shuffled and scurried into crevices of basalt to watch the confrontation.

He balanced the heavy steel rod in his hand, rolled the warm metal in his fingers, then spun it like a flag twirler's baton. The weight of the weapon felt natural, a comfortable extension of his own arm, similar to a lance he once wielded for the Fisherman in another life.

A battle. An ancient pleasure. One to enjoy. Michael grinned.

His stride was confident as he closed on the men, cloaked monsters, like the faceless orderlies, bullies inflicting their will on the weak and infirmed. A lifetime suffered as a caged animal, he would unleash an unbridled fury on the thugs, and yet his heart rate remained steady. Just a game. A training session to regain skills unpracticed for eons. Everything in this land of monsters happened for a reason, and the seven men blocking his course had their own.

You toy with me, Father, or does this serve a greater purpose?

He bared his teeth as his adrenaline surged. The steel rod paused its spin.

The hulks freed cancerous arms from their robes and spread out to surround him. Weathered skin, melanomas, wrinkled bearded faces aged a hundredfold by a bright sun piercing an atmosphere depleted of a protective ozone layer. Aluminum baseball bats, sharpened metal bars, and a machete glistened in liver-spotted hands.

The Moonie audience hiding in the cracks crawled over rough stone to watch. Some barked for battle, others shouted encouragement to members of the gang. The noise was benign, a fuel for human gladiators in ancient times.

Michael twirled the bar above his head and marched forward, switching the spinning weapon from one hand to the other. "Come to rob a naked beggar? Leave now or feel my wrath,"

But his impotent words carried no weight.

The big man in the center slapped an aluminum bat on his hand. "Wrath? We want nothing but the reward on your head, white boy."

Violent gusts of wind ripped blue and green tarpaulins free to flap noisily with each burst. Michael felt his nakedness, and he crouched like a predator, tapping the end of the metal rod on the asphalt as he eased forward with deliberate steps, envisioning every move each man would make. And his own countermoves. Three, seven, a thousand humans could not best him in mortal combat. Did the Fisherman intend to give him confidence? Or temper his cockiness?

Two men flanked him on each side. Still others scrambled up the rock embankments to enclose him from behind. Michael straightened his spine and inhaled a deep breath. He stared into the sun. Its fury burned his retinas, but he held its gaze. He soaked up a warmth denied for fifteen years, bathed in the forgotten light and infinite power of His creation.

He leapt like a big cat, his legs complimenting the metal rod as it lashed out in wide violent arcs, inertia and kinetic energy removing knees and shattering ankles. Defeated men writhed and moaned. Squirming on the asphalt, the leader screamed for help, waving his machete over his prone body to ward off Michael.

He knocked the big blade away and straddled the man's chest to point his bloody rod at his heart. Screams for vengeance lifted the rod higher. A violent gust of wind shot sand into his eyes. Michael blinked away the grit and found himself surrounded by hundreds of cloaked faces hoping to witness a death. The bright sunlight illuminated the flecks of black dotting the grey cataracts in the man's eyes.

The eyes of a monster, evil incarnate, without redemption, a charade. A demon of Satan.

With a primordial scream and downward thrust of his arms, Michael felt his redemption as he twisted the staff, grinding the metal deeper into the monster's heart. The final beat of the dying man's muscle vibrated up the iron bar and commanded another guttural scream from Michael.

His eyes narrowed as he bared his teeth. His arms trembled with bloodlust. The remaining gang members scrambled towards crevices, each eyeing him with utter horror. The circus of tarps flapping violently in the wind quelled. Silence followed the vanquishing of men and monsters. He stood and pulled the spear free from the chest with a sickening, sucking finality.

He bared his teeth and challenged all with his metal rod dripping with blood. Moonies scurried for escape, quick as the wind, down into crevices or caves covered with tarps. Michael struggled to ignore the lepers as he continued his journey down a road pitted with potholes, darkened with rain, and extending unobstructed towards the White Clouds. Blood dripped from the spear, dotting the white stripe centered on the highway.

Plumes of smoke and soot laid flat by the stiff wind, the granite spires of the White Cloud Mountains stood supreme, majestic, and snowcapped. The reasons for his years of imprisonment, his immunities to disease and pestilence, and ultimately his escape plagued Michael's thoughts as he concentrated on each footfall. The father of the young girl mentioned others like him, from the labs. They would need to be found, set free. Long ago, the Fisherman had commanded him to assemble armies, mold the soldiers into an unstoppable force, then lead them into the final battle. Was that his purpose?

The final battle.

The tarp-covered caves of Moonies disappeared as the road descended through long stretches of sagebrush and cheat grass, winding like a serpent through grassy foothills. The desolate road allowed Michael to consider his past and predict his future. His thoughts drifted back to the girl strapped to the gurney, and her baby. His promise to return was nothing more than a silly fantasy.

But the Moonie girl? Something equally strange about her, something special, and yet he couldn't say what that might be. Perhaps because she was the only girl he had spoken to, probably because she was the first girl he'd ever kissed.

Gusts of wind herded stampedes of tumbleweed to roll across his bare legs, biting him like prickly dogs of war. He stopped and gazed towards his destination. Arco. A once-forgotten town wallowing in a narrow valley separating two magnificent mountain ranges. A flash of grey bucking the wind made him turn his head. A small grey robe kept low and hidden behind thick patches of tall sagebrush. The young boy who had been hunting snakes shadowed him, and was doing an excellent job considering the bright sunlight.

Michael continued his trek, wary of the tiny wraith. The road dipped over a gulley before ascending a steep hill. He jumped off the highway into the dry gulley and hid in a wide-mouthed drainage pipe spanning the road. He backed up, deeper into the ribbed pipe, the darkness hiding his presence. Cold metal soothed his skin.

The boy played a game of hide-and-seek, but now he was it, whether he knew it or not. Like any good player, Michael waited with the patience of a stalking lion. After long minutes, he wondered who was the genius, or the fool? He used his toe to sift through a pile of trash scrambled into the bleached river rock. Translucent plastic bags, an Arkoff Happy Meal carton, a paper cup emblazoned with the Arkoff Industries logo, and a jumble of thin plastic food wrappers he didn't recognize.

The wait gnawed at him. The boy was getting the better of him in the silly game. Michael dropped to his knees and crawled toward the pipe entrance. He froze as a thin shadow split the light. He tensed, crouched, and readied for an attack.

The tiny shadow disappeared, replaced by a looming dark, with a familiar baritone voice. "The boy won't bother you. Even those from the labs need to eat, and you'll have to be starving."

The girl's father, and maybe the boys? A man he almost murdered out of simple curiosity. Why would this man want to help him?

"What did you give Myra? To heal her skin and eye? The boy swears you're the angel he's prayed for." His voice quivered with uncertainty. "Tell Seth it's not true, and we'll be gone."

The man held the high ground. Michael winced at his miscalculation. An arrow or spear could easily find him if he crawled out. Michael growled and rolled out into the gravel gulley, into the bright sunlight with sharp stones and sticks biting his skin. He stood with his arm poised to throw the steel rod like a javelin. His target waited up on the road, behind a short metal guardrail, his robes noisy in the busy wind.

Cradling the baby, Myra sidestepped to shield her father. The small wraith followed suit.

His arm trembled with a murderous mind of its own. Michael resisted letting the rod fly.

The boy tossed a bundle down to Michael's feet. "Better get with it. Even angels can't be walking around naked. You gotta grow wings. Angels always have wings."

The boy's eyes were wide and white, and he beamed with hopeful anticipation, his chatter cut short by his father squeezing his shoulder. Michael narrowed his eyes on the girl and the pair of tiny fingers wiggling free of the grey cloth strapped to her chest. He lowered the spear and picked up the bundle, a grey robe of the Moonies.

He glanced toward his destination. Arco remained a full day's hike, and he was hungry, and tired, and alone. The Fisherman would provide what he needed. But Michael knew to recognize His gifts if presented.

"I gave . . . Myra got what God intended for her to have. What she does with it is up to her." He shifted his eyes to Myra. "The baby doesn't need—"

The small family scattered. Myra started down the steep embankment as the boy and his father jumped into the gulley. Michael raised the rebar. His aim wavered. The father rushed to help the girl down the loose gravel, Myra whimpering as she struggled to carry the

child. The boy grabbed Michael's hand and pulled him towards the drainage pipe.

"Drones. Get that robe on, and get in the hole," Seth said as he searched the sky.

Michael looked into the sky but saw nothing but isolated puffs of white drifting east on the wind.

"Thought you were supposed to be like . . . smart and stuff," Seth said. He pushed Michael backwards and into the pipe.

Myra and her father ducked into the pipe. With deceptive strength, Seth dragged Michael deeper into the pipe.

Spreading his arms to block the pipe entrance with his robe, Seth grinned "Lots of drones, a whole freaking formation. Man, oh man, they must want you bad. You gotta be an angel."

"Boy, put that robe on for the sake of common decency," the father said.

So many words spoken to him, and all at once, and all as if what he did or said mattered now, as if he now truly existed in this strange new world. Michael untied the bundle and put on the grey robe. The coarse cloth rough on his virgin skin, foreign, but oddly welcoming, he stroked the baggy sleeves with his soft fingers, pausing at Myra smiling at him with an impish grin.

The baby was quiet. He sensed something wrong. He picked up the rod and balanced the length in his hand. Myra began to rock the baby gently. Noisy slurping coming from the swath made her smile.

"He's hungry today, eating like he wants to catch up to Seth," Myra said, fussing with the ratty shroud about the baby's face.

"Maybe the father is Sammy. He was a gluttonous punk of a man," her father said.

Myra's smile faded, and she returned her attention to the baby.

"Maybe the baby is why my Father released me," Michael said. "Maybe the baby has a destiny. Maybe the baby's father —"

"Incoming!" Seth said. He stepped deeper into the pipe.

The buzzing whirr of a swarm of tiny propellers hovered outside the pipe. Followed by the deafening roar of a jet engine flying low overhead. Michael covered his ears. The father moved deeper and crowded Michael, his breath reeking of decay. The pungent aroma of unwashed bodies wrinkled Michael's nose yet provided a pleasant change from the sterility of shaving gel and antiseptic alcohol.

The father leaned closer. Melanomas and cancers riddled his scalp and neck. He whispered, "What do you know of a baby? You're a freak, an outcast. God has no room in heaven for the likes of you. You got the best of me back there, but there's no room for your fancy fighting in here."

"Pappa, he's an angel. You can't talk like—" Seth said.

"Shush, boy. This is between *men*."

In a single motion, Michael flipped the rod around and jabbed the sharp point up into the man's chin. The man's eyes grew wide, and he pressed his back against the pipe.

"Seth has a point, and now you do too," Michael said. He increased his upward pressure and let a spot of blood slide down the metal. "Myra's child needs a grandfather, a protector, a provider. If you wish to resign the position, I can provide the means."

The man sneered then slid away.

Michael inspected his filthy garb, like nothing he had ever seen on the data streams. People, even the poorest of the poor always wore pants, shirts, and hats. Robes were for priests or monks, or false shaman.

"Why do the Moonies wear these?" Michael said.

"Geez, for an angel, you are dense. Maybe you landed on your head?" Seth said and picked up a handful of pebbles to toss each at a crumbled metal can. "Keeps the bad sun from roasting us but . . . doesn't always work. Myra still got that major noma on her face. But hey, look at her eye. You did that, didn't you?"

He narrowed his eyes towards the stain of a cancer marring half her face. The immunity he transferred worked magic on the cancer, and her right eye had lightened, gaining color to match the other eye. Cures for the monster's diseases pulsed through his veins. Why? And he wasn't sure why he'd kissed Myra. She was barely a teenager. Maybe anger and rage at the monsters forced his lips onto hers. Maybe revenge for their injustice. He didn't want anything in return, but he certainly hadn't expected them to follow him either.

Prodded by her father, Myra shimmied deeper to the center of the metal to become a huddled shadow.

Seth sat opposite Michael and sighed. He flipped his hood back and shook out a mop of long auburn hair, an eight-year-old face bronzed by sun exposure but devoid of cancer or blemishes, his hazel eyes sparkling with flecks of gold. With small, crooked teeth, he beamed a disarming smile. "Got me a real angel. Who we gonna help first? Maybe just grow your wings out and knock those drones to the ground. I won't tell anybody."

The whirr of drones departed, but a high-pitched beeping announced their proximity.

Michael offered a half-smile. "How come you know so much about angels? And drones?"

"Myra reads the Bible a lot, and she's teaching me . . . but a lot of the words are hard." Seth paused. "I like to play around with the drones. It's like having my own air force except I don't get to control them." He threw a stone out into the sunlight and stared. "Well, not like I wanna."

The boy spoke with confident wisdom. Michael tapped Seth's foot with his staff. "You believe in the Bible? In angels? In Heaven? I read all religion had been banned?"

Seth dropped his jaw with an incredulous look. "Heck, yeah. I mean, we got parts from the aid workers, but we weren't supposed to tell. Like, don't you? You're here, aren't you."

Michael shuttered his eyes. Indeed, he was here, in a foreign land, with strange devices. And hiding from faceless enemies. A chess piece in a game he did not quite understand. "The drones? How do I—we get out?"

Seth rubbed his palms together. "That's the thing. You play with their brains if they got one. Rattle them by turning to stone. Then they lose interest. Or confuse them with something they don't recognize."

Michael stared intently at Seth and absorbed his insightful dissection of drone behavior. A kindred soul. Too young to realize danger and too smart to avoid it. Fatigue gripped him, from his escape, from his battles, and the daunting realization the Fisherman had set in motion a plan that would require all his strength.

His eyes grew weary as he listened to Seth ramble of teachings of the Bible, incongruities, sexism, the unfairness bludgeoning his small world dominated by poverty and survival. The cool shade, and a pleasant voice lulled Michael to sleep.

Michael stood naked on a rocky riverbank, a long fly rod dangling in his right hand. Dense summertime willows crowded the shoreline, branches and leaves crawling with swarms of yellow mayflies amassing for a mating ritual. Across the emerald pool of the river waited a familiar rock jetty, the same one he had jumped from before, or had he? His short silver hair dripped water down his face. Inspecting the rod, he followed a neon pink line strung through the eyelets and a fuzzy insect imitation hooked onto another eyelet near the reel.

"You can't catch fish if you don't have your fly in the water." The thick brush parted, scattering the mass of bugs to take flight and swirl into the air. The Fisherman stepped through the willows as easily as a ghost.

Michael tried to speak, but his vocal cords choked. His Father stood a mere two feet away. His wide brimmed hat rode on His back. Flecks of silver hair peppered His beard, His nose sunburned and scarred.

The Fisherman smiled beneath eternal blue eyes and caused Michael to swallow a lump. "You don't have a back-cast with these willows, so you're gonna have to roll cast."

"I . . . I don't know how . . . I can't . . ."

"I'll teach you." The Fisherman smiled again with a tanned face weathered by patience, wrinkled with infinite understanding. "That was a tough swim, getting across that current, was it tricky?"

"It was freaking cold." Michael shivered then chuckled. Memories returned, not of prisons, or cyborgs, or humiliation, but of the Fisherman. The Father radiated beauty and allowed Michael to free himself from a prison of his own making. Emotions hidden from the world, and himself. The Fisherman understood his torment, understood his soul.

"Unhook that hopper from your rod, and let's warm up."

Michael's fingers fumbled nervously to release the fly from the eyelet. The Fisherman instructed Michael, guided him at each step, and soon he smiled as he flipped the fly twenty feet across the pool of water. He watched the bug swirl, then disappear in the white foam floating on the eddy. The Fisherman instructed him about the fluorescent fly line, how it reacted to the various speeds of different currents. Michael reveled in the scent of the Fisherman's breath, a spring rain, the smoke of a distant campfire, fresh-cut grass. He concentrated but bungled the maddening speeds of different forces working the lengthy pink fly line into a snarl.

"Lesson is over today," the Fisherman said. "Remember. Read the water before you cast. A river has a lot to teach if we listen. Practice a bit more, and we'll talk later."

As if a warm blanket was pulled off his chest, he awoke to stare at dusty cobwebs hanging from galvanized metal ribs. His tight chest trembled.

He squeezed the metal rod and checked a black and moonless night outside. Michael bolted for the opening, stumbled over loose robes, stepped on sharp stones, and pointed sticks of driftwood. The dream had filled him with an intense purpose.

A windless night. The drones would not take long to track him down. Michael crossed the road and ran up the gulley. The high-frequency beeps of drones surrounded him. He hopped on one leg for one minute, counting in five second intervals, then fell into a motionless fetal position for thirty seconds, then crawled hand over foot for ninety seconds, then jumped up to run again, sideways. His moves erratic and rarely duplicated, he headed into the foothills of the Boulder Mountains, the little sisters of the White Cloud Mountains.

Seth spawned the idea, and the Fisherman's instructions about river currents solidified his plan. He would play games with the drones, confuse their pattern recognition software, confuse the tracking system with erratic behavior, until default programming might require one to fly into range of his skill. Michael spun and hopped up the gully, eyeing the night sky for a red light, listening for the whirr of propellers.

Bouncing like Tigger, he aimed higher up the streambed until he found a drone hovering above a flat plateau. He lifted his staff, juggled the weight until the staff felt balanced, then threw the rod like a javelin. The duct-taped end wobbled as it flew past the drone. Moving on four downdrafts of air, the drone inched closer to inspect the strange anomaly.

A stone smacked the fuselage, and the drone spun in a clockwise wobble, then gyrated wildly as another rock found one of its four propellers. Michael turned to see the boy ten yards behind. A sneaky one indeed.

"Knock it down!" Seth yelled. He threw stones as fast as he could stoop down to reload. "Fire. Fire. Fire. C'mon, you stupid angel, fire away."

And mimicking Seth's arm motion, Michael learned a new talent. His fourth rock found the target, and the drone's heart. The four-propeller device dropped like a stone. Seth whooped a victorious scream as he ran to catch Michael.

"Perfect shot, angel. We smited it, huh?" Seth said.

"Right out of the sky." Michael ruffled Seth's hair and turned to retrieve the rebar. "I need to get to Arco."

"Wait. They'll regroup to fill in the blank spot and come at us again. Maybe we should keep doing your goofy dance until the sun comes up? One comes around now, I bet you'll take it out with one throw. Freaking angels. Man, oh man. I finally got me an angel." Seth said and began prancing through the dense sagebrush.

Three additional drones downed, the tiresome, goofy pace slowed as he rounded an escarpment of basalt jutting from of a steep hill covered in dense sagebrush. Cold wind bit his face. Sulfur and bitterness accompanied a stiff breeze rolling down from the Lost River Mountain Range. The gusty wind was sure to keep the drones grounded.

The bright lights of Arco illuminating his goal, Michael jogged along a narrow game trail of steep switchbacks, the steel bar in tune with the swing of his arm. He thought of his dream. Water currents were no different than the wind in the air, and he increased his speed.

The black of night surrounded Arco, held back by bright floodlights bordering a T-shaped intersection of two state highways. Golden arches shone high into the night. Bright neon billboards blinded Michael's search for the green dinosaur of a gas station blurred in a distant memory. The wind whistled in his ears. Women chortled at men begging for companionship. Fun and laughter, and drunkenness, and screams, and gunfire. Michael increased his pace, ignoring the pain of the thorns and sharp stones stabbing the soft soles of his feet. *Skin into callous into leather*. Shoes would never sheathe his feet.

He thought of his dream, and the Fisherman, and relaxed. Alive again, and with a purpose, and in service to a teacher he would die for again. He considered the many decisions he would make, and like the Fisherman's fly line drifting on the river surface of his dream, some might stall his course in slack water, propel him in the fast main current, or even drift backwards in a swirling eddy. Michael lifted an ironic grin. The Fisherman continued to teach with metaphoric lessons, even to the oldest of children. Were the others schooled in their dreams? Regardless, it was wonderful to smell fresh air again, feel the cold wash over his skin, and carry the invincible weight of steel in his hand, honored to be part of God's plan.

Wherever it might lead.

Arco was a modern boomtown fueled by unregulated timber harvesting, and mineral strip mining executed at a frenzied pace, with the extraction of resources helping to provide necessities for the twenty billion people barely surviving on the planet. Highway 224 was inundated with gigantic Holo-screens displaying vids offering excitement and gaming action at small casinos. Pawn shops offered top dollar. Sex shops offered quality choices, boys, or girls. Restaurants offered prime cuts of synthetic beef and vat-grown seafood.

The town of Arco festered on the skin of a depleted and dying Earth like a neon bubble.

Michael scrambled down a steep footpath leading to a subdivision crammed with single-wide shipping containers acting as homes for workers. Otter Road sounded familiar, but he couldn't be sure. Moisture and the scent of willows steered him toward a narrow two-lane bridge. He hoped to find the Fisherman waiting beneath the bridge and shifted his grip on the piece of steel as if it were a fishing rod.

Seth had disappeared hours ago. Smart kid. Stayed true to his family, and security, and . . .

Michael's throat went dry, parched like the riverbed below. No fisherman would ever stand on the riverbank at which he stared. Trash and desiccated willows lined a gravel riverbed sucked dry by the monsters upstream. Suffering a lifetime of horrors, of imprisonment, only to find a wasteland of discarded alkaline batteries and fast-food containers, old plastic water bottles, piles of human feces.

What are you telling me, Father?

The steel rod felt like lead, his legs wobbled, and his bruised feet screamed at him to rest. Michael hung his head and slid down the steep embankment to crouch beneath the bridge and escape the wind. The urge to continue waned as Michael sat on shards of broken glass and rusty metal. He curled into a tight ball, murmuring a childish prayer calling for his Father, and fell asleep.

"Mastering the current with that fly line is an endless endeavor. Watch it float on the water, each section traveling at different speeds. Each bend in the line needs to be accounted for."

Michael's elation, that of a first date, that of a first kiss or losing his virginity, paled in comparison with the presence of the Fisherman. The fly rod bent hard in his hand as the braided neon line was dragged downstream by the swift current.

"I can't cast it!" Michael lamented

A warm hand rested gently on his naked shoulder. A pressure melting his frustration, a touch answering his uncertainty, a steady hand guiding his own with the intricacies of the fly rod. "Know exactly where you want to cast that hopper. Behind that rock is calm water, a place fish might wait for a meal, but you will have to contend with the faster water on each side. Or maybe that riffle along the other bank. Your path is your own, just like the bug you cast, but your reward is dictated by your effort. Mend your line to match the currents, mend your ways, mend your course, adapt to the currents of the landscape you travel."

Michael flipped the line upstream and watched the water turn the line ten different ways. He groaned. The Fisherman moved close to his back. Michael swallowed hard, afraid to turn around.

"Currents reflect those who live on this world. Fast, slow, chaotic, stagnant, many have sunk into the deep pools of Satan. Others float on the current effortlessly like the blessed children they are. Most know not what they are. Most have lost their connection to us. It is up to you to help those find that connection again" The Fisherman pointed at the tip of the long rod. "Fishing demands a hundred different skills—knot tying, casting, reading the water—and we haven't even gotten wet yet. What you learn with me will serve you in the challenges this world will offer. Remember the currents. Wind, water, and people. Master the currents, and you master yourself."

Michael flicked his wrist and tossed the hopper upstream again. He played the rod like an orchestra conductor. The rod responded. The line flew upstream in the quick current. He flicked again, and the line straightened into the seam between rock and rapid. The rod felt no different than his spear, used for different purposes, but his command of the tool returned.

"That's it. Strip some line out of the reel, and let's try a longer cast."

Michael did as he was asked. Confident he could make the line dance across the river for his teacher, Michael stepped deeper into the frigid water.

He blinked awake and stared at shattered remnants of swallow nests, cobwebs, and neon graffiti announcing the end of the world. The rising sun cast golden light through the willows dying branches crying out for water. He rubbed grit from his eyes. The Fisherman guided him. Cryptic. Mysterious. A puzzle he needed to complete.

He stood and flicked his wrist much as he did in his dream, then picked up the metal rebar like a fly rod, but the bulky weight felt too heavy to finesse. His stomach gurgled. He climbed back up to Otter Road and began walking towards the main thoroughfare. Old Arkoff and Fords whizzed by. Car horns blared to interrupt what should be the peaceful quiet of a new day. Middle fingers protruded from windows to wave good morning to him.

Lost with deciphering his dream, lost for a direction, Michael turned and walked up a side street set back from the busy highway. Old weeping willows shouted spring's arrival with pumpkin-yellow fronds drooping into the front yards of centuries old brick homes. Mailboxes waited at street curbs. With the shattered windows boarded up, a red brick LDS church advertised an upcoming Sunday service that never happened.

Nothing in the neighborhood looked familiar. Was his brief childhood in the town a fantasy? Were the faint memories of a mother and sister manufactured to maintain his sanity in the prison? *Find the Sinclair gas station, then the tiny brick home just two lefts and a right turn.* Yes. He remembered the directions his mom made him memorize. He had been a child in this place, he had a mother, and a sister, and he had finally returned.

The morning sun heated his scalp. Michael pulled the hood over his head and increased his pace. Vehicles slowed. Drivers glared and yelled obscenities about the impurities of his kind. He thought of currents, and the Fisherman's words, and ignored the noise of men screaming at him as though *he* were the monster.

Michael looked up to the sky hazed with dust. *They have indeed lost their way.* "You can't help those that are lost in the current, Father. You can only cast again."

He heard the answer or imagined the Fisherman's response in his head. *Then guide those that can be led.*

The main highway bustled and boomed. Michael waited at an intersection. A left turn led back to the foothills. A right turn led to the sin and decadence of downtown, and maybe the Sinclair. He pounded the metal rod into the asphalt as he debated his direction. Decisions were currents.

Master them, the Fisherman had warned.

Michael turned towards downtown, just a quick look, steal some food, maybe salve for his feet, then travel north to Mackay. Others like him would not live in this town; they would seek seclusion, protection, and anonymity. *Others like him.*

His stomach knotted as mayhem streamed up and down the main highway, busy with Arkoff logging trucks hell bent on reaching a mill, tanker trucks sprayed fountains of water to minimize the clouds of dust raised by an endless convoy of two-story mining haul trucks bullying their way up the muddy thoroughfare. Electric automobiles darted through gaps between the monstrous trucks. Horns blared like an angry orchestra.

Michael sat on the curb, observing an anthill of futility. The advertisements spoke and flashed. Auntie Em guaranteed the finest girls in town. The Cottontail Saloon offered a happy hour buffet—*All You Can Eat, All Appetites Satisfied.* Instant paycheck loans with easy interest.

A boot struck his thigh. "Get outta here, ya scum," a man said then hurried downwind, glancing over his shoulder to make sure his words weren't followed.

"This is Satan's dominion, Father. Do not waste my time," Michael said. A battle on the streets would only call Satan's acolytes. And he had no stomach for them, at the moment.

Michael stood and followed the man down the sidewalk, peering into blackened storefront windows for what was advertised. Pawn Star Jewelry. Google Girls. Fast Cash for Sex, or drugs, or money. One blasphemous evil to purchase others. Why had the Fisherman guided him to this place? A safe house for Satan's work. In another

life, he would have called down the thunder, or lightning, or summoned Gabriel to blow his horn.

The Fisherman was the teacher and had His reasons, but this . . .

Water dripped from a small copper pipe protruding from the red brick of the Loco Lizard Cantina. Michael squatted and cupped his hand, lifting rusty water to his dry lips. The bustle of electric cars, robotic delivery trucks, solar-powered motor bikes, all busied the town's grid of streets, like ants foraging for a queen-less colony. Package-carrying drones flittered above his head. He peered up the dusty asphalt highway, hoping to see the face of an old green dinosaur.

This home he hadn't seen in fifteen years was a trick, a deception of Satan, and yet offered hope that others from the prison might have passed through. Hundreds of children had been stolen from Arco. Someone would know the direction his kind had traveled.

A commotion down the street caught Michael's attention. A small crowd of men gathered in front of the Cracked Egg diner yelled obscenities as Myra and Seth approached on the sidewalk. A few yards behind the father assisted another diminutive Moonie hobbled with a limp, their face cloaked deep within their hood.

Seth had disappeared, only to return to his family and lead them to follow Michael.

Seth pulled his hood off and pointed up the street, gesturing to his father to hurry. Five men dressed in dirty cargo pants and dirty white T-shirts emblazoned with *Arkoff Industries* followed ten yards behind the family, each dangled a hammer or thick crowbar in soot-stained hands. The men quickened their pace to close the gap. A convoy of three behemoth Arkoff mining haul trucks cut off his vantage. The haulers ripped loose with their air horns, as if celebrating. Black diesel fumes hung low and thick.

Michael stepped off the curb. Rumbling two-story synthetic tires rolled across his view. Michael darted between two lumbering Kenworth's as their air horns blasted a nasty warning.

The street was empty. The helpless Moonie family had disappeared.

CHAPTER FOUR

HER EYELIDS GLUED SHUT BY crusty mucus, Cyd swiped at her face with the back of her hand and groaned at the bright sun blazing through the open bedroom window. The muted brilliance accompanied birdsong and crisp pine-scented air. Zac's rasping snore brought back sketchy memories of last night's festivities, and the drug-induced nightmare that followed.

A foreboding dream of a faceless stranger lurking beyond her bedroom door, rapping on the hardwood to announce his presence. The stranger called out to Cyd, begging to be let in, but she stood firm and refused to flip the deadbolt. The cougar, Sheba, wandered around the bedroom nervously until the one-hundred fifty-pound mountain lion wrapped itself around her legs like a giant housecat purring for dinner. Cyd scratched the cougar behind the ears with one hand, the other hand frozen on the deadbolt. Zac and Jurgens called to her from an alcove behind the bed, to return to the party table piled high with blue powder. A hit of 3Bz waited. Sheba snarled.

The man on the other side of the door implored her to come out, called to her with a silky baritone voice. He had something wonderful to show her.

She awoke with guilty ambivalence and a scorched throat.

Cyd stared out the large four-pane window at an azure sky transforming to pale blue as the sun crested above the forested foothills.

Daddy did it again. Distracted her with hope, and promises, and then disappeared, leaving Zac and Jurgens to ply her with 3Bz, and drag her back down into hangover hell. Confronting Daddy with her demands, only to wake up the next day in the same bed with the same hangover. He continued to play her like a six-string guitar.

She resisted waking Zac with an angry punch to his stomach. He wasn't the problem; she was. She was her own worst enemy. And 3Bz. The drugs barbed hooks had sunk deep into her psyche. Daddy had to know, pretended like he didn't, but he had to know. She climbed from the bed and put on sweatpants and a tank top. She stared at the zookeeper, a muscled piece of brain matter staining her mattress. *Don't be mad at him. Blame yourself.*

She brushed her teeth and stared into the mirror. *My. Freaking. God! Sixteen, and with the hair of a witchy grandmother.*

Puberty had widened her hips, and she was too freaking tall. Boys definitely didn't like tall girls. The hormones gave her breasts that would never need augmenting, and in return, DNA had provided her with a head full of thick silver hair. Platinum. Zac said it sounded sexier. But it was silver, senior-citizen silver, a color that went out of style decades ago along with forehead piercings and holographic 3D tattoos. A silver-haired almost seventeen-year-old actress. Yeah, right, she might as well join one of the many freak shows performing everywhere on Boob-Tube-Plus.

The dream of the faceless man returned. She should have let him in. She should have unclicked the lock, stood back, and watched Sheba rip his throat out, but the cougar wouldn't have reacted that way. She was always a big kitten in Cyd's dreams. Probably a manifestation of some psychobabble term for her drug addiction. Sheba ought to take Jurgens for dinner, tear him to shreds, end the old man's nightly 3Bz party.

Cyd slipped out of the room then hurried down a long hallway towards the grand front entrance of the Old Faithful Inn. She passed a huge river-rock fireplace rising five stories then down another hallway lined with rooms that tourists had occupied decades before she was born. She stopped at room number 133 and held her hand on the chrome handle. She pressed her ear to the door and heard Daddy ranting. Like he always did. About nothing, or everything. About how he would change the rules of the game. About some fool named Michael being no match for him.

Dumbass Michael. No one had ever gotten the best of Daddy, in anything, ever. Michael and his whatever company were doomed to go broke, just like all the others that had tangled with Arkoff Industries.

Cyd dropped her hand from the handle and leaned against the wall. She wasn't much different from Michael, both manipulated by a master, both players in a game governed by rules Daddy seemed to revise with one of those stupid fucking blood-red ink pens he loved to use. She and Michael would both be bankrupt, emotionally, and spiritually, and soon. Cyd inhaled a long deep breath and put her hand back on the handle.

Anna was pleading with Daddy to slow down his verbal instructions. Stupid, condescending, a total bitch. Daddy's personal assistant had been Cyd's nanny for her tween years, and she was only nine years older than Cyd. She was Daddy's plaything then and his slave now. Two people made for each other. Anna interrupted Daddy's droning voice with a clearing of her throat.

Daddy raised his voice. "Oh, screw Michael. Get me that executive with Gryphon Studios. He owes me a few favors and can get Cyd started in a reality series. Maybe he can persuade her to take acting classes first. Then get us a rental in Malibu, beachfront only, or just buy it if Cyd approves. Being away from Cyd will crush me, but I can't abandon the animals, either."

The dialogue behind the door switched to muted whispers. Cyd stepped back from the door. Her hand trembled. Her thoughts raced. Hollywood. On her own. No 3Bz. A driver's license. Weirdos. Parties. Sunny beaches. *Screw the doubts, girl. You are an Arkoff.* And she would be just like Daddy. Successful. Respected.

Cyd stepped away from the door. Maybe she would take a run to clear her head then peruse the latest fashion actresses were wearing, and how to control her online presence on hundreds of different social media sites. A major turn of events, magnified. Then a celebration, fine wine, and the latest California music, and, well, maybe a little bit of 3Bz.

Just till she settled in Malibu.

———

SAMUEL SHOOK HIS HEAD AT Cyd's gullibility. The young girl knew security cameras covered the Lodge grounds, the kitchen, the servant quarters, and his own small office. He had watched her enter the hallway and ignored her approach until just the right moment. Cyd couldn't determine which way was up, or down, and the 3Bz took all the credit. On his holo-screen, Cyd retreated down the hallway, a giddy pep in her step.

Centuries to hone his superior intellect, but Samuel Arkoff's guile ruled the past, present, and the future. It always had, always would. He twitched his jaw in three motions and heard Jurgens respond in his earpiece.

"Increase the H, and the fentanyl. Screw the cocaine. Dub in some meth, too. I'm tired of being nice." He jutted his jaw and disengaged the link, then narrowed his eyes at Anna. She sat with legs uncrossed, ample cleavage advertising for sex, her bewitching sky-blue eyes focused and screaming, "Screw me."

"You cut your hair again, didn't you? You know I don't like that." Samuel walked around the desk and stood behind her.

"There are a lot of things you don't like lately, but you'll just have to suffer with the rest of us. You don't like your body looking like it does. And you don't like that Michael escaped." She shifted in her seat as Samuel stroked her neck. He let his long fingernail rest atop the Arkoff Port inserted below her left ear.

The Arkoff Port, a miracle of modern technology. Upon insertion, tendrils of fiber optic filaments sprouted and weaved between muscle fibers until reaching the cerebellum, facilitating a link with computers controlled by proprietary Alternate Intelligence. Goods, services, anything bought or sold or shipped to Arkoff Industries mandated the use of an Arkoff Port. For a century, the general public resisted using the implant, citing religious and privacy concerns, but the number of users soon exploded exponentially, bankrupting tech giants Apple and Google until the service ports became as common as toilet paper.

Each device imprinted with Samuel's nearly invisible three-digit number as homage to the banned book of God, and registration numbers prefaced with serial numbers once tattooed on the wrists of Jewish prisoners of years prior, Lucifer's technological mark of the beast was worn by eighty-four percent of the world's population.

After centuries of silence, the Father sitting atop his throne in an ethereal dimension once known as Heaven had started His games again. Michael, Raphael, Gabriel, all the soldiers of His silly outdated army had arrived in the world. Yet, the Father fumbled the placement of His game pieces.

Samuel pressed his fingernail into Anna's port. She was becoming old and stale, and cocky. As Cyd's nanny, her eighteen-year-old body fulfilled all his physical needs. She refused to partake in the 3Bz, but now, perhaps, she required forceful persuasion to truly experience the pleasures of his corrupt world. Then she might learn to appreciate all his gifts, again.

"Michael is none of your concern," he said. He increased the pressure on her neck. He pulled her up out of her chair, ignoring her protests. He could smell her scent, just as Rondo might have. He pushed his weight against her small frame, pinning her against the desk. He grew hard.

She needed to appreciate his stature. He ripped her skirt off her legs with one hand as the other hand muffled her scream.

She needed to appreciate everything the beast could offer.

MUDDLED WITHIN THE CLAMOR OF Arco's early morning awakening, a girl's high-pitched scream pierced the dusty air. The memory of the pregnant young girl strapped to the gurney in prison invaded Michael's thoughts.

The scream sounded again, louder, painful, and Michael bolted towards the sound. He bared his teeth and ignored pedestrians and shopkeepers shouting rude slurs. He slowed, cocking his ear to listen. Seth's squeaky voice. Men laughed and shouted. He turned up a street shadowed beneath old growth cottonwoods and weeping willows. Dense shrubs shielded high-gabled clapboard buildings with spray-painted plywood signage announcing a low-rent business district. Flashing neon from the Lotus Flower Massage Parlor sign welcomed customers. He paused and cocked his ear again.

A chorus of masculine laughter erupted from across the street. Grunts and the scuffling of shoes on gravel. Seth's tiny voice shouted warnings.

Michael pulled the robe off his body. The fabric chafed his skin, stunk like feces, and was too cumbersome to answer the call to battle. The metal bar gripped in his hand hung at his side as he searched up driveways and alleys separating the old homes and businesses.

Seth's voice again, weak and sobbing. Michael swallowed a rising anger with a wad of gritty phlegm stuck to the back of his throat.

Gray robes huddled as one against a rickety garage door at the end of a narrow concrete driveway. The weathered outbuilding wrapped with leafless vines was shaded beneath a canopy of old maples. Michael stabbed the rod into the concrete, once, twice. The third caused a tremor to command the attention of a small boy hiding in the mass of gray fabric.

Seth peered out of an opening, his eyes and cheeks wet with tears. The boy broke from the group and ran to Michael. "They stabbed Papa, and they got Myra. We gotta smite 'em, angel."

Michael tightened his grip on the rod and inhaled a deep breath. He flicked his chin for the boy to continue. Where?

Seth pointed. "They got her inside that house. Lots of 'em. And they got guns and knives. Smite 'em, angel! Smite 'em." Seth sobbed as fresh tears streamed down his cheeks.

Michael balanced the rebar in his right hand and aimed for the porch stairway leading up to the rear door. The Fisherman had made him human, flesh and blood, easily capable of dying. A hint of fear stayed his hand. An urge to raise his face to the dirty sky and ask why faded with Seth's sobs. A demon could smite him from across the room with no more effort than squeezing a trigger.

His hand relaxed as he stared at the doorknob. Death was life. Life was death. His essence lived eternally, and yet . . . the Fisherman had rebirthed him as human for a reason. A reason he should never question. Faith was armor-less; faith was weaponless. And faith in the Creator wielded limitless power.

Michael pushed Seth back and mouthed, "How many?"

Seth flashed a filthy hand. Five.

Michael pointed his finger at Seth and shook his head as a warning to not follow him. Endorphins flowed. A runner's high of adrenaline.

His heart raced. The Fisherman created him for battle, for moments such as this, to command the Army of God again.

"I am not going to worry about you, Seth. Go back to your Papa."

Seth frowned and sighed.

Michael growled. "You asked for an angel. Now go."

Seth pulled his hood up over his head but didn't move.

Michael reached back and flipped the hood off. "And how are you going to help?"

Seth stooped and picked up a handful of rocks.

"Where's the baby?" Michael said.

Seth whispered, "He's with Gramma. I'm gonna help smite 'em, too."

"You protect your nephew," Michael said and tapped the rod twice. "So let it be written, and now let's get it done." He offered the boy a stern face.

Seth stuck his tongue out, turned, and hurried away. Michael watched him until he was sure he would not try to return. Naked, no weapons other than a rusty piece of rebar, and the disciples of the Fallen One waited inside.

Now let them witness what he truly was.

Michael climbed the stairs and tapped the door window with the pointed steel. The planks of a subfloor vibrated beneath his feet. The boisterous voices inside faded into whispers.

The door opened. A long-haired bare-chested man looked him up and down, then smirked. "Run along, naked boy. Timmy's Tots is down the street. They'll have what you want." He started to close the door.

Michael shoved the steel between the door and jamb. The door flew open.

"Naked and a hearing problem. Maybe I'll use that rebar to poke some sense into you." His thick beard grown down to the sweaty tuft of black hair matted between his flabby nipples, the monster blocked Michael.

In a flash, the sharp tip of the rod lifted the man's chin, and his eyebrows. A trickle of blood oozed from the greasy hair.

A gravelly voice deep inside the home spoke calmly. "Let him in."

Michael took two steps and entered a storage room stuffed with musty cardboard storage bins. The air reeked of putrid body odor, black mold, old semen—the unpleasant scent of Satan's minions. He would smite each as Seth demanded, if only to clear the stench from his nostrils. He stepped forward into an empty living room lit by the bright morning sunlight of unshaded windows.

Myra sat huddled like a grey lump in the corner, cowering from the violence to come. Or the rape she had endured. She refused to look up at him as her body trembled with rolling spasms. Michael surveyed the stinking—fat, arrogant, ruthless monsters with unkempt faces. The rod eased through his fingers in incremental lifts, searching for the perfect balance.

"Pussy *and* a prize," the gravelly voice said.

The long-haired man stepped back to reveal a gray-haired man rising from a tattered armchair blocking the front door. He bared tobacco-stained teeth, a thin growth of beard marred by a postage stamp scar below his razor thin lower lip.

"My lucky day." He lifted a sleek carbon handgun and aimed it at Michael's chest.

The stink of monsters closed in. The steel bar was torn from his hand. Michael studied Myra. Had he failed her, and the Fisherman? Would the Fisherman summon him home so soon?

"Samuel Arkoff is gonna set my soul free." The man eased closer. His chin scar glowed yellow in bright sunlight busy with floating motes of dust. "He's gonna have a fling with you as guest of honor, and then we'll all get back to business. And I'm gonna be the CEO of any dotcom I choose." He laughed with a smoker's throat.

Lucifer's alias caused Michael to tense, ball his fists. He closed his eyes, pictured the possible reactions of each filthy member. He heaved a sigh.

"I'll empty this clip into you so fast even your big buddy in the sky can't save you, angel."

How did Chin Scar know what he was? Did it matter? Myra was his only concern. The here, the now, he was certain this challenge would define exactly who he was. Arco *was* a cesspool, of monsters, godless men serving only Samuel. Yet with blind faith and hoping for miracles, Seth, and Myra, and their family, had followed him. For that, he would grant Seth's wish.

Michael offered his wrists for binding. "Take me to your leader, douchebag, but let the girl go."

The others shuffled their boots and grumbled. A potbellied slob said no way was the girl not getting his hunk of love

Chin Scar narrowed his eyes. Michael smirked. Chin Scar's eyes darted to his posse, and he swallowed, undecided. The protest gained volume.

Michael closed his eyes. "Screw it. Keep the girl." He smiled at each pair of soulless blank eyes. "I'll trade her for a bottle of water."

The Stink rushed into a frantic search of cabinets and backpacks. Michael watched Myra. She lifted her face. The black growth plaguing her cheek and neck had faded into a plum splotch, a simple birthmark that would soon disappear. Michael met her gaze, his expression impassive and emotionless. Then he winked.

A young man yelled and held up a half-empty flask of water, as if a trophy from winning a contest.

Chin Scar motioned for the man to give Michael the water. "You cannot lie, cheat, or steal, Michael. You are bound by your word."

Not only did Chin Scar know what he was, but also who. Information he hadn't known himself till days ago. Samuel had warned them. A beast determined to divert the Fisherman's great plan.

Michael unscrewed the bottle top. "A little boy wants you thrashed, but you have my sword, and all I get is a bottle of . . ." Michael sniffed the water. "Nasty water."

He glanced at Myra, and she pulled her knees tighter to her chest.

Chin Scar grinned and stepped close to jab the gun barrel into Michael's chest. "She's all yours, boys. Me and the right hand of God will be leaving."

Michael tilted the bottle to his lips and let the foul water flow into his mouth. He swished and mixed it with his saliva. His cheeks bulged with water.

I heal myself with all I say and do. I heal myself with all I say and do. But not this time.

Michael sprayed the water to hit the closest three men with surprise. Another quick mouthful sprayed the others. The monsters recoiled, wiped at fat cheeks and black eyes, their voices shouting distaste at Chin Scar. The ruse would allow him to sweep their legs, swat their hands and arms, and kill each monster as he saw fit.

Instead, he watched a young boy's plea for vengeance unleashed with the Fisherman's dragon.

One monster bolted for the front door, tripped over a shirt, and fell dead. The skinny water contest winner stuck out his tongue then bled from his nostrils and ears. The others died with hemorrhaging eyes, noses, mouths. Each dropped like a blank domino, gurgling tainted blood.

Chin Scar dropped the pistol, shuddered with a molten hot fever. His jaw muscles convulsed in violent spasms.

The monsters twitched on the dirty floorboards. The stench of blood and excrement overpowered Michael's nostrils. Myra watched in horror, her eyes wide and white, her hand slapping frantically at the overspray of water on her naked body.

A demon's soul shimmered as it fled Chin Scar's body. Wisps of ephemeral white smoke laced with evil and deceit rose then hung like a wispy cloud in his face.

The Archangel Michael, a seasoned judge of the Fallen's acolytes, blew a puff of air as his verdict of the demon's soul. He corrected the demon's assertion.

"Not the hand of God. The sword."

CHAPTER FIVE

CYD PUSHED EVERY OUNCE OF her weight against the door as an angry wind buffeted the bedroom. Her heart thumped, seeking to escape her chest. Perspiration plastered her platinum hair to her forehead. A tiny trickle fell to sting her right eye. The sweat reeked of the acrid smoke of 3Bz.

Samuel cowered behind her bed. He screamed at her to keep the door shut. Zac stirred in the rumpled sheets of the bed, a useless body in a drug-induced coma. Music erupted on the other side of the door, a female's melodic voice, a favored R&B tune of an artist she adored for her empowering lyrics.

The door cracked open. She braced her feet and pushed the door flush into its frame. Samuel shouted a list of unspeakable horrors she would endure if she let the evil inside. Rape. Murder. Mutilation. Cyd pushed hard and turned the deadbolt.

Cyd sat up in a jolt. Her heart pounded. Her jaw ached. Her molars throbbed.

Fucking 3Bz and their dreams.

———

SAMUEL PUCKERED HIS LIPS AND appraised the young girl's curvy rear end as she pulled the office door open and departed. The new springtime policy of requiring skintight leggings for all female employees looked like a success. Fat or skinny, the stretchy fabric performed miracles for any female's bottom He leaned back in his leather chair and steepled his fingers beneath his chin.

Michael roamed. In search of his destiny, though predetermined by Him. Cyd grew restless, as Samuel had expected. She would require additional distractions, more than the 3Bz could provide. Most teenagers would be down on their knees, in front of anything or anyone, just to get a single dose of the synthetic pleasure. Cyd appeared too lucid in the mornings, too aware of her environment, and too damned determined to distance herself from his influence. And now her True Father was close to breaking down the door to reveal Himself to her.

Distractions, like guile, could be very powerful.

Samuel twitched his jaw to open a communication channel to the security captain on duty and said, "We'll be taking a trip to Sun Valley. Get my ride ready." He twitched his jaw and terminated the link.

Samuel rubbed the tiny plastic nodule beneath his ear. The Arkoff Port was a marvel of Jurgens' innovative thinking. Implanted just below the hinge of the jaw, its tendrils spread like a spider web to five lobes of the human brain controlling five autonomic senses. Years of research were misspent assuming manipulation of the interface might be controlled through ocular manipulation, but the optic nerves already received and processed an overwhelming amount of data, hence the Arkoff implant's command system was controlled by mandibular movements customized to each user.

Samuel walked out of his office, down the hallway, out the back door, and stared at the assortment of wire enclosures and wooden cages for animals indigenous to Yellowstone. The air was heavy with dung and urine. Fifty-meter-long rows of pens constructed atop the asphalt parking lot of the Lodge, just for Cyd. He steered left, to the predator aisle.

Zac waved at him from across the rodent cages. He ignored the simpleton.

The muscled boy wasn't a *big* enough distraction. Perhaps a well-endowed porn star might provide the distraction Cyd needed. He twitched open a link and said, "Get me a list of big Johns from the Adult Video Awards show in New Vegas. Contact info, and discreet files. And no, Anna, they're not for you." Samuel smirked and twitched the link closed.

He strolled down the aisle of oblong wire cages. Coyotes and foxes cowered in the corners. Bobcats slept. A cougar paced nervously. Samuel stopped at Rondo's cage to admire a magnificent beast relegated to an eight-by-twelve polymer wire enclosure. The wolf was asleep in a shaded corner. Its flanks rose and fell in an easy rhythm. Samuel shook the wire fence vigorously to wake the beast and laughed.

Cyd turned away from the marmot pen she was cleaning with a garden hose to glare at him. She must have heard the clamor. He smiled and waved her over. If she only knew what she was, Samuel had no doubts she would grab a sharp object within reach of her long arms and bury it in his eye. He studied her as she approached. Long tan legs moving in a purposeful stride, her breasts bouncing beneath her dirty white T-shirt, her spooky amber eyes hidden by dark sunglasses. All the luxuries and excitement provided by youth. Oh, how he missed those days. Perhaps he should wean her off the 3Bz, chain her to the metal columns in the basement, let her finally experience what precious *Daddy Dearest* really was.

"How are our furry friends today, Cyd? The new sunscreens helping them to stay cool?" Samuel said. Furry friends indeed, he would just as soon spray the hideous zoo with mustard gas, or maybe a blast of sarin gas concealed with the other weapons of mass destruction stockpiled throughout Yellowstone's three thousand square miles.

Cyd eased closer like a wary cat but remained out of reach.

"I assume you're all packed. The shuttle is coming," Samuel said. He grinned as the statement slapped the scowl off Cyd's face.

Cyd's jaw dropped. "Wait, what? We're leaving now. Holy shit!"

"What did I tell you about cursing, dear?" Samuel said.

Cyd checked her shirt. "Oh my God, I'm filthy. I need to shower. I have to pull some outfits together."

"Slow down, girl. We're just flying to Sun Valley for a few days," Samuel said. He saw her shoulders sag, her enthusiasm melt, and he loved it. "We're staying at Sterling Moore's house. I thought he could give you some perspective on the film business."

Cyd's enthusiasm returned. "Sterling Moore's house? Oh. My. Freaking. God. He was the greatest in *Kachina Children*. Maybe he can get me a part in the sequel. They have to be doing one."

"Go, Cyd. The chopper's leaving when you're packed."

She bounced up and down and squealed. He stiffened as she pecked him on the cheek with wet lips. She turned and sprinted towards the Lodge. Samuel wiped his cheek with the back of his hand, her saliva burning his skin like acid.

The endgame was building like a sudden summer thunderstorm. All the players assembled in the deserts and mountains of Idaho and Montana. No national anthem for this event. Destruction would rain like confetti.

Samuel removed his own dark glasses and stared into the burning sun. He felt His presence. Felt His embrace even now.

Come to me, Father.

Teach me what I need to learn.

Then get the fuck out of my way.

MICHAEL PICKED UP THE METAL staff. He pitied Myra with her face buried between her knees, her arms clamped tight around her head.

The sickly ruin sprawled across the old hardwood floor had already summoned black flies to swarm over the thick, bloody goo still oozing from Chin Scar's mouth. The death of billions might follow, transported by His smallest creatures. Sickness and disease mingled like old friends in Michael's blood, the worst of the worst, the quickest of the quick, a super strain of plague unmatched in history. And he could wield it like a scalpel, slicing those that deserved it, and healing those he chose.

Michael picked up Myra's robe crumpled in a corner and offered it to her. Did the gift of a cure cause Myra's violation? Did cleansing the disease that marred her face cause her rape? Every action, every decision produced a current in this world.

Guide those still with hope.

"I hear the baby calling for you," Michael said.

Myra lifted her face, her eyes puffy and red.

Michael's knees weakened in her gaze. "Seth needs a bit more learning. He thinks I'm some sort of smiting angel. Look around, Myra. Does this look like the work of an angel?"

Myra looked at the blood and bodies and nodded. She pulled the robe over her head and glared. "It looks exactly like what I prayed for."

She swept past him, sidestepping bodies and blood spilled over the floor, her stride filled with purpose.

Guide those still with hope.

Michael juggled the staff in his fingers and followed her outside, sneering at the blood and gore that might cleanse the world as easily as Noah's calamitous flood, should He pass final judgment.

Myra ran across the driveway to crawl into the huddle of gray robes with Seth and the others. She wailed. The grey mass of her father sat motionless, darkened with blood, murdered by a monster's knife. Seth peered out from the cluster of gray fabric, his cheeks stained with tears. He stared at Michael, furrowing his brow with uncertainty.

An ancient woman with a leathered face spotted with cancerous lesions gazed up and offered a bony hand bloodied by the father's lethal wound. Her pale blue eyes flecked with tarnished gold unnerved Michael. Her eyes belied her soul's true age and teased a faint memory from eons past. She grimaced and attempted to stand. Myra held her back.

Seth emerged, cradling his nephew. "Did we smite them, Angel?"

"As only angels do," Michael said. The air above the canopy of ancient elms and weeping willows fluttered with whizzing drones. Sirens blared in the distance. "The Fisherman has smiled down on us. Of that, you can believe. But if you still have hope, you'll need to follow me, and now!"

Michael hurried down the gravel driveway, stooped to pick up his discarded robe, then searched up and down the empty street. The wounds on his feet pained him with renewed vengeance. The huge cottonwood canopy would stifle the drone's search. He turned right.

Seth's small hand grabbed his finger and held tight. The boy walked in silence, his young soul without a scent. Michael shook his head in amazement but grinned down at the bright blue eyes of a child touching him without his consent. The boy carried hope like a backpack. One of the mortals the Fisherman had encouraged him to help.

"Put it on, angel," Seth said and pointed at the robe. "You're like a lantern for moths."

The boy's voice was a placid current in the river of irritating noise. Peaceful, and guiding.

"And so are these robes," Michael said.

More tiny drones whirred above the treetops. Michael slowed, unsure of his direction except to locate a green dinosaur of a Sinclair gas station. A home conjured from silly prison fantasy. He lifted his face as a lash of wind battered the canopy above. The noisy drones would flee. The Fisherman provided respite. In ancient life he could have ushered in tempests, called down lightning bolts to destroy the flying annoyances. But this strange new world offered unique challenges.

"Let's get inside until dark. Let the drones think we escaped," Michael said.

He glanced over his shoulder. The old woman carried the baby and pulled Myra away from her dead father, whispering for her to hurry.

"How did they know about us so fast?" Seth asked.

"The demon. He was one of Lucifer's," Michael said as he climbed into his robe.

"Holy crap! Angels *and* demons. Just like the Bible says," Seth said.

Michael led the group up a treacherous concrete path of buckled concrete and exposed tree roots. Seth bolted ahead, up to the front porch of an old brick home, and pressed his nose to the glass door. A tiny solar-powered delivery drone whizzed beneath the canopy. The sirens fell silent.

"We can hide with the cows. Or maybe find some trucks to climb into," Seth said. He shot ahead against Myra's weak protest.

"Your brother seems made for this world. A clever tactician," Michael said to Myra.

The old woman spoke. "Made for this world, he is. But you aren't. What are you? A blessing?" She nodded towards Myra's unblemished face. "Or a harbinger of the end times?"

"Neither, old woman. Either way, I will have no problem judging your soul."

She huffed. "Been there, done that, and here I am. Right smack in the middle of His plan again."

Michael narrowed his eyes. "And your name is . . . ?"

"Mary. This time around. But I might've answered to Maggie, Lillith, or even Whore to some, or whatever name you might see in my eyes. My son was David, and now he's dead. And he's with Him." Her face furrowed with unprocessed sorrow, she lifted her chin and met Michael's gaze. Her eyes challenged him, though the tone of her words were spoken with the wisdom of a prophet. He slowed, and she hurried to block his path, then she glared. "Myra's baby has no name. Shall we give him one? Michael, is it?"

Michael flinched and stepped back. A corner of Mary's mouth lifted as if she'd won a victory. She tickled the wisp of a distant memory. A soul he couldn't quite place. An untouchable woman.

Seth ran up and pointed ahead. "We can hide over there. A couple of Tubers live in that house," he said before grabbing his knees to catch his breath.

"You sure?" Michael said.

"Duh, angel. Two guys asleep in bed with wires and water bags. I'm a kid but not stupid."

Michael had read about the cultural phenomenon of Tubers. Using an implementation of the Arkoff Port, die-hard video game players immersed themselves into complex live-action games, playing for days, even months, as computer-generated avatars. Feeding tubes provided the nutrition, catheters facilitated the disposal of waste byproducts, and the players survived as data-eating zombies. Michael never understood the allure. Escape this world, only to flourish, or die, in an artificial world. The Arkoff Port had provided both options.

The others followed close behind until he reached the rear porch and tapped his staff on the door's glass window. No answer. He stepped into a pantry stocked with canned goods. He scanned the labels—beef stew with vat-grown beef, GMO refried beans, clam chowder imitation clam bits, butter-flavored Snap To-It Popcorn. His stomach growled with the choices.

Seth slid past him, down a wallpapered hallway with missing picture frames outlined by clean paisley flowers. Michael followed, checking two bedrooms and a tiny bathroom. The front room down from the kitchen held two recliners, and the Tubers. Godless monsters. Bags of saline dripped, nearly empty. A second tube connected to empty bags of colorless gunk. The zombies lay motionless, their faces and ears covered with thick black masks. Thin translucent sheets covered hairless torsos with pasty white skin rivaling his own. One was a female.

Michael relaxed as Seth helped Myra up the steps and into the house. He swallowed a mass of saliva gathering in his mouth. The old woman helped herself to the cans of food, shoving her selections into pockets stitched on the inside of her robe.

"Later," Michael whispered.

With a defiant voice, she said, "They can't hear you. They're Tubers. They might not wake up till they reach another level. Maybe never."

Seth shoved a handful of cheese puffs into his mouth and offered the bag to Michael. Michael arched his brows then leaned in closely to peer inside the flimsy clear bag filled with bright orange puffs. His mouth watered. He pinched a single puff and examined it as Seth shoved handfuls into his mouth, letting crumbs and yellow dust fall over his robe and down onto a dirty woven rug with flowery designs. Michael touched the puff to the tip of his tongue then pulled it away. Saliva flowed. The strange taste of chemicals, salt, and imitation cheese. Nothing like the bland prison slop he'd eaten all his life. His stomach rumbled. He placed the puff on his tongue and closed his mouth. The food dissolved. He swallowed and moaned with pleasure.

Seth handed him the bag and continued searching the pantry. "This is almost like getting a puppy. Man, oh man, these people eat good."

Michael walked through the small bungalow, shoving handfuls of cheese puffs into his mouth. The two vacant bedrooms were immaculate, sheets and blankets folded and placed on the ends of the beds. The windows and blinds raised six inches for small cuttings of herbs on the sills to gather sun and fresh air. The rooms were void of any personal statements.

Myra nursed her baby but refused to lift her head. Seth fidgeted with the Tubers' wires, tubes, and attachments. He poked the two bodies with his finger, looking for a reaction.

A twinge of the Fisherman's lessons tickled his thoughts. Tubers existed like the foam in a back eddy of a river, trapped in the endless rhythm of a current going nowhere, one only nature could change.

Or God.

Michael reached for the bowl of steaming broth Mary carried in. The old woman dodged him and kneeled before Myra, offering her the meal. They whispered, but Michael heard each word.

"I'm not hungry," Myra said.

"Eat. For the baby," Mary said.

Myra slapped at her wet face then pulled the baby tight to her chest. "Papa's dead. Seth thinks this is a game, and you still think we should follow this psycho."

"Girl, the most precious gift suckles you. Give him what he needs."

Myra lowered the baby to her lap and took the bowl. She sipped the thick soup.

Mary moved as nimbly as a teenager, gently pinching Seth's neck to usher him into the kitchen. He pulled off his robes to reveal skinny arms and battered kneecaps. Fresh scabs on his elbows oozed blood. His dirty T-shirt and tattered jeans were three sizes too small. She set a bowl of stew in front of Seth sitting proper at the table. Seth dug in like a starving miner, shoveling thick stew into his mouth, only pausing to blow quick cooling breaths before another bite.

Mary looked back at Michael and motioned him to an empty chair. "An angel's still gotta eat, lest I don't know my scripture."

Michael sat and spooned exquisite potatoes and gravy into his mouth, gobbling the stew until his stomach bulged and threatened to explode. He leaned back in his chair and twirled his spoon. Waiting for more of . . . anything but synthetic oatmeal and fake eggs. He rubbed his swollen belly and smiled at Mary as she spooned canned peaches into his bowl.

He suddenly understood why people often said a prayer of thanks before a meal. Hunger was cured by the blessings of the Fisherman. A slippery peach dropped from his spoon, and Seth giggled. He reached into his bowl for another. The little buggers were cagey, but his spoon would not be denied, and he laughed at his own ineptness.

Seth laughed, spraying syrup across the table.

The sudden giddiness prevented a spoonful just inches from his lips from entering his mouth. The boy's gleeful sound was infectious, and disarming, and like nothing he had heard before. The monsters in prison never laughed.

Seth yawned and staggered over to Mary standing by the sink. She pointed at a bedroom door, and he disappeared, still grasping the tablespoon.

"Why are you back?" Mary said as she wiped her hands with a dishtowel.

"Why do you care?" Michael said and continued his battle with the peaches.

"I've lost a son because of you!" She limped towards the table and pointed a wooden serving spoon at his face. "Because I have grandchildren that should be running from the likes of you, and . . . and they follow you like rats charmed by music."

"Wasn't my idea. I'd be long gone if it wasn't for you," Michael said.

"You'll never be gone." She turned her back. "Ever."

Michael set his spoon on the table, cocked his ear at the sound of tires crunching gravel on the driveway outside. He peered out the window just as a car door slammed shut. He motioned Mary to join Seth in the bedroom. The kitchen sink was stacked with crusted saucepans, the table strewn with crackers and puffs and dirty dishes. Keys jingled in the porch door.

Michael stepped barefoot behind the door just as it swung open. Lavender and horse manure greeted his nostrils. A sweat-stained straw hat shadowed the window. The wearer paused at the door threshold to survey the mess inhabiting the kitchen.

"Tuber idiots," a female hissed. "They're paying for this."

The hat came off, and she took a hesitant step inside. In a single motion, Michael closed the door, moved behind her, and engulfed her neck in the crook of his arm. Her brief scream was choked to a gurgle.

"Shhh," Michael said. Her sharp fingernails dug deep into his forearm, and he squeezed tighter. "Shhh. No harm. No foul. We'll clean it up." Her fingers relaxed. Her skin was soft and smooth on his own. Strands of her long auburn hair tickled his face. "Will you let us clean up and leave?"

Her head flinched, then she nodded vigorously. Michael released her, and she stepped forward to turn and face him. "You're gonna pay . . ." She took two tentative steps backwards. "They're hunting you everywhere! And you gotta freaking hide here?"

She was exquisite. Her tan skin contrasted beautifully with straight white teeth. Her thick shiny hair was split into long ponytails. A beauty seen only sparingly on a prison one-dimensional screen.

She turned to begin clearing the mess of dishes on the table. "You people keep coming. Stupid lost sheep looking for a pasture. The vids say you're the last. God, I hope so." She dropped the plastic dishes into the sink and turned. "Are you him? You're the last one? You're the one that idiot keeps waiting for?"

Michael stepped forward and asked, "The sheep? Where are they?"

"I ain't gonna tell you crap," she said.

Michael retreated a step. She was defensive of someone, but she knew of his kind. Who was the idiot? Idiots waiting for other idiots? He clenched his teeth. He was the idiot.

He moved with quick, silent precision, picking up a sticky fork glazed with syrup. He pushed the girl against the sink. Pans and bowls clattered to the floor. Her eyes blinked rapidly, as if to ward off the sharp prongs pointed at her eye.

"I'll judge your soul right now if you *ain't* telling crap." Michael cocked his wrist to thrust the fork into her eye.

"Michael! No!" Seth screamed.

The boy's voice disarmed him. His muscles went limp, the fork dropped from his trembling hand. Seth walked into the kitchen, his small hands rubbing at sleepy eyes.

"Michael?" The girl looked up to the ceiling. "You *are* the one the idiot has been waiting for." She laughed mirthlessly.

"Where is this idiot?" Michael said.

She dropped a handful of bowls into the sink and sneered at Michael. Grabbing his hand, she led him down the hall and into the living room. Frowning at Myra and the baby asleep in an oversized armchair, the girl pointed at the male Tuber lying motionless on the reclining couch. "Ralphie. There's your idiot."

Michael hovered above Ralphie to stare at a large pasty sack of skin easily mistaken for a corpse. Ralphie's pinkie finger twitched. Michael looked at the girl and shook his head.

The girl moved slowly around the bed, widening the distance from Michael. "The Arkoff Ports, Ralphie's got three, thinks it gives him an edge on the competition."

Michael glared. "I've never read anything about that."

She smirked and shook the saline bag with half an inch of liquid at the bottom. "It's all the rage. But having more than one ain't legal."

Michael shook his head in exasperation. His time researching history might have been better spent on learning of Satan's accomplishments as opposed to ancient wars, plagues, and failures. But the technological innovations of the last decade held little interest. His prison had managed to show him every technological marvel imaginable—cyborgs, clones, and the invasive Arkoff Port. The thin clear wires extended from a flat black box and inserted into Ralphie's neck were intriguing. The actual connection was hidden by Ralphie's heavy black beard. Michael yanked the wires free.

The girl reached. "No! No! Don't pull his links, ah . . . you idiot." She reached for the wires hanging from Michael's hand, but he clutched them protectively to his chest.

"My little brother did that," she said. "Once." She stepped away from the Tubers, and aimed for the kitchen, pausing to issue a warning: "You woke him. Now, you get to play with him." She hurried down the hallway.

Michael expected the back door to slam shut with her escape; instead the clank of steel and porcelain said the kitchen would be cleaned first. He looked at Ralphie, the fingers on his left hand twitched like Chin Scar's jaw had. He ripped Ralphie's mask off, sweat and sweetness filled the air. Unshaven, smooth pasty skin, Ralphie slept in peace. Michael looked at the wires dangling from his hand, then at both Tubers. He curled his lip. He threw the wires on Ralphie's rib cage and turned away.

They lose their connection to you, Father. Lucifer offers earthly satisfaction. His dominion over humanity is nearly complete.

No answer.

But the Fisherman's puzzling game had added another piece.

Michael returned to the table in the kitchen. The girl busied herself with cleaning. Mary whispered to Seth in the bedroom, comforting him from almost witnessing another murder. He picked up Seth's spoon and began licking it like a popsicle.

"You know who I am," Michael said.

The girl stopped her chore and lowered her head. Time and silence filled the room until she turned to face Michael. "It's like I was supposed to do this. I could've been working in Sun Valley, making bank as a massage therapist, a legitimate masseuse for the bougie rich crowd. But something said I needed to do this, take care of those idiots living in fantasy land." Her eyes filled with tears. "My mother said I was schizoid. *Take some drugs*, she said, fuck, I tried, but they didn't work . . . Nothing did . . . I . . . God warned me you were coming." She wiped at a tear falling down her cheek. "So why the hell are you here?"

Her emotions pained him. Her blind devotion to the Fisherman made him swallow a lump. He placed the spoon on the table. "Does He talk to you in your dreams?"

She scoffed and wiped snot from her nose. "I wish. I might've blocked that out." She gurgled a laugh. "He talks to me when I'm driving. Can you believe that? Sitting at a stop sign, stuck in traffic, it doesn't matter, but mostly when I drive here from Idaho Falls. A good ole chat with God every minute of every mile. Six times a week. Coming and going. He tells me how treasured I am, how unique I am, tells me I am His child, tells me I am loved, and He will provide. Provide. Ha. And here I am changing two morons' diapers and dripping baby food into their stomachs."

"And yet you still do it?" Michael asked.

She lowered her eyes and kneaded her hands. "And I still do it."

Michael frowned. "Do you think they hear Him? The dummies in the living room?"

"No, I think they escape. Live in a world—*live* isn't the word. *Exist* in a world made by men and machines, see what they want you to see. Feel what they want you to feel."

Michael felt a strange empathy for the girl. Felt her torment akin to his own years of despair caged in a tiny room, and yet he still chose to believe in God even as he curled his legs tight to his chest and cried each night. She was a prisoner, as he was, a soul unwilling to abandon faith. Michael fidgeted as she told him of driving to St.

Luke's Hospital in Twin Falls, cursing God and his incessant conversation for a hundred miles, and then sitting in a dark parking lot and crying for hours. And yet, God only reminded her of His love and endless patience, no matter what path she chose.

He reached behind his neck and pulled his robe off. He lifted his chin and inhaled to expand his chest. "Now you see what He wants you to see. Now you are as close to God as you can be in this mortal world."

The kitchen lights flickered. A nova of white sunlight brightened the kitchen. Michael approached her cautiously, and her face relaxed, her arms hanging limp with surrender.

"Now He wants you to feel His embrace," Michael said and spread his arms like wings, his pasty skin gathering a golden hue from the sunlight. His shoulder blades tickled as he waited for her. The touch of God, his own wish each night in a cold sterile cell, would now be granted to the girl.

She took a cautious step. Her eyes darted from the ground up to his steady gaze.

Michael nodded, unsure if she'd accept his gift. She crossed her arms then eased a step closer. Her eyes watered with confusion, settled on his, and then widened at something beyond his shoulder.

"Dear Lord," she said. "No, Ralphie!"

Michael ducked and slid across the slick linoleum floor to confront a Tuber charging into the kitchen trailing wild plastic tubing and wire.

Ralphie roared. "Mother. Jesus. Fuck. Who disconnected my—"

Michael ducked beneath Ralphie's weak attempt at a punch and stepped past a man eight inches taller. Michael rose up behind Ralphie and clasped the Tuber's neck into a jujitsu arm-bar. He squeezed hard. The awkward position allowed Ralphie to knife a hand in to ease the pressure on the carotid artery. The Tuber was deceptively strong for a semi-comatose zombie. Michael tightened his grip and used his other arm to leverage the pressure.

Ralphie gagged but managed to worm his fingers between Michael's forearm and his own neck, his long fingernails drawing blood as he pulled to loosen the headlock. Michael clenched his jaw and pulled with all his strength, adding every ounce of his weight as if he were a human backpack. His shin was raked by Ralphie's soft-soled foot, but Michael held tight.

Ralphie turned like a drunken miner, stinking of feces and old sweat. Michael thought of releasing the drunken bull to offer a compromise. Ralphie was supposed to be like him, an escapee from the labs. But he couldn't be sure. Not based on the words of a caretaker. Ralphie's wild arms wiped the table clean as he backed Michael into the door, shattering the glass.

Give me the strength.

"Please . . ." the girl whimpered.

Michael pulled the headlock with all his strength, and yet it only enraged the man. Michael spun with Ralphie's wild thrashing, his back stinging from the broken glass. Releasing his grip, Michael fell backwards and scrambled to grab the steel rod still propped up near the pantry.

Six feet away, the steel bar wouldn't miss its mark, and Michael readied the bar for a short thrust. Ralphie trashed the kitchen, ripping cabinet doors from their hinges. The girl took refuge beneath the table shoved against the wall. Michael sneered. He would end this madness now.

Ralphie's eyes were clouded with glaucoma. Michael aimed his strike at Ralphie's sunken chest, and yet his arm acted as if it wasn't his, as if he were handcuffed. Michael stepped back and growled, torn between the rage of battle and the Fisherman's interference. His own unbridled anger was unfamiliar, and he didn't care for it.

A faint memory tickled. Michael growled again. A compromise would satisfy the Fisherman.

Michael sidestepped over to the giant and slammed the heavy rod atop Ralphie's skull. Ralphie crumpled, taking plates and cups with him to the floor. The noise sent the girl scurrying into the pantry. Michael's heart slowed as his curiosity piqued.

Currents.

Humans lived as currents—air, or wind, or water, slow, fast, or stagnant. The type mattered little. The caretaker lived her life wallowing in a foam-filled back eddy, never enough strength to climb on to shore or move ahead with the main current. Ralphie was no different, except he resided in a murky bottom where light rarely shone.

The Fisherman's metaphors were plain to see. Why was it so

important for Michael to understand the volatility or futility of humans?

Ralphie moaned. His long arm slid across the wet floor. His fingers scratched the surface as if digging for something. The spaghetti tubes slithered like serpents biting at his pallid skin.

"Don't hurt him. He's not a bad man," the girl said.

Michael checked the hallway, half-expecting the other Tuber to stagger in, requiring a dose of what Ralphie received. It was empty. He tightened his grip on the rod, frustrated. The totem writhing on the floor couldn't have hailed from the lab. No way could he know where the others had fled. Ralphie had checked out. Ralphie lived in Samuel's domain, down in the abyss of darkness.

And yet Michael had been prevented from killing him.

Michael picked up his robe and put it back on. "Help me with this freaking pile of meat."

Silence.

The girl sobbed uncontrollably. Water stains darkened her blue medical scrubs, her hands covering her face. Michael squinted, confused. She lowered her hands to stare at him with puffy red eyes then wiped snot from her nose.

"No," she said and started laughing. In broken sentences, the girl stammered, "You, you . . . o-,o-, owe me. He says to get w-, w-, what's mine." She wiped her face. "He's talking to me right now, telling me to get what I wanted. I gotta be crazy. I ain't driving, and I ain't in my car. This is nuts."

Michael stepped to the table and offered his hand.

She looked up. "I gotta know you're not the man in a white jacket. Gonna load me into the wagon of no return." She frowned then offered her hand to let Michael help her up.

Michael smiled thinly and took her fingers in his. "You must warrant a special place in our Father's plan." His words caused her eyes to blink rapidly as he lifted her weight. "Not many may touch Michael and live to tell about it." He smiled with perfect teeth. "And the woman that may brag about this feat in Heaven shall be called . . ."

"Serah, but I don't . . ."

Michael hugged her, squeezing her response short. He inhaled sweet lavender and whispered, "Our Father has a plan, Serah. Could we ever think to know it. The prison you have lived is no different than my own." He felt her relax, suffering and torment fleeing her muscles. "You believe unlike any I have encountered. I feel it. And here we are." He squeezed her tight. "I need your help."

Serah's body was stiff and rigid in his arms. He released her, but she wouldn't let go.

She trembled. "He said you would embrace me, give me what He couldn't. He said to hold on as long as I wanted." She shivered again. "He's talking to me. No driving. No potholes. He's fucking talking to me right here, right now." She laughed and cried.

Ralphie groaned and started to rise.

Michael reached for the bar leaned against the table. Ralphie was deaf and blind to his world. Why had the Father allowed his soul to sour the earth was . . . He raised the bar to stake the man to the kitchen floor. Ralphie coughed and vomited a wad of ugly brown liquid. The idiot deserved nothing more.

Serah stayed his hand. "Oh, my heck. He says your idiot brother needs your help."

CHAPTER SIX

FAR BELOW THE SHARP SILVER wings of the hover-jet, the land-scape's geometrical shapes passed faster than Cyd could focus her attention. Circles of green farmland, scars of upturned soil, the lines of black and red oxide asphalt highways, expansive tracts of arid sagebrush bleeding into an umber stain of lava rock stretching as far as she could see. She pressed her nose hard against the window. A parade of blue and green tarpaulins dotted a bleak landscape remind-ing her of leathered animal skin.

"Is that the Craters? Is that where the Moonies live?" Cyd said.

"I suppose," Samuel said.

She looked at him, waiting for him to add something else, but he sat absorbed in the holographic images floating in front of his face. She shook her head imperceptibly then pressed her forehead back on the tinted glass that transformed the world outside to appear as if a giant shadow had blocked the bright sun. Her dark eyeglasses added to the desolation passing below.

The depletion of the ozone layer had caused a thousand-fold increase in skin cancers, glaucoma, and cataracts, but supposedly preventable if she wore eyeglasses and UV-resistant clothing. Cyd wasn't ignorant of the increasing maladies spreading over the planet. She managed to slip into Anna's office and surf the info nets for an hour, maybe two, every other day. *Do this, don't eat that.* Misery, and war. Blogs recommending an organic diet and synthetic supplements to live beyond the average lifespan of fifty-six years often filled the banners of websites she visited. She was pretty sure Anna knew of the intrusion.

She lowered her sunglasses and watched the miniature world below pass like a We-Tube video played at Arkoff speed. She checked her short skirt and UV leggings. Sterling Moore waited for her. The first step to freedom and a new life. New people, fancy restaurants, and movie premiers, the glamorous life she had always dreamed of. Daddy's influence would help a smidge, just till the producers and directors saw her talent. The script said to act afraid—heck, she would stretch and wrinkle her face as if Rondo was about to attack. The director said kiss Matthew Depp—well, he was kind of gross, but she could suck his face like she did Zac's. No problem.

The aircraft crossed a mountain range, and the landscape below changed to dense forests spotted with high mountain lakes and the lush green squiggles of creeks. Small, isolated cabins dotted the thick green blanket of trees. If she failed as an actor, she could always run away and live in the mountains as a reclusive anarchist, poach endangered elk, hide in a secluded bunker to avoid detection by drones and satellites. Survivalists probably ate their own children if the rare harsh winter came around, but if she failed, she would join them rather than listen to Daddy lash out with his razor-edged tongue.

Cyd looked at her father and felt a tinge of guilt. After all, he had gotten Sterling to share his house. Had he just protected her until she was old enough to deal with the chaos of the outside world? Tutored, babysat, and protected since before she could remember. Maybe letting go was hard for Daddy? Samuel swiped away holoscreens to be replaced by others for him to tap with nimble fingers.

She scoffed silently. *Letting go? He never latched on.*

The aircraft banked hard, and Cyd held tight to the armrest. Her stomach sank. A murky river sparkled in the sunlight. Sterling's house was definitely waterfront, had to be; he was the biggest movie star ever imagined. The pressure in her ears popped as the aircraft descended.

"Feeling okay, Cyd?"

She looked at Samuel and smiled thinly at his concern. She nodded and turned back to the window. The thought of the small

stash of 3Bz inside her suitcase lifted the corner of her mouth. Anticipating the relocation to Malibu, the elation, the sadness, and trepidation tempered her emotions at the possible loss of 3Bz. The drug was super expensive, limited to the ultra-wealthy, elite and powerful. Jurgens undoubtedly used his position as chief of staff within Arkoff Industries to maintain an ample supply. But the feeble old mad scientist looked like he might croak any day.

Be strong, Cyd. Be strong. This is what you wanted.

The aircraft skids touched, bounced lightly, then flattened out as the vertical thrust of the engines died. Cyd unbuckled her seatbelt and stared at the door, waiting for it to fall open. Daddy tapped his port and closed the screens floating at his face.

"This is just a prelude, Cyd. A snapshot of what you can expect in Malibu." He checked the surroundings outside his window and grunted disgust.

She swallowed a lump and nodded. "Let's hurry. He might be waiting."

Samuel smirked. "Undoubtedly. Remember, we fly home tomorrow."

He slid out of his seat but allowed Cyd to rush past him and wait at the stairway. The first step was always the hardest. She pushed her glasses up her nose and squinted at a cloudless hazy sky. People paid millions to witness an unpolluted blue sky in the temperate Antarctic. How magnificent would it be to feel the sun. See the blue sky without the UV filtering glasses. She reached to pull the glasses off her face then felt Daddy's hand on her wrist.

"A second of that sun will ruin all your dreams," Samuel said and released her.

"Got it," she said and scrambled down the stairs.

Cyd turned in a slow pirouette, arms outstretched, absorbing the heat of the sun with the distant noise of jet engines and sirens. She was finally birthed into the real world.

The limousine's stop-and-go ride up the crowded highway was totally marvelous. Cyd kept her face glued to the window. A massive three-tiered mansion overlooking the Big Wood River had to be Sterling's. No, too small, and too close to the highway. A superstar needed seclusion from the adoration of groupies. She curled her fingers into a ball and let her sharp nails bite the palm.

Stop it! Stop acting like a giggling schoolgirl pining for an autograph.

Cyd sat straight and spoke up. "How long until we get there?"

Daddy patted her knee, but the driver spoke through the thin translucent film between them. "Busy highway, Miss Cyd. This traffic stretches all the way back to Twin Falls. We'll hang a left a few miles up and call for a few drone zaps to eliminate any paparazzi following us."

Cyd leaned forward. The chauffer's hair was groomed immaculately, his jacket shimmering with fine threads. Twin Arkoff Ports, below both ears. And his wrists sparkled with red neon light pulsing from just beneath the skin. The man had Smart Arms, prosthetic limbs that could crush rock, fire lasers, even shoot old-style lead projectiles if required. She sat back in her seat.

Each street on the left had to be the one. Clusters of people shouted and waved signs at the electric Porsches and Town Cars easing past their corner.

"Ungrateful peons," Samuel muttered.

This meeting was huge. A big movie star met by a future big star. The worker bees wouldn't understand. They couldn't fathom the destiny being shaped by a meeting arranged by Samuel Arkoff, the richest, most powerful man on the planet.

The driver turned left and increased speed. The limo bottomed out crossing a bridge spanning a swollen Big Wood River. They slowed to a stop. A series of muted pops. Cyd looked out the rear window as an armada of drones swarmed the air above the bridge. A white car spewed steam twenty yards behind them. Two hovering drones fired tiny missiles at more cars jammed behind the steaming wreck. The rockets exploded with huge balls of flames mushrooming into the air. Cyd shrank into the comfortable leather seat.

The recently enacted Celebrity Act had given politicians, movie stars, or those with notoriety the legal basis to protect their privacy. The law was vague, as it was designed to be, provided legal grounds for the use of a wide variety of violent acts in order to protect the privacy of individuals from the snooping and surveillance of paparazzi and gossip websites, which ironically only increased the fervor of the stalkers. Disappointment weighed on Cyd's excitement;

an aspiring actress needed all the exposure she could get, even from ruthless paparazzi.

She looked at Samuel. He sat engrossed in his holo screens. She shook her head with exasperation.

The limo rolled past high masonry walls and gated enclaves, fortresses shielded beneath massive pines and cottonwood trees. LED warnings flashed on reader boards of the carrier drones intercepting vehicles entering its observation zone. The shadowed haven of technology moguls, the ultra-wealthy, and the famous, all beholden to Arkoff Industries. Sycophants escaping the world they helped create.

Cyd huffed. The exclusive neighborhood was a slum compared to the majestic compound of Yellowstone, but no one was as rich as Samuel Arkoff.

The car turned onto a gravel driveway guarded by massive iron gates. Cyd watched the driver tap icons on a red holo screen projected within reach of his right hand. He repeated the input on the screen several times. The gates remained closed. Cyd looked through the gaps of the metal spires to check out the elaborate peaks and gables of a Tudor-style mansion. The driver tapped the screen again with frustration. An almost invisibly thin glass window rolled down.

"I'm sorry, sir. The house security system won't recognize our presence. I've tried—"

Samuel swiped a hand to eliminate his screens. His jaw worked. A single screen blinked back into view. His fingers wiggled with anticipation. "Open the gate, Sterling, or I'll wire the media that picture I just sent you. And let the crows have their lunch."

Cyd groaned inside. Meeting the biggest movie star in the world, with Daddy's threats as an introduction.

Samuel smirked and looked up at the gate. Cyd stared at the black carpet. The car inched forward, and then crunched gravel at an easy pace. She thought of the vial of 3Bz in her pack. The house would have a zillion bathrooms she could excuse herself to. Just a small snort. It would burn her nostrils and she would need time for the calming effects to kick in, but a hit might take the edge off the approaching confrontation.

The car stopped beneath an Italian brick porte-cochere, and Cyd scrambled for the door handle but found it locked. She looked at the driver, then at Daddy.

He had that revengeful expression on his face again. Like he'd been crossed by Anna or saw something he didn't approve of on his fucking holo-screens.

"Sterling, get the fuck out here and open the door for my daughter. Cydney Arkoff will be greeted as her name commands," Samuel said. He looked forward in a blank stare, and his jaw twitched twice."

"Don't talk to him like that," Cyd said and shrank back from the door.

Samuel's commanding tone was often frightening, occasionally intoxicating, considering he wielded greater political power than any President of the United States. Private teachers, private tutors, and completely isolated within the confines of Yellowstone Park, Cyd had rarely witnessed her father's notorious dominance.

Cyd's eyes darted from the massive front door back to Daddy swiping fresh holo screens, then back to the house. Daddy glanced out the window, and his jaw twitched. The happiest day of her life, and it was about to blow up like a Razzi drone.

The massive iron doors of the house opened wide, and Cyd sat up. Reaching for the door handle, Cyd looked back at her father. He bared his yellowed canines. No!

Sterling hurried out the door dressed in a baggy T-shirt and droopy gym shorts. Cyd scrunched her face. The door locks popped, and she opened the door. As she climbed out, Daddy's hatred flowed out with the air. Screw him. She was out of Yellowstone. She was free. She resisted an urge to duplicate the rejuvenating dance she performed on the tarmac.

"Cydney Arkoff," Sterling said. He opened his arms wide in a greeting. "You are nothing less than the beauty your father had described."

Cyd swallowed as the man approached. This wasn't the great Sterling Moore. He was shorter than Zac, his stringy long black hair streaked with grey, the saggy muscle on his arms rivaling Jurgens' old body.

Her voice failed. "Hi. I . . ."

Sterling grabbed her hands and smiled up at her. "You're so gorgeous. You'll make my arm candy jealous." He bent over to peer inside the limo. "Samuel, I was preparing for your visit and must've forgotten to program the system for your arrival." Sterling jerked his head back out, his eyes wide with surprise, or fear.

He turned his attention to Cyd and put his arm around her waist. His fingers squeezed the fold of skin above her hip. Oh. My. Fucking. God. Sterling Moore was fondling her as if she were a groupie.

"This is a beautiful home—"

"Yes, it is. And you haven't even seen the best part," Sterling said. He stared side-eye at the darkness inside the limo and swallowed hard. "The Arkoff patriarch has work to do, but we don't. Do we, Cyd?" He led her towards the front door. "Such a sexy name in a masculine sort of way, and your hair . . . Platinum might become the rage again when Tinseltown gets a load of you."

Cyd's heart drummed as Sterling led her into the house. He was nothing like she pictured, his prominent chin shadowed with a week's worth of stubble. His famously brilliant blue eyes bulged beneath loose flaps of skin.

The familiarity and safety of Yellowstone beckoned. Her stomach fluttered with nerves as she walked down a hallway adorned with pictures of Sterling—perpetually grinning, embracing rock stars, shaking hands with world leaders, or donating millions to the starving children of Mexico.

What did you expect? Jeez. She hugged herself as Sterling led her into the grand room. Gigantic sheets of clear glass offered a view of the swollen Big Wood River splashing foam and froth over huge granite boulders. The fireplace burned red with fake wood and neon embers.

Sterling showed her to a sunken living room. A brunette girl no older than Cyd used a razor blade to chop sky-blue powder piled on a mirror. A lithe blond woman supervised then looked up at Cyd and smiled. She rubbed her girlfriend's backside then looked back down at the powder.

"Arelia and Princess. They will show you to your room." He squeezed her butt. "And whatever pleasures we may conceive."

———

DISGUST ALMOST FORCED THE FOOD in Michael's stomach to return to the sink. He wiped his mouth and turned to face an audience. Myra sat and suckled the baby. Ralphie sneered and yanked on the cloth straps binding him to a kitchen chair. His jaw worked hard, biting the air like a zombie seeking a victim. Mary leaned against the fridge with her arms folded across her chest. Serah lifted the faucet lever and let rusty water run.

Currents. Each different, each required to be dealt with by a different mend of the line.

Mend, Michael, mend.

"Each of you hear the Father," Michael said. "And He has His reasons. And I have mine. I am here for a purpose. One. Single. Purpose."

"You're an abomination," Mary said. Her withering gaze was resolute with conviction.

"He's God's angel," Seth countered.

Mary shot the boy a scowl. Seth glared and stared down her warning.

"Your pride, or your ego, or your beliefs won't protect you from what He has armed me with," Michael said. "The Fisherman has charged me with . . . all of you!" He grabbed Ralphie's long black hair and pulled, tilting the Tubers face up. Michael sneered at the Tubers' milky grey eyes clouded from years of wearing a black VR mask.

Brother, indeed.

He released his grip on Ralphie and squinted at Serah. She smiled a wry grin, a deceptive face that said she knew something he did not. He balled his fist. Mending fly line in this chaotic windstorm was impossible. Michael closed his eyes, hoping for a whisper of help.

He inhaled deep and heaved, then opened his eyes, and surveyed God's new army. *Women, children, babies, and zombies. This is what He has armed me with.*

So be it.

Currents to manipulate, and control.

"Wake up that other Tuber," Michael said. *Mend, Michael, mend.* "Serah, my *brother* needs your help. Obviously, our Father must have some use of him in this world."

Serah grabbed a dish towel and moved to Ralphie's side. "We have to bring his senses back slowly, as if he were in a coma." Serah smiled at Seth. "Junior bug, get something to shove into his ears." Ralphie thrashed and growled as she tied the towel around his eyes for a blindfold and took Seth's offer of a paper napkin to shove into his ears and nostrils.

She stood back from her work and laughed, a hearty sarcastic laugh, as if an artist had just failed at creating a masterpiece. "All these years I thought I was fucking crazy." She laughed again, a vocal release of an internal torment. "Ralphie's gonna be pissed. But I'm coming with you."

Michael silently groaned. *God's Army. Indeed.*

Michael walked back into the living room and studied the motionless woman lying on the gurney. He put his hand on her wrist. A rapid heartbeat. Her adrenaline surged. A glimmer of her mind's eye flashed in his own, of dark tunnels, menacing doors, sick abominations appearing from around corners to attack, silly weapons, and fake ammunition as rewards. He pulled his hand away, and the vision stopped.

Lucifer's world of deception.

Michael slumped down into the armchair. *You kept me sanitized, isolated for almost fifteen years just to witness the world as it truly exists. I understand now, Father. But don't anchor me with mortals and let me float like flotsam on a swirling eddy.*

Serah walked in and kneeled next to his chair. "I'm sorry. I didn't mean to sound so . . ." She placed her head on his thigh. Michael stroked the back of her head. In prison, her silky hair would be a fantasy. Now, the pleasant sensation only tickled his fingers.

She looked up at him with teary eyes. Moisture glistened on the tiny hairs on her cheeks, illuminating a tiny crescent-shaped white scar beneath her right eye. She chuckled, a nervous noise. "I hear Him. Sounds like my baby brother sometimes. Do this, don't do that, but . . ." She squeezed his leg and giggled nervously. "He says relax. Go with the flow."

Her final word confirmed the Fisherman did indeed talk with her.

Ralphie roared from the kitchen. Glass shattered, wood splintered, and Michael pushed Serah away. She stood and held up her hands, motioning for him to stay seated, and she hurried to the kitchen. Silence. Serah whispered. Her voice calmed the idiot beast. She was cute in a tomboy sort of way. Why had the Fisherman brought her into this destiny? Any of them? Did it matter? But she was kinda pretty.

Seth shook him from his fantasy and said, "We got problems."

Michael's face flushed, and he adjusted his robe. "My life is now one big conundrum. Please throw another on my plate."

Seth scrunched his face with confusion.

"What's the problem?" Michael said.

"Well, I checked the others while you were playing goo-goo face with that girl, and we need a bunch of stuff. Like baby milk stuff, more food, and water jugs."

Michael frowned. "What are you talking about? The pantry is full of food, and Myra can feed the kid. Wait . . . what others?"

"Um, maybe you didn't notice, Mr. Angel, but like, uh . . . a lot of Moonies think you're some kind of savior, and they're following us," Seth said. He folded his arms and glared.

Michael arched his brows. "And you wouldn't have had anything to do with that, would you, Seth?"

"Hey, go talk to Myra. She's the one who kissy-faced that stupid Davis goodbye. They heard what you did and started to follow us."

Michael frowned.

"Well, I helped a little. Told them the Archangel Michael was heading to Arco and, well, maybe they should follow us," Seth placed his hand on Michael's shoulder. "C'mon Michael, living in that trash dump and then a guy like you just comes walking in. What'd ya expect?"

The boy was right. What did he expect? A memory of the prison's white cage entered his thoughts, the tortuous grooming, and the relentless blood draining. The endless futility of his life. Moonie life was no different. Michael stood up and nodded his reluctant agreement.

He followed the boy down the hallway, paused at the kitchen to watch Serah dab a wet cloth on Ralphie's head wound. They stepped out the back door. Shaded by a thick canopy of tree branches, the bright sun felt warm, nonetheless. Seth waited at the street curb, waving for Michael to hurry.

The buckled sidewalk ended at a gravel road. Hundreds of identical black cows congregated near the wire fence of Milsap's Cloned Beef and Manure. Seth shooed the beasts away and climbed over a gate. The stench of cow dung and ammonia made Michael's eyes water as he leaned the steel bar against the wire fence and hopped the gate to follow Seth. His bare feet sank into hefty piles of squishy manure. The blisters on his soles tingled. Seth bolted, aiming for a grove of old cottonwoods spewing fluffy seed pods to scatter into the brisk wind.

Michael halted and considered his impetuous act. Clothed but defenseless, he would be relegated to flinging cow pies at anything that chose to attack. He seethed at everything waiting beyond the trees. The brisk wind was relenting and wouldn't keep drones from finding them for long. He glanced back towards the house and thought of Serah.

A high-pitched whistle, and Seth's waving arm, called him.

Michael searched the field for anything to use as a weapon. Cow patties, dried and fried by the intense sun, or squishy, or buzzing with flies. He gave up the futile search. Seth scrambled down an embankment as Michael grew close.

Hundreds of huddled grey lumps lined the dry streambed. The robes of Moonies flapped in the wind. Faces concealed in hoods, they stared down at their own tattered sneakers or dirty bare feet.

Michael looked to the sky and closed his eyes. *Oh, Father. Why?*

Seth pranced up and down the riverbed, shouting at the Moonies, "I told ya. I told you an angel was gonna help us."

"A bunch of bull manure is more like it," a male voice said.

Michael balled his fists and searched for the man. The words infuriated him, not because they might be the truth, but because they spat on a young boy's faith and hope. Michael had read stories about human friendships. Some spanned a lifetime, others hurdled insurmountable obstacles, some were severed then reconnected, some ended with the death of one and within days the other. Seth's companionship was welcome and easy, and without commitment.

Michael pulled off his robe and climbed down the rocky embankment into the dry streambed. Naked, and defenseless, he walked the dusty river channel staring at anyone brave enough to challenge him. *Grow gossamer wings and the Moonies would cower. Sprout a golden halo, and they would kneel.* The Moonies watched with expressions half-hidden behind hoods held as masks.

"Your faith in me is blind," Michael said loudly, then turned a full circle. He felt their eyes watching him, but nothing moved. "Follow me, and your faith will be tested, your hope sucked to the marrow. Follow me, and your obedience shall be absolute and voiceless." He waited for someone to move away. "Hope is all I can promise. And the protection of a steel rod."

The wind lulled. He pushed his face at Seth. Widened his eyes in a *Now what expression.*

Seth pointed upstream, towards the smoke and dust billowing off the distant mountains. "We're gonna find the other angels, your friends, up there in the mountains."

Michael narrowed his eyes. "How come all of a sudden you know so much?"

"Duh. It's where Ralphie wanted to go. And you were going that way, too. Two plus two still equals four, angel."

Seth was hiding something. The Moonies would never leave their meager homes because of something a boy said. He was clever beyond his years.

Seth offered him his robe. "Drones don't care about Moonies unless we try to mix with people. But we escaped the Craters, so now they'll keep watch and make sure we keep going."

Michael pulled the robe back on. His skin protested the feel of the thick UV-resistant fabric. He studied Seth's wide-eyed, innocent face. He couldn't quite discern an odd feeling rising in his chest. He took a step downstream, back towards the Craters, and his prison, then looked upstream towards the town of Mackay and the White Cloud Mountains.

An imposing mountain range of ugly granite spires jutting out of steep slopes covered with sagebrush, deep crags forming sharp incisors to bite at the hazy sky. An impressive Lost River Mountain range defeated by a mechanized assault of strip miners swarming up from the arid bottomland.

Michael kneeled and closed his eyes. "Father, I have failed at what you have taught. Forgive me. This body, this mind, I am directionless at every turn. I beseech you. The currents pull me one way, then another, and yet I have no chance to mend my line." He felt reluctant to stand, face Seth, face Moonies who hoped to believe in an omnipotent angel, one that didn't quite believe in himself.

"We got incoming. Ready your arms and load up!" Seth shouted.

Adrenaline surged. Michael's heart pumped as his eyes followed Seth's point. A drone flying low in the channel aimed multiple beams of red light to scan the huddled Moonies. Cries of fear sounded. He

stayed Seth's arm and pulled him into a huddle. They waited and touched foreheads as the drone engines whirred close overhead.

"Battle isn't always the best course, but don't let me say that too often," Michael said.

"Tell 'em to keep moving upstream until we can catch up," Seth said. "We gotta get Myra and the baby, and Grammy, and food, and Ralphie."

Michael stood tall, expanding his chest as he inhaled air laced with odorous sulfur from the mines. He walked up the line of robes huddled on the rocky riverbank and slapped hoods. "You, and you. Ready yourselves for battle." He chose using their eyes, skipping the defiant or suspicious, and even passing on the eager. Frightened eyes suited his purpose best.

Michael led a troop of twelve robes through the field of cow dung, scattering slow-footed cattle. At the gate, he turned and warned them, "All the houses on this street are fair game. Stuff your robes and backpacks with canned or packaged food. Don't waste your time on water, or whiskey, or anything that might piss me off. Don't believe everything Seth said about me. Put a pint of booze in your pack, and you'll regret it. Now spread out and steal. Your robes will scare them. Any trouble, scream out like your fingers were cut off. Let me deal with the people. Now go!"

Michael grabbed the bar as he watched them climb over the railing to scatter towards the homes. *Currents, Father. Your sword in this dry creek just created a new current. A hydraulic of your making, one that may pull all of us down.*

Three drones dropped from the tree canopy across the street and hovered twenty feet above his head. Fan blades whirred in the dying wind. Each rotated, confused, then shot out to follow the scavengers spreading through the neighborhood. A small odd-looking object dropped out of the trees and fluttered thin translucent wings to maintain a steady position in the wind.

Seth threw a clod of manure at the insect-like drone. The dragonfly dropped ten feet and released a puff of smoke, rotated, and re-aimed its bulbous eye-cameras. It fired a needle. Michael threw the javelin. The mechanical bug ejected another puff of smoke as the rebar split the aluminum body.

Michael ignored a pinprick of stabbing pain in his chest. Seth jumped and thrust his fists into the air. A simple dance of a boy cele-brating victory, before he folded and crumpled to the ground, a tiny metal dart pinning his robe to his chest.

Michael looked down at his chest and saw an identical dart. *I heal myself with everything I say and do. I heal myself with . . .*

His empty hands balled. The monsters and their machines would find his retribution. The monsters would regret . . .

Michael dropped to the ground. His robes flapped in a warm breeze wafting of human ignorance.

Michael's cheek sucked heat from a slab of sun-bleached river rock. He stared at a two-inch salmonfly crawling atop the crusty rock, its long antennae twitching for scents hidden in a gentle breeze. Michael willed his legs to move, but his muscles were paralyzed. A ragged boot landed inches from his face. He was lifted like a ragdoll. He stared at eyes blue as midnight, an infinity speckled with tiny points of light.

"Didn't expect you so soon," a pleasant basso said.

Michael worked his jaw, but his voice was gone. Calloused hands soothed his disorientation, and the Fisherman's face came into focus. His nose scarlet from a burning sun, a beard riddled with strands of grey, the Fisherman cradled him as if he were a newborn child.

"Look at that water, Michael. The river runs turbid with the spring runoff. The currents are muddied and full of flotsam. The bugs can't mate, the trout can't eat, and you were still caught, hooked like a fish."

Michael could only gaze into the beautiful eyes of a depthless night sky.

"But I found you and now release you back into the river. You'll be stronger, wiser. Faster," the Fisherman said.

Michael fell in a freefall, a ride into oblivion.

Instead of Salmonflies, Michael stared at maggots burrowing through a dung heap. He twitched his leg, then his arm. Stronger. Wiser. Faster.

As if forged in red-hot steel, the Fisherman's words resounded. Michael cursed the robe as he struggled to stand up. The Moonies had fled. How long had he been asleep? An eternity could pass bathing in His glow, listening to His words, and yet only seconds had passed.

Seth stood in his shadow, slapping cow dung off his stained

robe. An inkling of Seth's presence in his dream passed. Four drones hovered like four horsemen and surrounded them as he pulled the needle out of his chest.

He clenched his teeth. Faster. Stronger. Wiser.

Michael picked up clumps of dry manure and looked at Seth. The boy's eyes widened, and he nodded. Battle. Michael hurled clods of manure, each piece compressed by an angry fist, each piece a missile of divine making. The drones rose to avoid the attack and hover beyond their range.

Thwack. Thwack. Two drones dropped to the field. *Thwack.* Another fell.

"Uncle Zeke! Get that last one. Get him. Get him!" Seth yelled.

Michael picked up his steel rod. A giant Moonie with thick forearms covered in scales of dried skin and ugly carcinomas aimed a small slingshot at the last drone. Naked except a long loincloth and tattooed from neck to ankle in elaborate designs and colors, Zeke leaned on a prosthetic leg attached at the knee.

"Little fucker ain't getting away," Zeke said.

Thwack.

"Ya got him. Ya got him!" Seth pumped his fist.

Zeke put on a Moonie robe two sizes too small but shadowed his face within a deep hood. Michael approached to within inches to peer closely at his weathered face until an apparition raised its head to peer over Zeke's shoulder and glare, a translucent face identical to Zeke, unaffected by the wind, riding on the man's back like a rucksack. Michael frowned and stepped back. The ghost was a twin, a lost soul who hadn't or couldn't pass over to His realm.

He stared at the angry soul but said, "Get the Moonies moving. Upstream. Get them far away from this place." He pressed the point of the steel rod to the man's chin and lifted it. "Move them fast."

"Is that why you think we follow you? That bloody steel rod? God has many weapons and treasures. God will deliver us," Zeke said and made the sign of a cross over his chest.

The man was right. God would dictate every step. The Archangel Michael was no different than Seth, Myra, Mary, or Zeke. And he was human now, and unsure of anything except to lead the Moonies far from Arco.

He recognized the man as one who fought at Myra's father's side.

"You're right, Uncle Zeke." He lowered the rod and bowed his head. "God does have a plan for all of us. Thank you for—"

"For knocking the crap out of those drones," Seth said.

Michael gave Seth a sideways glance. "The Fisherman . . . eh, our Lord commands me to lead these chosen . . ." Lead them where? The mountains, the coast, freaking Alaska? And yet the Lord had always provided. Every soul on this planet was given what was required to flourish. But he was human now. The concept remained disconcerting. The Fisherman would provide.

"We need to move your—our people upstream," Michael pointed the rod towards the mountains. "They . . . We need to move fast."

Zeke laughed and shook his head. "The Fisherman, you say. Is that what an angel calls our Lord?"

The Lord was known by hundreds of names. The Lord spoke with infinite voices. "He speaks to you through him. Doesn't he?" Michael asked.

They locked eyes. He saw and heard all he needed.

Zeke narrowed his eyes.

"He speaks to you through your dead brother," Michael said.

Zeke recoiled, as if his face was slapped, then said, "Go to Hell."

Michael smiled a crooked smile. "I judged his soul. I allowed him to pass into His arms, but He refused and closed the gate. His spirit still has work to finish."

The propeller of a downed drone died in a mound of dung as Michael watched the man melt.

Zeke swallowed hard and said, "He keeps saying the good times are coming. Tells me our Lord is coming to reclaim His kingdom. We saw what you did for Myra! We all saw it! It was a fucking miracle! So, we followed you." Tears streamed down his cheeks, and he swiped at them angrily.

"The Fisherman says we need to go. And now," Michael said.

Zeke ignored him. "What did I have to lose? We had nothing on the Moon except bugs and rats. I said why not? Been hearing about deliverance since . . . Why the hell not? Maybe I'd get a little revenge, maybe I'd find a . . . And then . . ."

Zeke dropped the slingshot, fell to his knees, and sobbed.

Appraising a human was infinitely more difficult than judging a soul. Michael approached and tapped Zeke's shoulder with the steel rod.

Zeke looked up, dark tears at the corner of each eye. He laughed, a roar of odd laughter. "He was right, angel." He wiped his nose. "He's been with me the whole time. Telling me things would change." Zeke chuckled humorlessly. "He said that when shit hit the fan I would know. Over and over, he kept telling me to wait until the shit hits the fan."

The large man rose from his knees and straightened his back, then pointed at a drone dying on the turf. "Shit has hit the fan. But I'm gonna guess this dung heap we be standing on is just the appetizer."

"Man, you need to get the others moving," Michael said. "And don't stop. Shit is going to hit the fan, and we can't be here when it does. Now, move!"

Zeke wiped snot from his nose and glared. "Why didn't he get in? Why did God stop him"

Michael grinned. "The Fisherman makes angels where He sees fit. And I'm not sitting on your shoulder, Uncle Zeke. But he might be!"

"You mean he—" Zeke heaved a sigh then picked up his slingshot. "We'll follow the riverbed up to Mackay. I'll post lookouts every so often, to help the scavengers. We got women and small children, but we'll move as fast as we can."

Michael looked toward Arco and saw the first Moonie returning with a heavy pillowcase hanging from each hand. Seth ran towards the Moonie girl. Michael gazed up at the hot sun and felt the light burn his eyes.

He had lied about judging Zeke's brother. He might never know why the twin still wandered the earth. But the words felt right, and the deception caused no shame. Memories of Michael's past lives sprouted then withered quickly. The Fisherman had his reasons. And he was no different from Zeke's brother, a tool for Him to sow His garden.

Ancient memories returned—sharper and focused.

He was a garden tool, a hoe, and a shovel.

A scythe against the coming storm.

CHAPTER SEVEN

SAMUEL CLOSED NUMEROUS HOLO-SCREENS FLOATING in the tiny office and chuckled as he considered how his unthinkable gambit would play on the news channels. News anchors and pundits were sure to label him a raving fucking lunatic. A madman. An evil mass murderer. And with a few commands issued through Arkoff Ports he could eliminate all discussion of the matter. No one wanted to cross him—better yet, no one could deny him, let alone endure the wrath of Lucifer. His dominion over mankind was absolute.

Samuel stood up from behind the security officer's desk and said, "Detonate that tactical nuke on top of that shitty little town, Captain."

A nuclear strike on American soil, a treasonous demand if there ever was one. Captain Boatman would have every justification to slap handcuffs on him and escort him to whatever silly court governed this bleak excuse of society.

Captain Boatman lowered his eyes. "Sir, we can't do that. Maybe drop some napalm or maybe carpet-bomb the target, but—"

"Can't or won't, Captain?" Samuel walked around the oblong conference table and crowded the big man standing rigidly in a military *at ease* posture.

The young officer outweighed him by fifty pounds, all pure

muscle. Even so, he could lift the officer with a single hand and send him sprawling across the room. Boatman wouldn't meet his eyes.

Samuel backed off. "Tell me again how your surveillance drones and satellites seem to have misplaced our friend Michael?" Samuel flared his nostrils to inhale the sweet scent of fear floating in the warm stale air. He waited for an answer that was utterly irrelevant.

"We find him, and then we lose connection to the drones," Boatman said. He initiated a holo-screen an arm's length away. The red borders flickered then vanished. "See what I mean. Satellite surveillance is useless due to the intense solar storms bombarding us constantly. We can't seem to—"

Samuel let his thoughts slip. "The master piddles with pawns."

"Sir, I don't understand?" Boatman said.

Samuel faced Boatman. "Of course, you don't. That's why you are going to take a team to the coordinates I transmitted to you and retrieve one of the tactical nuclear devices I have hidden." He raised his hand to fend off any questions. Boatman's jaw quivered. "Arco has been subverted by terrorists. Anarchists. Maybe Islamic jihadists. But the who matters little. The town is owned by Arkoff Industries and will be destroyed in any manner I see fit."

Boatman shifted his stance. "I'm not gonna be the man responsible for detonating a nuclear weapon on U.S. soil. I'd be treated like a pariah, forced to live in a hell of my own consequences."

Samuel smiled. "Admirable, Captain Boatman. But if I'm not mistaken, your daughter lives in that hellhole, doesn't she?"

Boatman shuffled his feet but said nothing.

"Would you vaporize that town to liberate your little girl from the chains of that nasty 3Bz? There are treatment programs I can get young Vanessa into, get her clean, and ensure she doesn't walk down that dark alley of addiction again."

Boatman bit his lip then opened his mouth to say something.

Samuel continued, "The whoring, the violence, the pimps. She won't live to see twenty. Vanessa's salvation depends on your decision. And I'm sure you know that a deal with Samuel Arkoff is as solid as one with the devil himself."

Boatman almost whispered, "They may be gone by the time it detonates."

"They? Do you think I want to obliterate the town just to kill a few Moonies?" Samuel chuckled and walked away, confident the fish was hooked. "We need to wipe out what young Michael has unleashed. A curse, a plague that will ruin this world for our species."

Boatman cleared his throat. "Vanessa's in Atlanta with her mother . . ."

"But nowhere is safe from what Michael has unleashed. Afterwards, she will receive only the finest care. Captain, you've reviewed the files from the labs. The plagues Michael has been exposed to. The death and misery that boy carries inside him."

"But he cured everything he'd been exposed to. The virus—"

"Yes, the anti-bodies made us a lot of money. Plain and simple. The cure for Ebola alone made this company over three trillion dollars. But now it's time to pay the piper," Samuel said.

Boatman frowned.

"It's an ancient proverb. All debts come due. Michael may have cured the world of many diseases known to mankind, but *you* let him escape." He let the accusation sink in. "And flee with the most lethal combination of disease and sickness known to man. He is patient zero. He is the vector that will plunge this world into the apocalypse. You might be vilified, maybe for years. But if mankind survives, you may well be deified."

Boatman looked away for a long minute, then snapped to attention. "I don't have the expertise to detonate a nuke, sir."

Samuel chuckled. "Who does? Except the military. The bomb you are going to retrieve is a black-market suitcase model Arkoff Industries purchased to prevent it from falling into the wrong hands. Apparently, the instructions were included with the purchase. What was I to do? I stored it. I forgot about it. Until now."

"I . . . I . . . can't just . . ."

'You can, Captain!" Samuel said. He approached to within inches of Boatman and stared at his bloodshot eyes. Was the security officer also enjoying the pleasures of 3Bz? "Would you pilot a jetliner into the ground if you knew it would save thousands? Would you have assassinated Hitler to save millions of innocent lives? These questions are easily answered by saying yes. Who wouldn't? Michael is worse than Hitler. Michael is a jetliner aimed for the skyscraper of humanity. Michael is a walking time bomb. A mortal danger to everyone he comes in contact with."

"But a nuke. On American soil?" Boatman said. His shoulders sagged.

Samuel bit his lower lip to feign concern. "I know. I know. I will take full responsibility for this. Let the chips fall where they may. But we need to be diligent. Act before Michael can spread the plague outside the containment zone." He could simply access Boatman's consciousness using his Arkoff Ports and order the man to carry out his wishes. But then what fun would that be? "We will save billions. Vanessa. Our wives and children. And our future." He wiped at his eye as if a tear fell.

Boatman twitched his jaw, working it as if eating a meal. "I have the coordinates, sir. Estimated time for pickup and delivery is fourteen hours. Detonation estimated at twenty-two hours from this mark." Boatman kept twitching his jaw. "Will that timeframe end the scourge?"

"Accelerate it! This plague must be eliminated. Now! Or we all . . ." Samuel let the statement hang. He turned away to smirk.

Sending a pawn to do a king's job, but a move He would have predicted. Samuel felt his skin shrink, tighten in on his old bones. He clenched his fists. The paradox of predetermination could often make Samuel feel like a helpless fetal child. A feeling only serving to enrage him. God could not know everything. Could not be everywhere. Could not know what would happen every second of every day of every living thing on the planet. Nothing Samuel had invented, or conspired, would command that infinite knowledge, that infinite power.

But if that power did exist, Samuel would have it for himself.

He turned to face Boatman. "Why are you still here?"

The man flinched, then turned on his heels and walked out the door.

Twenty-two hours, indeed! Get the fucking bomb near city center, and he would detonate it himself with a simple twitch of his jaw. Simpletons. Piddling with pawns. This game was for all the marbles. Maybe that simpleton Boatman needed an explanation of what a game of marbles entailed. He chuckled.

A bright red alert icon flashed on his holo-screen.

Urgent! Urgent! Urgent! The world operated in an urgent state of flux. Maybe he should let Michael decimate the world, and he could simply rule the ruins of an apocalyptic kingdom with fear and guile. Screw the stress. Screw technology and the decisions they entailed. He could sit as king on the throne of Yellowstone and dish out edicts, take the maidens that suited his fancy, supervise the peons as they constructed stone monuments to deify him. Been there, done that.

The technology allowing his consciousness to meld with the wolf, Rondo, would be destroyed. No. He had to ride that beast again, and again. He had to feel the warm blood, the life essence of a kill, blood dripping off his jaws. Primal and glorious.

Samuel twitched his jaw and read the message. From Sterling. He chuckled.

Cyd succumbed to his rituals.

Debauchery and deceit did rule the world.

Cydney was key to winning the game. The red queen, a stupid virgin angel whose death was required. He could drop a nuke on every city on the entire West Coast, and it wouldn't matter. Not if she remained free.

But she needed to die at precisely the right moment.

THE VISION ACTED AS A plague on Michael's thoughts—the brown murky water, violent whitewater roiling hefty tree trunks like broken toothpicks, the water level rising quicker than he could retreat up the bank. The vision was . . . a simple metaphor, a portal through which He spoke. And issued commands. But the Fisherman had been absent from the nightmare. A flood, a storm, a mysterious cataclysmic event was coming. And soon.

Myra led the two Tubers to join the procession of Moonies. Her hood off, she carried the child in a sling held against her chest. She looked at Michael with pleading eyes as she steered the two lurching half-dead gamers up the rocky riverbed. He pursed his lips and gazed up at the sky.

Dear Lord, you have made me a nursemaid. But if that is what you require . . . then so be it.

He jumped up on a crumbled rock jetty and yelled, "Move faster! If we are still in this valley when that sun disappears, then we die. Your . . . The Lord . . . Move! Move like your life depends on it!"

Michael searched downstream, hoping to see Seth. The boy came and went with boundless energy, assisting the scavengers returning with food or supplies. Burdened with cans and packages of food, Seth handed them off to other Moonies, then disappeared in search of more. He would prefer the boy at the head of the pack. To sound a warning of approaching drones, or even the police.

Michael jogged ahead, passing Moonies who grumbled with doubts and dissension. He found Zeke carrying a toddler in each arm and leading the procession at a plodding pace. The man ignored Michael's presence. He searched the cavities of his mind for the memories of a kind soul. The memory greeted him and showed him a story. And then fled like a wisp of smoke.

Zeke grunted an acknowledgement.

Michael crowded the bigger man. "Let's get it straight, big man. A tsunami is coming. Now!"

Zeke increased his pace for a few steps, as if he simply wanted to get away from Michael.

"What's it gonna take?" Michael said.

Zeke stopped and glared. "Uh . . . Mr. Angel. It's gonna take more than you."

They locked eyes. Michael felt as if he was kneed in the groin. He stood dumbstruck as Zeke shook his head and kept moving. The procession of Moonies ignored him as they passed.

He was Michael.

He was an Archangel. The mighty sword of the Lord of Lords.

And he would weigh their souls.

But how could Zeke or any Moonie truly know what he was or had been? He was nothing but a man—a boy, really—carrying a silly piece of steel. His cheeks flushed, and he squeezed the steel with strength surging from anger. His vision fogged with grey robes and whitewashed rock glowing red. The steel bar burned hot.

He would confront Zeke and show him what he truly was. Show him he wasn't to be trifled with. Show him what an Archangel was truly capable of. He would carry the whole motley lot to safety if that was what the Fisherman required.

A warm sensation tickled his toes. A trickle of warm water wetting his feet as if to cool his temper. A rivulet of muddy water coursed through the river rock. Thin grass and black specks floated with the brackish water. The water gained speed like a miniature torrent, as if running away from his feet.

Another warning from the Fisherman!

Panic replaced anger, and Michael ran. His feet squished and slipped in the fresh mud.

The huge bulk of Zeke's robe was easy to find. Michael placed his hand on the man's shoulder to turn him. "This water we're walking in is a warning. The Lord is telling us that something is coming."

"And what do you propose, Mr. Angel? Gonna build us a boat, too?" Zeke said. He waved to the others to keep moving.

Michael glared, the sarcasm tempting him to swing the steel rod like a bat and send the man's head into the bleachers of the distant mountains. Metaphors. The Lord spoke in metaphors. "What would stop this water from making mud beneath our feet?

Zeke scratched his beard. "Dam it up. Or get upstream of the source."

Michael searched his memories, of maps and geological formations near the location of the prison. Information he would require for a successful escape attempt. Mackay Reservoir and its rock dam.

Michael's anger returned. He shoved the point of the steel rod beneath Zeke's chin and lifted his face. "I'm going to be the angel you require, sit on your shoulder, and shove this steel up your ass every time you don't move these people faster."

Zeke huffed and stared at him.

Michael's next words came from a distant realm. "Do your job, big monkey. Do as the Lord commands."

"Fuck! Why'd you say that?" Zeke said. His fists balled, and he bared his teeth.

Michael lifted the steel bar to push firmly on the man's chin. "Your mother's spirit also remains on this world. The Fisherman speaks through her. Or are you too stupid to listen, big monkey?"

Zeke swatted the steel to the side as if it was an annoyance. "He has a plan for you too, huh, boy? Didn't give you those wings, or that sword, or that Almighty power you're used to. You're no angel."

Michael calculated the balanced movement for a leg sweep, followed by an arm bar, to take him to the ground. Then what? Make him say uncle? And Zeke was right. The Fisherman had made him human, required him to feel pain, doubt, and joy, regardless of the deadly scourge coursing through his veins and in his spittle. His final judgment for all His blessed creatures if need be.

The Archangel stabbed the iron rod into the ground. "You're right. You doubt who I am? Ask me a question only your mother would know, and let's settle this discussion."

Zeke released a deep breath and rubbed the back of his neck. "When I was seven. Our mother got us something for Christmas. What was it?" Zeke pushed his substantial bulk close and stared deep into Michael's eyes.

The pale gray eyes opened Michael's mind to a childhood memory, or perhaps the vision belonged to Zeke's mother. A leafless tree branch strapped to ugly water stained walls and illuminated with tiny glass bulbs of light. Blue and green and yellow and white lights blinked and towered above young twin boys, giggling and shaking packages wrapped in colored gift paper. A mother and father beamed as the boys settled to sit cross-legged on a water-stained plywood floor and began tearing open the gifts. The boys each held their gifts at arm's length, expressions of confusion and surprise twisting into disappointment. The spirit whispered in Michael's ear.

"She gave you a tradition," Michael said.

"Son of a bitch," Zeke said. He started screaming, "Move. Move now! Run if you fucking have to. Manny, help those youngsters. Goddamn it, go! Go!" Zeke started downstream then turned back. "Just so we don't have any doubts, what was it? The first one."

Michael smiled. "The year of the socks."

Zeke grinned and nodded. He barked at the herd to increase the pace, faster, faster. He directed the meandering procession like a seasoned range boss.

Michael searched the lengthy procession of Moonies. Seth had been missing far too long. Maybe he found trouble. The cuts and abrasions scabbed on his feet screamed as he began a slow jog atop the dry, crusty rock.

"Hey, where ya going?" Seth shouted.

Michael stopped and peered over his left shoulder. On a cut riverbank, Seth stood naked, his alabaster skin free of blemishes common to the Moonies, his bony torso rippled with protruding ribs and the maturing muscle of a fit young boy.

"Going the wrong way, ain't ya, angel?" Seth said.

"Where are the scavengers?" Michael said.

"I got 'em all. No more houses until that next town." Seth read Michael's questioning expression and jumped off the embankment. "Hey, if you can go naked, then so can I."

"Get dressed and head towards the rock dam past Mackay." Michael prodded the boy forward. "Help Myra, and your grandmother. You hear me, Seth?"

"Yes, sir. The angel speaks in direct ways." Seth saluted.

Michael watched him jog ahead, dragging the robe across the rock. The boy was a savior, a tactician, a second-in-command. A breath of fresh air.

The blazing sun dropped behind the mountains to paint a hazy gray sky with angry shades of crimson, abandoning the dry riverbed to spawn dark shadows in the rapidly cooling twilight. The pace of the Moonie procession slowed. Zeke caught up to Michael and reported endless troubles with the troop. Old women faltered, young men whined, mothers fought over food to feed their children, and worse, an overwhelming dread that the next sunrise they witnessed might find them returned to their concentration camp in the Craters of the Moon.

Michael kneeled and prayed. *Help me. Guide me. They want to believe. But they walk with little faith. Let me show them. Show them You are walking with them. Lord, allow me something, anything to inspire them, to lead them with.*

Seth tugged on Michael's robe and pointed upstream. "It's ready."

Myra had steered the procession into the backyard of an abandoned ranch-style house with a shingled roof ripped open by wind and age. Tall grass and thick tumbleweeds shielded the yellowed clapboard home graffitied with black swastikas, pentagrams, and inverted crucifixes. Symbols of Satan. Children scampered through doorless openings and taunted others through the shattered window frames.

An old oil drum sliced lengthwise hung from the chains of a child's rickety swing-set erected above a smokeless fire. Wisps of steam swirled above the drum to dissipate into a dying breeze. Michael's nostrils flared with an appetizing scent.

"We gotta feed the troops, right, angel? Mary put a bunch of stuff we collected into the pot, and hello," Seth said. He ran off to join other children near the front of the chow line.

Michael joined a group of stragglers and listened to the joyous greetings of familiar souls reconnecting, mixed with disgruntled grumbling and whispered words of doubt. The yard was crowded with robes, as each filed past the cookpot to accept paper plates or empty cans of hot food served by chattering old women. Michael weaved through the assemblage, checking the whining and complaints that went silent with his approach.

Michael's stomach rumbled as he resisted the urge to cut to the head of the food line. The defeated chatter grated on his psyche. A young family huddled together as the father portioned his own share of food to his three children. Myra joined a group of teenagers sitting atop a flattened stack of rusty metal cars to conspire with other young girls. Michael surveyed the crowded yard of tired people. They wouldn't move again, not with warm, full bellies.

He looked north towards the mountains. *Just go. Live the life of a nomad. Solitary.* Responsible only for himself.

Now, Lord. They truly need to see You are guiding them. And me.

He pulled the robe off and watched heads turn in his direction. He lifted his arms, like wings, pointed the steel rod to the sky, and let the Lord's prayer come out of his mouth.

Elder Moonies bowed their heads, though most remained unmoved by his words.

Michael waited, lingering like the disappearing sunlight. The silence was deafening. He lowered his eyes, picked up his robe and began a retreat, telling Seth he would check for stragglers downstream.

They need to believe!

Naked and alone on the grassy bank of the dry river, Michael stared aimlessly as the valley downstream disappeared in the quickening shadows. A bright red star hung above the horizon. Mars, maybe Jupiter. *You teach me to read the water, you teach me how to cast a line, and I believe. Give me my sword. Give me my wings. Return me my gifts if I am to battle Lucifer.*

Michael's nostrils flared with moldy, damp soil wafting of poison and futility. He swallowed a lump. The steel bar dangling is his hand was a weighted anchor. Was he really an Archangel, or some lunatic who believed he could peddle an ancient myth? He hadn't done anything extraordinary. He'd performed no miracles. Sure, his spittle could kill, but that was a curse provided by the human monsters. And his kiss healing the maladies of an unfiltered sun could be explained by the science of those same monsters. Michael sighed.

Behind him, the murmurs of Moonies who had silently followed gained volume to rise to a fevered pitch. He glanced over his shoulder. Many stood and pointed at him. The freak. A pariah for their amusement.

He dropped the robe and steel to stretch his arms wide. His shoulder blades itched with relentless mosquito bites. The Moonies dropped to their knees and . . .

Laughed? Sobbed?

Seth weaved his way through the garden of gray robes. A smile stretched wide across his face. "Let me see. Let me see."

Michael expanded his chest, pinching his shoulder blades forward and back, shrugging to loosen tight muscle. A lightning rod of pain shot down the length of his spine and into his feet, reversed course, and shot up into his neck and head.

He screamed with intense agony. The pain unbearable, he dropped to his knees. Punishment for his doubt. Penance for his demands. Tears streamed down his flushed cheeks.

The pain disappeared in an instant. Seth stood over him, his small hand stroking Michael's smooth scalp. His touch was nothing more than a whisper. And yet his touch soothed. The hems of tattered robes crowded around him. He felt small, helpless. An idiot. Murmurs and gasps.

"That's a pair of wings coming out!" Seth shouted. "That means Michael's a young angel. He needs time to let 'em grow out."

Michael sank onto his elbows. Soiled fingers and palms touched his hot flesh, soothed his pain. He kept his eyes shut and allowed himself to bathe in miraculous adulation.

Never again, Father. I will never doubt again.

The Fisherman's whisper escaped from the crowd's rising clamor. *Never again.*

Michael gobbled up the bowl of Moonie stew with quick spoonful's, staring in the direction of the Mackay Reservoir's rock dam miles away. He bit down hard as he checked the sprawl of tired bodies allowed an hour of rest. Prodding the people who had restored their faith in him would be difficult. Every minute of the hour was agonizing.

And amusing.

With a rope leash, Serah led Ralphie around the yard like a blindfolded dog. The giant stumbled over stiff tufts of grass attempting to reclaim his balance or struggled to break the cloth binding his wrists. He cursed like a seasoned convict. The Tuber didn't fit in this world, wasn't one of His chosen. But Serah believed Ralphie was as much a part of His plan as any of them were.

Zeke began the dirty work of kicking and shaking the Moonies, yelling at them to get up and move. Michael winced with the pain screaming from his shoulder blades but followed Zeke's lead. Flashlights and tiny solar headlamps lit up.

Seth appeared at his side like a flesh-and-blood wraith. "The river road is a dead end. The highway is close by but has a police roadblock. Whatcha say, angel? Let's take it out and give 'em a smooth road ahead?"

The flock could move faster on flat ground, and be open to drone attacks and surveillance cameras, too. He was the Lord's General, and the decision was his alone.

"Let's take a look," Michael said.

He followed close behind Seth. The boy's night vision was extraordinary, slowing to warn Michael of a barbed wire fence or irrigation ditches hidden beneath tall grass. They ran through an empty field, then sprinted along a narrow cattle trail to a metal gate.

"Just past those two houses. Demons with guns," Seth whispered. The boy smiled, an impish flip of his lips. He moved close as if to whisper in Michael's ear; instead, he rubbed Michael's shoulder blades with a feathered touch. The pain vanished. "I'll get Uncle Zeke to move everybody up to this gate while you smite 'em, angel."

"Why do you call Zeke your uncle?" Michael said.

"Cause it made people think twice about jumping me back on the Moon. Nobody wanted to mess with Zeke, especially if he gets mad."

Michael nodded then angled his face. Seth wanted men murdered, rationalized them as demons maybe, but they were still human. Or did they differ on the definition of smite? Maybe Michael didn't lead this carnival; maybe it was the boy. But it didn't matter—the goal was the same.

"Okay. Bring them up the road. I'll do what I've been sent to do."

The boy scampered into the growing darkness, full of energy, full of life. Was this another reason Michael was born human, to experience the beauty and frailty of the human body, witness a vibrant young soul with a heart bursting with hope? Questions he would hold on to, then ask the Fisherman.

Michael climbed over the gate and put on his robe. He jogged on gritty asphalt until he saw the police barricade. Three Idaho State Police cruisers formed a Z and blocked the two-lane highway, allowing only a single vehicle to pass slowly. Resting on four thin legs, the sleek semitransparent polymer hovercraft blazed red, blue, and white light into the dark scrub beyond. A line of vehicles shining bright headlights busy with flying insects waited for their chance to escape Arco. As he walked towards the roadblock, he checked the waiting cars and trucks loaded with people and belongings. The Fisherman had given them a warning. A vivid dream, a ghostly premonition, an ethereal voice, a sudden epiphany—the Fisherman worked in many ways.

The bumps on his back burned and stiffened as he hobbled into the pretense of a limp. He hid the steel bar inside the robe then stumbled as he neared the bright lights. He feigned the rod as a splint for an injured leg.

AI-driven threat assessment scanners whirred from atop the cabs of the vehicles, firing red lasers in random patterns to search for any possible threat. Intense beams of red light focused on Michael, bright white light erupting from another vehicle illuminated the landscape for a radius of twenty meters.

A lanky uniformed officer checking a vehicle raised his head then aimed a bright flashlight beam at Michael.

"Moonie boy. Hold up there," the officer said.

"The Lord commands you to abandon your trespass!" Michael shouted as he moved closer. "The Lord commands you to obey His warning."

The incredulous deputy shook his head and scoffed. He was joined by two other uniformed men.

"The Lord commands you to let these people pass. Let them pass!" Michael said. With his palm, he slapped the hood of a car waiting near the front of the queue. "Let these people pass, or you will feel the wrath of the Lord."

Michael hid a smirk. He enjoyed his reenactment of the centuries-old dramatic movies he had been allowed to watch in prison. Lots of cheesy dialogue, loaded with hell hath no fury, and the good and righteous protagonists always victorious at the end. Predictable. Yet satisfying. Michael hunched his back to imitate the posture and gait of the ugly Quasimodo who hid in the Notre Dame centuries ago. A character the movie audience was asked to love and made to cheer. Until the monster was enraged

The three men readied handcuffs as they spread out to surround Michael. He looked at each. Lost souls, but not demons. Michael kneeled on one knee and bowed his head. He calculated the thrusts and kicks necessary to subdue the men. The steel bar poked out from beneath the hem of the robe.

"Weapon! Weapon!" an officer shouted.

He heard weapons unsheathed, feet shuffling nervously on gritty asphalt, orders to lie down and submit. He closed his eyes then stood to his full height, using one arm to lift the robe up over his head. He dropped the steel rod to clank at his feet. He raised his arms in surrender. "Don't shoot. The Lord commands it."

"Freak," one said and stepped backwards.

"Get the cuffs on him," another said.

All the three men eased closer. One talked rapidly into a headpiece connected to his Arkoff Port with a micro-thin fiberoptic wire.

Michael moved like a wisp of smoke and sent the man in the center tumbling backwards with a palm thrust. The man on his left went down as Michael jumped to hit him with a spinning back kick.

The last man, the guardian of the roadblock, was too slow. Michael knocked his weapon aside and grabbed his head and spun, turning the man's neck faster than a spine allowed. The crack of bone. Michael smelled the wisp of his soul as it abandoned the body.

Cars sounded angry horns. Drivers opened doors and climbed out, their backlit faces frozen with panic.

"Go! Now!" Michael shouted.

He stepped through the jumble of bodies towards the configuration of the police vehicles blocking the road. He slammed his heel into an officer's temple to quiet his moans. He opened the door of the police vehicle strobing an angry red light. Red holograms flashed above the dashboard, above the console and over the passenger seat. He sliced his hand through the lights with no effect. A chubby woman's holographic face stared at him, then shouted questions about needing assistance.

Michael stabbed his finger into the eye on the holo-face with no result. Cool.

"Cam, talk to me. C'mon. Help's on the way," the lady said.

Michael looked at the steering pad, a square patch of transparent plastic with odd, embedded icons flashing red. He couldn't operate a car. He couldn't operate any machinery. Automation and technology had never summoned his attention while surfing the limited web browsers.

A drum reverberated in his head, a methodical beat that slowly increased with deep basso and subtle percussion. The pain in his back shot lightning bolts down his arms into his hands. His fingers clenched into rigid claws as he screamed.

Metaphors. *He speaks in metaphors.*

The winglets hadn't only brought His grace, but His strength.

Michael climbed out, closed the door, and walked to the front of car. He clenched his jaw, squatted to face the plexiglass windshield, then lifted the graphite car and heaved it into the drainage ditch beyond the shoulder of the highway. His expression contorted by the effort, he turned to a crowd of faces shocked with disbelief.

The anger and pain fled with each fresh breath he inhaled.

"Now go. As fast as you can." Michael put on the robe and kept his eyes trained towards the direction from which the flock would arrive. The distant shady outlines of Moonies grew closer as vehicles shot past him every few seconds.

Seth ran up to him, out of breath. "Smited them, didn't we, Angel?"

"Indeed," Michael said.

"We ain't gonna make it, Angel. Too far to go before . . ." Seth said.

Michael squinted. The boy did know of the warning. He knew enough to be forthcoming. "You know Lucifer's evil is coming, don't you?"

"Well, duh?" Seth said and rolled his eyes. "I could read your face like a picture book . . . if I knew how to read . . . but you were pretty obvious."

"You know how to read. You said you read the Bible?" S e t h held up a single finger. "No. I said Myra was teaching me to read the Bible. But it's all goofy words and stuff. I'm going to write my own Bible someday. People will eat it up."

The Moonies crowded the road and shoulder as vehicles weaved carefully through the narrow gap between the hovercraft.

"Go! Go!" Michael waved the cars forward.

Zeke walked out of the congregation of Moonies growing in size by the minute. "You know those cars could help us."

Michael looked at Zeke. Seth nodded. Michael swung the rod down to smash the hood of a red sedan approaching the gap. "Stop!"

Seth put his hand on Michael's wrist. "Tell 'em to open their trunks."

"Excellent," Zeke said. "I'll go with the first. Show 'em where to pull over."

Zeke grabbed the sedan's door handle and pushed his face into the window. "Pop the trunk. You're gonna give us a ride."

Car horns trumpeted impatience.

Zeke looked to Michael and raised his eyebrows.

"The reservoir. Get 'em behind the dam. Down close to the water," Michael said. He closed his eyes and pictured the bulky berm constructed with hefty boulders and hoped the location was the correct decision.

Zeke nodded and opened the door to crowd into the back seat stuffed with luggage and moving boxes. Seth prodded three Moonies to hurry and sit in the open trunk. Two others joined them in the cramped space. Zeke slapped the car door to get the stunned driver moving.

Would there be enough cars, and space, for hundreds of Moonies? It didn't matter. They were moving again. Quicker than he might have hoped. *The Fisherman will provide.*

Hours passed with Michael playing traffic director. His white naked body with inflamed bulbous knots protruding from his back caused vehicles to halt yards from the loading zone. Too often he had to hustle to a waiting car and slap the steel rod across the hood or push his face at the driver and bark commands. The people sneered and cursed, but their scared eyes revealed their desperation to escape.

Just as his own eyes might.

"That's it, Angel," Seth said and swatted at the swarms of flying insects attracted to the bright lights. "We got all the Moonies."

Seth looked back down the highway towards Arco, and Michael followed his gaze. Stalled headlights snaked down the highway. He grabbed Seth's robe and started to lead him up the highway.

"Stop!" Seth broke free of his grasp and shot Michael a scrunched expression. "Stupid butthead. They count too, you know. We can't just leave 'em."

The boy's indignance wicked every ounce of Michael's resolve. "And what do you want me to do? Drive them?"

"Get them moving. Wave 'em on. There just scared of you. Put your robe back on and make 'em go." Seth handed Michael the grey bundle he must have been hiding beneath his own robe.

Michael stopped a tiny E-vehicle with a single passenger and ordered Seth to climb in and go. He instructed the young driver to take care with his new friend then implored the driver to move fast. Michael growled as he donned the robe, its thick, rough material abrasive on his tender backside. Michael tapped the steel bar on hoods, windshields, and fenders of a parade of vehicles easing forward to the roadblock, waving each to hurry. After what seemed like an eternity, the chain of cars escaping Arco picked up speed.

CHAPTER EIGHT

CYD SHRANK INTO A COMPACT ball, grabbing her head as if to protect it. Her eyes squeezed tight as grating termites gnawed deeper into her ear canals, penetrating up into her temples. The stranger banged on the bedroom door, demanding to be allowed inside. She wiggled beneath the bed to hide. Sheba eased in next to her and purred like a concert sub-woofer. The big cat comforted her. She blindly stroked its soft fur as the pale blue termites of 3Bz receded and left her wide-awake.

"Get the king crab. I don't care if they are a protected species. Bribe a ship captain," Sterling said. He swung his legs off the edge of the bed.

Cyd turned her face on the soft pillow to gaze fifteen feet up to an octagonal ceiling painted with a mural. Horned red devils carrying pitchforks danced around a white pilgrim wearing tiny white wings and roasting on a spit over a hot fire. The odd artwork was surreal and probably the cause of her nightmare. The dark room was too warm, and the windows' heavy purple drapes blocked all but faint slivers of moonlight from penetrating the room.

She blinked away the goo of sleep blurring her eyes. Princess and Arelia lay sprawled together on a long plush couch near the window. The two women appeared comatose, their breathing barely notice-able. Faint memories of last night returned. Shots of expensive Grand

Marnier, the techno-vibe of superstar Darius thumping exotic music to ripple pleasurable vibrations through the air, the synthetic floorings' intricate sound webbing vibrating in rhythm with the music. The generous helpings of 3Bz. A pleasure palace of debauchery.

Oh my heck, what have I done!

She ran her hand over her nude body. Did she have sex with Sterling? She couldn't remember. Oh my God! Did he enjoy it? Should she reach over to touch him?

"Fine. Send the stealth drone to pick them up in Seattle. Off," Sterling said.

Sterling turned to face her, but she closed her eyes to feign sleep.

"Things I gotta fucking do." He groaned. "Accept call . . . Samuel, just getting ready to call you back. Uh huh," Sterling said. He stood up and pulled on a pair of black boxer briefs.

Cyd rubbed the grit from her eyes and sat up against the headboard of the Texas king bed, an enormous circular mattress overpowering the large bedroom. She looked at the girls on the couch then remembered snorting 3Bz off the nipples of Princess as she lay on the bed like a serving platter.

She groaned and rubbed her temple. *Oh, what have I done!*

"She'll be fine here. Plenty to entertain her," Sterling said then looked at Cyd and winked.

She closed her eyes and fought through the 3Bz fog clouding her memory. Nothing to complain about—she had been treated like royalty, showered with attention, and alcohol, and plenty of blue powder, everything to silence the tiny voice that sat on her shoulder wagging its finger and telling her she was a fool. A spoiled rich girl who could not see her surroundings for what they truly were.

As more memories returned, Cyd shrank into herself. She was only here because Daddy said she was born for greatness, as an actress, as a beautiful woman, as the only woman capable of bearing the Arkoff family name. It didn't matter that she was adopted; it made her more sympathetic to the media, racked up big points for the benevolent Samuel Arkoff. But the nagging perception that every detail of her life was contrived and manipulated haunted every realization. Her own father had escorted her into Sterling's world, dropped her off like a schoolchild in need of corruption.

"What do you mean? What does it matter? She's fine. Doing

everything you asked," Sterling said. He looked down on his sleeping arm candy naked on the big couch.

Cyd stretched out her long arms and massaged life back into her tight muscled thighs. A jog would clear her head, prepare her for the day, but she forgot to pack workout clothes. Poor Sterling, getting an earful from the doting father before breakfast, or was it dinnertime?

"I got it, Sammy. Hunker down with the window shades drawn. Until when, and why?"

Cyd perked her ears. Nobody called Daddy anything less than Samuel. She blanched at Sterling's thick, hairy backside dotted with ugly black moles. Overweight, almost bald, obnoxious, he was nothing like the heroic protagonists he played in the movies.

And yet you lie in his bed, the little angel said.

And because of you I snort 3Bz, she thought.

Sterling raised his hands in frustration. "She's not going any-where. Now what the fuck is this all about?"

Daddy had planned something. Something big. And he wanted her protected. Or out of his way.

Enthralled by Sterling offering promises of movie auditions, she stuffed her nose with 3Bz until her body wilted like rubber in a hot sun. She had laughed and giggled at being included in Sterling's weird game of snakes and blood. A bizarre ritual he claimed would cleanse her soul, but the odd game of sacrificing rattlers and boa constrictors to tasting its blood like each was fine wine only repulsed her. Or was it a 3Bz hallucination? She couldn't be sure.

The ultimate manipulator, the master puppeteer, Daddy had to know. She was simply one thin string tied to hundreds of his wag-gling fingers. And Daddy only showed his true self when his plans went afoul like he did a decade ago. Destroying the Miami mansion after the Miracle Marlins won the World Series, throwing priceless vases at priceless paintings because of a freaking baseball game. Cyd hid in her bedroom closet with her favorite stuffed kitty-cats to protect her, each one her favorite that day, listening to his violent destruction and ranting a "wasn't supposed to happen" mantra he kept muttering for months.

Jeez, a freaking baseball game.

The urge to get out and breath fresh air overwhelmed her. She would jog up the quiet streets until her legs had nothing left to give. Screw Daddy. Screw Sterling. Screw this place.

She slipped out of bed and found her bra, panties, and T-shirt and dressed quickly. Her sneakers spotted beneath the party table, she eased on the balls of her feet to retrieve them.

"Going somewhere, beautiful?" Sterling said. He checked the half-empty vials of 3Bz on the table,

Cyd crawled beneath the table to grab the shoes. "Gonna take a run. Be back in a few."

"Samuel said you need to stay inside. And away from the windows. What the hell is he planning?"

"I really don't care." Cyd countered. "I need some fresh air."

"Sorry, baby, can't let you out right now. Doctor's orders," Sterling said. He knocked on the glass tabletop. "Plenty of the blue stuff right here. How bout we get high and screw again? Seems I remember you being a real wildcat last night."

Cyd groaned silently. She hated herself every morning, hated the sex and debauchery she was powerless to resist after snorting, or smoking the synthetic blue drug.

"Not now. I need to get outside," Cyd said.

She stood up and aimed for the door. Sterling blocked her. His white flabby belly hanging over the too-tight briefs.

"Daddy dearest says you need to stay inside. C'mon, let's wake up the girls and play some more," Sterling said. He leered a malicious grin.

She loomed eight inches taller than Sterling, though he outweighed her by a hundred pounds. She could dodge the shapeless old dog without much effort. "On second thought, maybe a snort might clear my head."

"Now you're talking, baby," Sterling said and clapped his hands at the others. "Girls! Girls! Time to party."

Cyd used the distraction and aimed for the hallway door. She reached for the doorknob.

Sterling grabbed her wrist and twisted it free of the knob with a deceptive strength. He smirked and said, "Better than you have tried that move."

He squeezed her wrist hard. She winced. "Daddy will feed your balls to the wolves."

Sterling chuckled humorlessly. He slapped her face. "My balls would be a small price to satisfy Daddy."

Hot tears rolled down her stinging cheek. Cyd's anger boiled. She twisted her wrist free with a strength she had rarely employed. Sterling raised his hand to slap her again.

Cyd caught his wrist in her hand and squeezed hard. She heard a bone crack then felt another bone snap. He screamed and crumpled to the floor, but she held on. What had she done? He was only trying to help her.

Believe in you, the annoying little angel said in her thoughts. *Believe in yourself.*

She released him. Sterling writhed and howled as tears flowed down his cheeks. She hurried to the front door then glanced over her shoulder at the party girls stooping to help Sterling. A famous movie star on the carpet. 3Bz waiting for her on the table.

Cyd swallowed hard. *Believe in yourself.*

Cyd found a bench in the mudroom and fumbled tying the laces of her thin Kevlar sneakers. She refused to allow tears to fall. What had she done?

Believe in yourself.

She found her way outside into the darkness of dawn chilled with pine-scented air, hurried to the front gate, and climbed over the wrought iron to begin an easy jog down the street lined with spindly lodgepole pines and aged cottonwoods. She tried to concentrate on each footfall as she wiped tears and snot off her face. A left turn on Wood Loop to cross over the Big Wood River, she paused on the steel bridge spanning the torrent of murky water ushering trash and flotsam downstream.

Hypnotized by the endless cascade of icy water, Cyd resigned to slip into the churning chaos beneath her. Let the water take her wherever. Nothing in this world could save her from the 3Bz. Nothing could free her from a domineering father. Nothing could save her from herself.

She sidestepped over to a crossbeam and stared at the violent river with blank unseeing eyes. The swift current would carry her downstream forever, free of the Arkoff prison. She stepped to the end of the beam. Her hand slipped on a guide wire. She swallowed hard. Her muscles tensed. A simple leap to end the pain.

The emerging sun brightened the neighborhood of expensive mansions crowding the river channel. Daddy's people. Money and power. Falseness and ego. She looked down to find her landing spot. A huge flat boulder bucking the swift current, one sure to snap her neck if she dove headfirst. A man knee-deep in the torrent of murky water waded against the current beneath her perch, his green vest and waders darkened by water splashing against his thighs.

Cyd blinked back tears and chuckled mirthlessly. A stupid fisherman just happened to be wading beneath the very spot she chose for her death. Even irony offered her no pity.

The fisherman tilted his head back and looked up at her.

They locked eyes. She gazed at piercing sky-blue eyes transcending the shadows beneath the bridge. He was old yet extremely handsome. She narrowed her eyes and cocked her head as he performed an odd gesture. He pulled a sweat-stained fedora off his head, swept it across the water as if to offer an obedient bow.

As if she came from a noble heritage.

Or he was introducing himself.

DRAINED OF WATER, MACKAY RESERVOIR sat as a dusty tub basin for decades, managing to suck the remaining trickles of the Big Lost River down into the layers of lead and arsenic sediment lining the lake bottom, seeping into a subterranean aquifer of radioactive groundwater. The Moonies congregated near the tiny rivulet of a river once notorious for inexplicably disappearing into its riverbed near Arco.

Infinite stars of the night sky faded with the breaking dawn. Michael paced an overgrown access road atop the reservoir's rock dam. Beyond the river valley, past the tiny burg of Mackay, the neon abomination of Arco burned bright. Headlights of vehicles escaping Arco on the highway aimed toward Challis had petered to an occasional vehicle speeding recklessly as if chased by brutality. An assortment of vehicles crowded a defunct campground on the rim of the lakebed. Townspeople and Moonies wandered aimlessly on the dusty lakebed.

Michael had missed his opportunity to sleep and possibly dream of the Fisherman. The long night held no opportunity for even a nap.

He stabbed the metal rod into the dirt and looked over his flock. His flock. The words caused his teeth to grind. He had become a shepherd, for boys, and lepers, and even Tubers.

Wedged between hefty granite boulders, Myra and Seth slept close to Zeke. Serah slept sprawled atop a flat boulder; the leash tied to her Tuber ward dangled in her hand. Ralphie rocked back and forth as if mentally challenged. Regardless of the blindfold, the Tuber seemed oblivious to the world around him.

Brother indeed.

A tiny meteorite streaked in from atop the mountains to the north.

Michael lifted his face to follow the point of light, following its course over the crags of the Big Lost Mountains, gliding, until it fell and detonated over Arco. He turned and roared at the Moonies to cover their eyes and heads. He turned back to face a brilliant, scorching sunburst. One the Creator had not summoned.

The instantaneous white flash burned his retinas. The ground beneath his feet buckled. He raised his arms like wings and braced his legs to accept the churning wave of dirt and flotsam rolling towards him at an unbelievable speed.

Yanked backwards by the hood on his robe, Michael tumbled down over huge, chiseled boulders as the maelstrom of debris stormed over his head. Glass and sharp pebbles pelted his face. A blistering hot wind howled.

He landed hard on his back. His breath was crushed from his lungs as a heavy weight landed and covered his body. The storm waned.

A gigantic soft hand patted his chest. "You are a boatload of trouble, brother," Ralphie said. "Get to see what you needed to see?"

Michael blinked dust out of his eyes and tried to push Ralphie's heavy weight off. The Tuber's face hovered above his own. Close enough to kiss. Ralphie's breath reeked of tooth decay or foul meat.

"Didn't think the final battle was all about you, or did you?" Ralphie said.

"The Moonies?" Michael said. "Seth and Myra?"

"Interesting turn of events," Ralphie said as he pushed his face closer. "The Michael I used to know was only interested in black-and-white judgments. Cared little about the sheep."

Michael looked deep into eyes glittering with specks of heaven's light. Ancient memories flashed in his mind. Death and battle with Lucifer and the Fallen. The Archangel Raphael grinned.

With a grunt, he pushed Raphael off him. "And safeguarding pilgrims was supposed to be your lot."

***

CYD CROSSED OVER THE OLD bridge to help the crazy fisherman, just as he'd asked. Her excitement heightened with each step. Was it the prospect of finally meeting a normal person, one out of Daddy's sphere of influence, or maybe because her suicidal thoughts disappeared after the old sportsman claimed to have lost his cherished net and needed a set of younger eyes to help him find the thing in the dim light beneath the bridge.

She slid down a steep gravel embankment precarious with loose stones and grass slippery with morning dew. Cyd found the net's lacquered wooden handle leaning straight up behind a girthy log beached beneath the bridge.

He heaved a sigh of relief. The old man leaned his flyrod against the gnarly root-ball and sat, hanging his head as if in defeat. She crossed her arms and stared at him. What was such a feeble blind old man doing wading in that raging water?

"I know. I know. You think I'm crazy for being out here." He took off his fedora and scratched a full head of hair peppered with grey. "But it's the only time of day the drones don't chase me off. And finding a good fishing hole is tough these days. You live around here?"

"No, just visiting." Cyd shuffled her feet as she checked the bridge's rusty steel rafters covered in spiderwebs and the shattered shells of swallow nests. "You trying to kill yourself out there?" The irony in her question made her pause a deep breath.

He chuckled. "You ever try fly casting?"

She shook her head and gazed downstream as the swollen turbulence became clearer with the sunrise. "Seems like a silly game, throwing fuzzy fake things at fish. Probably hurts their mouths when you catch one too."

He patted the log with his hand in an offer for her to sit. "Now see, that's what I thought at first. Then you go find a nice spot all to yourself and commune with nature. You're so busy tying knots and leaders and casting and wading and changing flies nothing else gets in your head except what really matters. Puts your mind right most times. Got any places like this where you live?"

Cyd chuckled and sat. "A bazillion. I live in Yellowstone."

"Wow. I haven't been there in a long time. Love to see that place again."

"But you won't. My father has the whole park sealed off."

"Hmm," he said and nodded.

A deep *boom* rattled the cold air and sent gravel sliding down the river rock embankment. Dirt and dust fell from the steel beams overhead. A subtle vibration penetrated her sneakers.

Cyd brushed dirt out of her hair. "What was that?"

"Sounds like a war just started," he said.

"Pffftttt. Wars are always starting somewhere." Cyd shook her head, dismissing the statement.

"True. Except the next one might be the last. Faith against technology."

Cyd bit her bottom lip. "Hmm. I'd bet on technology then."

"And I might have predicted you'd say that. Faith has become harder and harder to find these days. People only believe in what they can see and touch and buy with money." He squinted to check Cyd's neck. "I don't see one of those Arkoff Ports on you. Maybe technology hasn't bought you yet."

"I'm not old enough yet. But I'll probably get one," Cyd said and touched the spot beneath her ear where one would be implanted.

"Some say you sell your soul to Satan when you get one. Believe that?" he said.

"Gotta believe in God to believe in Satan, and I want no part of that silly religious dogma," Cyd said.

"And if I told you God does exist, everywhere, in everything, what would you say?" he asked with his hands offering the beauty of the river.

"I'd say you are an old man that can believe anything he wants to make himself feel better about dying. Sorry . . . but you asked."

"And what would have made you feel better before jumping off that bridge? Sorry . . . but you started it."

Cyd recoiled. Was her intention so obvious? She swallowed hard and tried to stand, but her chilled legs felt locked tight. Her hands trembled.

The old man withdrew a green oblong box from his vest and opened it, revealing swarms of fuzzy fishing flies sorted by size. He unhooked a dull bullheaded grey bug accented with bits of yellow and red trim, tiny rubber strings for legs, and held the fly up for a close appraisal. "Dave's Hopper. One of my favorites. You should find a rod and tie one of these boys on when you get back to Yellowstone. Maybe find what calms you."

The distinct whirr of Razzi drones hovered above the bridge. Cyd closed her eyes and flinched from the dirt churned into the air by the big propellers.

The old man patted her leg. "They found me. They always do." He stood up, picked up the long rod, and started downstream of the bridge. "Find what calms you, young lady," he said before disappearing over the steep embankment.

Cyd's muscles relaxed. A Razzi drone hovered ten yards upstream, almost skimming the water, bulbous eye cameras pointed straight at her. Sterling and Daddy and the whole world would soon be coming straight at her. But they wouldn't learn of the suicide she had contemplated. She had simply gone for a jog.

Nothing had changed.

Except a brief talk with an odd senior citizen.

3Bz still lurked, just like death.

Still, the old man had suspected, talked to her like some all-knowing guidance counselor in one of the e-novels she had managed to pilfer from Anna's computer. The thought of Malibu no longer excited her. Acting and the bright lights of fame seemed shallow and unfulfilling. Soon Daddy's hover jet would land on the road near the bridge and he would emerge to hold her close and swear to never let her leave his sight again. The falseness of his words oozing deceit with each syllable.

Nothing had changed.

Cyd climbed up the embankment and crossed back over the bridge to sit on a boulder overlooking the river. Three drones hovered. Others buzzed like wasps. Red laser beams sliced the air around her. She shook her head at the constant turbulence, in the air, in the water,

in her own life. She stretched her neck to focus on the boulder she'd chosen for her death.

That old man could have drowned in that raging river. She shook her head with disbelief.

The arrival of the hover jet sounded in her ears minutes before its landing. She would go home to Yellowstone, have nothing to do with Daddy, or Zac, or Anna, or 3Bz. She would immerse herself in the daily chores required of the animals. She would have faith in their care. She groaned. But for how long? How long before the boredom and 3Bz sucked her down again?

She inhaled a long breath as the shuttlecraft landed and the door slid open, and the stairway lowered. She stood and brushed dirt from her leggings then stumbled over a loose shoelace. She bent down to retie the lace and froze.

A big Dave's Hopper was hooked to an eyelet. The steel hook pinched tight to prevent it falling off.

Cyd huffed as a sad smile lifted the corner of her mouth.

———

LIKE GIANT BLACK CONDORS, THREE huge, winged ships topped the granite ridges of Borah Peak, skimming above the steep slopes then accelerating over the sagebrush foothills. Razor-thin profiles and silent, the aircraft split into a pronged attack formation.

Michael lifted his face and watched the hover drones dive into the lake basin and raise clouds of toxic dust to obscure their attack. Human screams filtered through the storm of wind and dust. Automatic gunfire blasted projectiles across the mountainside opposite the empty lake.

"They all die, Michael. Unless you step into the net."

The command boomed from a hover-drone easing into a position directly above him and dangling a heavy corded net.

Raphael pinched his shoulder from behind and whispered, "I'll take one, and you take the other. Then we race to get the third. What say you?"

"With wings, I would take you up on that." Michael replied. He pointed at the farthest drone armed with twin multi-barreled cannons aimed at the Moonies. "That third one will kill hundreds before we get to it."

"The war has started. Casualties will happen. You have to know that?" Raphael said.

The nuclear blast had signaled the beginning of the war, the battle for the soul of the planet. But the Fisherman had plans for the Moonies. Seth and the others would be defenseless. Their safety was paramount.

"We need to get the Moonies up the river, into the White Clouds. And you need to lead them," Michael said.

"I have just awakened. I have no wings. I have no—"

"Were you so fucking asleep in that fake world that you remember nothing?" Michael slapped him hard. "Wake the fuck up. Remember who and what you are. These people will die if you don't."

Michael raised his arms in surrender then walked towards the drone lowering a cargo net to spread flat and wait like an unbreakable polymer cage. He searched for Seth or Myra, but the wind and dust obscured everything on the lakebed. He paused at the edge of the net and swallowed hard. Swap one prison for another. Undoubtedly his new warden, Lucifer, waited at the other end.

Michael stepped into the center of the net and braced his legs. The drone lifted, the corners of the net followed, and he was hauled into the air. He held the net tight as it spun in quick rotations, rising higher, until he glimpsed Seth sprinting up a buckled concrete boat ramp and waving to him. The boy raised his fist and punched the air, his face scrunched with anger. Michael watched the flock grow small as the dust blew south and the ground fell away.

I asked for wings, Father. Just not this kind.

The aircraft aimed north, crossing over a mountain range of sharp granite teeth, eleven peaks rising above an elevation of eleven thousand feet, each capped in dirty grey snow, the remnants of a meager winter snowpack. Hundreds of fires burned where Arco had been. Plumes of smoke obscured the graveyard with a blast zone scorching sagebrush for miles beyond the lava fields of Craters of the Moon. Highways smoldered with blackened vehicles and buckled asphalt.

Michael shuttered his eyes at the destruction. The opening salvo was impressive, intimidating.

Lucifer's power on earth had magnified.

Michael began to shiver as the thin frigid air bit through his robe. Circular swaths of agriculture, oblong patches of cornfields, dry aqueducts like veins intersected the land beneath him. Vehicles buzzed over an interstate highway bisecting Idaho Falls, seeking to escape the radioactive fallout sure to arrive. Hovercars plotted their own course yet maintained proximity to the asphalt road. The magnificent crags of the Teton mountain range grew closer, and the already cold temperature plummeted. Peaks he had once flown above centuries ago, folding his wings to dive in a freefall, twitching back and forth as he swooped through narrow granite chutes, sudden death but a few inches away.

With every moment, his memories slowly returned and yet he remained human. He shook his head with the perplexing question. Why clothe him in the frailty of flesh? But faith would guide his course, and he would not waver.

The snowcapped Tetons passed beneath, and his course turned north into vast swaths of untouched forests. Swollen rivers ran glacier-blue and turbid. Herds of bison and elk grazed. Pockets of steam from small geysers rose into the frigid air. The Yellowstone Caldera remained a pristine, elegant ecosystem. The aircraft descended, aiming for an antique wooden high-rise surrounded by an expansive gravel field crammed with wire cages and animal enclosures, pole barns and maintenance outbuildings.

The aircraft hovered above the dormant Old Faithful to allow six mechanized cyborgs to take up positions around the perimeter of the landing site. His hands and feet left unbound, maybe he could overpower his new guards. A consideration Lucifer would not have ignored.

A chubby middle-aged man pushed open heavy doors at the old Inn's main entrance and walked briskly towards the landing zone. Tall, with a prominent hawklike nose, bulging midsection, balding hair, dark sunspots marking a tanned face and neck. The Fallen One had aged badly, yet maintained the calculating eyes of a hyena eons had never dimmed. Lucifer twirled his hand as a signal to lower Michael to the ground.

Michael adjusted the robe over his body. "Samuel Arkoff. Maker of false dreams. The prince of false hope. You look like shit."

Samuel lifted the corner of his mouth. "Michael, Archangel of filthy Moonies, judge of no souls. Weak and helpless. You look like a prisoner."

Michael raised his arms out of the robe. "Not yet. Shall we battle here and now? Winner takes all."

Samuel chuckled. "Those are stakes even you can't offer." He cocked his ear and frowned, feigning to listen. "Nope, your heavenly backer isn't chiming in, so I think you are a prisoner."

Michael shrugged and stepped forward.

Samuel retreated a few steps and held up a single finger. "Not that easy. You follow the cyborgs to your holding pen. You will be strapped and caged and eliminated from our Father's game. Or else."

Michael eyed the cyborgs closing in, then lifted his chin towards Samuel.

Samuel wagged a single finger, then flicked his head back towards the doors. "I might have my fun with her, but she dies a horrible death if you try to sprout those fucking wings and leave that cage."

Escorted by two male cyborgs, Myra shuffled out of the hotel entrance to wait in the shade of the carport. The swath on her chest hung empty.

Samuel chuckled mirthlessly. "Why the Father made you human is a question I haven't quite answered yet. But with His precious enforcer out of commission, time is on my side."

Michael stared at Myra, but she refused to look at him. What deception had he missed back at the lakebed? When was she abducted? Where had he been at the time? Who had helped Samuel? The answer was hidden on Samuel's expression.

"And just to be clear . . ." Samuel raised his hand again and stepped closer.

A lithe woman exited the hotel, cradling a child. She leered at the baby in her arms then lifted her face and offered a row of sharp fangs as a smile.

"I'll feed that baby to the wolverine if you even take a piss without my permission."

Michael swallowed hard and heaved an exasperated breath. "For the last three centuries, our Father has given you everything you wanted. Wealth and power. He has allowed you dominion over billions. Why do you need more?"

Samuel narrowed his eyes and chuckled. "My reasons make a

long list. Heaven still yearns for my return. Revenge. Even your job, weighing the worthiness of souls, makes the list. I haven't tasted that power yet, but that position may have an opening soon. I am very tempted to have those Borgs slice and dice you into pieces and feed the cubes to the predators, be done with you, except . . . except that won't satisfy my curiosity as to why you were born human."

Michael shrugged. "Then show me to my room. I had a computer screen to amuse me in my last prison. Any chance at the same courtesy?"

Samuel laughed. "Maybe that's why you're human. God has finally given you something you never had. A sense of humor. That sarcasm might serve you well while you rot in your cage." Samuel signaled for the borgs to take him away. "Remember, children and babies. And if you're not there to meet their souls, yours won't be far behind."

The cyborgs crowded him as they wrapped polymer bands to encircle his torso with his arms cinched tight to his sides. A cyborg prodded him forward with the sharp point of a metal claw grafted to its hand. He walked past small pens holding raccoons, geese, ferrets, hares. The animals slept or hid beneath wooden benches. The scent of dung and urine hung in the warming air. An odd stench of chemicals overpowered the forest's pleasant pine aroma. Mechanical air distribution units the size of train cars blew plumes of warm, moist air up into the sky.

Towards large overhead doors fronting one of four oblong metal pole barns, Michael gazed up at the morning sun burning bright in a cloudless blue sky.

And heaved a huge sigh.

CHAPTER NINE

CYD JIGGLED THE DOOR LEVER again, then turned to fall on her rumpled mattress. She stared aimlessly at intricate swirls and divots texturing the ceiling paint. She fumed with the injustice. A prisoner, and by her own father's doing. Who cared if she broke Sterling's wrist? He deserved it. He should never have tried to stop her from leaving. Daddy should have been proud that she stood up for herself. Maybe she should have told Daddy what Sterling was really like, a lecherous fat pig who thought he could control any girl stupid enough to walk through his front door.

She screamed and pounded the mattress furiously with her fists. Almost seventeen and fucking grounded like some silly tween. Her heels joined the drumming of the soft bed.

She paused the assault on her bed. Maybe the discipline had a silver lining. She blanched at the thought of using 3Bz. The lure of the drug with its incessant little voice amplifying her cravings to find and use, smoke and snort, was now easily swatted away since that day . . . that . . . awakening.

Awakening. She liked that description; it was an easier term than suicide. Daddy would explode if he learned of the suicidal thoughts she had almost acted upon. Or would he? He had delivered her to a house of debauchery, then said goodbye as if Sterling's palace of devil worship was a playroom. No loving father could treat a daughter like that.

Cyd stilled, then eased her head high to listen.

The whirling beat of a large air chopper thumped louder. It sounded as if it might land in the vacant lot next to the Old Faithful Inn. She jumped up to peer through the louvered windows. She moved around the wide window, flicking the slats of the blinds to find the best view. Choppers were not uncommon but usually only transported cyborgs or security soldiers dressed smugly in pressed uniforms.

She squinted to see between the dusty blinds, angling to see towards the front door. Cyd jumped back and forth across the window, up and down. She rapped on the Polymer glass, then pounded the fiber-hardened plastic until she screamed. She used her back and slid down the wall. She screamed again.

A metallic click on the door lock.

She narrowed her eyes and crawled on her hands and knees to the door. The sound must have been her imagination. She tried the lock and found the lever swung free. She pulled the door open, then released a held breath. She stared at the ugly wallpaper curled at the top corners and stained by years of roof leaks.

She pushed her head into the hallway and checked each way to see the hallway was empty. Whoever released her didn't want Daddy to know. She jumped up and hurried down the long hallway lined with locked guest room doors, tourist space never to be used again.

A large pane of glass provided sunlight at the end of the dark hallway. Cyd eased to the dirty window to see an animal capture net descending from the sky. A strange looking man rode in the net, his gray robe pressed against his body, the hood riding on his back flapping with the turbulent downdraft. A Moonie. The young man lifted his face to the sky as the net fell around his feet and released him. Cyd pressed her nose against the glass and squinted. Maybe a monk or a beggar but probably a disgusting Moonie crawling with cancers. A day's worth of silver stubble shaded his scalp and beard, his skin white as bleached flour.

Her father exited the front door as if headed to meet the chopper. What the heck? Daddy never met anyone at the landing pad; the courtesy was beneath him. Visitors always had to make the effort.

Daddy shouted at the Moonie pauper, the words muted by the thick glass. Cyd pressed her ear to the glass and closed her eyes, focusing on the sounds. Michael. Game. Eliminated. Cage. Die.

Cyd stared at the prisoner. Couldn't be. No way. Michael the Monk frightened Daddy.

Daddy offered his hand toward the grand entrance. Cyd switched cheeks to see a young girl walk out, escorted by two cyborgs. Her robes matched the man in the net. Her face was splotched with a rose birthmark. Cyd pulled back from the glass and frowned. Why would Moonie beggars interest Daddy? He would spit on the homeless living in the streets as easily as offer them a chance at a new life with an Arkoff Port.

The beggar waited on the flattened net as the main cord fell at his backside.

Daddy offered his hand again to the other side of the building. Anna was cradling a beggar baby.

Oh. My. Freaking. Heck.

Cyd pressed her ear hard against the bulletproof glass. The muted, indecipherable words made her palm slap the wall. The chopper flew off. The beggar stood stiff like a marble statue as the borgs wrapped thick yellow straps around his arms and body then escorted him into a pole barn once used to store Yellowstone OHVs and snowplows.

Cyd slid her back down the wall near the window and brought her knees to her chest. Michael wasn't the CEO of a company to be chewed up and spit out by Arkoff Industries. The Moonie girl and that baby . . . Daddy despised young children.

What the heck was happening?

———

AN UNUSUAL CLARITY, GAINED FROM spending a lifetime in prison, now offered Michael multiple insights into possible escape. He sat on the cold asphalt with his upper arms strapped tight against his torso but allowing his arms movement below the elbows. The shadows of cyborgs circling the prison routinely blocked the sun penetrating through a thin gap beneath the building's metal siding. He sucked on a tube feeding him liquid tinted in turquoise, like a hamster but without a wheel. He spat. The chemical taste was bitter and obtrusive. Then he sucked again.

I heal with everything I say and do.

The empty pole barn contained numerous EV battery chargers mounted to the metal columns, yet the air wafted of ancient petroleum and oily dust, and windowless except for a tinted transom window above the coiled overhead door. He adjusted his position against the heavy metal bars of the square eight-foot cage to face the door.

A side door opened, and the shadow of a backlit zookeeper stretched inside before she stepped in. The bright light caused Michael to wince and narrow his eyes.

"Time to change the bucket," the shadow said with a smoky feminine voice.

Michael took a suck of water. "Maybe time to change this shit-for-water you're feeding me."

The girl posed her hands on her hips as if irritated. "Slide back so I can get that shit bucket changed out."

Michael shimmied back into the corner, sick of the stench of his own feces. The girl kicked an empty white five-gallon bucket into the cage, as if afraid to touch it with her hands. She stepped inside. A tiny flash of red and yellow pinched to her running shoe caught his eye. The bullhead and color configuration were unmistakable.

"Dave's Hopper. Deadly if presented exactly right. Or so I'm told."

The girl looked down at her sneaker. "Yeah, well, doesn't seem you'll get the opportunity to see one in action."

Michael huffed. "Probably not. The Fisherman sure seemed keen on them though."

The girl paused her chore. "Don't try any hocus pocus, mumbo jumbo shit with me. I got my own problems."

"Don't we all," Michael said.

———

CYD PULLED THE DOOR OPEN and recoiled from the stench of feces and urine. The cyborg at her side growled and stepped back. She put down two empty buckets and covered her nose with her sleeve.

"Fucking Zac didn't do his job. Again!" She scowled at the guard. "Why don't you change the buckets this time?"

The cyborg clicked his tongue and waited for another mechanized guard to approach. Their jaws worked as if they chewed gristle, subliminal communications flashing through their optic enhancements.

"Proceed," one said.

"Yeah, figured you'd say that," Cyd said. She picked up the buckets and stepped inside the pole barn. The shadows of the twin cyborgs dimmed the sunlight illuminating the interior walls and asphalt, and she turned and motioned them to step back to allow light inside. They didn't move. She groaned and shook her head.

"You stink like nothing I've ever smelled before," Cyd said. She flipped the door latch and stood at the open cage door. "Both doors are unlocked, and you still sit here like a lump of shit. I'd be gone so quick."

Michael stretched his neck and shoulders within the confines of the straps wrapped around his torso. "What's it like being the daughter of the great Samuel Arkoff? Cleaning shit buckets and sliding slop into cages seems a bit beneath your title."

Cyd glared. "Better than what you got. You're one of those weirdo Moonies that thinks Daddy Dearest is the reincarnation of the devil. Probably why you're strapped and prepped to be dropped into one of the geysers."

"Can you check my water?" Michael said. He spat colored phlegm. "The chemicals keep me up at night. A last request from a dying . . . a dying man."

"I don't do the water. Jurgens has that pleasure," Cyd said. She stepped back out of the cage and motioned to the borg that she was finished.

"Thanks for the consideration," Michael said.

Cyd approached the pole barn, an odd enthusiastic pep in her step. Over the past two weeks the revulsion of cleaning disgusting feces and acrid urine had become irrelevant as she neared the door. Often positioned like a filthy Buddha sitting cross-legged in the center of the cage, Michael intrigued her, a disgusting yet pleasant distraction from the mundane routine of caring for the inhabitants of Yellowstone's silly petting zoo. She had spied Jurgens playing with the contents of the dispensing tanks on Michael's feeding tubes, adding scoops of chemicals that matched the turquoise color of 3Bz into the whey powder mixed with water every day.

Two cyborgs met her near the door.

"Getting old, guys. If you wanna change the buckets, just let Daddy know, and I can take the day off," Cyd said. She offered two empty buckets.

"Proceed."

"Yeah, thought so." Cyd pulled the door open, and her heart sank. A dying animal waited huddled into the corner, its life force withering, its will to live resigned to a slow death. No different than the orphaned wolf pup she helped capture when she was ten. She had watched it pace the small cage for weeks, refusing food and water, until it slumped into a corner to lay its head on its paws and wait to die.

She entered the small cage, full of purpose. Cyd dropped the empty buckets at the door, hoping the echoing clang might startle Michael to raise his head. His dark scalp sprouting thick hair had turned splotchy, like cancers from the sun had found its latest victim.

"Yo, yo. Getting the buckets," Cyd said. She stepped toward a bucket buzzing with black flies but kept her eyes trained on the stilled hunch of Michael. "C'mon, I need a little acknowledgement that you're still alive."

Michael nodded with an almost imperceptible movement.

"I changed your water feeder. I think Jurgens was feeding you 3Bz. And I asked the cook to add some supplements to your gruel." Cyd reached her hand out to stroke the head of the dying animal, then pulled it back. She swallowed hard, then picked up the bucket and turned for the door.

She pivoted to look back at Michael. "Look before you crap."

MICHAEL TESTED HIS WINGS WITHIN the tight confines of the heavy straps, flexing and expanding his chest, convinced one mighty thrust would snap the thick fiber. Not yet. The circumstances had not changed. Samuel still held Myra and her baby captive. Plus, the chemicals in the water needed a few days to filter out of his kidneys.

Maybe the Fisherman would visit his dreams again to provide guidance.

He wondered about the tall girl, Cyd. She didn't act like the usual monsters he had encountered in the prison lab. She had a tough exterior but inside beat a kind heart. A soul that genuinely cared. She had left a packaged protein bar in the bottom of the empty bucket, and his effort to unwrap and consume it without the use of his arms would make even the Fisherman proud. Cyd could not be the blood offspring of Samuel. Adopted, maybe. But why would Samuel desire a daughter, especially one that didn't carry his cruel essence in her blood?

Michael flexed his chest and heard more tiny fibers of the straps stretch and snap. He relaxed and stood up, then shuffled backwards to lean against the metal cage.

The barn door clattered as it rolled up. Bright sunlight assaulted his eyes. He blinked rapidly against the brilliance as tall dark shadows waited at the threshold of the open door. Pine-scented air mixed with the putrid stink hanging in the barn like a cloud of flies. The fresh air caused his nostrils to flare and stiffened his spine. The bitter chemicals in the water had not only muddled his thoughts and stifled his dreams but dulled all his human senses.

Samuel walked in, followed by Myra and two cyborgs. The young mother dressed in jeans and a denim work shirt kept her head lowered. He spied Cyd waiting at the entrance, hugging the door jamb as if she feared what Samuel might do.

Samuel stood safely behind the knot of metal bars and thick wire. "Day fourteen, Michael. You've been a good boy, so I'm gonna let you see Myra. Just so you know, nothing has changed outside. You escape, and she dies, and I feed the baby to the ferrets. And what a slow, painful meal that would be."

Michael swallowed and relaxed the tight ball of his fists. "Since I'm outta the game, what's your goal? Is the Fallen One to rise up to Heaven and take the crown from our Father?"

"Of course. To rule Heaven *and* Earth. And I'm halfway, maybe more than halfway with you out of the picture. You thought to lead His army again, but there you stand—excuse me, sit. In your own shit." Samuel stepped forward and gripped the cage. "Five hundred fucking years I've planned this. I see what He sees, I hear what He hears, and you sit here like the fucking impotent Archangel you've always been."

"Ouch," Michael said. He glared at the black soulless eyes responsible for an eternity of torment and pain. "Your ego hasn't aged well. It still coats your words with slime. And yet here I am. Human. Easy to murder. Do it, Samuel, or shut the fuck up and let me keep sucking on my feeding tube."

Samuel chuckled. "You can goad all you want, but the bait isn't taken." He waved Myra to come forward. The girl eased forward as she stared at the floor. Her plum birthmark had completely disappeared, replaced with the silky soft skin of youth. Samuel yanked her to his side. "She will make a fine addition to my dominion if someone doesn't fuck up the agreement."

"Myra," Michael said. "Don't . . ."

Myra shrugged off Samuel's grip and hurried for the door. Cyd offered a sympathetic hand. Myra spurned the offer and kept running.

"Must be suckling time," Samuel said and chuckled. "The endgame is here, Michael. I've seen it coming, all of it, and you're not included."

"Since I'm irrelevant, then how about a bath?"

Samuel shook his head and walked away. He turned back, started to say something, then kept going. He ignored Cyd as he exited through the door to disappear into the sunlight. Cyd opened her palms and shook her head, confusion scrunching her face.

She rushed forward to the cage. "What the hell is happening? Who are you? *What* are you?"

Michael slumped to the floor. "My story for an energy bar."

———

CYD OPENED THE CAGE DOOR and stepped in. Michael waited in the corner. His head drooped between his dirty, blackened knees. Cyd tried to swallow, but her tight, dry throat rejected the effort. The bucket sat empty. The end of the feeding tube was crusted and unused. The water tube dripped tiny drops into a puddle of green, fuzzy algae. A caged animal waiting for a slow, miserable death. She stepped closer and tapped a shoe into his bare foot rippled with purple veins and emaciated bones.

Cyd had endured the deaths of countless animals brought to the zoo. Food rejected or vomited or left uneaten, water consumption reduced to a few drops, but the eyes losing the shine of life always turned her stomach. She had managed to save a few raccoons and a few squirrels. Sheba was her crowning success. The young cougar had curled beneath a wooden bench, shrinking into the shadows further each day until even a quarter flank of elk meat wouldn't coax her from her death bed. Cyd had shaken off the zookeepers' protests and entered the enclosure to hand-feed the feline small bits of meat. Tiny cubes of elk or venison became slices as she sat and coaxed the cat to eat each day.

Growing up lonely and isolated in Yellowstone, her reassuring conversations with Sheba soon surpassed any she held with imaginary best friends. She had pleaded with Daddy to collar Sheba and let her walk the big cat along the many trails leading from the former resort.

Someday, he said. Always someday.

She nudged Michael's foot again. "You said I'd get a story for a granola bar. Two bars mean I get a bestseller. Eat up, Michael. And I hope that story includes what you know about this silly fishing fly permanently attached to my shoe."

Michael lifted his head a few inches, just enough to stare at her shoe.

MICHAEL FINISHED THE SECOND ENERGY bar and stretched his neck to lick his fingertips. With one hand he folded and pressed the wrapper into a flat square to be hidden in feces. He tilted his head back and stretched his neck at all angles allowed by his spine. The food was exquisite. He flexed his chest, but the wings resisted their birth and remained dead weight, like a rucksack of stones. He sighed.

Father, what do you want from me? To die? Then take me now. To fight? Then release to me my sword. To play spy? Then I am at the end of my mission. Please, Father, the currents swirl like spring runoff, and I float as a naked helpless soldier in Your service.

The metal door opened, allowing a sliver of brilliant moonlight to mix with the blackness of the unlit barn. A shadow darted inside, and the door closed. The shuffling of feet slowed as someone approached his cage. The pleasant aroma was unmistakable. Myra.

She pushed her unblemished, youthful face against the bars and wire. "My prayers have been answered. Take my baby and fly. Fly, angel. Fly. Seth would tell you the same thing."

Seth. The boy's name fluttered within a special place of his heart.

Michael looked at his feet. "I can't."

"No. You mean you won't. The baby is all that matters. Take him and fly away!" Myra spat at his feet.

Michael stared at her then heaved a heavy breath. "Then you die."

"And that's okay. But my baby will live. And live a life protected by angels. What more could a mother ever ask for?" Myra frowned with her sad resolution. "In my dream, He said you would judge my soul. Do I get in, Angel? Do I?"

"I don't think this is the time . . ." Michael said.

"Faith. I think that's what you don't have," Myra said. "Except I have faith, enough for both of us. I give you permission to leave here. Take my child back to the Moonies. Mary will provide for him."

Michael bit his lower lip. "Let me think . . . What you're asking . . . I . . . I'm not sure."

Myra stepped back. Her eyes darted around his cage. "You need to fly, Michael. My dreams promised you would soar with the wind, up into the sun. They promised."

"I'm not sure I can fly. Trusting me with a child . . ." He shook his head. "Maybe I . . ."

Myra gripped the metal bars. "Tomorrow morning, I'll bring my baby. Before sunrise. You need to be ready. If he discovers us, then . . ." The skin on her hands paled as she turned to leave.

Cyd's voice whispered a warning outside the pole barn, and Myra ran to hide behind bags of animal feed stacked against the far wall. Cyd stood in the doorway, an ominous dark shadow, and searched the pole barn with catlike eyes glowing in the faint moonlight.

She turned to face someone outside and offered her hands above her head. "Maybe your fucking optics need a diagnostic. I don't see anyone here. But hey, come on in and help. Shit waits for no one."

Twin laser beams sliced the interior air, scanning for Myra. A single cyborg stepped close and scanned Michael. Its infrared beam lingered on him as he sat down on the bucket. *Enough of this.* He rose and flexed his chest. Faint twangs of fiber snapping caused another laser sight to aim at his chest. Two additional cyborgs rushed through the door and targeted his forehead with their red beams.

"Just squatted you boys a fresh specimen. Did Samuel tell you my history? I am a living, breathing germ factory, and just the whiff of my crap might kill millions." He eyed Myra huddled in shadows then stepped to the front of the cage. "Come on then, change the bucket or use it yourself. But hurry up."

Cyd snickered and offered upturned palms to two additional cyborgs joining the others inside. "I'm going to dinner with Daddy. You want me to tell him something is up? He can call in reinforcements. But I don't see anything but a Moonie and a bucket of crap."

Laser sights mixed and crossed as the cyborgs communicated subliminally.

Myra had shimmied between the stacks and into a gap against the wall. It was Cyd who had helped the naïve girl enter the barn to offer her own brief life as a sacrifice.

He flexed his chest and popped the straps. Laser lights targeted his face and chest. Cyd shouted and waved her arms, hoping to distract the cyborgs.

Michael flexed and stretched virgin ligaments. One violent thrust, and his robes would shred. His mighty wings would unfurl to crush the metal cage, allow his escape through the flimsy metal roof. He would soar again. Stretch muscle and tendons atrophied for centuries. Revel in the awesome power the Fisherman had bestowed on him.

Michael calculated the oncoming violence, just as he would in prison. The cyborgs would die in a rush of air and feathers. Myra would scream as he lifted her high above the landscape. Cyd would perish for her treason. The baby would be lost to Samuel.

And the Fisherman would frown on his impatience.

Michael sat on the bucket, and released a loud belch.

CHAPTER TEN

FOR CENTURIES, SAMUEL ARKOFF TOILED between ruling subservient minions or battling disgusting righteous believers in God. His influence limited by the capabilities of human communication, Samuel dominated the souls that amused him, tortured those who refused his demands, and amassed unfathomable wealth, concealing the ill-gotten riches from discovery until the time was ripe to flaunt it. Years ago, an opportunity too magnificent to ignore spawned ideas.

To avoid default on trillions of dollars of debt, the United States Congress elected to auction off Yosemite, Yellowstone, the Great Smoky Mountains, and even the Grand Canyon. The sell-off hadn't stopped with the privatization of the National Park System. National forests, BLM-managed grazing land, Scenic By-Ways, a total of ninety-eight percent of all federal land was sold. Purchased by the only parties that could afford it: wealthy individuals and corporations, or friendly nations, all intending to rape and pillage the resources for monetary gain.

Samuel Arkoff purchased the area known as Yellowstone National Park for the equivalent of sixty U.S. dollars and absolved the federal government of sixty-three trillion dollars in bonds that Arkoff Industries held in trust. He considered buying other large national parks, but none held the allure of Yellowstone's large caldera, an idling volcano waiting to erupt and spew misery across the globe. The subterranean lava tubes, geothermal heat, and abundant clean water formed the foundation of an idea to connect heaven and earth, to be remade in Samuel's image. Corrupt, vile, violent, a heavenly landscape befitting a fallen angel.

And not enough.

Samuel manipulated governments into war and famine. His conglomerate of companies devoured the environment to accelerate a tsunami of natural disasters. He set religions to war against each other.

But it was the sweet aroma of souls ascending to the Father's Kingdom which assaulted Samuel's senses. Each beyond his reach, destined to return to Samuel's domain as a squawking human child. Their innocence reeked of newborn ignorance, and their return made Samuel's dominion incomplete. He would decide who his kingdom accepted. He would decide what manner of soul would bow down on their knees to worship him. Eliminate the ceaseless catastrophes boiling with unsavory acts of human kindness or revolting displays of compassion.

The war for domination had been a standoff.

Until Jurgens perfected the Arkoff Port.

Samuel reveled in a superiority rebirthed from the earliest centuries, spawning a fresh boundless energy for manipulating government edicts and rival corporations by requiring the invasive neural connection for any business transactions conducted with Arkoff Industries. A snowball of manipulation that simply rolled downhill, money and greed driving the pandemic of neural connectivity. The Catholic Church resisted for seven years until their isolation within the world community gestated an epiphany from the Pope. God would accept the new device.

Samuel smiled as he manipulated the new world order like a game of children's checkers. Wars ceased. Governments cooperated. The final domino fell as hospitals and healthcare institutions required Arkoff Ports for admission, for life-sustaining treatment, for pharmaceuticals. The technological virus was complete.

The Arkoff Port ushered in peace, prosperity, and utter subjugation.

Samuel chuckled with his reminiscence. The odd cluster of children born in the backyard of Nowhere, Idaho was so cliché. The

Father's baby pawns. Easily taken by Samuel's acolytes, to be swept off the gameboard. Except they had proved useful and enriching, until almost all disappeared from confinement.

Michael's escape had unnerved him. Until he gazed down at the mighty Archangel squatting over a bucket of feces, handcuffed by righteousness and human ignorance.

He looked up at the blank ceiling and chuckled again. "Father, why, after centuries do you choose to stick your face into my affairs? This world is mine. Even you can see that from your lofty viewpoint. I control everything, everyone, everywhere, just as I set out to do. Now, I will come for you. And you can't stop me."

He looked down at the security holo-screen floating near his face to see Cyd walking down the hallway towards his office. She had changed since returning from Sterling's residence. She was compliant. Soft-spoken, and easily manipulated. He could only imagine the debauchery Sterling and his crew had employed on her during her brief stay. Was a gang rape all that was needed to mold her into a compliant slave girl? She continued her uptake of 3Bz from Jurgens lab, but the drug's effect on her personality had changed. He liked the change but would keep a close eye on her.

He watched Cyd bow her head and knock on his door. He unlocked the magnetic door with a simple twitch of his lower jaw.

"Come in, Cyd," he said. "You know you never have to knock. My door is always open for you."

Cyd nodded but wouldn't look him in the eye. "That Moonie thing you have locked up in the barn needs to have a firehose taken to it. It reeks worse than dead skunk. The zookeepers won't go near it, and the Borgs want to terminate it. What should I do?"

Samuel sat back and steepled his fingers. She would never have asked for his guidance before. She would have told him what needed to be done and then did it anyway, regardless of what he decided.

"Do you know what that thing is?" Samuel said.

"The zookeepers say it's an angel, but I think it's a freak of nature you plan to use to make more money. Either way, it needs a bath."

"Do you think it might be an angel? Do you believe in them? In God?" Samuel asked.

"I believe you will try to convince people that's what it is." Cyd looked up to see her father's reaction. "But I think it's one of Jurgens' experiments he hides in the basements of the other barns. Maybe like Sheba and Rondo except . . .”

“Except what?”

“Except that he is human, and nobody should have to live like that.”

“You’re absolutely right, Cyd. Maybe my orders have been too harsh.” Samuel entwined his fingers. “Let’s give it a bath and go from there.”

Cyd looked up at him, her eyebrows arched. “Really? Um. Okay, I’ll get everything ready.”

“Excellent. I have meetings all morning and into the afternoon, so let’s say four p.m. I want to be there. I would think all the keepers, even the staff, will want to see exactly what we have inside the barn.”

“Um. Kinda dehumanizing. To do that in front of everyone.”

“Cyd, you seem to have changed since coming back from the Sterling trip,” Samuel said. “Is there something I should know? Did he do something, something I should confront him with?”

She bowed her head and shook it. “I’m a zookeeper. I just want the best for the animals. Even a mutant like Michael is no different.”

“Ahh,” Samuel said. He stood up from behind the desk. “You’ve been talking to it. Michael . . . What has *Michael* been telling you?”

“He doesn’t talk. I got his name from Myra. She said he was an angel. Whatever. That robe has to come off, and he needs to be sprayed down and checked for head lice, maybe inoculated from disease.”

Samuel chuckled. “He will never need a vaccination.”

Samuel paced as he counted down the hours then the minutes until Michael’s bath time. Centuries, eons, and never a spectacle the likes of which would occur in the courtyard outside the metal barn. Two thousand years ago, Samuel would have commanded the bath to take place in front of a riotous mob filling the seats in the Roman Colosseum. Now the humiliation of the Father’s enforcer would be broadcast worldwide using every media outlet and streaming service he controlled. A soul-sucking humiliation of the righteous Michael. The filthy individuals still resisting the Arkoff Port, and his influence, would flock to his implant clinics, clamoring for a connection.

Samuel paused his pacing. The pole barn doors slid open on

his holo-screen. With the twitch of his jaw, he released weaponized drones to fly a surveillance grid pattern above the courtyard.

Cyd hurried inside the barn.

"Fuck," Samuel said. She was early.

He hurried out the door and down the hallway, the silver holo-screens floating at his face keeping pace. He slowed and heaved his breath. Cradling the baby, Myra waited at the front doors, two cyborgs as escorts. He sniffed the warm air, relaxed his shoulders muscles, and aimed for the front doors. Anticipation lightened his step. Anna came out of her office and followed. Jurgens hurried up from the basement stairway and trailed after Anna. Samuel pushed open the heavy wooden doors and stepped out to a pleasant sunny afternoon.

Samuel lifted his face up to the sun and smiled. He sniffed the air, then curled his lip at the revolting stink of a fresh-bathed baby. Regardless, the day was glorious. Maybe he would celebrate later, shove Myra down onto his bed and show her what she should fear most. A glorious day indeed. He beckoned Myra to come closer. He snickered as she closed the swaddle around the child's face, as if to prevent it from seeing what she secretly desired. Myra stepped in front and bowed her head. He signaled a cyborg to come close then reached down to pull the child away from Myra. She resisted.

"He will not be harmed. You have my assurances," he said. She looked up at him. Her turquoise eyes were beguiling, her skin flawless, her adolescent female scent intoxicating. "I promise."

She adjusted the swath and offered the baby. He smiled then grabbed the child as if it were a football and handed it to the cyborg. The half-human recoiled, then took it with one hand and one metal pincer.

"No. Don't," Myra said and reached for her baby.

Samuel swatted her arms away then gripped her cheeks in his hand. "Do as I say, or I'll feed that child to the wolf."

Two cyborgs appeared from each side of the pole barn, slicing the air in all directions with laser targeting. Two cyborgs led Cyd as she emerged from the dark building, guiding Michael with a ten-foot-long polymer strap as a leash.

Samuel smirked and pushed Myra aside. His mandibles twitched with a subliminal order for the cyborg to take the child to the wolf enclosure and wait. He approached Cyd and ordered the bath to begin, then returned to Myra to stand behind her and rest his bony, liver-spotted hands on her shoulders.

Cyd dropped the leash and approached Michael cautiously. Using a pair of laser-assisted-Scizors, she cut the polymer straps to fall at the hem of his filthy robe. She turned her head to catch a breath of fresh air. Cyd reached out to Michael with a slow, trembling hand, as if he were a dangerous feral animal.

"The robe's gotta go. I got Myra's robe I can give you after the . . . the bath," Cyd said.

Samuel stepped forward, pushing Myra to remain in front of him. "Michael needs nothing except his Father's acceptance. Cut the robes and douse him like the scum he is."

Michael stiffened.

Samuel pushed Myra closer. "Our deal."

Cyd rolled her eyes and shook her head, then sliced the robe top to bottom. The fabric fell and crumpled around Michael's feet. She gasped and stepped back. Her eyes widened.

Michael craned his neck in wide circles, arched his back to expand Herculean pectorals. He flexed knotted forearms and biceps. Hairless genitals hung between the muscled legs of a marathon runner. He lifted his face and let his bone-white skin bathe in the hot sun. Massive five-meter wings unfurled in slow increments, reaching high above Michael's head. The white wings extended outward, allowing thick, sturdy feathers to warm in the rays of the sun. Michael extended his arms to his sides and clenched his fists. Loosening bone and sinew cracked in the stillness.

Samuel stepped forward and sniffed the air. "Again. Our deal."

Cyd signaled Zac to open the hose bib, and she aimed a violent stream of water at Michael. The force of the water deflected upward and outward as if hitting a brick wall, showering Cyd and the borgs. She screamed then laughed, her platinum hair dripping water down her face. She aimed the water to clean each limb until she directed the water stream back towards the barn. Her eyes remained glued to the beautiful Michael.

Michael shook his body like a wet dog. He grinned and retracted, then extended his wings and shook again. A shower of water flew like a magical fountain.

Samuel dropped his hold on Myra to shield his face with his arms as each water droplet burned his skin like wasp venom.

Michael loomed within an arm's length, separated only by the trembling Myra. The girl's knees buckled, but Samuel held her upright.

Samuel's pulse quickened. His throat was parched. He stared into Michael's eyes, endless blue pools, a color reeking of God's ethereal paradise.

Michael grabbed Samuel's throat.

"Our deal, Michael. I will eat the soul of this girl if you—" Samuel choked, a vise squeezing his airway.

"If I don't choke the life from you first," Michael stated.

"Then the baby dies," Samuel said. He grabbed Michael's wrist. The grip on his neck was unbreakable. "And I'll return in a few eons to start again. I don't think so. Father didn't birth you and your magnificent fucking self to play the game again."

Michael squeezed harder. "Conceit and snake oil. Nothing's changed."

The cyborgs rushed towards them. Michael flapped his wings, and a powerful backdraft of air sent the cyborgs flying backwards to crash into the barn's metal cladding.

"The baby will die. You have my word," Samuel said.

Michael scoffed and released Samuel. "Your word died when Father threw you out." Michael pulled Myra out of Samuel's grip and held her tight to his body. "The baby is yours."

Myra screamed.

With a single flap of white, unworldly wings, Michael lifted Myra into the air to hover a few feet above the asphalt. Powerful feathers fluttered gently in the warm air.

Samuel coughed and spat. Missiles, lasers, and flamethrowers waited to be launched with the twitch of his jawbone, but he hesitated.

"I will feed that baby to the wolf before you get out of Yellowstone," Samuel said. "You judge its innocence then, Michael. Sit high and mighty and judge its eternal soul."

Michael snarled at Myra flailing in his grasp, then fluttered his wings to move closer. "Your nostrils have grown old, like you. The child carries no soul to judge. A vessel born for a demon."

Samuel frowned with the statement. Michael couldn't lie, or could he? Michael rose hundreds of feet above the asphalt, then folded his wings to swoop like a falcon and snatch a stunned Cyd. He rose higher with easy swipes of massive wings.

Fucking Michael.

Samuel ordered every drone, cyborg, and weaponized aircraft within a hundred miles to follow and shoot down the fucking white bird. Anna placed a hand over his wrist. He bared his teeth at her. The two women struggled in Michael's arms, tearing at his skin with fingernails, reaching to gouge his eyes. He held on with little effort then barked basso commands at his captured prey. Each girl went limp. He dropped like a stone to hover and face Samuel from a perch of superiority, his wings fluttering thick feathers to maintain position.

Strategy manifested in many forms. Samuel suddenly felt the fool. Did he think a captured Archangel would sit quietly and wait out the end game?

Samuel cancelled the kill order. Michael hovered closer. The cyborgs regained their positions and aimed plasma beam weapons at Michael. The kill zone was sure to roast Anna and Jurgens—and irritate the fuck out of Samuel.

Michael tilted his head. "The child is an empty vessel of no value. Hand it over. Maybe a good deed might sway His judgment of your black soul when the time arrives."

"I judge the souls on this world!" Samuel roared. "I dictate who lives and dies. You have no conception of the army coming for you. Your kind is obsolete, Michael. Short-sighted and damned by arrogance. Are you going to save everyone? Or just those two? I have been grooming this world for centuries, just for this day. You . . . you escaped a silly prison, with my acquiescence, and now you think to ask me for my obeyance."

Samuel stepped back and offered his right hand. "Michael, meet Rondo."

The wolf's leap spanned ten feet as it aimed for Michael's throat—only to collide with a wing wrapping around the unconscious Cyd. Michael dropped to the ground but held the women tight. He used a wing to slap the wolf aside and send it tumbling into the zoo's wire enclosures.

Samuel offered his left hand. "And Sheba."

The cougar attacked with lightning speed. Its sharp claws raked Michael's thigh. Michael roared and flicked his wings to rise. Sheba snarled and leapt like a house cat chasing a dangling toy. Myra screamed as sharp claws found her calves. Michael flapped his wings again to shoot high into the sky. His drizzle of blood fell like a pleasant summer rain.

Samuel watched the wounded fowl disappear over the horizon. Sheba curled her taut, muscled body around his legs and sat. Rondo approached cautiously, sniffed Samuel's leg, and slumped down on the opposite side. Samuel stood quiet as he sifted through thousands of camera shots until he found the perfect angle to broadcast to the world. Michael's weakness and cowardice. A call to arms for the millions of his acolytes.

Lambs and donkeys at the manger, replaced by cougars and wolves controlled by his acolytes, each waiting for the arrival of God's next child. A divine meal.

Then Samuel would sit on Heaven's throne.

And laugh.

CHAPTER ELEVEN

Alone, on a chunk of bleached stone at the base of the empty reservoir's rock dam, Michael hung his head and stared aimlessly at his bare feet poking out from the dirty robe. Guilt and self-loathing festered on the lacerations scarring his legs. In his absence, the Moonies remained bogged down at Mackay Reservoir. Campfire smoke drifted over tents, tarpaulins, and lean-tos scattered across the lakebed's dusty sediment.

Raphael approached cautiously. Michael waved him away. He felt innumerable eyes watching him, disapproving, and condemning. Only Seth had dared to approach within five yards, close enough to toss him a new robe. Michael had pulled the robe over his head with the wings folding tight to his back. The boy offered an innocent wave before running away.

Myra's leg wounds would heal, but her heart was broken beyond repair. And he was to blame.

The zookeeper, Cyd, was another matter. Seething with snake venom and spite, she had jogged up the main highway, then turned on Trailside Road heading west towards Sun Valley. Attempts to dissuade her had been met with expletives and rocks. Her escape was thwarted by Raphael jumping in front of her path to threaten her with plastic restraints and a driftwood club.

Michael liked the younger girl. Her history seemed oddly similar to his own upbringing. Subjugated by evil, escape impossible and yet maintaining a stubborn will to be free. Her skills as a caregiver were immeasurable. Animal or human, the young woman bandaged, stitched, set bone, equal to any skilled surgeon. In just a few days, her status among the suspicious Moonies had risen quickly. And yet she remained a mystery as to why Samuel had kept her close, an adoption that might dismay even the Fisherman.

The Fisherman.

Michael's dreamless sleep was disconcerting. Was the Fisherman disappointed with his impetuous outburst, abandoning a baby to Lucifer's possession? Had Samuel known about his dreams and destroyed his ability to communicate with the Fisherman using the contaminated water? Samuel had indeed magnified his power on Earth in the last five centuries. Was that influence enough to usurp the Fisherman in this decaying world?

A wasp stung his neck, and Michael slapped at the annoyance. Another stung him above his ear. Michael slapped at the perceived swarm only to hear laughter. He rose to his full height, baring his teeth as his wings exploded from the confines of the robe.

"Myra won't forgive you. Cyd thinks you're a freakin dork. Raphael thinks you're still stuck in your eggshell, whatever that means. The Moonies think you couldn't tie your own laces even if you wore shoes."

Michael spotted his brave tormentor. Seth hid between two large boulders, his hooded head bearing an expression of humorous evil intent. Michael heaved a breath and waved his tormentor over. Seth sat on a boulder a few feet away. His company comforted the distress rattling his thoughts.

"Cyd thinks I'm a dork?" Michael said.

"Well, you are. Kind of," Seth said. He tossed the last of his ammunition to bounce into the dark crevices between boulders.

"I saved her from—"

"From nothing she couldn't have saved herself from. She's awesome."

Michael nodded. She *was* awesome. "Myra wants to slit my throat and–"

"I can handle Myra," Seth said. He tossed his last pebble hard and watched it clatter over the rocks. "Rocks I throw never bounce the same way twice. Why is that?"

Michael looked at the wise old soul disguising itself impeccably. "I'm not sure. What do you think?'

Seth raised a single finger. "Chaos theory. Each rock has infinite paths. I could throw a million rocks, and none of 'em would bounce or land in the same spot twice. Except . . ."

Michael tilted his face. "Except what?"

"Except certain things don't change. Like the big boulders my pebbles bounce on. Or maybe this whole dam of big rocks. Things that don't move. Whatcha think?"

"I think you should be a university professor somewhere," Michael said. He studied Seth.

"Nah, I like hanging out with you. Nobody gets an Archangel for a best friend. I'll just have to watch over you, make sure you do the things Archangels are supposed to do."

"And what are those things?" Michael said.

"Like protect people. Smite demons. Make the world okay."

"And what if there are too many demons or they're too power-ful?"

Seth stood to leap over a crevice to sit next to him, their legs touching. "Then you get help. Soldiers, more angels, and then you smite them." He punched the air with a grimy fist.

Michael gazed up at the hazy gray sky. Seth was right. Raphael had been the first. Michael was Patient #173, then logic would dictate one hundred seventy-two others had been imprisoned with him.

Seth knocked his leg. Michael looked down at a pair of beguiling azure eyes boring into him.

"You're supposed to listen to me. I mean, that's what my dreams say," Seth said. "But I don't know. An angel taking orders from me seems kind of silly."

"Who have you been talking to? Zeke? Raphael? What are they telling you?"

Seth hung his head. "No. I'm supposed to give you . . . direction. Whatever that means."

"And you would direct me where?" Michael said, intrigued by Seth's dreams.

Seth pointed towards the White Cloud Mountains. "Up there. That's where the others are hiding."

"Who? And hiding from whom?"

Seth shrugged. "Myra told me what happened. You shouldn't have let that demon take the baby. He's going to turn it into something terrible."

Michael stood and looked away. "I get it. I screwed up. Nothing can change that now."

"Except Cyd says if the baby is still alive, she could save it."

Michael growled then faced his tormentor. "Does everybody in this fucking camp talk to you and not me?"

Seth nodded furiously. Michael groaned and sat down. He dropped his face into his palms and massaged his temples. Tiny fingers began to massage the crown of his head. Soothing. Comforting. A pleasant sensation unfelt since before he could remember. The loving touch of another human felt divine.

"So, what do you think I should do?" Michael said.

"Well, actually, I think *we* have a lot of options. We should have a powwow. Bring in all the big guns and come up with a plan."

Michael turned and frowned at Seth. "You're how old?"

A powwow was exactly what Seth orchestrated. A blazing campfire snapped and crackled and shot hot embers into the cold night sky like miniature meteorites. The boy pulled unwilling and resistant attendees to the fire then commanded each to wait as he ran off to find others.

Michael stood and watched the coals flicker and flame. His position was preposterous. He was the Archangel Michael. And yet he waited quietly like a camp rat for others to arrive. He turned to leave and found Seth holding up a single finger and a forceful expression commanding him to wait.

Cyd eased in and stood opposite him, keeping the flames as a buffer. She held her hands out to warm. Myra limped in to sit behind Cyd, sulking in her filthy, tattered robe, wearing a heavy hood like a death shroud. Raphael paced in the shadows, as if his nerves were wound too tight. Zeke eased into the circle, outmatched, yet cocksure. Serah stalked behind the expanding circle of bodies, the firelight shadowing her soft features like menacing rouge. She set a stack of metal cups and a plastic pitcher of brown liquid on a boulder.

She pulled her sketchpad from her backpack and readied charcoal pencils. Seth prodded Serah closer to the circle then rushed over to Michael and nudged him to begin.

Michael stepped closer to the fire. "My inclination is to . . . to . . . I have no inclination. We're here at our Father's urging. And I don't have the slightest clue what that is."

Zeke shook his head and waved the gathering away as he side-stepped closer to Serah's pitcher of tea.

Cyd chuckled with disdain. "You pissed off the most powerful man in the world, and now you want to play the moron. That's just precious. I have just one simple question, well, maybe two, but why the fuck did you bring me here!" She bared her teeth as if resisting more choice slurs.

Michael swallowed hard. He had no answer. Only that the impulse to snatch her from Samuel felt right. "I don't know. I . . . It . . . felt like the right thing to do."

"Like leaving my baby with a monster," Myra said. Her face stayed hidden beneath the hood.

"If the road ahead is paved with bad decisions, then I'm not one to travel it," Zeke said. He eyed the tea beneath his fingertips.

"People, let's not forget who got us out of Arco before that atomic bomb exploded," Raphael said. His dirty robe was stretched tight across his torso with maturing winglets.

The powwow erupted with argument and dissent, each member stating their objection to standing exactly where they currently stood. Moonies emerged from the darkness to envelope the meeting, joined by casually dressed people that had escaped Arco. The arguments, the animated voices, the shrill tones grated Michael's fragile emotions until he turned to walk away.

Seth blocked his way, as if the young boy had foretold his path. Seth grabbed Michael's hand and turned him back to face the flickering brightness of the fire then lifted a hefty boulder at his feet and heaved it into the fire, spraying ash and embers into the crowd, and silencing angry voices.

Seth took Michael's hand in his again. With a defiant posture and a stern expression, he dared anyone to speak. Minutes passed. The fire burned bright with driftwood tossed in by Zeke.

Seth spoke. "I prayed to our Father for an angel to help us. And guess what I got? A freaking Archangel. Our Father asked what I would do with an angel. I didn't know, but I knew he could kick ass and fly and smite and set the world right. And yet he kept asking me the same question. What would I ask of it? My prayers were answered, and I still couldn't answer the question. And I still can't. And . . . and . . . that's why we're all here. Michael flies blind. We need to help him find the path the Father has set before him."

Cyd smirked. "You're how old?"

Seth stepped forward with a knotted brow and a stern aura. "Old enough to see what's ahead of us."

Cyd raised her hands in surrender. "You people do love drama."

Michael shook his head. "Open your fucking eyes, Cyd. The world set at your feet is painted with Samuel's misgivings. Your father, adopted father, is Lucifer, and his dominion over this world is nearly complete. The Arkoff Ports have spread his influence over the entire planet."

"You people should have stayed in the Craters and—"

Raphael moved like a phantom and grabbed her throat from behind.

"Enough!" Michael said. "Release her. Now!"

Cyd coughed and spat and eyed venom at Raphael.

"God's foolish cabal wars with each other," Grandmother Mary said as she stepped into the light. "Samuel would dance and rejoice at the sight." Seth hurried around the fire to embrace her. She smiled and held him close. "My boy speaks wisdom for the ages. Now does anyone hear him? Answer his questions? You all see the world with different eyes." Mary pulled Seth tight then pointed at each. "The wealthy, the poor, the artist, the revengeful, the buffoon, and our own Archangel, the lost. Perhaps the gifts our Father has given each of us should be returned. Perhaps that is Michael's path, to fly each of you up to His Kingdom and judge your souls. But I think not. But an old woman's opinion in Samuel's world means nothing."

Mary pushed Seth back towards Michael then continued. "Michael's right. This is Lucifer's world. A world he has cultivated for centuries while the sheep slept. Whether you accept it or not, you are at war. Lucifer reigns. And we are nothing but irritants in his grand plan."

Cyd stepped forward to point a sharp finger at the woman.

"You're a Moonie. You don't have a clue. The charities he sponsors are off the charts. And war . . . You people are nuts. The only war that's gonna happen is when my father finds out I'm living in this pigsty."

Raphael shook his head and barked at Michael, "You brought her here, why?"

Seth backed up to wait at Michael's feet then gazed up at him with an expression pained for answers.

Michael raised his voice. "We pack up at first light and follow the river upstream. Raphael stays back as a rear guard. Serah, pick two Moonies and gather all the medical supplies, take inventory, and give me a list of what we need most. Zeke, you take point and lead this ragtag group. Follow the river until we find the others like me. Let's get some sleep tonight."

"It's been fun, but I'm going home," Cyd said and stepped back from the firelight.

"I'm sorry. No," Michael said. "You're coming with me. Up high or down low, but you will be at my side."

"What the fuck? No way," Cyd protested.

Enough of the self-doubt. Enough debating. Was he human or heavenly? Michael stepped barefoot into the blazing embers of the fire. Flames roared and bit at the hem of his robes. Sparks and smoke obscured his face. He sneered at the pain. Human or divine? Let the flames burn their judgment.

"All you've heard tonight, and still you want to return to the fallen angel who plays at being parent!" Michael yelled. "Does my image in this fire conjure any memories?"

Cyd swallowed, frozen in the shimmering waves of heat erupting from the fabric incinerated in an instant. Hot embers swirled high, burning ash fell at his feet, leaving Michael naked and unscathed.

Michael stepped out of the fire. "You are the puzzle piece I find difficult to place. And I always liked to possess that one final piece. Just for that aha moment."

Cyd stepped back. "You're sick. If it wasn't for those wings, I'd think you—"

"You'd think I was just as bad as Samuel. And you do," Michael said. "Except what I need is this . . . this cabal . . . this war council to believe in me. Follow me. Help me."

Michael stepped back into the fire and spread his massive wings thick with glistening white feathers and let the flames tickle the tips. Energy surged through his limbs as iridescent sparks crackled. Blinding neon auroras swirled about his body like a ghostly mist. Michael spread his arms in front of his wings. A bright meteorite flashed through the night sky.

"From the pit of hell, and into the fire, I have finally risen. My rebirth is complete. And now I begin a journey to give hope to the hopeless, to usher in a new beginning, to bring the new Kingdom of our Father back into this world." Michael fanned his wings once, lifting flames, spark, and ash into the dark sky. "You all have a part to play. No greater or less than mine. Choose now."

Michael folded his wings and aimed an intense stare at Cyd. Her throat swallowed a dry knot. Her defiant eyes drifted to the others as if asking for guidance. Michael stepped from the fire and stood before her.

"You left that baby to the wolves." Cyd's words barely a whisper.

Michael stepped from the fire and crossed his arms. "Perhaps. Maybe that's what Samuel needed to believe. That the child was soulless and his to demonize. Samuel's own guile used against him."

Cyd scoffed but nodded. "So, you could go back and rescue him. Nice. Except Daddy will expect that, so you're screwed."

"Not if I have help. From someone who knows the zoo and people and the layout."

"You want me to betray my own father? Good luck."

Michael chuckled mirthlessly. "Your one true Father hooked that Dave's Hopper on your shoelace for a reason."

Cyd narrowed her eyes. Her jaw clenched. She turned to walk away.

Michael raised his voice. "Do you know who your real parents were? Where you're from? All humans want to know such things."

Cyd turned to face him. "I really don't care. I have a life most people would kill for. So, no, I don't know. Do you?"

Michael smiled flawless white teeth. "I spent fifteen years in a prison of Samuel's making. Skinned like a helpless animal each week and drained of blood each month. And the reasons why become clearer every day. Your false father had reasons to *adopt* a child with no history. Keep her close to his side. Then he allows his precious daughter to be flown away by a sworn enemy without even a . . . Please. You're not stupid. Ignorant, maybe but—"

Cyd stormed off.

Michael groaned and swept his wings once to rise a hundred meters into the night sky. He hovered, regretting his sarcasm and accusations. Perhaps the grasshopper hooked to her shoe was meant for him, a subtle reminder of the currents swirling about him. Gliding silently above the Moonie camp, he spotted Cyd and dropped into her path.

Cyd checked her escape routes left and right, then crossed her arms.

"I apologize for the . . . the . . . inappropriate insults and my tone. Except I really do want to know about your—you . . . and I have never ever talked to a girl, so I plead forgiveness . . . and I'm big on that, you know. I know I can come across as some arrogant angel, but I'm still me. Patient number 173 is all I've ever known, so—"

"What do you want from me?" Cyd said.

"A truce."

"Fine. We're best buddies now," Cyd said and went to step around him.

He extended a wing and stopped her. "Let me show you something, and if you still want to go back to Yellowstone, then I'll fly you there myself."

Cyd sulked but pondered the offer. "And you'll fly me right back to—"

Michael pulled Cyd tight to his body and shot into the night air. Silent flaps of his unworldly wings lifted them higher into the night sky, quickly turning ice-cold. Her body began to shiver and tremble. He pulled her close to his body as he plunged down toward a peak jutting prominently from a rugged spine of mountaintops. He landed gently on a pair of giant granite boulders and released his grip.

Cyd stepped back and stumbled, causing Michael to grab her to prevent a nasty fall. "Mount Borah, tallest peak in Idaho. I think I remember telling my human mother I would climb it someday. Just before Samuel's minions stormed the house to take me *and* my baby sister. That is the last thing I remember. The rest became a blur. Still is. Prison. White walls, always white, floors, furniture, even the food.

Kind of started to hate white and look at me now. White. Head to feet."

Cyd pushed away. "But your hair isn't. Its platinum like mine."

Michael stared at her. "Platinum like yours."

Cyd lifted her eyebrows. "Oh no. No. No. No. Don't try to tell me we . . ."

Michael pulled her into his arms and jumped. Spreading his wings, then retracting them to form a streamlined fuselage as they accelerated in a free fall towards the dark lakebed spotted with hundreds of campfires. Cyd's screams of terror became lost in the blurring whoosh of wind.

Michael grinned and reveled in the exhilaration of total freedom even as death drew close with each passing breath. He resisted an urge to roar at the face of death, spit in its face. He acquiesced. Seconds from hitting the rock dam, Michael spread and angled his wings to hover above the Moonie camp, fluttering the tips of the feathers to maintain his position.

He bellowed a primordial scream, blessed with the Father's approval, every ounce of air in his lungs fueling the announcement of his true rebirth.

And the silence that followed humbled him. He gazed up at a full moon shining down like a heavenly spotlight, and he smiled. His wings flapped with unearthly silence as Cyd whimpered. They circled the camp like a hawk, growing nearer with each iteration.

Michael leaned close to Cyd's face. "I'll be back in the morning. We both have a lot to think about. I'll accept your decision."

Michael lowered Cyd by the bonfire, as easily as an eagle might drop a fish into a nest full of hatchlings. He rose high to survey his . . . Samuel's kingdom. Smoke and fire continued to consume the tiny town of Arco. Hundreds of strobing blue and red lights rimmed the perimeter of the blackened devastation. The missile strike wasn't close enough to harm him, or the Moonies.

The bomb that decimated Arco wasn't meant for him. And Samuel wasn't prone to such miscalculations or mistakes. But he might be inclined to wipe away the recriminations of Michael's viral retribution on his acolytes before the plague could spread. Samuel didn't want to destroy this world. Not now that he owned it.

Michael's nemesis had aged, far more than he expected. Had

Samuel imprisoned Michael and the others to steal blood in a fruitless search for youth? Too simple. Michael could have easily snapped Samuel's neck.

But Samuel was a mastermind and was planning something monumental, mischievous, something even the Fisherman feared enough to give birth to His army again. Other than to rule the heavenly realm, Samuel's true intentions remained a mystery.

But by manipulating Cyd, Michael would find out.

———

CYD HURRIED BACK TO THE fire and held her hands out to warm, then turned slowly like a spitted hog to warm her torso and legs. The cabal was gone. The *cabal*. The word made her chuckle. She would go to sleep tonight and wake up tomorrow knowing the pine-scented air of Yellowstone's pristine forest waited for her return. She'd take a run to sweat out the residual effects of Moonie hallucinogenic mushrooms Serah must have spiked the tea with. Maybe even synthetic LSD that was all the rage. The whole night was a bad trip. Angels and devils. The fate of the world. Serah had picked some bad mushrooms. Super bad.

Cyd turned to let the fire warm her backside. She glanced over her shoulder as Raphael slogged into the firelight. He mimicked her posture and warmed his backside.

"I don't believe any of this shit," Cyd said.

"You got to ride with an angel up toward heaven. Why wouldn't you?" Raphael said. He turned to push his palms closer to the heat.

"Because I've been drugged or maybe I've turned Tuber. You people are all nuts."

"And what if we're not?"

Cyd pivoted, as if she wanted her front side to warm. "Then you're fucked. Samuel controls everything, everyone, and nothing can stop him from getting anything he wants."

"That's what the ancient prophecies said. Except . . . the predictions written centuries ago don't always sit true. That angel you just . . ." Raphael waved his hands above his head like a crazed man, twirled then faced her. "That angel that just dropped you here speaks nothing but the truth. Knows nothing but the truth."

He approached as her a predator might, eyes narrowed and shoulders hunched, lips glistening with saliva, his bearded neck elongating like a viper easing to its prey. Cyd glanced at the fire for a possible weapon, then held Raphael's rapturous eyes. Down, down, down she fell into an abyss. The bottomless well of his green eyes offered safe harbor and excruciating pain with equal allure. Raphael loomed and drew his face closer, sniffing her scent like a dog, his jaw working as if . . .

"Hey, what are you guys doing?" Seth said. He wiggled in between them and tugged on Raphael's robe. "Zeke is looking for you, Ralphie." Seth tugged on the robe again. "I mean Raphael. We gotta start calling you by the right name. And Cyd needs to get some sleep cause she hasn't slept since getting here."

Seth looked up at them, turning his head back and forth, waiting for the trance between them to be broken. "Earth to people. Earth to people. We're down here now."

Cyd shoved Raphael away. "What the fuck did you just do?"

Raphael lifted the corner of his mouth in an evil smirk. "Just trying to help." He turned and hurried out of the firelight, the bulge of immature wings slicing the thin fabric on the back of his robe.

Cyd shuddered as she watched him go. The morning couldn't come quick enough, and Michael's promise of a flight home. The dark night felt like a suffocating coffin, regardless of the firelight. Raphael had unnerved her. His eyes had burned holes in her psyche. He was supposedly an Archangel like Michael. Not like Michael— the exact opposite.

"Earth to Cyd. Earth to Cyd." Seth tugged on her robe.

Cyd shook off the dazed thoughts and frowned down at Seth. "What? Are you going to escort me home, little man?"

Seth beamed. "My heart's desire. Do I get a goodnight smooch?"

Cyd chuckled. "Maybe. If you age ten years before we get there."

"So, wait. If in ten years I walk you home, then you swear you'll give me a smooch?"

Cyd ruffled his hair. "If in ten years you have the opportunity to escort me home, then I will fold up into your arms and let you have all the lip gloss you desire." She chuckled again.

Seth raised his fist and hissed a yes. "You can sleep with Myra tonight. She's conked out. Sad about the baby. I think Michael should just fly back there and smite those devils."

Cyd took Seth's hand and let him lead her deep into the Moonie camp. Tiny fires illuminated poverty. Empty tin cans beckoned hunger. Crying children wailed with sickness. Violent shouts announced dissent and abuse. And this destitute tribe of Moonies had just been ordered deeper into the unknown. Angels and devils. The world was mad either way. She would be happy to get home, to the zoo, and to . . .

And to what? Caged animals with sad eyes beseeching their own freedom? Or more 3Bz to numb her own overwhelming desire for escape? Or she could continue to sprint across meadows and through forests hoping to forget the pointless existence she endured.

At the front flap of a flimsy tent, Seth shushed her. He pointed to the back corner just big enough for an eight-year-old boy. She smiled and prodded him inside, then zipped the flap shut.

Hugging herself as she walked through the sleepy camp, gazing up at the infinite starlight, she found a dark crevice between two large boulders at the base of the dam and wedged her body inside to keep warm. She sat mesmerized by the amazing sliver of night sky. The stars. So many stars. Different from the hazy dark sky above Yellowstone. The light of infinite galaxies sparkled down on her, as if she was someone special. She shimmied deeper into the crevice and snuggled tight into her robe.

Sleep came quick.

Angels and devils.

And Seth. What a charmer.

Seth's incessant tugging on the hem of her robe awakened her. She groaned and shushed him, but he was persistent. Cyd tried to turn away, but her torso was pinched impossibly tight between the boulders. Her right arm wouldn't budge. Her left arm was numb. Her legs were useless unless she could power-squat tons of rock. Panic shot bolts of lightning into her heart. Her breathing turned quick and shallow. She opened her mouth to scream.

"Pretty cool that you can do that," Seth said.

"Get me out of here. What did you do to me?" Cyd said.

"I didn't do nothing."

"Then go find Michael and tell him I want to go home," Cyd said. She tried to twist her torso, hoping to find feeling in her arms.

"So, you're not gonna help get Myra's baby back?" Seth stepped closer and shaded the crevice from the faint morning light.

"After you people did this? No way. I want to go home." Cyd continued her futile struggle against the boulders.

"We didn't do nothing. You did this. You pulled the rocks closer like a blanket."

"Seth, go get Michael. Tell him I've made my decision, and I want to go home," Cyd repeated.

Seth dropped his head and nodded. "I thought you were home."

Cyd watched the boy turn and plod away, her rejection a heavy cloud above his head. She swallowed hard. "Wait up." She began to shimmy and slide and ooze her body through the crevice until her left arm was free. "A little help."

Seth hurried back and took her arm and pulled. His effort was meaningless, but invaluable to restore his enthusiasm. "How'd you get in there?"

"It wasn't this tight last night. Maybe an earthquake." Cyd disbelieved her own premise.

"I didn't feel anything," Seth said. He kept tugging.

Sunlight crested the eastern hills to shine warmth and bright light on the lakebed and rock dam. The shadows of marmots and birds flittered across the boulders as tarps and tent flaps announced the awakening of the Moonie camp.

Seth released his grip and stepped back. "We might need to get help. Maybe find some grease. I don't know."

A shadow high in the sky darkened the morning rays of the sun then landed silently behind Seth. Michael folded his wings and crossed his arms. Cyd groaned with the awkward position of her body, the helplessness, and the last person she wanted to witness either. She hid her eyes as an audience of Moonies closed in around her.

Michael stepped closer and peered into the crevice. Cyd shunned his eyes. He wafted woodsmoke.

"How'd you get in there?" Michael said.

Cyd bit down until her teeth hurt. "Maybe you did this while I was asleep. Just a little nudge from the great angel to keep me here."

"I absolutely want you to stay, but not if we have to drag along heavy machinery for your sleeping preferences."

"Very funny. Get me out of here."

"I'll try." Michael looked at Seth. They both shrugged.

Michael offered Cyd a plan. She had to squat and shimmy beneath his legs while he unfurled his wings to spread the boulders.

"Fine. Fucking fine. Just get me out of here."

A few positioning adjustments, and Cyd crawled from the crevice to roaring applause from the Moonies. She slapped her robe free of dust as the adulation made her crack a sarcastic smile. Myra offered her a flask of water. Zeke clasped her shoulder, then hugged her. Serah offered to doctor her abrasions.

Cyd melted and found the outpouring of love and comradery overwhelming. She pushed her face into her hands to sob and laugh with equal vigor. Serah's warm hand pulled at hers. Seth tugged on her robe and pointed her to review the dark crevice she had just escaped.

Michael waited, his face confused, as if sad and happy at the same time. His eyes were intent on hers. Cyd worked her mouth, biting her bottom lip, then she relaxed to inhale a quick, deep breath. She stepped in front of Michael to thank him.

Michael smirked and pointed at the rock crevice. "A word of warning: our Father likes to speak in metaphors. You can take that little crisis a lot of different ways. But it seems you were either just reborn, or He didn't want you to leave."

"I want to go home," Cyd declared.

Michael spread his wings and offered his hand.

Cyd squinted at his azure eyes. "The baby *was* in room 541. But . . . I'll need to double check. And I'll need a believable story of how I escaped. And a few days to make sure Daddy doesn't suspect anything."

—

SAMUEL STRETCHED HIS LEGS OUT on the recliner and intertwined his fingers behind his head. He glanced at numerous holo-screens floating near his face, then studied Jurgens tapping an old plastic QWERTY keyboard to manipulate the flood of numerical data processing on a wall crammed with old HD monitors. He allowed the eccentric scientist his quirks, old screens, old keyboards, old drug habits. The Arkoff Port implanted on Jurgens' neck gave Samuel unfettered access to anything the old man did, except the consciousness transfer he was preparing to embark on. The mathematics and mechanics of inserting his mind into a wild animal still escaped his comprehension. The alpha wolf, Rondo, sat caged thirty miles distant, near a herd of elk, zookeepers waiting for a signal to release him for the hunt.

Samuel licked his lips. "Let's go. I think my steed might be hungry."

He ignored the warning icons flashing on the holo-screens. The alerts had been endless after the toilet named Arco was decimated by the detonation of a low-yield tactical nuclear device. Media pundits screamed for accountability. The Greenies' coalition decried the permanent loss of valuable resources. The climate activists shouted impending doom as the radioactive fallout encircled the globe. It was the atheist collective narrative that always made Samuel smile, spouting their faithless dogma like scripture, even as they propagated his goals with their ignorance. What would the silly atheists say should they witness the mighty Archangel Michael flapping his wings over Times Square and staring down at them?

"Are you ready sir?" Jurgens said. He reached a shaky hand to insert a fiberoptic filament connection into Samuel's neck port.

Samuel flicked away the bony hand. "You couldn't plug in a lamp. I'll do it." He took the jack from Jurgens and narrowed his eyes. The man had lost a step, perhaps three, but . . .

Jurgens offered a distraction. "The new warrior is almost ready. If this goes well, we might try—"

Samuel reached out and squeezed Jurgens' wrist painfully hard, the brittle bone ready to snap. 3Bz would placate his painful transgression. "Cyd has returned. We need to move up our birthing day. Michael will surely follow. And I want a front row seat to witness our Father's favorite warrior slain by the inexplicable."

"Yes, sir. I will need to download that operational system you wanted. And the enhancements you requested will need time to grow."

"Do it now. After infinite millennia on this world, my time has come, and I intend to enjoy every minute."

Samuel plugged the jack into his port. Screens flashed at his face. Warnings. Data streams. His heart rate accelerated. Biometric data filled the screens. And the wolf, Rondo. Body temperature, his and Rondo's. Respiration rates flashed. The assimilation had commenced. Entering Rondo's consciousness, he would be vulnerable for a few minutes. But Jurgens turning on him was inconceivable.

Samuel convulsed with back spasms. White light filled his sight. Sagebrush scented his nostrils. He opened his eyes to a wire enclosure. Pine, grass, mold, the olfactory overload steered the white light back into his sub-vision. He steadied his breathing, the panting, and let the scents drift like spores until Rondo's heightened senses identified each. The white light faded. He focused on the sharp angles of the rectangular cage. Angles incongruent with nature dominated his surroundings. A sharp voice echoed in his ears.

Rondo rose onto four legs to reach out with his front paws and stretch. He yawned. He twitched his lips; the best smile Samuel could manage. Shadows blurred the opening of the wire fence. An open meadow. Water of a meandering spring and scented with willows gurgled a hundred yards down the hill. He sat on his haunches and allowed Samuel's consciousness to settle into the beast. He sniffed. The scent of blood, tinted with fear, prey ready to flee. The delicious aroma quickened his belonging.

Samuel issued a low growl.

He relived Rondo's memory of his teeth sinking into the neck of a newborn buffalo calf, the warm tang of copper, its sweet life tickling his jaws. Rondo battled Samuel as he spasmed and nipped at his own hindquarters.

Enough. Samuel cleared his mind from the rush of senses, the overload of confusion, and took control. He lifted his leg and urinated. He turned his head to see a zookeeper holding one end of the wire gate open, then rotated his neck to study the young zookeeper Zac easing open the other side of the enclosures gate. He became irritated by the dull boy's lethargic movements.

The boy spoke loud and forcefully. "C'mon, Rondo, you don't have all day."

A bluff. Samuel could sense the human's nervous fear.

Samuel stepped forward slowly, cautiously, sniffing the air, as any wolf might. He inched past the fence line, freedom a few steps away. He growled at Zac's verbal prodding. He flinched from a stone landing at his feet that the boy had thrown. Samuel calculated the distance between them, eyed the fleshy part of the boy's neck.

He leapt, and with three bounds, he found Zac's soft throat in his muscled jaws. He clamped tight as they both fell. His prey thrashed and punched his flanks, its moans muffled, then it spasmed. The boy's feet pushed against the pine straw as he attempted to crawl backwards.

Sweet death kept his mouth clamped tight. The scrumptious warm blood pulsing down his throat was magnificent. Unimagined ecstasy.

Shouts of alarm. Samuel released the boy's neck and lapped at the delicious blood flowing into the dirt. He looked up as if awakened from a trance. The other zookeeper had fled, screaming for help fifty yards away.

Samuel stood and raised his bloody snout to the sky.

And howled.

CHAPTER TWELVE

THE ACCOUTREMENTS OF SAMUEL'S REVENGE waited below, like an outdoor concert waiting for the headliner to take the stage. Michael flapped his wings gently to circle the arena constructed atop the Old Faithful Inn overflow parking lot. The top rails of metal grandstands were decorated with crimson and black pendent flags flapping in the warm thermals rising off the hot pavement. The bleachers were crowded with monsters waving and twirling black and red hand towels. Small tents and kiosks surrounded the arena, selling the wares and drinks of Samuel. Alcohol to rile up angry emotions, spices to stir up bile, drugs to heighten savagery, a crowd bent on bloodlust, an audience once suited for an ancient Roman Colosseum.

The spectators spotted his arrival and let loose with roars of approval followed by basso boos. Why had he been greeted by this odd spectacle? What had happened to Cyd? He came to locate a child, not be party to Samuel's silly games and displays of cruelty.

An announcement of his arrival blared from loudspeakers mounted on poles rising high above the metal bleachers. Michael flapped his wings once and considered the purpose of the arena. He was supposed to fight someone or many, all for the amusement of godless monsters. But what purpose did this serve Samuel? Revenge topped the list, maybe sprinkled with the humiliation of Michael's defeat. The Fallen One would rejoice in witnessing his death, sending his soul back to the Father as a message, an intention both malicious and final.

Michael dropped to the center of the arena floor, a hardpack of sandstone clay, pine needles, and forest detritus. The restless crowd erupted with cheers and boos. He took three steps and extracted a piece of rebar stabbed upright in the soil. He twirled the bar. The balance was off, with extra weight wrapped in shiny new duct tape. He squeezed the tape and crushed tabs of lead wrapped clumsily beneath the tape. He twirled the bar again. Better.

The crowd roared at his prowess with the bar, then began a sick chant of "Kill. Kill! Kill!"

Michael spread his wings outward and fanned a stinging blur of stones and twigs into the crowd. The chant died before the monsters roared for vengeance from his petty assault. Their breath fouled the air. Their insatiable bloodlust corrupted the arena. These were Satan's acolytes. His fellow Fallen. The same demons Seth might ask him to smite. The stage was set.

But he didn't like that Samuel had total control of it. He thought to rise, hover out of reach, search the crowd for the baby—and Cyd. The crowd erupted with applause and cheers.

At the open end of the stadium, twin cyborgs entered aiming red targeting lasers at his chest as they escorted Cyd up a set of stairs to a shaded dais erected in the center of the top three rows. Her face was painted red with a harlot's rouge. Sweat tinted with black mascara trickled down her cheeks. Her eyebrows knotted in defiance, her long fingers worked to loosen the thick opaque straps binding her wrists.

Michael narrowed his eyes. Her role in Michael's silly deception and inept rescue plan had been discovered. His human sister, now a pawn Samuel undoubtedly hoped to employ as leverage, or bait. But what could Samuel have planned for her here, at this very time, except as a distraction? And a distraction was all Samuel might need to—

A small boulder struck his backside between his wings. The kinetic energy sent him face-first into the dirt. He gasped, then clenched his teeth and pushed off the dirt. Collapsing his wings tight to his back, Michael crawled forward to grab the rebar knocked from his grasp.

He masked his shock and surprise, then feinted right and rolled left, coming upright to see—

An impossibility.

Myra's baby fluttered across the arena floor using tiny black bat wings ten times the width of its chubby naked body. It rose into the sky. Its white-less eyes appeared confused, until its face focused on him.

Myra's child smiled a toothless grin as it hovered thirty feet above his head. The demon folded its wings and divebombed, its tiny hairless head aimed directly at Michael's chest.

He sidestepped the assault at the last second to let the tiny demon hit and tumble over the dirt. The thing scrambled like a grounded bat, using its chubby legs and spindly wings until rising into the air again. A sick childish chuckle accompanied a squirt of black feces.

The vile abomination demonstrated that Samuel's trickery held no limits.

Michael dodged the demon's airborne assault with ease until he grew tired of the game and set his stance.

The demon baby dropped like a plump football. Michael swiveled the steel to meet the demon for it to impale itself. Black wings flapped furiously. Brackish black blood gushed. A grey mist hissed as it swirled out of its orifices. The crowd roared with approval.

The demon's soul descended like heavy fog, spreading onto the soft loam, permeating the churned soil. A corrupt soul banished to Hell. Michael grabbed the body and crushed its wings in an angry grip, then tore it free of the steel rod. The baby's true soul of life, its essence, drifted like a subtle fragrance fighting a headwind, rising high into the pine tops in search of Michael's judgment.

He slammed the meaty remnants of the demon into the ground. He eyed Cyd standing frozen in the shaded dais, a horrified scowl cemented on her face. He felt his own soul shrink.

He spread his wings and roared, "Enough games, Samuel! Face me!"

A shadow flittered across the field. Another demon soared high across the bright sun, its winged shadow circling Michael. It descended, its true size growing with each pass over his head.

Michael saw his own face. Or an excellent rendition. The clone flapped its wings with short, abrupt strokes, landing clumsily on the tarmac, unsure of the lift and torque its mighty wings commanded. The clone landed a few yards away. Its skinny naked body sported flushed skin as if it had just stepped from a hot bath. Its eyes cloudy gray, a pair of Arkoff Ports were inserted beneath the ear.

Michael stepped closer. "And what demon might you be?"

"We are you, Michael." The clone balled his fists and flexed his pectorals. "You will fight yourself. The winner gets Cyd. The loser gets . . . well . . . gets Cyd."

"What have you done this time, Samuel?"

"All those years in that prison, and you still haven't figured it out. My dominion over man is complete. My revenge on His great army will be wrought by . . ." It chuckled. "His great army. Perfect copies, all at my command."

Michael narrowed his eyes. "A new low, even for you."

"On the contrary, I will elevate to His kingdom and take my rightful place at His side. My stormtroopers at my feet. Picture it, Michael. And I know you can. And I know you will. This world and all the others ruled by our Father, as I rule Him." The thing folded its wings, took two steps to its left, and feinted an attack.

Michael rose a few inches off the soil but held station. He squeezed his fist as anger molded the end of the rebar with an imprint of his grip. "Since I am about to die, tell me about the girl. Your daughter. Your adopted daughter. My human sister. And Samuel . . . I am truly mystified as to her nature in your grand plan."

The thing spread its wings to rise, easing closer to face Michael. The screams of bloodlust and victory filled the stadium. "You will have eternity to solve that puzzle, Michael. Rotting on a boulder while the flames of Hell taste your flesh. My minions will tantalize you by whispering clues that lead nowhere, or maybe somewhere. You'll be blind, wishing for another chance to face me, wondering how Cyd could do what she did."

Samuel's bluster caused Michael to squeeze the steel bar to the breaking point. Everything the Fallen Angel said or did was a lie, or maybe the truth, but embedded in deceit. Infuriating and baiting.

Michael aimed the steel bar at his foe. "In a way, you have finally regained your wings. Here at our Father's feet, which death suits your ego best?"

"Is there a difference?" Samuel said. He swept his wings forward to crush Michael between them.

The clumsy attack allowed Michael time to rotate the steel rod horizontally as a wedge between the wings. He pried open the feathered vise, then returned the favor, unfolding his wings and sweeping them inward.

The demon's wings crumpled as if made with brittle bone and weak cartilage. Samuel shrieked as he flapped into the sky like a wounded bird. Michael followed. Wary of a trap.

Flapping broken wings to stay aloft, Samuel shouted. "You think you've won?"

Michael frowned.

"To the death, Michael. Right now. Down there. For the whole world to see," Samuel said. He retracted his wings and dropped, spinning like a weighted feather, down to the center of the arena.

Michael lifted his face towards the sun to bathe in its heat and magnificence. Everything felt wrong. He was being led, like an animal herded to slaughter. And yet what waited below wasn't Samuel, though his mind, his consciousness, somehow controlled the clone of an Archangel. He wanted to scream at the Father, make Him truly see what this corrupt world had birthed. Help Him to understand.

The arena crowd chanted for battle.

Cyborgs streamed into the arena, readying their armaments.

Cyd struggled against her restraints.

Samuel waited on the arena floor.

Michael lifted a corner of his mouth into a half-smile. He looked down at nothing but a silly skirmish. This wasn't the final battle. Samuel waited somewhere safe, his decayed mind watching through the eyes of a clone, his mind commanding the clone's muscles and wings.

Cyd screamed at him, but the words were lost in the clamor of spectators. She struggled and pulled free of the monsters at her sides. Michael bared his teeth and rose. He flapped his wings once and skimmed over the grandstands, silencing the bloodlust. He landed and faced Samuel.

The clone swept a single wing in a wide arc, pushing wind and stones across the field into the crowd. Sycophants erupted with shouts of painful pleasure.

The battle played out, two powerful Archangels circled each other on the ground, in the air, feinting, each seeking an opening to deliver a death blow. The crowd quieted.

Michael smiled. A clone wasn't born with the knowledge of ancient martial arts in its chromosomes. Samuel expected brute force in an arena of sticks and stones to prevail.

Michael stepped back and extended his wings. Fighting Samuel was inevitable, the time and arena ambiguous, though irrelevant. The ancient proverb of *Use you against you*, Samuel had taken it to a new level. But why not?

"Enough!" Michael twirled his rebar. "Finish it."

The final round was quick and decisive. Michael's experience with wings used as a shield, or scythe, or pointed battleaxe was too much for the old demon residing in a younger body.

Samuel struggled to stand, but his shattered wings were useless weight, limp on the ground. His hands scratched at the dirt, as if he were trying to crawl away. Michael stood over Samuel and raised the steel bar to impale the abomination.

He hesitated, stunned by strange and unwelcome emotions. Pity. Mercy. Attributes bestowed on other angels. But not him.

The steel bar held high over his head and primed for the killing blow, his hesitation turned debilitating.

Samuel retrieved a weapon buried in the dirt and swept a flimsy wing inward as he rose to his full height to face Michael.

The thrust was unavoidable. The depth of the impalement foretold.

Michael looked down at a shimmering silver blade piercing his abdomen. Red blood oozed from the wound. Impossible.

Samuel rammed the weapon hard, and deeper, until his face was inches from Michael's. "I have lived eons for this day. Your fucking righteous sword waiting in my basement. Until now."

Samuel twisted the hilt of the sword and chuckled.

As life drained from Michael's thoughts, Samuel laughed and continued his torture by twisting the hilt. The Fisherman drifted in and out of his fading consciousness. Why was his weapon withheld for this battle? Why would the Fisherman . . .

Michael coughed, specks of spittle and blood striking Samuel's face.

Samuel licked at the slight with a serpent's tongue. "Die, Michael. The final battle will not include you."

Michael coughed again, and again.

The black eyes of Samuel widened as if struck with a sudden incredulous realization. He stumbled backwards, drawing the sword out of Michael. Samuel's head twitched in sudden convulsions. Foam trickled out of the corners of his ugly frozen smile.

Michael grabbed his side, then the sword. He lifted a bloody hand to his face and looked down to inspect the mortal wound. Another impossibility. Cyd crashed into him and screamed at him to go.

Blood oozed from beneath the hand pressed to his side.

His sword for eons, a weapon he wielded like an appendage, heavy in his hand.

Was he truly mortal?

CYD WATCHED WITH HORROR AS Michael struck down the tiny, winged child, a cherubic monstrosity with blank black eyes, black wings, and a malicious toothless grin. She covered her mouth as Michael seemed to snarl at a wispy grey mist steaming out of the dying thing, sinking into the loose soil. Michael kicked at the apparition as if to prevent it from disappearing, his lips moving as if he was talking to the mist.

Cyd pulled one arm free from the borgs' mechanical grasp and smiled at Michael soaring up in the sky to circle above the arena, to be joined by another. Now, two angels circled each other like two apex predators.

Cyd pulled her other arm free of the cyborgs' restraint as the arena erupted with deafening noise. The other angel was identical to Michael. The cyborgs reacquired their grips on her biceps as she stood mesmerized by the two mighty winged creatures circling each other in the air like competing eagles.

Cyd winced at the cyborgs' tightening their grip. She looked at each cyborg, then shouted, "Enough!"

The mechanized men flew backwards over the bleacher railing as if struck by a punch of wind.

Cyd watched the surreal cage match unfolding before her. Her fingernails kneaded her palms, her thighs twitched with an energetic rush a million times stronger than any dose of 3Bz. Electric tension coursed through her body.

The fake Michael fell and lay scratching at the dirt, defeated, with the real Michael hovering. The real Michael. The distinction was as easy as black and white.

Pleasure excited her skin. Pain coursed through her veins. Purpose bludgeoned her stiff legs into action. Cyd flew down the stairs, leapt over the guardrail, and aimed for the arena. Cyborgs rushed in from beneath the grandstands, and with quick sidesteps, she dodged their lumbering bulk. A burst of adrenaline flooded her nervous system and fueled her taut leg muscles as she aimed for the center of the arena.

Michael stood over the defeated angel's body, readying a death-blow with the bloody steel bar. Cyd slowed down and opened her mouth to shout for mercy. The defeated angel turned over to witness its own death then retrieved a heavy white sword buried in the soft soil and rose up to stab into Michael's midsection.

A single held word finally erupted from her mouth, "No!"

Michael pulled the false angel close and coughed blood and spittle. Cyd dodged the protective wings at Michael's side and stood between two wounded angels. Her expression matched Michael's incredulous face as he lifted a bloody hand up to his face.

The other angel gagged and choked. Its muscles spasmed in violent convulsions, blood trickling from its mouth and nostrils. A tear tinted in crimson fell from its eye. The incongruity of an angel dying such a violent death commanded her eyes. The realization of Michael dying at her side made her reach out and help him stand.

"Go, Michael. Fly me back to the Moonies," she said with no humor.

Michael's knees buckled as he stared at her with unfocused eyes. "My sword. He used my own sword to kill me."

"Not dead yet, brother. Three swipes of those wings, and you can glide us back to camp."

His eyes glossed over. Blood ran down his hip and leg to pool at his bare foot.

Cyd held him upright and slapped her hand over the wound. "Three swipes, Michael. And I'll tell you everything."

"My sword," Michael said and pointed to the bloodied sword in the dirt.

She moved with lightning speed to grab the weapon and return to support his body. "Three swipes. And I'm counting. Three."

Michael spread his wings and flapped once to lift them a hundred yards above the arena.

"That was a flutter." She slapped his chest. "We agreed to three big swipes. You moved a mountain with those things, and I want one big one. Now!"

Michael flapped, and they soared high until the crags of the mighty Teton Mountains filled the horizon.

"Need one more, Michael. Get us over that mountain range you tried to impress me with."

Michael's face blanched, but his wings responded, and they shot straight up. The air turned frigid and lacked oxygen. Cyd gazed down at the world, sprawls of cities and townships, circles of crops, lines of highways. No different than looking out the window of a hover jet flying over landscapes her father boasted to dominate.

Except Daddy didn't command the warm body she held tightly. He wanted to kill it. Tried to kill it. One of his tricks. Another deception.

Cyd turned Michael's head with her hand. Defeat and blood loss paled his skin. She slapped his cheek.

"One more swipe, Michael. Just to turn us towards that stack of smoke. Your friends are waiting. And Seth."

Michael jerked his head free of her hands. "Hold on."

They dove like cliff-diving lunatics, aiming for the smoking husk of Arco. The rush of frigid wind stung her face wet with tears. She buried her face into Michael's neck. His skin was cold, and paler than minutes ago. His silver hair grown out two inches, stood straight up and resisted the wind howling into their faces. The identical hair color as her own.

Michael was not her brother. He could not be. How could she be the sister of a heavenly creature? She hadn't an inkling of who her birth parents were. A subject forbidden by Samuel. Why was her heritage off-limits unless Daddy wanted to hide something or shield her from a notorious family history? She had thought long and hard on the matter but was too fearful to push the subject further with

Daddy. He would always sidestep the issue, turning violent if she persisted.

But the family dynamics had changed. Daddy had changed. His pleasing nature was too easy to see through. His kidnapping of Myra and the child was despicable. The imprisonment of Michael was inhumane. A cage fight between angels and demon babies. Monstrous clones of Michael and Myra's child. The world had fallen into a hellscape of unbelievability except . . . here she was in the arms of an angel, maybe her brother, miles above the earth, falling to her death.

Cyd gripped the hilt of the sword tight to her breast and squeezed her eyes tight. Wind roared in her ears. She braved a glance. The ground was coming up too fast. She shouted at Michael, but he didn't respond.

She bit his shoulder with her sharp teeth. He groaned, but their suicidal descent continued to gain speed.

Her screams lost in the rush of wind, she struggled to revive Michael. The impact inevitable, Cyd stretched her neck up to whisper in Michael's ear, telling him of her suicide attempt on a bridge, the odd appearance of a fisherman and how the silly bug became hooked on the lace of her sneaker.

She kissed his ear. "I'm gonna give you the bug. Hook it on your robe. You better remember me."

The descent was buffeted by crosswinds and thermals. The columns of smoke rising from the Moonie camp became distinct and numerous. Seconds to live a lifetime, and she'd finally be gone. Cyd held the sword tight to her breast and squeezed Michael's neck, then closed her eyes and awaited her death.

CHAPTER THIRTEEN

SAMUEL STOOD AND BRUSHED TINY copper fibers off his pants. The frayed fabric of the consciousness transfer recliner would require an update with more sophisticated sensory netting. The sensory electrodes embedded in the fabric's weaving reacted sluggishly and caused the transfer of sensations to remain a shade off from claiming the ultimate possession of a human body.

"He's gone, Jurgens. Flying away like a smug prick," Samuel said. "Just like we thought."

Jurgens swiped at holo screens hovering near his face, tapped keyboards only visible to his optical implants. The relinquishing of his preference for nostalgic firmware was a pleasant development. "This data is invaluable. Our next attempt will be an improvement."

Samuel took three long steps and stood behind the scientist to pinch his bony neck between his fingers. Beneath the soft skin, he felt the Jurgens' pulse quicken. "An improvement? Do you think this is a research lab for synthetic food? You lay off the 3Bz until everything is dialed in. Exactly as I have specified."

Jurgens howled and pleaded for forgiveness.

"The child was as expected. Weak and impotent," Samuel said. "Regardless, continue accelerating the development of our other children. I will assign acolytes more capable of inhabiting the bodies. If nothing else, the crowd was enraptured by those little demons. That much I could sense."

Samuel released his grip and began to pace along a lengthy wall sheeted with opaque glass. Jurgens' lab was equipped with computerized technology unknown to the world. VR matrix servers blinked red lights. Artificial intelligence programs employed cutting edge fractal geometrical algorithms to complete subroutines in light speed. Godspeed, Samuel liked to call it. He paused at the end of the window, appreciating the reflection of his face plum with victory. Red lights of computer servers blinked, a pair aligned with his own eyes in the reflection, as if casting beams of scarlet light from his eyes. Smirking with the visual analogy, he considered the infinite possibilities of his plan.

Coincidence or circumstance. Samuel shook his head and looked up to the concrete ceiling. Coincidence was a bumbling tool of His meddling. The Father saw everything Samuel did and more, and yet He was hesitant to dissuade Samuel of his actions, including the thrust of heavenly metal deep into His favorite Archangel.

His own reflection unnerved him, and he twitched his jaw to switch off the opaque filament embedded between the glass panes. The glass cleared. A cavernous lava tube the length of a football field presented, one of many buried beneath the dormant geysers prominent in the dormant Yellowstone Caldera. Bright lights hanging above numbers of cylindrical vats brightened. Clones floated as adult fetuses in clear fluid bubbling in the wombs. Children. Men. Women. Michael. Cyd. The corrupted representation of his life's work endless and waiting for his command to rise, go forth, seek, or destroy.

"Uncork another Michael," Samuel said. "And a Cyd. She might come running back after she sees what the media feeds are reporting. But I think we'll need to replace her for appearances' sake."

Samuel swiped at a holo screen, following him like a puppy. The glass dimmed, returning his reflection with the same beady red eyes staring back at him. Michael regaining his sword was worrisome. Perhaps Samuel shouldn't have shown his hand so quickly. The clones. The sword. Forcing Cyd to choose her inevitable destiny. To actualize her true existence.

Doubt was a miscarriage of ego. And had no place in his domain. All was foreseen.

———

A REBEL YELL PIERCED THE torrent of air buffeting Cyd, daring her eyes open. The campfires and colorful tarpaulins on the ground continued to grow larger and brighter. Michael's eyes remained closed. A pair of filthy hands attempted to loosen her grip on the sword.

Raphael cackled and pulled at the sword as his wings flapped in the raucous wind. He yelled over the noise, "Let loose, and I'll escort you down to the ground!"

Cyd gazed at the identical green eyes she had fallen into once and knew the angel was lying. Raphael tugged on the sword again and again.

Cyd refused. Michael would be allowed to die with the one thing he appeared to cherish.

Raphael leveraged his legs against Michael's body, then spread his great wings, slowing their descent. He yanked hard for the sword. Her grip loosened with the angel's immense strength.

No. She would die before she relinquished. Let him pry it from her cold dead hands.

She screamed her rage. The violent rush of air exposed three Arkoff Ports camouflaged by Raphael's heavy beard. Daddy's pathways of influence.

She leveraged her own legs and pushed against the angel's chest, the sword held between them. Her heart pounded in her throat and mouth. Cyd released Michael but the near weightlessness kept her secure in the crook of his shoulder.

A stalemate of angels. But who was she to battle an otherworldly Archangel? Raphael could rip her arms out of their sockets. Tear her throat out.

"Enough!" she shouted. With her free hand, she gripped the soft flesh beneath Raphael's neck and squeezed hard.

Raphael clipped the spread of his wings and sent them into a tailspin, his intense eyes smiling maliciously at Cyd, hypnotizing her to relinquish the sword.

"You know what I am! Who I am!" Raphael shouted. "Let's hit that rock below and see who survives." He softened his pull on the sword.

"Pull up, Raphael. Pull up now!"

Cyd waited long seconds until Raphael unfurled his wings to slow their descent but not enough to prevent her from splattering on the rocks.

Cyd softened her grip on the sword and slapped Raphael. "Snap out of it!"

His expression remained blank but resolute. She slammed her fist into his chin and winced from the pain. Then her teeth followed. She opened her jaw wide and lunged for his neck. Her mouth clamped down on rough, wiry hair. Her tongue probed the skin until it found the three Arkoff Ports. She bit deep through hair and gnawed at his flesh.

Raphael roared as he tried to pry her off. She held tight.

Cyd spat nasty bits of skin and bloody hair into the wind, followed by the Arkoff Ports' plastic nodules trailing thin filaments.

Raphael released his grip on the sword and pushed away, spreading his wings to soar high, anger and revenge snarling his face.

The pyramid of boulders on the dam just seconds away, Cyd pushed her bloody face into Michael's neck and waited for the impact, and death. Tears fell and dried in the blast of wind. Dying wasn't difficult. Death with a million questions buzzing through her scrambled thoughts was agony.

Cyd adjusted the hilt of the sword, pressing the blade against Michael's chest as if he were a Viking warrior laid on a funeral pyre.

She closed her eyes. *Be kind when you judge my soul, Michael.*

The sword flared a hot white, as if a tiny sun had exploded. A nova of brilliance illuminated the blue sky. Cyd tried to squeeze her eyes shut and yet couldn't. The blazing white light commanded her to witness its glory.

The rush of air quieted. An impossible stillness enveloped her. The earth below disappeared. Specks of illuminance pulsed with the beat of her heart. White motes of dust danced like fireflies at her face.

Death was beautiful. Why would people fear such a glorious event?

Michael put his hand on hers and pressed the sword tight to his heart.

And they fell. Together, entwined.

She stood naked on the rocky riverbed of a gentle turquoise river.

Waves of rolling mist floated across the sky. Steep pine covered hills disappeared into the heavy fog melding with the sky. The river disappeared beyond a sharp bend narrowing into a towering canyon of sheer granite cliffs. Waterfalls fell from the rock painted with a rainbow of colored lichen.

Cyd looked down at her genderless naked body. Modesty, embarrassment, the irrelevant emotions of her past life made her grin. Michael lifted his face and snorted the air like a bull. His sword was missing. His wound had healed.

A shout of excitement sounded downstream.

Cyd looked at Michael with a furrowed face.

Michael offered his hand. "Did you bring that Dave's Hopper on your shoe?"

"I don't have shoes," Cyd said and looked down at her running shoes, a big bullheaded bug hooked to the lace. "I guess I do."

They stumbled to cross shallow braids of cold running water. Michael refused to release her hand, until they stood side by side on the shore of the main stem of the placid emerald river. They soaked up the magnificent beauty of the water. Deer and elk grazed tall grass growing lush at the water's edge. Bull moose lifted huge antlers at their approach. Yellow mayflies dabbed the deep pools to lay eggs.

Cyd's thoughts synchronized with the calm river. Her turmoil and anger disappeared. Her heartbeat relaxed with contentment and happiness.

A shout downstream sent the animals fleeing into the forest.

Michael led her downstream. She giggled as her feet slipped on river rock slick with algae. The bond of their hands held firm. They approached a sturdy bearded man fly fishing in the middle of the river, intent on flipping a fly into a narrow pocket of calm water behind a submerged boulder. The angler ignored them. Until he groaned, threw up an arm in frustration, and slogged across the knee-deep current back to the shoreline.

"I hope you had better luck than me," the Fisherman said. His smile was genuine as he held Cyd's gaze. The same man she had met beneath the bridge. "That hopper I hooked on your shoe. Try it yet?"

Michael squeezed her hand painfully hard.

Cyd smiled. "I know you."

He returned her smile. "Excellent. Most people have forgotten me."

"Where are we? What is this place? Am I dead? Are you—"

"This is a place Samuel strives to achieve. And one you must protect. And not yet."

Cyd tilted her head and frowned. "Huh?"

"I answered your questions," the Fisherman said. He unzipped a pocket flap on his fishing vest and removed a bright green fly box and flipped it open. "These fish are crafty devils . . . Oh, sorry . . . crafty *creatures*, and I just don't seem to have the right fly to entice one to rise."

The Fisherman glanced at Michael, then held Cyd's stare. Michael squeezed her hand hard. She shot him a glare then realized what he was doing.

Cyd looked at her sneaker. "How about a big Dave's Hopper? Just happen to have one ready, willing, and able."

The Fisherman ran a finger through the assorted flies in the box. "Hmm. Maybe that might do the trick. I taught your brother how to fish, but I think maybe you should learn too. Let's wade back out to that rock and give it go."

Michael released her hand as the Fisherman took her other hand and led her into the tranquil water. The river current softened five yards upstream as they waded across river rock and squishy gravel, the gentle current an exquisite sensation on her now shoeless feet.

The Fisherman stood next to her and fumbled tying the fly to the thin monofilament line. Cyd reveled in the calming noise of the river, the smell of pine and willows, the abundant fauna that continually dared to approach the riverbank. He handed her the flyrod and instructed her how to cast and mend line and point the tip of the long rod to follow the big hopper as it floated downstream.

The Fisherman paused her hand from a cast. "Samuel has achieved all his desires. Now he strives to rule this kingdom. If he succeeds, he will rule this world as he does yours. All you see will be gone." The Fisherman lowered the rod trembling in her hand. "You are a beautiful creation. Like Michael . . . yet different. The Alpha . . . and Omega. For millennia I considered and fussed over your design, divine and human, a woman of infinite power and wisdom, but unlike Michael and the army that he leads, you haven't had time to grow and understand what you truly are. And it would appear time is not on our side."

"What exactly are you—"

Cyd felt the rod jerk from her hands as if a fish had struck the hopper. She stumbled on the slick rock and fell backwards, back into the swift torrent of cold air buffeting her face.

Michael unfurled his wings and fought their freefall, spreading his feathers as a parachute. He groaned with the effort to tilt the wings and slow the rapid fall until the arc of their descent equaled the tremendous uplift of his wings. They hovered a mere hundred feet above the Moonie camp. Roars erupted from the camp, fists of victory held high, the Moonies converging on the main campfire.

Michael winced as his hand found the wound nothing more than inflamed pink flesh.

Cyd pressed the hilt of the sword onto Michael's chest as her thoughts remained in the beautiful canyon with the overwhelming abundance of peace and comfort. She hoped for an opportunity to fish with the Fisherman again. "Wanna explain our little side trip? Did you hear what the Fisherman said? Where was that river—"

Michael pressed a bloody hand over her lips. "What the Fisherman tells you is just for you. Share. Don't share. But never pretend to know what truly transpires in His kingdom."

Cyd jerked his hand off her mouth. "Samuel's coming for heaven, that much I can tell you. And don't ever put your hand over my mouth again, brother."

A flutter of feathers stilled the air, and they studied each other for a long moment. Cyd wondered what Michael had seen, or heard, or had they both experienced the same vision?

"I might still be bleeding," Michael said.

"I smell Mary's cooking," Cyd said.

MICHAEL HELD CYD'S HAND AS he led her towards a huge bonfire in the center of the camp. His warmth and grip were pleasant for a change. Moonies bowed with reverence as they passed. Cyd's robe had been dyed black by Mary, attempting to hide nasty stains. Preparations for the final push into the imposing White Cloud Mountains were evident with backpacks and duffle bags stacked near the flaps of tents, hand carts and old school bicycles chosen as dependable transportation. Sandals and sneakers sat washed and mended.

Cyd chuckled and shook her head.

Michael glanced at her. "What?"

"Nothing," Cyd said.

"From royalty to pauper. And I'd wager you wouldn't change a thing," Michael said.

His words said everything. She wouldn't change anything. Except to find her way back to the Fisherman. The serenity and mystique of His domain. The simple pleasure of lying in a grass field and absorbing His abundance.

Michael squeezed her hand gently. "What were you feeling standing all alone on the bank as He taught me to roll cast?"

"Excuse me? How did *you* feel standing all alone while He taught *me* how to cast that hopper?"

They stopped and chuckled together.

"We will never understand that which can't be comprehended," Michael said.

Cyd turned Michael's face to look directly into his eyes. "Enough with the biblical crap. If you want to understand anything, just look around."

Cyd released his hand and aimed for the fire. The presence of an angel followed as she passed tents busy with Moonies packing measly belongings. The Moonies hurried to escape their meager existence, no different than her desire to escape the opulence of Yellowstone. Both of their worlds had radically changed. And in just hours.

Cyd stopped to help a young girl fold a large, tattered sheet of blue plastic into a small square. The Fisherman's warning of Heaven threatened by a malevolent caretaker had spread and seemed to provide the impetus and motivation for the bustling activity of the camp.

Michael whispered in her ear, "I think we all heard the same thing. Them too."

"He said I was like you, but different. Alpha and omega. Do you know what he could have meant by that?"

Michael frowned and considered. "After Lucifer was cast out, the Fisherman refused to create any other heavenly souls such as us.

I hate to speculate, but I think He was supremely disappointed with Lucifer's vast ego. Then He was crushed by Lucifer's involvement in His only son's crucifixion. You might be the first new angel he has created. And the last one. You'll hold a special place in His heart."

Cyd followed Michael into the light of a voluminous campfire. Women suckling young children covered their breasts and started to flee their approach.

She pushed past Michael. "Stay. All of you with babies. Soak up the heat. Maybe you men can gather wood and help with the dirty diapers." She appraised the crowd of men surrounding the fire. "Anybody that has a problem with that, come see me." She glanced at Michael hovering behind her right shoulder. "Or my brother if you think I'm too much of a bitch."

Cyd warmed her hands on the fire as the Moonies offered respectful bows before receding deeper into the tent camp. Seth grunted with Herculean efforts to forage split logs and drop each on the fire to maintain the flames. The child's robe was wet with perspiration and his face beet-red with exertion, working so hard as if evil might invade the camp if the fire died.

Michael unsheathed the sword to slice the air, and parried, and twirled the weapon as if he had found an old friend. Cyd stepped back into the shadows and chuckled as the mighty Archangel played with his old toy. Streaks of light shot across the night sky.

Serah joined Cyd as a group of Moonie men circled the fire, closing off the firelight from others. Serah's hand found Cyd's. "He says the time has come for us to finally rise up and take our place in the world. Whatever that freaking means."

Cyd tilted her head. The girl that supposedly talked to the Fisherman. Serah's cherub face bathed in the dancing firelight became shadowed by the dark robes of uninvited men. Cyd held tight to prevent Serah from retreating and disappearing into the darkness. She flicked her chin and motioned for her to listen.

Moonie men gathered, voicing dissent and petty disagreements. Moonie men argued against the treacherous trail ahead. Moonie men raised staffs of steel and wood to mimic angels. Moonie men shouted at women to gather more wood to enlighten the decisions of the chosen Moonie elders. A Moonie man kicked Seth in the rear end and laughed, then ordered him to hurry with more firewood.

Cyd bit down on her tongue and tasted blood. Masculine laughter and male ego summoned bile from deep inside her. She released Serah's hand. "I'll show you exactly what that freaking means."

Cyd rushed forward, pushed through dense robes, and bared a mouthful of sharp canines and incisors. Her fingers elongated from her palms, muscle and bone stretching, fingernails lengthening and curving into sharp claws.

The passage of time had stopped.

She attacked as a blur of teeth and fingernails to slice robes and nip throats. Nothing moved. Flame or smoke. Flesh or light.

Cyd exacted her anger on the helpless, paralyzed men, finding their eyes wide and suspended in timeless limbo. She gazed deep into the whites, to witness their souls, finding many with Arkoff Ports. She tore the devices of Samuel's corruption from their throats.

Michael stood still as a statue as she screamed a pent-up vengeance at his face. He blinked but was helpless just as the others were. Cyd surveyed the carnage, ran her tongue over her bloody lips, looked down at bloody hands, and licked the fingers.

And she let time begin again.

Cyd stood atop the bonfire. The red-hot embers tickled the soles of her bare feet. The flames licked her black robe, yet the fabric failed to ignite. She turned in a circle, gazing at the stain of blood on her hands. The screams of terrified chaos invaded the camp.

What had she done? What had she become?

And yet she knew.

Seth sidestepped bloody men and robes to approach the fire, wide-eyed and burdened by a hefty, split log cradled in his arms. Michael remained unmoved, his expression confused. Serah stepped close to the flames and lifted a corner of her mouth into a knowing, victorious grin. She nodded acceptance to Cyd.

Myra pushed through the mayhem and tossed swaddling clothes to burn. Mary limped forward, holding her cane like a totem, and tossed an ugly wool blanket into the fire. Young women tossed brassieres, undergarments, and old robes into the fire. Old women circled the fire, bowed their heads, and began to pray.

Cyd spun her vision in every direction, staring at the women filing into the firelight to toss something into the fire. Her eyes caught Seth standing at the stone fire ring, the split log still cradled in his arms. She tilted her face. Raised her eyebrows. And offered a wan smile.

Seth shrugged, and his innocence shone.

Cyd smirked. "Throw another log on the fire, my little charm."

Seth tossed the wood into the flames, sending hot embers floating up with the thick smoke.

Cyd stepped up to Michael and locked her eyes onto his. Split seconds or infinity could pass between them. The choice was hers.

He narrowed his eyes and tilted his head.

Michael shot up into the dark sky.

—

SAMUEL WATCHED THE PROCEEDINGS AT the campfire as if he stood within the circle of robes. The sudden maiming of his acolytes was unwitnessed. The speed at which the assault occurred told of an unrealized force.

An Archangel.

A formidable addition to the brethren of the Lord sitting so high and mighty. Unique, untamed, unseasoned, and his daughter.

Cyd.

Samuel cracked a smile. A false expression practiced for the throng of media, for clicking cameras, for handshakes often required at functions celebrating the ruse of child hunger, or a conference bragging to save the planet dying beneath the withering stare of the sun.

His smile faded. Cyd was his, or was, or would be again. In one form or another. Regardless, she would die at the appropriate time.

Samuel startled at the soft knock on his office door. The sensation of surprise tingled his arms and hands. His heart raced, a sensation unfelt for centuries. A sign of the end times. He checked the surveillance view at the hallway and pushed an entry code into his holoscreen to allow the door to swing open.

Captain Boatman knocked again then stepped forward to stand at attention.

Samuel waved him to leave. "Your report is irrelevant, Captain."

"On the contrary, sir. I'm sure you are aware of the increased solar flare activity. Geomagnetic storms have rendered wireless connectivity sporadic. Arkoff Ports are experiencing unprecedented interruptions. Shipping and supply chains are failing. Social disruptions have increased one hundred percent. Riots and looting have occurred in seven major population centers. Several governments have abandoned positions of authority. Shall I continue?"

"And do you think I don't know this already? Please offer me something I don't know."

Boatman stepped closer to Samuel, his jaw working the connection ports. "Vanessa is missing from the rehabilitation center in Atlanta."

Samuel stood up and stretched his neck, rotating his arms in their shoulder sockets. He blew out a deep, exasperated breath. Immature black wings stretching fabric of his jacket attempted to unfurl on his back. A priceless painting of Michelangelo's *Creation of Adam* crashed onto the floor behind him.

Samuel walked around the desk and extended his hand in a show of appreciation. He moved quickly to squeeze the man's throat to crush his windpipe. "Poor Vanessa. She will be well taken care of. Trust me." He tossed the large man across the room to crash into a concrete wall. He watched the essence of a soul rise like boiling steam.

Samuel stood over the body. "Piddling with pawns has ended. Warring with queens and kings begins."

CHAPTER FOURTEEN

THE RAGTAG PROCESSION OF LEPERS and misfits followed a trickle of dirty water up to the headwaters of the Big Lost River. The journey might have required two hours of driving time if Michael had allowed vehicles to transport the Moonies. Instead, the procession of hooded figures pushed and pulled wheeled carts or burdened their own backsides with packs and frames rigged to carry tents, camp stoves, and foam sleeping mats. Covering eight miles through dense sagebrush and thick willows was considered a good day, and the riverbed provided an abundance of driftwood for the campfires at night.

The main campfire burned brightly near the confluence of two creeks forming the main stem of the Big Lost River. The shallow clear water was a welcome change from the algae-laden and polluted water coursing through Mackay Reservoir's dusty lakebed.

Michael dropped into a flat gravel area and retracted his wings, the articulating bone folding in on each layer. He thought to put on a robe, but the masquerade now felt silly, though maybe necessary at times. The twilight shadows of Moonies gathered around the fire. His reconnaissance held nothing new. The location of others who had escaped the labs remained hidden. Hidden from him, then maybe hidden from Samuel, though he doubted it.

And Samuel watched everything. Watched them even now. He might drop another nuclear weapon once the enclave was discovered.

Samuel's strategy had to have been disrupted by Cyd's sudden transformation. The bloodletting, the stoppage of time itself at the campfire, the female Moonies showing her extraordinary reverence, Cyd's not-so-subtle impersonation of Joan of Arc burned in his thoughts. The Fisherman's creation was nothing like he had ever experienced.

And she was his sister.

Michael strode into camp, his sword hanging from a leather strap melded to the feathered armor plates that had formed over skin. His chest plated with a mold of hardened white feathers, a white Roman skirt hanging as a shroud to protect his waist and thighs. Familiar clothing. Comforting armor. Was his transformation any less astonishing than Cyd's? The deeper the tribe trekked into the remote White Clouds, the faster the metamorphosis quickened.

Cyd often sat alone. Seth and his innocent demeanor braved her stern, worried face to offer food, water, or lighthearted conversation, yet she remained an isolated queen, one confused by her royal duties.

Michael feigned warming his hands by the crackling fire, but the heat of burning wood held no comfort nor issued pain. Even the thin frozen air high above snowcapped mountaintops caused little discomfort. Anticipation of tomorrow's begrudging miles gritted the faces of the Moonies scurrying through the bivouac. Their unreconciled motivation sucked at his heart.

Michael stepped into the fire, letting the embers and sparks swirl about his body. Moonies gathered around the fire. "What we seek is just ahead. The burden of your trek, the trail of your tears is also shouldered by Him." Michael unsheathed his sword and stabbed the point into the embers. "My purpose is to lead you to a promised . . . a village of His choosing."

He shuttered his eyes and groaned inwardly at his own silly words. Words that might have once enraptured the ignorant or commanded respect from frightened pagans' eons ago, but now . . .

"Maybe. Just fucking maybe, this world will be vaporized by Satan. Just maybe our Lord has chosen you to survive the fucking shitstorm that's coming. Whether you're worthy is irrelevant. You've been chosen, and for reasons I don't even begin to understand. Some of you almost died after kicking Seth like a dog. Yesterday the young girl Lilith traded sex for extra bits of beef jerky"—he scanned the crowd—"and were answered by Cyd's wrath. You. Have. Been. Chosen. Each of you. Conduct yourselves as such."

Michael pulled his sword out of the fire then stabbed it back into it, issuing a rush of heat, sparks, and smoke. "Why? Ask yourself, why? What heavenly purpose do you serve?"

A great rush of wind sent ash and smoke swirling in the dark sky.

Raphael dropped next to the fire and folded his wings. His hair remained long and unruly, but his face was clean-shaven. The crowd of Moonies moved back into the shadows. Raphael's white skin was molded and melded into feathered armor much like Michael's. Two curved blades sheathed in old leather hung on a belt around his waist.

Michael picked up the sword and held it angled down against his chest. Raphael nodded a greeting to Michael then stiffened as he watched Cyd glide into the arena. Michael frowned as he checked the hem of her robes. The black fabric floated inches above the gravel. No visible movement indicated she had even used her legs. She moved like a true wraith, floating, gliding, as if her feet never touched the ground. Michael swallowed hard, then returned his gaze to Raphael.

"Do you bring a message from your new Master?" Michael said.

Raphael chuckled. "I serve only one Father."

Cyd pulled back her hood, exposing narrow feline eyes, sharp canine teeth, and a long mane of platinum hair tinted with streaks of a golden sunset.

Raphael smirked. "How'd I taste?"

She spat at Raphael's feet. "I still taste your treachery with every bite of food. I should have taken your throat."

Michael stepped from the firepit.

"But you didn't," Raphael said.

Cyd's robe dropped from her body like a stage curtain, the fabric magically clawed into long ribbons and gathering at her feet. She stepped forward wearing shiny silver fur melded to her skin to form a tight dress, silver pelts forming a plate of chest armor molded to her breasts. Her bare feet sparkled in the moonlight.

Raphael unsheathed long, curved blades, his fingers kneading the solid pearl hilts tight to his palms.

Michael stepped between them and faced Raphael. "Say what you gotta say and go."

Raphael stepped closer to Michael. He blinked, and lifted the corner of his mouth, acknowledging Cyd waiting behind him. "I got no beef with you, brother, but your little sister needs to hear a few things."

Michael felt Cyd's strike coming, a premonition, the foretelling of an ancient tragedy. The prelude to a death that might alter the future of an infinite universe. In a blur, Michael raised the tip of his sword and lifted it into Raphael's chin.

"He's all yours, sister," Michael said. "But let's hear what he has to say first. Then we can roast angel wings over the fire."

In the bat of an eye, Cyd was behind Michael's right shoulder, her movement undetected.

Raphael chuckled mirthlessly, then sheathed his knives. "Everything I saw or heard . . . Samuel experienced too. That fucking puke imprisoned me on a gurney using those things inserted in my neck. Then dear sister rips the things out of my neck like she was . . . some kind of vampire, and . . ." Raphael unsheathed a knife and tapped the sharp point into the ragged bite scar on his neck. "And the Lord led me on a treacherous trail leading down into a dark canyon, taught me to scale cliffs, taught me to survive. Just His presence—"

"Offered you the shelter of His love, and guided you here after warning you of a coming calamity that may end the universe," Cyd finished for him.

Raphael sidestepped Michael to face Cyd. "The canyon bottom stretched farther and deeper than any I've ever experienced. The Lord's face looked pained, as if the life-giving river at the bottom of the canyon might run dry."

Cyd grabbed Raphael's face to turn it and check the scar. She closed her eyes and nodded.

Michael stepped between them, unsure how or when he had lost his position between them. He placed a light hand on Cyd's wrist.

Cyd shrugged off the restraint and glanced over her shoulder at Michael. "The Arkoff Ports. His dominion over man. He sees and hears everything."

Raphael stepped back and warmed his hands with the fire. "Worse than that. My time wearing those Arkoff Ports is still fuzzy, but I remember screaming like a banshee when I was taken from the white prison. I was maybe a year younger than Seth. They said having the implants would grant me freedom." He scoffed. "Like I even had the choice to refuse."

Raphael unsheathed both knives, his front teeth biting down on his lower lip. He swallowed a lump. "I was a fucking child." He looked away. "The rest is history, they say, except . . . Samuel doesn't hold dominion, doesn't just control them. He *is* them. His essence lives inside anyone with a port. Fucking Lucifer times ten billion. Think we can still win this battle, even if we locate our brothers . . . and sisters?"

Michael scoffed. "We don't have an alternative. But it's worse than that. When I went back for Cyd, I had to fight a clone. Of myself. The thing was made of everything I am except it was missing a soul. Samuel didn't just control that thing; his essence was inside it before I killed it. There are probably hundreds or thousands. Of you, me, every one of the children from the labs. We'll be fighting ourselves and Samuel."

"He can't control so many all at once. Impossible," Cyd said. She held herself as if a cold wind chilled her bones.

"That's one word I refuse to use around Lucifer," Raphael muttered. He turned to Cyd. "You held a special interest in Samuel's strategy."

Michael blinked. Cyd stared into Raphael's eyes from just inches, his own knife now pointed at his throat.

"Enough!" Michael shouted. "Raphael, your meandering words will get you killed, and nothing I can do will stop it."

Raphael smiled. "Tell the rookie about me, then. Tell her I'll keep coming back over and over until He sees fit that the job is done. Kill me here, and I'll be back tomorrow. This rookie needs to know this is war, and renegades always lose."

"He's correct, Cyd. If, in fact, that is the true Raphael." Michael said. "Maybe you should slice him up now, and I'll go save us a share of Mary's stew."

Raphael groaned.

Cyd lowered the knife.

"Sister, I meant no disrespect." Raphael said. He scowled then spat. "Samuel used me to spy on everything since I was awakened, but he has a strange fascination with you. He adopted you. Raised you. And he had a big reason for providing that servitude because that runs against his nature. We need to know why, maybe use it against him."

Cyd stepped back and found a boulder to lean against. Her eyes downcast, she said, "He's right. Samuel was grooming me for a reason. But I don't know why."

Michael walked away, giving Cyd time to think.

Seth tugged on Michael's elbow. The boy could be stealthier than Cyd. He motioned for Michael to bend down and listen to a secret. "Cyd doesn't look so good. Give her my share of stew tonight."

Michael nodded, then glanced up to see what Seth saw. A young woman changing into something new, powerful. A human transforming into a . . . god? Bitterness and anger narrowed her eyes. She sat alone, aloof. Not even a faint recollection of past lives to help guide her. A new Archangel challenged by inexperience, corrupted by her upbringing, the daughter of the Devil himself.

Michael tilted his face and blinked back a tear. She was alone and afraid. And he needed to act the big brother.

Michael pointed his sword at Raphael. "What say you get us a side of beef for a feast. And a few bags of wine."

They locked eyes, and Raphael nodded with an unspoken understanding passing between them. Raphael shot into the sky.

Seth tugged again. "That's not what I meant, Michael."

Michael smiled at Seth. "It's exactly what you meant, young sir."

The bonfire roared high into the night air. The flames roasted two sides of beef. Grease dripped into the fire and sizzled. Seared animal flesh sailed a scrumptious aroma throughout the camp. Mary worked as only a tireless grandmother could, cutting slices of meat and placing them onto the serving plates for children, women, and finally hungry men. She chided for all to come forward, regardless of their Moonie robes or how much they had already eaten. Firelight glistened on the oily faces of satisfied Moonies.

Michael took another sip of red wine. He pondered where exactly he was, or why humans sought the effects of the fermented juice, then he frowned at his empty cup and wondered where the little black box of wine had escaped to. Cyd sat surrounded by women, refusing to partake of the beef, and grimaced at any offer of wine.

Michael stepped into the waning fire to spread his wings slowly, gently. "This was always story time for me. Full bellies, wine, the anticipation of music and dancing. That was an eternity ago, and time can be daunting. Traditions, memories, each a gift from our Creator. Each of you will speak a story from your heart and let us all revel in the joy He has bestowed."

Michael poured the last sip of wine down his throat. "But let me begin. I was made to gaze down on the creation of this world. Made by our Lord. Then remade again, and again, and again to suit His needs when called upon. This sword, this armor, this body. Each occasion familiar, challenging, and victorious. I look deep into this firelight and see centuries past. I see familiar friends. And face familiar foes. Except this time, I see new challenges, faces of new friends. I see my baby sister sitting over there like the smug pug she pretends to be and dwelling on herself. Tales told by the fire never lose light; they live eternally, live in books, stories handed down as if time held no barrier. I see my sister at her first firelight, as she truly is, the alpha and omega of His plan. I see my sister standing in this firelight and telling her first story. Words that will transcend time and be written by some sneaky soul conspiring in the shadows."

Michael stared at Cyd. His eyes glistened with unfallen tears.

Cyd stood and approached the fire. Michael bowed at her approach and stepped aside. She took a deep breath and exhaled. A knot in her throat struggled to work its way down. "I am—was—a tormented soul, probably no different than billions of others. And I should be dead, a piece of meat for the insects and fish living in the river. And now I can snap my fingers and achieve anything I desire. Except . . ."

Cyd choked on her words. She hid her eyes and started back to her perch on the boulder. Seth walked out of the shadows and embraced her leg. She smiled down at his uplifted face full of wonder and affection.

She regarded hundreds of enraptured faces. "Except I found Michael, and he needed a bath."

A chorus of laughter.

"And I found myself needing one too. I was soiled and needed cleansing from the nasty influence of . . . Lucifer . . . Samuel . . . my adopted father. And the Fisherman gave me something I hadn't experienced my whole life—a purpose to fill the emptiness in my heart. Kindness. Compassion. Patience. Michael was all those things and—"

Raphael spoke up. "That's not the Michael we know."

Another round of laughter.

Cyd grinned. "My story starts here. Now. If somebody in the shadows chooses to write it, then beware. I hate typos and misinformation."

Cyd hugged Seth and let him lead her out of the firelight and back to her perch. Seth sat with her, wrapped his arm around hers, and shimmied close. She relaxed and absorbed the comforting firelight dancing over his grimy face.

The fire burned into the early morning as Cyd sat surrounded by a growing throng of women enjoying a unique sisterhood. Serah sketched shadowed faces backlit by firelight. Men and Moonies offered tales of faith and bravery, though Michael thought most were fables. Women spoke of love and children and a feeling of empowerment Cyd had brought into their lives.

And in the wee hours of dawn, Seth told a story that captured Michael's heart. How he wandered into the Craters of the Moon as a dirty, hungry four-year-old, naked, and afraid of the menacing eyes peering out of the dark, foreboding hoods. How he hid in narrow crevices only a child's slight body might squeeze into, stealing a soiled rag and using it as a robe to blend in, scrounging for food, begging for water. Seth stood next to Myra and proclaimed the young girl saved his life, protected him, fed him, resisted the protests of her father and grandmother, until each accepted him as a member of the family.

Myra turned away, her tears wetting the black robe draped over Cyd's shoulder. Peppered with questions, Seth could only shrug and yawn for sleep.

Michael stood alone by the dying embers.

There was more to the boy's story that was not spoken. Much more. And he intended to find out.

CHAPTER FIFTEEN

A MUFFLED MORNING SUNRISE WAS delivered in a gray haze, as if a forest fire had raged throughout the night. A thick layer of soot hanging over the camp like the umbra of a poisonous mushroom.

Michael allowed the Moonies to sleep in as he paced through the camp and eyed their collection of meager belongings. The flock had swelled to nearly a thousand since the nuclear detonation. Perhaps it was the return of heavenly creatures, or the fear of the radioactive poisons floating invisibly in the air, or to escape Samuel's morbid dominance. The infinite reasons intersected into a singular mystery, but the goal remained clear. Michael thought of the ancient Hebrews unfulfilled journey to find the Promised Land centuries ago. But the Moonies' journey had been promised nothing, fueled by a blind loyalty to him, and Cyd, and the unyielding faith in the Fisherman.

Michael lifted his sword and appraised the razor-edged blade. The white sharpness held no value in this modern world, and a blade dripping with demon blood would shock no one. Except as a prop, the sword was feared only by small children or zealous prophets. He ran his finger along the edge.

"A bit dated, huh?" Cyd said.

Her stealth continued to unnerve him. "You read minds too?"

"The look on your face said it all." Cyd clasped his arm. "Nice morning. Let's walk."

She led him along a narrow trail through a desert of thick, blue-tinged sagebrush. On the gravel road pointed towards low foothills, Moonie backpacks and wheeled carts lined the edges, preparation for the day's coming journey. They walked up the road arm in arm.

"Why are we here, Michael? I can't seem to wrap my head around this. Not to mention my new outfit."

Michael snickered. "Your garb befits an Archangel. Feminine but regal. Intimidating and functional at the same time. Don't even try to guess why. Eons of doing His work, and I am always stumped by the why. Millennia may pass before I might say, 'Ahh, that's why.' But that was before when people were simple, their lives focused on survival, their beliefs simple. And now with all the technology, people's lives have become complicated, and not for the better. Meanness and ugliness flourish alongside the new technology. We fight with family and neighbors because of tech. Humanity has lost themselves in technology and forgotten what truly matters. Love. Family. Faith. Not sure all that smart tech was smart."

Cyd stopped and stared at the gravel, hesitant to continue. Michael let her sort out the thoughts anchoring her feet. After a long minute, Michael squeezed her hand. "If you can't tell your heavenly brother, then we're all lost."

She smiled thinly but kept her gaze aimed at the gravel. "I had found the perfect place to end my empty life. Found the perfect place to crack my head open and drift away." Cyd sniffed back snot and tears. "And that crazy Fisherman comes wading into my landing zone. I thought I'd be pissed, but He waved me down to help him find a silly fishing net. I know. I know. In hindsight, it all fits. But I've mostly forgotten the conversation we had beneath the bridge. I remember the loud boom and the ground shaking. Obviously, Arco was being vaporized at the time. He said it sounded like a war had started, and I said something an immature teenager might say . . . The war . . . was a . . . That the war was between faith and technology. And I said I'd choose technology, and He . . . He moved away when the drones found us." A lump stuck in her throat. "I said I wanted no part of religious dogma. And I still don't. Except . . ."

"Except what you said is complicated. The reason might become clear after a generation or two passes. I think the reason–"

A pebble struck the crown of Michael's head, followed by a hailstorm of small rocks falling out of a dark, murky sky. Cyd grunted as a stone found her ear. Michael unfurled his wings to shield them from the torrent.

"Protect the Moonies!" Cyd shouted.

Michael swiped his wings once and rose above the rain of rocks. The relentless source of the assault was spread wide around a warren of bunkers and crevices riddling a hillside that shielded the attackers.

He pulled his wings into his chest to release a powerful torrent of air. The projectiles stopped mid-air and reversed course, pelting the hazy hillside. More rocks passed the retreating stones midair, signaling a clever mastermind had employed a staggered strategy to circumvent his winged response.

Michael swiped his wings again, and the rocks retreated, only to be followed by another round and another, until a rigid schedule of flying rocks ebbed and flowed. The artillery was a cunning deterrent to attacking the launch site.

Michael choked off a scream at Cyd to flee.

She was gone.

The assault stopped in an instant.

Cyd waited beneath him, restraining a young girl struggling to get free. Her soiled clothing nothing but a pillowcase with cutouts for a neck and arms, her ratty, dirty-blonde hair riddled with small twigs and fragments of dried leaves, her face streaked in warpaint of charcoal and white ash.

Michael landed and arched his brows.

"I think we've found the others," Cyd said. "Or their children."

———

MICHAEL PRODDED THE FERAL GIRL forward, glancing down at her often with the hope she might speak. Cyd disappeared untold times, for brief moments, until she returned too exhausted to continue her reconnaissance. The valley beyond the sparsely vegetated hillside was riddled with hundreds of narrow crevices to be used as bolt holes and sapped her strength like a magnet. Michael relinquished the girl to Cyd and shot high into the sky to soar like a hawk, circling and searching for prey.

The main road ascended a formidable mountainside using a corkscrew of switchbacks before finding the summit, followed by a steep descent into a narrow valley thick with aspen groves and lodgepole pine. A long crescent-shaped lake fed by three springs glistened in a reflection of the White Cloud Mountains rising like a buttress against the elements.

Fierce winds buffeted his wings. Maintaining altitude proved difficult and tiring. Rapid strokes of his powerful wings kept him mere feet above the thick canopy of trees. Tendrils of smoke from distant campfires lifted straight up into a blue sky and appeared unaffected by chaotic gusts of hot thermals Michael battled.

Michael bit down hard and paddled out of the valley like a drowned gosling, giving a Herculean effort to reach the summit before Cyd appeared in his view. He let out an exhausted gasp before folding his wings to glide toward his target. A simple maneuver. Fun and games. Now one that suddenly required every ounce of strength to unfurl his wings and brake to avoid requiring a headstone on the side of a road.

Michael grabbed his knees and sucked in huge gulps of air. His great white wings collapsed to the ground. Cyd's soiled sandals appeared in his vision, barely touching the ground.

"I should've warned ya about that fortress against heavenly creatures," Cyd said. "That place sucks the life out of you."

Michael gritted his teeth and stood high and proud, like the Archangel he was born to be. He pushed his face towards Cyd. "Yeah. Nice warning. That fucking chip on your shoulder will get us both killed. Think, Cyd. Think. This is a chess match. Lucifer against the Fisherman. I'm a pawn. You're a pawn. Maybe we're bishops? Who the fuck knows. Strategy and foretelling will decide the victor. And you've had a taste of both."

Michael grunted as he folded his battered wings. He aimed an evil stare at the young girl restrained by Cyd. Her expression remained amused by her capture. Been here. Done that.

"Was the wind sucked out of your lungs up there?" Michael asked.

Cyd turned her face away but nodded. "More like walking in wet concrete for me."

Michael smirked. "Then let's arrive like the Moonies we lead."

Michael and Cyd led a bedraggled procession cursing and crying with discourse. The Moonies' difficult trek was amplified by the thick, opaque air. The wheels of carts rumbled, and weary shoes scuffed gravel. Burdened with the weight of homes strapped to their back, the Moonies struggled to ascend the steep switchbacks. The next U-turn was simply a deflating mirage that disappeared into the hazy mist from hell.

Michael carried a toddler on his shoulders, the stink of feces and urine leaking from its soiled diaper a perpetual source of consternation. Cyd cradled a baby girl in each arm, regularly shooting him a challenging glare as if chiding him to pull his weight.

The summit offered an expansive wide gravel turnout to beckon a break. The sky beyond the valley offered unequaled shades of dark blue to serve as a backdrop for a lemon sun. A dark portal of infinite stars hovered above the valley like a tunnel. Distant galaxies and spiderlike nebulas floated just beyond the horizon. An earthly impossibility.

The thin blue mist suspended over the valley reflected the turquoise water of the lake below. His wings sluggish and temperamental, Michael tempered his urge to soar. He sat on a boulder as Raphael escorted the oldest members of the tribe to a welcome rest. Cyd kibitzed with Serah and Myra, her eyes darting towards the valley floor, her blossoming anxiety easy to recognize.

Michael waited at the cliff edge. Would his wings fail if he jumped? Just a leap. Headfirst. Soar down into the valley and crack like an egg. He chuckled at his own absurd thoughts. Faith stayed warm in thin or thick blankets, the insulation value always precarious.

Cyd offered the feral child a drink of water and giggled as the orphan sucked greedily from a rusty metal canteen. Michael's sister held a place special in the Fisherman's heart. His first. His last. The alpha and omega. What did He intend for her?

Michael wiped a drop of liquid falling from his eye and stared at his own wet fingertip. Wet, like a tear. His first. His last.

Michael began to understand the unique and fragile human existence.

Michael waited at the head of the Moonie herd, his wings spread wide and regal to hold back the procession. "This descent will be far harder than that little hill we just climbed. What you think you know of the world will wither and die. What you truly desire waits at the bottom. A home. A community where you're not outcasts but survivors. This land before you is His special place on Earth, free of the ills of Satan. Even I, the Archangel Michael, have never been allowed to experience heaven on earth. You have been deemed special, and you shall act accordingly."

Michael's wings slumped. The speech practiced in his head for hours barely raised a weary head. A speech uttered eons ago that could incite a rebellion, lead a suicidal charge into battle, or offer assurances of salvation. Michael licked his lips, then waved the sluggish Moonies to begin the descent.

"That was sweet," Cyd whispered in his ear. She pecked his ear lobe with soft lips. "That hocus pocus, mumbo jumbo doesn't work anymore. Same crap Daddy might've said to a bunch of people barely hanging on to a thread of dignity, only he would snip it and laugh as they fell into a hell of his making. I know. I was there."

Michael swallowed. A moment, and Cyd was whispering in his other ear. "Samuel thinks the same way—old school, dominion-over-the-world-of-man crap, except . . . What if the Fisherman—"

"Thinks the world of mankind is over," Michael finished. "Maybe the dominion of women should take its place."

"The alpha and the omega," Cyd said. "Wanna guess what we find down there?"

Michael pulled Cyd into a playful headlock and squeezed. "I'm gonna guess I'd find myself holding an armful of nothing should I ever want to snap your neck."

Cyd chuckled. "You wouldn't or couldn't or can't. Take your pick. I see my purpose. Do you, brother? Let me go, or the wraith of time might gnaw on your flesh."

Michael stared at a pair of deep pools of azure masqueraded as her eyes. He relaxed his grip. "That was the old-school me. The same one Samuel wants us to stick to. You know I never had a sister before, not even a true friend, and especially not one like you. I think back to the many souls rising . . . to be judged together, burdened with betrayal, or bursting of unflinching love . . . Mostly the love. The love . . . It helped me weigh judgment. We both have a lot to learn. Maybe that's why we were born as humans. A notion that would totally piss off Samuel. Born human to simply . . . appreciate their complexities."

Cyd scoffed. "He'd never believe it. Why did the Fisherman create someone like Samuel? He thrives on the pain and misery of people . . . sucks it up like a vacuum. Plays with people's lives like he is . . . God."

"He wants to be God, but it's not possible. Maybe sitting by His side and ruling the realms is the next best thing, but that isn't possible either." Michael shook his head. "Samuel would never admit to himself those impossibilities exist. So, he keeps trying to defeat Him, to return and rule."

Cyd spoke over Michael's shoulder. "So why not just kill him in a rockslide or let him drown in some weird boating accident? Get rid of him."

"Samuel or even someone like him will always be required to balance the intricacies of humans. Can't have the good without the bad, I suppose."

Cyd faced Michael. "So, if I just jog back to Yellowstone and eliminate Samuel, this will all be over, for at least a time?"

"And if I held onto you, could you take me at the speed you travel?"

Cyd whispered in his ear. "Nope. Been there, tried that with Seth."

"Hmm. As soon as we start the descent, your time tricks will fail, just like my wings."

Cyd nodded, but her gaze remained on the road they had just traveled.

"Sister, I feel your urge to return," Michael said. "And let it rip if you need to. But I sure could use . . . some moral support for whatever waits for us down in that valley."

Cyd scoffed. "The great Archangel Michael nervous about meeting new friends. Sounds almost ridiculous. My own brother introducing me to the old gang as the Archangel Cyd. Sounds like I should—"

"Hold my hand when we tell them to go screw themselves." Michael smirked and offered his hand.

Cyd took his hand.

The old wagon trail sliced from a granite cliff face by prospectors and miners of another era appeared unused for years as the mile-long procession traversed the narrow dirt doubletrack overgrown with tall cheatgrass. Moonies towing carts stayed tight to the shear rock face with ample cool springs trickling out of the rock and narrow crevices ripe with lime moss and neon-colored lichen. A wayward child or loose wheel might cause a kneejerk reaction accompanied by a five-hundred feet plunge into a densely forested valley below. The soft soothing rush of a swollen creek piggybacked on the tendrils of mist floating skyward.

Michael walked at the head of the procession, using his sword as a shepherd might. His folded wings felt shriveled with each step lower into the valley. Babies wailed, and older Moonies shuffled close behind him until he reached the bottom. He slowed as the road diverged into well-worn footpaths spreading out like capillaries into a beautiful valley rich with human activity.

A small log cabin spewed woodsmoke a few hundred yards down a well-traveled trail. Rectangular plots of fruit trees and lush fields of grain intersected along the shoreline of the crescent lake. Abundance and prosperity stretched beyond the farthest shore to disappear into the blue mist creeping down from the hazy sky. As if abandoning their harvest, field workers emerged from the orchards. Children fishing near the lake inlet paused fun and games to watch Michael lead the Moonies across the bridge.

Michael bowed his head as he crossed the sparkling clear water. *Father, we have arrived.*

Seth raced past him, jumping, and punching his tiny fist into the air. The boy shimmied and danced across an empty circular gravel plot beyond the bridge, issuing victorious war whoops. Serah jostled his shoulder as she rushed forward, looking back to turn his frown upside-down by her sly smile. Others at his back joined the celebration. The Moonie procession flooded down the road, teeming across the bridge like a plague of lemmings. Michael kneeled and stabbed his sword into the weathered logs forming the bridge and resisted the joyous onslaught of salvation that flew past him like a steady breeze.

Numbers of farmers appeared from the rows of apple and pear trees and assembled into a large mob before striding toward the Moonies' raucous celebration.

Michael pulled his sword free and held it across his chest. He narrowed his eyes and studied the faces of the approaching farmers. He thought to recognize many, but he wasn't sure.

With eyes shaded by a wide-brimmed hat, an angular face concealed by a heavy beard, Uriel stared at him. Ariel wore a long denim dress, her blonde hair braided down her back, but her sweet cherub face was unmistakable. Nuriel and his knack for conjuring violent hailstorms. The beautiful Jophiel with hollow green eyes ever searching for the source of wisdom.

A lanky man wearing a red plaid shirt and blue jeans and carrying a long-handled scythe pushed to the front of the mob. Gabriel. He gestured for the others to grab garden tools, scythes, reapers to be used as weapons.

Michael swallowed road grit. This was not the greeting he expected.

Cyd grabbed his free hand. "Still wanna tell 'em to go screw themselves?"

The raucous celebration died as the mob of angels neared the crossroads beyond the bridge. The Moonies converged at Michael's back. Mob against mob. He and Cyd appeared no more than the Moonie beggars they led. Except for his sword, the Moonies were defenseless. Even after millennia, Gabriel had to recognize him. A thousand questions tempered his battle calculations. The magical valley housed all of His angels, masquerading each as a simple farmer. But why?

The angel mob converged and raised their tools as if preparing for a charge.

Raphael stood behind Michael's right shoulder and unsheathed his long blades. "They don't recognize us. We're just simple poachers."

Michael spun the hilt of his sword, turning it over and over in his sweaty palm, hoping the weapon might intimidate farmers wielding simple shovels and hoes.

He stepped forward. "Gabriel, self-professed leader of all His angels, I offer you His greetings." With an open hand, he offered the Moonies at his back. "And His chosen. They might not look like much, but most have His ear."

Gabriel stepped forward with three quick steps and pointed the tip of a razor-sharp grain scythe at Michael's face. "You have brought the black dragon with you. His shadow will now pollute our orchards."

Michael countered Gabriel's move and pointed the tip of his sword at him. "The mighty Gabriel. Afraid of a simple dragon? Maybe the world is lost after all?"

"How do you know my name?"

"I know all your names. Uriel, Moroni, Netzach, my brothers and sisters. Perhaps you have been asleep while plucking your apples and peaches off the trees. A humble life, character-building, but the time has arrived for His warriors to wake the fuck up!"

Gabriel looked back at his mob, as if gauging their temperament for a fight. Narrowed eyes and stern expressions softened as murmurs passed through the mob. With long, confident strides, Gabriel stood face to face with Michael. "One night. You can have as much fruit as you can carry, then keep going."

"Hmm." Michael appraised the mob. Dull witted, sluggish. Angels or not, they wouldn't mount much of a defense. "What will we find if—when we keep going?"

"Don't know. Don't care," Gabriel said with a challenging expression.

A bloodletting of angels, should he force the issue. "Thank you. We'll camp in the orchards for the night. But before we move on, can you tell me if others have passed this way?"

"Anyone passing this way has always chosen to join our collective."

Michael stabbed his sword into the dirt. "Last question. The black dragon. Have you seen it up close? Does it breathe fire? Should we prepare for a possible attack?"

Knotting his brow, Gabriel scratched his chin as if to give the questions deep thought. "You should be safe during spring harvest season. The breath of the beast will soon color the sunlight. Should it drop poisonous dung, we are forced inside caves or cellars for months."

"Kill the dragon, lure it down, and cut its throat."

Gabriel recoiled. "Samuel never descends into the valley. We can never kill it."

Cyd pushed forward. "Did you say Samuel?"

Raphael whispered in Michael's ear, "Feel the dumb invading your thoughts? I can smell Samuel's chemicals. We'll change. Become just like them."

Cyd turned to Michael. "He's right. The blue mist we saw at the top of the summit. 3Bz, same stuff you were fed. An aerosol."

"To crop-dust the valley." Michael frowned at Cyd. "The dragon is a fucking drone, but these simpletons wouldn't know the difference. I gotta get to the summit and get my wings back."

Cyd and Raphael argued over who would accompany him. Someone needed to stay and prevent a bloody confrontation. The angels residing in the valley would be useless—unless the source of the blue mist was destroyed.

Samuel would have calculated Michael's strategy, including his intention to destroy the dragon mist. Samuel had somehow foreseen the future, a gift only the Fisherman possessed. Was this sense of precognition luring Samuel to believe he could return to Heaven?

But he would need His blessings to enter the realm. Bribery. Threats. Negotiation. All useless. And all His children might perish before Samuel fought a way back in. And the Lord knew what Samuel planned. Two master chess players battling inside each other's head.

The thought befuddled Michael.

Regardless, the Lord would have his army resurrected.

CHAPTER SIXTEEN

SAMUEL THREW THE EMPTY COFFEE cup across the room and began using both hands to swipe the holo-screens relentlessly. His jawbone worked frantically to manipulate the Arkoff Port, switching channels, changing low-frequency data inputs, responding to emails and requests from acolytes for guidance. The normal workload exacerbated by the increasing frequency and intensity of the solar flares erupting from millions of miles away. Exactly as predicted. The heavenly Father's pitiful display of omnipotence.

But multiple layers of atmosphere shielded the Earth from true destruction. Minor disruptions to satellite communications, a loss of surveillance fidelity, glitches in the fast-as-light technology was merely an irritant, irrelevant to achieving the ultimate goal.

On an infrared display, Samuel watched two red splotches stumble like wounded insects ascending the access road leading out of the Valley of Dead Angels. Michael and Raphael, possibly Cyd, but confirming their identification was impossible given the surveillance disruptions. No matter.

Angel wings would succeed in sweeping the gas out of the valley, freeing Gabriel, and his band of nitwits to join the fight. In twenty-four hours, hundreds of His angels would rise and disperse into a sky Samuel controlled. Blind and without direction. Weaponless. Stupid hybrid angels with visions of grandeur. In twenty-four hours, he would defeat God's army, then with one more simple act, the heavenly doors to His kingdom would swing wide open, and He would invite Samuel to ascend the throne.

Samuel waggled his fingers as if imitating a child's Halloween witch. "Tell me to stop now. Beg me to rise and sit at your side. Promise me we will rule together. Tell me now or—"

A burst of static rippled his holo-screens.

Samuel lifted the corner of his mouth. "Your answer is loud and clear."

He terminated all screens except one. He enlarged it and initiated a link to Jurgens. The scientist's liver-spotted face appeared up close, unaware the camera spying on him was inches away.

Samuel rubbed his palms together. "Release those ugly little pets of yours."

———

MICHAEL TUGGED ON RAPHAEL, HELPING him ascend the last steep incline. The burly angel huffed and puffed as if the misty air sucked the wind from his lungs. Reaching the top of the steep road, above the layer of blue mist, Michael assisted Raphael to a boulder and let him rest.

Michael stabbed his sword into the hard soil and gazed down into a valley shrouded in a mist colored like the blue sky above. His lungs gained volume, his thoughts sharpened, and his wings sprouted like vibrant shoots in a warm wet spring. He gazed up at the orange sun shrouded in a layer of atmospheric smoke. He flexed and tested his wings.

Raphael stood and arched his back. "I've been here before. Over and over. A hundred thousand times. Lying on that bed, plugged into that Tuber gear. I played the same game over and over, dying over and over, each iteration ending in failure, never able to fight my way into the final level." He swallowed hard. "We all lived in a prison of Samuel's making. You. Cyd. Seth. Different wardens, maybe, but still prisons. My avatar inside that simulation never changed. No matter what I did, what I found, the demons and monsters inside that game always found a way to kill me. Just so I could start all over again.

I'm pretty sure Samuel had the game designed just for me, keep me occupied until I could be useful to him out in the world."

Michael nodded. "I'll bet he's watching us right now. He truly thinks he's God. His ego won't let it go."

Raphael spread his wings. "And I intend to make him pay for my imprisonment. I stood in this exact spot thousands of times in that game. Then the game changed. I found a young squire to assist me, point out weapons I hadn't discovered, show me power-ups I didn't know existed. Seth reminds me of that squire. I still fought demons and monsters, but I didn't feel so alone and destitute, and hopeless. That squire saved my life in that game, found me a weapon unlike anything else, and I fought like hell to save his ass. You have your Fisherman, and I have my Squire."

"Is there a point, Raphael?" Michael said. He flapped his wings once. "Did you beat the game?"

"I would have, but some idiot pulled my wires."

"Well, you needed a break."

"You're missing my point, brother. I've lived this exact moment over and over," Raphael said. He beat his wings and rose a few feet into the air to land next to Michael. With a single finger, he pointed north towards the Big Lost Mountain range.

A black mass enveloped the granite peaks like a seething thunderstorm, rivulets of black slime oozing down the cliffs and consuming anything in its path. Relentless and unstoppable, the black malignancy metastasized as it reached the dry lakebed of Mackay Reservoir.

Michael narrowed his eyes. Lucifer's legion was coming fast. Evil and ferocious. He looked back towards the crescent valley below, through a clearing in the mist created by their wings. A bloody massacre waited below, delivered by Samuel's abominations. Michael pulled his sword from the earth.

Raphael shook his head. "I have lived this moment every day for an eternity, brother. The little ones will get through no matter what we do. Let's clear this blue fog out and hope the others can recover. I'll fly out and greet our guests, let them have a taste of battle. You get back down and rally the simpletons."

Michael grabbed Raphael's wrist to prevent his ascent. "You bucking for General now?"

Raphael snickered. "Always. And I was gonna ask you to be my squire. Winning this skirmish cannot be left to those that have not experienced it. Just saying." He cracked his neck and fingers and stretched his mighty wings.

Michael scoffed. "And just in case I ever play this unwinnable game, what was the new weapon your squire discovered?"

Raphael grinned like a Cheshire cat, wide and white. "The Sword of Saint Michael."

Two Archangels attacked the hanging layer of blue fog as if herding a flock of sheep. Powerful strokes of their wings pushed the mist forward to gain volume, and mass, and speed, until the dry fog rolled up on itself into violent blue thunderheads. Bolts of dry lightning crackled and struck the granite cliffs. Rockslides rumbled down into the forested valley. The pair pushed the blue lightning storm towards the wave of black continuing to crest the granite crags to the east. At the end of the crescent valley, a prevailing thermal took hold of the storm, lifting it into the heated air to expand and intensify. Lightning flashed, and thunder split the air open as if the doors to hell had been blown wide open.

Michael hovered in silence, hypnotized by the violent blue maelstrom.

Raphael joined him. "I think we had help doing that." He unsheathed a single long knife and handed it to Michael. "For Cyd. I think if we can get 'em close to the ground, then that sister of yours can vent her frustrations."

Michael took the blade and beckoned for the other knife. He held out his sword to Raphael.

Raphael took it and ran his finger gently along the sharp edge. "You think my squire was telling us something?"

"I want it back," Michael said.

"Always, brother," Raphael said. He shot up and aimed for the center of the black storm.

Michael bit his lip and swallowed the dry blue dust coating his tongue. He should be at Raphael's side, but the plan to delay the black horde was sound. Defending his drugged brethren, and the Moonies, was paramount.

Michael turned and dove down into the valley, the warren of bolt holes and crevices used by the rock-throwing children passing beneath him. A rock struck him in the thigh. He flinched and flipped around. Each dark crevice or hole held a head of ratty hair with a dirty face, skinny bare arms poised to hurl sharp stones. Except one. A scrawny girl barely nine years old and dressed in a crude dress of rabbit pelts stood defiantly and lifted her chin as a challenge.

She stood her ground as he landed barely an arm's length in front of her.

She stepped close, inches from him. Her blonde hair stiff with tunnel dust, whittled twigs and sharpened rodent bones as jewelry. "We're here to fight. We know what's coming."

"You have no idea what's coming." Michael said. "Hide in your holes and—"

"We defend our parents in the valley. Against all comers."

Michael frowned. "Your parents? Do you know what your parents are?"

"It doesn't matter." She dared him with blunt hazel eyes. "We know they are like you. Except they're drugged and stupid and need our protection."

Michael nodded. "You live underground for protection from the blue—"

"You're Michael. His General. I'm Josie. My father is Gabriel."

"How long until Gabriel becomes . . ."

She shrugged and shook her head.

Michael rubbed the side of his face. Children should be protected, not fighting demons. Except they weren't normal children. Offspring of angels. Uncharted territory.

"We're gonna fight. Under your command or mine," Josie said. She showed a handful of stones.

Michael narrowed his eyes. She certainly acted like Gabriel. He pulled Raphael's knife from beneath a feather on his wing to point it at her face. He tapped the air with the blade. It might work.

"Are your archers good?" Michael asked.

"Nailed you, didn't we?"

"Indeed" He glanced toward the coming storm. "And their wings will offer a wider range of targets. Gather your troops and meet at the bridge crossing the river."

Josie squinted in mistrust.

Michael scoffed. "You'll be under my sister's command. She captured one of you earlier. Get moving."

Josie hesitated then waved her fellow badgers back into their burrows. "What about our parents?"

Michael considered the question. Children born of angels. The concept was confusing, the ramifications extraordinary, but he had no reason to doubt her. Were these children the reason His angels were born human? Were they half-angel, or half-human? What would these immaculate births offer this subjugated world?

"We hold the fort until reinforcements arrive, and your parents are the cavalry—if they can shake that . . . dragon breath."

Josie nodded. "They will."

"How long will it take you to get back?" Michael asked.

"The others are halfway home already." She pointed at the labyrinth of tunnels. "These holes lead to old mine shafts by the waterfall. The mist from the water keeps the blue stuff from getting in."

"Fresh air won't be a problem anymore," Michael said. He offered his hand and spread his wings. "Give you lift?"

Josies eyes opened wide as saucers, and she took his hand.

The ride was short but exhilarating as Josie whooped and screamed on a descent to rival any rollercoaster. Moonies scrambled and hurried like a nest of angry ants. Michael dropped at Cyd's side and released Josie. A quick introduction, but none were needed as the two girls hugged like old friends.

Michael offered Raphael's long blade to Cyd. She took it warily and offered a questioning look.

"The sky is black with them," Michael said. "He's buying us time to prepare. Josie's archers can clip a few wings and get 'em down to the ground. With that knife, you can finish 'em. But that's only a drop in the bucket."

"Seth and Zeke are arming the Moonies with whatever farm tools they can find." Cyd pointed towards an old log cabin. "Myra and Serah are hustling the old women and children to find a safe hideout."

Josie snapped to attention. "I can help with that, sir. I can show them the mine shaft."

Michael nodded his permission, and the wild girl bolted. He looked at Cyd. "The blue mist still slowing you down?"

"The effects faded pretty quick after you guys rolled that mist out of the valley," Cyd said. "The farmers will need more time."

"Hmm," Michael licked his bottom lip.

Cyd's face was inches from his, her breath hot and fast. "What? Talk to me, or I will put you in a headlock that even time can't pry open."

Michael chuckled. "I finally fit that last puzzle piece into the picture—you. You were born for this very moment. Nothing could stop that horde I witnessed coming over the mountains, even with Gabriel and the others. You. You're the Fisherman's white queen on a chessboard dominated by black pieces. Samuel might not have known that, and he couldn't control you."

"Telling me I gotta save the world or else."

"I'm telling you that if I ever find your soul in front of me to be judged, I will offer my hand and ask you to sit by my side, sister."

Cyd looked away and wiped her nose. "You remember our mother?"

"A little."

"Well, then, you've given me a big reason to smite some fucking demons. To use Seth's vernacular."

Michael smiled.

The bright sunshine dimmed as the leading edge of the dark storm flew over the White Cloud Mountains. The black sky rumbled as if a thousand train engines converged in the valley. Like hungry black flies' intent on consuming the corpse of a dead beast, the swarm of Lucifer's demons descended.

———

MICHAEL INHALED A DEEP BREATH and held it. The carnage grew with each exhale. At his feet lay mounds of wormy intestines, bloody claws, jaws full of sharp, canine teeth, mangled wings, limbs snapped like twigs. Blank eyes frozen on the bloodied faces of dead farmers stared at the sky. Dead Moonies gazed up at him from between pelts of bloody fur. Michael lifted his foot to avoid a pool of blood oozing from a wolverine's mouth of jagged teeth, then crushed its skull to mix with the numbers of pelts stacking up like cordwood.

Clones.

He wiped his long knife on the fur of a raccoon and watched Josie's archers launch another assault at more demons skimming over the battlefield. The carnage would expand with their clipped wings, Cyd removing hundreds from the battle before he could take his next breath.

The sun broke free from the restraint of the black swarm to shine hot streams of light down on the battlefield. The resident angels fought like frightened peasants.

Azriel defended her wheat field with a vengeance, swatting and slicing demons with a long wheat reaper, retreating into her field, leaving corpses to fertilize the ground, until the vast numbers bullied her up against a tool shed to fight to a certain death.

Uriel had screamed with each slice of his death scythes, his voice graveled with the onslaught, then silent with the magnitude he faced.

Chamuel had guarded a small log home, standing outside the front door, beckoning the horde to find him and not the windows or doors, to protect those hiding inside. The snarling bloodbath grew to his knees before he disappeared in the mass of fur and black wings.

Gabriel had roared his defiance at the horde as he ran through the apple orchard, ducking beneath apple trees then rising to slice open snarling bobcats and vampiric bats, tempting the demons deeper into the orchard and away from the village.

Michael pushed his legs through the weight of dead things, then unfurled his wings to rise above the massacre.

"I would love a set of those right about now," Cyd said, pointing a knife dripping with blood.

Michael looked over his shoulder at his sister, her platinum hair limp and plastered with blood and the sweat of a long-distance sprint. The luxurious pelt covering her torso was nothing but a thin cloth matted in blood, both red and black, her calves and thighs lacerated and bruised, her bare feet matted with the coarse hair of the dead. Cyd raised a single finger and disappeared.

Michael shook his head. The time disconnect continued to confound him. The possibilities endless, and yet it answered how the angels had so far survived the onslaught. Each and every Moonie, had been assisted—or rescued—by Cyd traveling through her own world. Her own dominion. Slaughtering Samuel's sadistic and warped spawn.

The black blots covering the sky thinned into small flocks until disappearing.

Cyd whispered in his ear, "I need a fucking nap. Can I count on you to keep the noise down?"

Michael grinned. "Always."

Seth led a procession of Moonies up from the mineshaft, each carrying a bloody shovel, or hoes, or wooden clubs. The group was loud and raucous with victory. Seth's stern face refused to join the celebration.

Serah stepped gently through the piles of skin and flesh, frantically sketching dead demons with her charcoal pencils. Masked raccoons, clawed skunks, striped badgers, wolf pups, razor-toothed predators cloned to inflict pain and death. Soulless demons created for this occasion. Serah paused her hand as she stood over a tiny dead bear cub. She bowed her head and wept.

Michael stepped toward the girl, only to find Cyd consoling her. The time distortion made him bite his lip. Cyd's compassion made him swallow a lump.

Tiny fingers pulled on his wing.

"We smited them, angel," Seth said.

"That we did, young master. You led your platoon well," Michael said. He placed a gentle hand on the boy's shoulder.

"Heck yeah, I did," Seth said. "And we'll do it again and again."

Michael frowned at Seth. The bloodletting had hardened the boy's gentle heart to seek rage and revenge. "You will do no more."

"That was just the first wave. Invasions always come in waves," Seth said.

Michael inhaled a deep breath reeking of sweat and death. Seth didn't lie. Samuel would send more abominations. "That is true. And how might we prevent that?" Michael knew the answer but waited for Seth to offer it.

The boy nodded and waggled his finger in the air. "Take the battle to them. Catch 'em off guard and then fucking smite them."

Michael nodded. "Then we agree. It's time we get the others aware then." Michael squeezed Seth's shoulder hard, enough force to cause discomfort. "Do as I say but not as I speak. Your f-bombs belittle your command. If I die today, then remember that much at least."

Seth lowered his face but nodded. "Do you really think I can command? Lead armies into battle? That would be so cool."

"I see no reason why you couldn't be a general someday," Michael said.

"Cool. My brother says I need to concentrate on learning about people. How they work and think and stuff. He always finds me by the water and tries to teach me about people and stuff."

Michael frowned. Was Seth mocking Michael's own dreams? He was sure he had never told the boy of the dreams "Your brother talks to you how—and when—in your dreams?"

"No, he visits me when I go to pee or poop, told me to do *my business* by the water but never in it. He just pops out of the trees and gives me a hug, then the lessons start. Ugh. The lessons are so boring sometimes."

Michael stared wide-eyed at Seth. "Why . . . why do you call him your brother?"

"'Cause he says he is. I'm his only brother, and he probably won't get any more."

Michael placed bloody hands gently on Seth's shoulders and searched the battlefield, unsure of what he was looking for. "Is this man the same man you asked to grant you an angel?"

"Sure. He can do anything." Seth glanced down at his bloody shoes. "He says I gotta learn to wash feet first, then the bigger stuff."

"Indeed, you will," Michael said. "Let's throw these drowned angels a life preserver. Better yet, let's see them sink or swim."

Michael aimed for the log house of Gabriel, keeping Seth's robes in his grasp. The resident flock had gathered to gloat and celebrate their victory. With farm tools, axes, scythes bloodied by battle raised to the air, Gabriel led the cheer. He was an imbecile. A warrior of centuries past. Lost in his new reality.

Michael held back ten yards and pulled Seth forward. "These angels still wallow in stupid. If you were a general, what would you order?"

Seth rubbed his lips with a bloody hand, as if the question was a crucial test. "Hmm. I think . . . no. I'd give him a choice. Let him decide."

"Decide what?"

Seth narrowed his eyes. "His path in life. I think that's what my brother would say . . . but that's what I'll say too."

Michael smiled. "I think your brother is wise. Stay here and watch. This should be interesting."

Michael flicked his wings and, in an instant, landed in front of Gabriel. The man bared his teeth and snarled at the intrusion, beckoning a smirk from Michael. He knocked the bloody club from Gabriel's hand and embraced him in a bear hug. His breath reeked of chemicals and death, the black iris of his brown eyes dilated, his teeth slimy with a transparent film of blood. Gabriel sneered his defiance.

"Let's take a ride, brother. If you return, then we'll know the answer," Michael said.

Michael embraced Gabriel and shot straight up, strong strokes of his wings lifting them high, then higher, and higher, until the air thinned and turned frigid. Still Michael flapped his wings, battling gravity and the heavy weight of the body he restrained. Seth's words echoed with each stroke. Gabriel squirmed and struggled.

The air depleted of oxygen, yet Michael continued the beat of his wings, rising high to see the full moon rise above a distant ocean. His wings found scant resistance. Oceans and islands. Clouds and continents. The beautiful blue world retreated beneath his feet. The sun's heat and radiation bathed him with His power.

Gabriel pounded Michael's flanks with his fists, his screams of terror lost in the near-vacuum of space.

Michael released his cargo and watched passively as Gabriel fell, his terrified eyes widening as he flailed, kicked, and swam as if he were drowning in water, falling into the abyss of life. Michael turned back to face the sun and watch the eruptions of plasma emanating from its surface. Geysers of protoplasm erupted, ribbons of light waves following, a massive storm unseen since before time.

Michael nodded and thought to understand the Fisherman. The planet below was a jewel in His kingdom, worthy of every effort to maintain its purity and splendor. A planet worthy of an offer of His second son, Seth.

Seth's arrival disguised as an orphaned Moonie was brilliant. Samuel would never suspect, not with so many angels birthed at the same time, clustered near the same location, setting the table for an easy feast for a spiteful fallen angel. An enigmatic quandary for Samuel's boundless ego.

The sun erupted again with a wave of plasma energy. Michael counted three waves rolling towards the planet. Michael narrowed his eyes. Another storm would erupt within minutes, its waves of electromagnetic energy arriving to assault the atmosphere. Like clockwork. An unflappable trait of the Fisherman—predictable, and unyielding.

A trait Samuel would attempt to use for an advantage.

CHAPTER SEVENTEEN

COMMAND AND CONTROL REEKED OF perspiration and anxiety as Samuel growled then swept away all but a single holo-screen. He opened a communication link to Jurgens and ordered the scientist to his office. His jaw twitched as if a piece of gristle was stuck in between his gums and teeth.

A grainy black-and-white image of the angels' camp appeared then began to focus and sharpen in metered increments, drawing closer as if he walked among the abundance of dead demons littered across the landscape. He issued a command to freeze the picture. He gave the order to disburse surveillance drones hidden in the valley. The command was rejected. Insufficient bandwidth due to atmospheric disruptions.

Jurgens slipped into his office and waited with his back against the door. The old man smiled nervously, not the typical subservient stretch of the lips Samuel was accustomed to seeing—but a smile expressing . . . true happiness. "Have you seen the satellite pictures of the skirmish? Absolutely fascinating."

Samuel frowned. Had Jurgens ingested 3Bz before he arrived? He was acting strange. Samuel sat back in his chair and steepled his fingers. "Nothing we didn't expect. I was hoping for Gabriel's camp to have spilled more blood but . . . why are you smiling?"

Jurgens offered his open palms. "I have known Cyd since she was a small child, and I never suspected."

"What the fuck are you talking about?" Samuel snapped.

"The skirmish." The smile dropped from Jurgens' face. "Perhaps you haven't seen the data from our Satlink satellite. The pictures and resolution are superb considering the sunspot activity. You must see for yourself. I transmitted the recording of the skirmish."

Samuel started watching the playback before Jurgens had finished his sentence. He narrowed his eyes as his demon menagerie died in waves at the hands of the stupefied angels and Moonie resistance. Michael had employed his wings like giant blades as he spun and sliced the demon horde like the impotent, brainless predators from which they were cloned. Cyd sliced and diced for a few seconds, then disappeared. To obviously hide. He replayed the recording, witnessing Cyd's cowardice again, and again.

Jurgens grinned with a childish *I know something you don't* expression.

Samuel refused the bait. "Accelerate the extraction countdown for the clones. Let Michael and the others fight themselves while we locate our quarry and walk unopposed through that heavenly door."

Jurgens stepped forward. "You don't understand. The recording played in real time is deceiving. The satellite camera records thirty-two images per second. Per second." He let the factor sink in. "Replay a small slice, study each micro-second, and tell me that is not the most amazing thing."

Samuel's fingers curled tight. Jurgens' Adam's apple bobbed in his throat like bait for his growing rage. "Provide that for me, Jurgens. Provide for your master."

Jurgens arched his brows and recoiled. His hands began to swipe frantically at holo screens popping up at his face. "I sent the file, the speeds reduced to allow you to see—" Jurgens stepped back. "You see everything, master. I am but your conduit."

"Hmm." Samuel narrowed his eyes as his jaw worked to scroll through the pictures inches from his face. The pile of dead or dying animal demons appeared to increase every few frames. A skunk baring sharp teeth was covered by a gutted wolverine only to be blanketed by two masked raccoons. Samuel restarted the pictures from the beginning, sure he had missed something. He paused the scroll then zoomed in to a curved silver knife held in a bloody hand. The hand was gone in the next frame. A dead bear cub flayed open from anus to mouth had joined the pile.

Samuel relaxed his fists and sat back against his chair. He twitched his jaw to access the file and play it at normal speed. His eyes grew wider as the slaughter of demons replayed. "Someone is very fast and very skilled with Raphael's knife."

"No." Jurgens shook his head. "It's not speed you are seeing. Or not seeing. The rate of killing defies speed. Unless someone can travel faster than the speed of light. Which we know is impossible. Someone or something suspends time itself, to murder the demons, at a leisurely pace if it chooses." Jurgens snapped his fingers. "Someone is not playing by the rules of known physics."

Samuel played the recordings side by side but couldn't synchronize the spectacle. "Is this all we have?"

"The Alternate Intelligence has compiled a new algorithm for dissecting the recordings as we speak. Only one surveillance satellite had the capability to record at that speed, so it shouldn't . . ." Jurgens manipulated holo screens floating at his face then lifted a wry smile. "I just sent you two frames that might hold the answer to this enigma."

Samuel sat up and opened the file. He narrowed his eyes and studied the two frames displayed at his face. The first showed a Moonie standing over a mound of dead demons, their blood-soaked robe shredded to ribbons, a knife held in its hand, a thin tendril of blood stretching from the curved blade down to the open throat of a bobcat. A hood hid its face.

The second frame caused Samuel to swallow hard, a knot unfelt for eons. Samuel checked the recording's timestamp then swallowed another knot. He twitched his jaw. The picture zoomed in on the Moonie standing atop an even larger mound of dead demons. Blood and matted fur covered its robe, its arms spread wide open. A bloody Archangel's knife pointed toward the sky as if the Moonie knew a camera watched from above.

A bloody, war-weary expression. Platinum hair.

Cyd bared her teeth.

Samuel inhaled deep and swiped away holo screens disrupted by the hard bite of his jaw. He refreshed the screens back into view only to wave each away. Static fuzzed the holographic displays. Samuel aimed his displeasure at Jurgens.

"I said this was amazing," Jurgens said. "Our Cyd. An assassin of demons. I would have never—"

Samuel flew around his desk and grabbed Jurgens' throat, moving at a speed to rival what he had just observed. He narrowed his eyes as they bored into Jurgens' frightened face. "Decant the clones. Send the access codes to Enoch and the others. The war comes here."

Samuel pushed Jurgens out the door and waited with his back to the door. He lifted his face to the ceiling. *Long ago, I would have asked for your guidance.* He pondered the ramifications of Cyd's abilities, but the infinite permutations bludgeoned all rationality. The universe existed on a linear timeline, an unspoken rule. Events transpired and moved into the past, souls died and were reborn, lessons learned or ignored, time and again, each traveling on a singular path towards . . . towards . . . a disposition dictated only by Him.

Hesitation and ambiguity were traits of weak humans, not suited for a god just steps away from the throne. Still. Samuel rarely experienced the debilitating emotions that fenced the human flock within its self-inflicted pasture. Never. Not through war or pestilence or tragedy did he doubt himself. The metamorphosis of his adopted daughter was disconcerting and unplanned.

Samuel tugged on a desk drawer near his right hand but found it locked. His anger yanked the drawer open, splintering wood and igniting holographic alarms to flash notifications of a trespass. He swiped away the red alarms throbbing at his face and lifted an ivory-handled knife sheathed in human skin tanned with past failures. Nero, Genghis Khan, Hitler, Pol Pot, Andaya. The supple muscle of their hearts had been taken at their death and formed into a stiff scabbard for his weapon.

Samuel raised the thick blade and rotated it, studied it, letting glints of sunlight sparkle off the blade forged from a dead angel's sword. At the proper time, he would slip the blade beneath the rib cage and shove it hard into the heart, then twist, and twist, and enjoy the sweet aroma.

A moment in time to stun the heavens.

Cyd's angelic power was impotent to stop the course of a new history.

Still.

Samuel peered over his shoulder as he checked his office. He swallowed hard.

———

CYD TRAVELED THE DIRT ROAD ascending out of the crescent valley, her legs, and sandals dark with dried blood. The world was silenced of birdsong, without a breeze to brush her hair, void of the soothing sounds of waterfalls cascading far below. The utter silence was sickening.

Her throat parched, she paused to take a sip of water from a spring wetting the stone cliffs. She sniffed back tears then reached her crimson hand out to catch drips of water. Drops of water suspended in time and air. She growled, then stepped back into the timestream. The onslaught of fresh air and pleasant sounds pushed her to press her back against the cliff face. She curled her fingers as if to grip the moss-covered stone then cried.

No one had seen the massacre she had orchestrated. Nobody could blame her even if they had. She could still travel to Malibu and become a movie star. She could. No one would know.

She slid her back down the wet rock face and buried her face between her knees. She was living a nightmare. She *was* the nightmare. Maybe the airborne 3Bz had caused hallucinations? Maybe she was nothing but a Tuber existing in an immersive computer game? Maybe nothing would ever explain her existence.

Except.

Beneath her arms, hooked to the leather strap of her sandal, the googly eye of a stupid fake grasshopper stared back. Its feathers and yellow yarn pristine as a Pacific island isolated from the chaos of murdering bizarre mutant animals. Like a lucky charm.

Cyd clasped her hands and squeezed her fingers tight. "I can't do this anymore. I want out." She rocked back and forth like a child, hoping the motion would wake her from the nightmare.

A shadow covered her. A warm wind lifted sand into her face. The silence faded. The crunch of gravel. Bloody, shoeless feet appeared in her sight.

"The others are afraid of you. Some think you're one of Samuel's demons."

Cyd looked up and glared.

Michael offered his hand. "I'd like to say I know how you feel. I don't. But this war is lost without you."

Cyd softened in a vast comfort as Michael helped her up and embraced her. She sobbed against his chest. His warmth penetrated her tattered robe. She inhaled deep, calming breaths. How long had she waited for love and acceptance? Not like the barren emotions offered by her father. Adopted father. Or the lustful coupling with Zac. But the unconditional love of an angel. No, that sentiment wasn't right. The love and protectiveness of a big brother. The unbreakable bond of blood and a lost childhood.

Michael held her tight and shot straight into the stratosphere. Continents and clouds swirled beneath them as he flew towards the burning sun. He offered a warning before diving toward the deserts of the Middle East, gliding over the Great Pyramids and the mighty Nile until they shot up again and soared over the dense jungles of the African continent, the friction and wind tearing the rat's nest of clothing off their bodies. Flying over farmland and busy cities, then accompanying broad-winged cranes shooting the gap between Everest and K2, then gliding inches above the cobalt water of the Pacific Ocean, letting the spray of endless rolling waves wash them clean of the blood of battle. They hovered above the gentle eruptions of Hawaii's Mauna Loa volcano and allowed the heat and spectacle to dry their bodies and feathers. Michael hurtled upward, powerful strokes of his wings defying air and gravity, until they floated at the edge of space.

"Thank you for this," Cyd whispered into his ear.

"Do you see it?" Michael said. He pointed at the sun. "The gold ring of His power aimed straight for us."

"They hate me, huh?" Cyd said. "Save their sorry asses and farms, and they think I'm the enemy."

Michael chuckled. "Gabriel started the rumor. He was so pissed I dropped him from up here that he needed to save face." Michael closed his eyes and bathed in the light.

Cyd frowned at his quiet acceptance but followed his lead and allowed the light to irradiate, answer her questions, cast doubt aside, direct her back onto the path of an inevitable destiny. Cyd snapped her fingers. The slow, synchronized movement of the vast, limitless universe paused. Clouds of swirling plasma halted. Michael floated, frozen in time.

Cyd dared escape from Michael's embrace. She twisted his arm and slid out from beneath his wing. Free of restraint, she gazed down at an agonizing and inevitable death when time and gravity restarted. If it restarted. Still. The incongruity of time and space beckoned only one question from Cyd.

Why me?

Images flooded her mind. A newborn baby cried with its birth near a drought-stricken river. A sickly old woman squeezed her husband's hand in the final moments of her life. Emaciated children suffered blistering winds in a fruitless struggle to survive. A young family braved the dangerous torrent of a swollen river attempting to flee a warring landscape. Each image pummeled Cyd as if she too had joined their struggles for survival.

Why not?

Cyd closed her eyes and groaned silently. The flippant response floated like a white balloon tied to a tiny thread, its end just out of her reach. She gazed down at the motionless world suspended below her feet. A chaotic world she had tried to understand but failed. A world she escaped in the mind-numbing realm of 3Bz, of the simplistic world of Yellowstone with its limitless opportunities to experience the compassion hidden inside her soul.

Images of humanity's misery continued to flash through her mind. Helpless people. Suffering children. A civilization demonizing the very world on which it had thrived for millennia. A species murdering itself.

Cyd swallowed but found no spittle. She sucked in a gulp of air yet found no oxygen. Swirls of plasma churned from the distant sun, and yet time had not restarted. She floated about Michael, moving across his chest, stroking the stiff feathers on his wings, studying their intricate texture. She moved up beneath his wing and found the position he would expect when time started. She stroked his hairless face. Her protector. Her brother.

Her Angel.

Cyd lifted the corner of her mouth and nodded. A golden wave of plasma erupted from the sun, a heavenly volcano firing waves of destruction toward the world suspended at her feet. An unimagined catastrophe, an onslaught that Archangels and demons were powerless to stop. Samuel would have contingencies waiting at his fingertips, even as the world burned in the golden light. His Arkoff Ports rendered useless, his wealth impotent, his influence isolated and humiliated. Unless . . .

She realized what she must do.

Alpha and omega. The first and last.

Close.

Cyd stared at the sun, an act to incinerate her eyes. That single word of God was as clear as her own voice. Not the first and last. The beginning at the end. She was just the first to usher in a new beginning emerging from the end of the world. The Moonies, the angelic farmers, Seth and Serah, all players critical for a new beginning.

A new world Samuel would attempt to rule.

Cyd snapped her fingers and let gravity pull her from beneath Michael's wing like a rock dropped from a cliff. She gazed at the brilliance of the Archangel bathed in golden light, his face wrinkled and frozen by her sudden suicidal act. Michael turned his body and aimed at her. She snapped her fingers again, freezing Michael in time and space.

Her brother hung suspended in space and reality, an unequivocal lifeline if she needed one.

Wind and air brushed her face as the blue planet rushed up. Cyd snapped her fingers, and gravity paused.

Suspended above the unspoiled Yellowstone Caldera, Cyd eyed her home.

And the inevitable confrontation with Lucifer.

CHAPTER EIGHTEEN

MICHAEL STARED AT HIS EMPTY hands as the continents drifted beneath his feet. Why had Cyd abandoned him and the protection of his wings? He considered his sister, her plight as the daughter of the devil. Prisons came in many forms. His own had been lonely, sterile, governed by faceless monsters, expectations rigorously enforced, but a chance at freedom always accompanied his next great escape plan.

Cyd rarely talked about her prison, but Michael surmised her upbringing was a prison unlike anything he might imagine. Isolated within nature's royal beauty with an evil egomaniac playing pseudo father figure, Samuel's parental guidance guiding her drug use, tempting her with carrots of freedom only to feed the vegetable to the rats gnawing at her psyche. Her resentment and hatred of Samuel simmered year after year, quite unlike Michael's disdain for the Fallen one. Cyd carried all the baggage of a tormented, abused child, caging her feelings, no mother to comfort her, no brother to confide in, only to have her concept of the world explode. Cyd would want answers, maybe revenge. Probably both.

And how did Samuel know about the cluster of children born in Arco, the angels, and Cyd? Did he know a second son had been delivered to the world? Was he helped by someone? But those questions were for the Fisherman to deal with.

Michael gazed down at wispy cloud formations and churning

storms blanketing the Atlantic Ocean. Cyd would go home. Back to her prison. Looking to permanently close the door on her old life. The immaculate beauty of the universe waited as a backdrop while Michael seethed with his impotence, his miscalculations. His sister wasn't ready, wasn't aware, wasn't versed in the ways of the Lord, or the wicked sin of Lucifer. She reeked of the impetuous innocence of youth. Acted on impulses of naivety. Confused by a sudden abundance of maturity, rattled by an infinite multitude of choices, empowered by her destiny, and yet she remained a silly human teenager. Her sarcastic retorts to his edicts. Her reckless abandonment of his winged embrace. She was . . . his sister.

And he . . . loved her.

And he would dive down into the gates of hell to find her.

Michael lashed out with his fist. Fucking Cyd. She was lost and alone after she dropped from his arms and . . . and she could be anywhere. Fucking Cyd. He kicked and screamed like a petulant child as the sprawl of bright city lights drifted beneath his feet. Bucharest, maybe Berlin.

Currents.

Michael spread his mighty wings and snarled at the city lights below. Time to show the faithless true retribution. Let them experience an Archangel's anger. Fire and flame might blacken his wings, but his wrath would rain down on the godless monsters.

Currents.

"That shithole waits for my vengeance."

Currents.

"No, no, no. Don't talk like you don't understand me."

And mend.

He turned away from the city lights and flapped his wings, anger stemming in his throat, then dove towards the planet. She could be back home by now.

Where Samuel waited and schemed.

———

CYD SWIPED AT THE STREAM of tears falling down her cheeks, then twisted another padlock to break open. She held the rickety chicken wire door open as Inky, Stinky, and Dinky scurried past her. The raccoons bolted straight for the pole barn that stored bags of animal food.

Fucking Zac. He hadn't fed the animals for days. The whitetail deer and elk had gnawed on the fenceposts.

She snapped the lock on Bobbett's cage, but the bobcat didn't move. Rondo's enclosure across the aisle was empty. Bobbett huddled inside a faux timber cave, panting, her eyes glossy and unfocused. Cyd opened the gate and stepped in. The water dish sat dry, the rim crusted with alkaline. Scat riddled the fence. Bile rose into her throat. Cyd snapped her fingers and froze the passing of time. She picked up the bobcat and carried it to a leaky hose bib that would drip water.

She placed the animal on a puddle beneath the spout and looked around. The zoo was nothing more than a mirage. To entertain her. To keep her occupied. And with no water. No food. Just pain. Just suffering.

She split locks and opened gates. Sheba the mountain lion was gone. Good for her. The zoo was closed. Permanently. Yellowstone was closed. For eternity. She looked around the hotel and parking lot expecting to see a cyborg or maybe hotel staff. It appeared both had already gotten the memo. The devil was here. She could feel him watching her.

She stormed inside, crossing the lobby and into the restaurant with empty tables holding upturned chairs. After today, only ghosts would be allowed to dine at the Yellowstone Inn restaurant. She shouted for service. The knife dangled in her hand, nervously tapping the clean, soft pelts. Cyd suspended time, walked into a camera angle she knew Samuel used to survey the room, and raised her arms in surrender. She snapped time on.

"Oh, Daddy! I'm home!" she shouted. "And now you have to deal with me."

Cyd paced the perimeter of the big room, checking the areas beyond the windows where a platoon of cyborgs might appear. Three rapid beeps sounded. She froze. Magnetic door locks clicked. The windows darkened as if a switch had been thrown. Security glass, impregnable and fireproof. Air vents shuttered. A television monitor recessed in river rock above the woodburning fireplace flickered with a single red dot in the center. Daddy's eye.

"Welcome home, Cyd," Samuel said using the soundbar beneath

the television monitor. "I wasn't expecting you so soon. You tripped the alarms. It'll take a few moments to reset."

"Really? You want to keep up that charade?" Cyd snapped her fingers. The room remained no different as she walked around the restaurant flicking stationary dust motes suspended in the glow of hydrogen light bulbs. She snapped her fingers to the grating chuckle of Samuel's voice.

"The remodel that you hated ten years ago." Samuel said. "You whined like the spoiled bitch you are. The security enhancements invisible with your silly predictable exuberance at having your own zoo. Snap time all you want. You'll spend eternity in that room."

Cyd lowered her head and nodded. "I remember. Did you know back then . . . ?"

"That you were one of His? Please . . . pulling you from Michael's arms was the one of the best days of my life. The little fuck tried to stop me. Can you believe that? A fucking toddler. Destined for the labs and still screaming like a pissy wildcat."

"And now you're here," Cyd said. "In this moment. At this place. And about to die."

Cyd snapped her fingers. The dark cavernous room weighed in the surreal, a dated spectacle she remembered for gobbling oatmeal breakfasts or omelets, a safe location to escape the responsibilities of the zoo or the uncomfortable aura of Samuel. Cyd slumped into a chair. Her childhood had been both lonely, and confined, manipulated by the power of money or the poverty of others.

Cyd stared up at the ceiling and stretched her neck, cracking ligaments, and bone. A weariness fogged her thoughts. The crush of eternal silence restarted time again.

"You just gonna leave me here?" Cyd said. She pushed her lower lip out in a pout. "I'll leave time on hold, and you'll never get what you want."

"That's a stalemate. No one likes those. Not you, me, or your benevolent master," Samuel said. A squirrel or raccoon scurried through the crawlspace above the front door.

Cyd thought about the statement. For once, Samuel didn't lie. "So come down for some lunch, and we can settle it."

Samuel chuckled. "Your life was always such a waste, Cyd. Drugs, sex, feeding the little kitties as penance. And now you've found Him. Or should I say He found you. How much faith do you have in Him?"

"I am the alpha and omega. That is enough," Cyd said.

"Really?" Samuel chuckled. "Then how do we settle this? Your faith against my technology? On a neutral playing field?"

Samuel's challenge made her swallow hard. Her mouth went dry. She snapped time off and paced the room, checking the doors with her blade or the security windows with the hard knock of her knuckles. Her own words haunted her. Technology had always won out over faith. People had always demanded it. She chewed her lower lip. The Moonies had no technology, yet they had won a benefactor, their freedom, a guardian of their faith. And Seth, he had even less, and he would grow into a fine man, a good leader, a faithful husband. Faith had many advantages. With one true God.

And the Archangel Cyd would prove it. She snapped her fingers.

"Open these doors, Daddy," Cyd said. "Time for a family reunion."

"Excellent. Come to my office so we can discuss the ground rules," Samuel said. "I'll make preparations while you find a way out." He chuckled loudly. "Don't be late. Time is a-ticking."

———

GREAT NUMBERS OF ELK MIXED with vast herds of buffalo to stampede down grassy slopes and into the grasslands surrounding dense forests. Even swollen rivers were no match for the huge numbers braving the dangerous water. Deer ran and leapt across abandoned highways to flee with rabbits and rodents. Huge formations of honking geese aimed south towards the high desert. Eagles, osprey, and hawks abandoned ancient rivalries to join ducks and waterfowl. All manner of forest creatures scurried from the dormant geysers of the Yellowstone Caldera.

Michael soared above the exodus of animals. The land swarmed with panicked wildlife. A warning from the Fisherman.

Flee or die.

Michael landed in the center of the abandoned arena. Polished black ravens, broad-chested mountain bluebirds, tiny redheaded sparrows escaped the protection of dense pine forests, squawking their warnings to flee. Michael picked up his discarded steel bar half buried in soil teeming with black beetles, spiders, columns of black carpenter ants. The smallest of His creatures also warned by the Fisherman. The ground vibrated beneath his feet.

The Old Faithful Inn waited as a haunted forest skeleton. Cyd's prison, no different than his own.

A conspiracy of crows erupted from between the gabled pole barns he recognized as his prison. He twirled and spun the bar like a marching band drum leader and aimed for the barn to stand at the open door for a look inside. His nostrils flared. Dark shadows and the stench of angel crap wafted like ghosts in the abandoned building. Noisy machinery clicked and whirred and tickled foggy memories of his drugged imprisonment.

The pole barns shielded behemoth mechanical equipment spinning huge fan blades. Warm air spewed the scent of his brethren. Michael walked and kicked the plastic trash that had collected against the equipment curbs, sniffing, letting the incongruent scent lead him. Like a viper concealed in a subterranean pit, the dormant Old Faithful hissed and belched a faint plume of steam.

Michael followed his nose to another barn. The doors spread open with his arrival, as if it were an invitation, or a trap. A tiny eight-by-eight pillar stood in the center, a shaft made of concrete with a single door and waiting like a beacon.

As if with a mind of their own, his wings trembled.

CHAPTER NINETEEN

THROUGH THE HEAVY METAL DOOR and down six flights of concrete stairs, Michael found an oblong vestibule. The scent he followed was muted, the dim light of a single bulb above his head. A polished black door at the opposite end of the vestibule was a mirror image of the rusty black basalt walls, almost invisible, the frame melded into the stone as if it were forged from hot lava. Michael stood back and bit his lower lip. No knob, no hinges, nothing to wedge a finger into or even a sharp blade, and yet hidden behind it waited Samuel's true intentions.

Seth's voice scoffed in his head. *You're an angel, ain't ya?* The boy's vulnerable innocence and simplistic approach to impediments made Michael nod and step forward to simply knock three times.

The heavy slab depressed, and the door slid open, a mechanism similar to the white door of his childhood prison cell. A rush of moist warm air flew in his face. He stepped across the threshold. He stiffened as halogen floodlights brightened one by one down a seemingly endless cavern. An ancient lava tube of immense dimensions. Hung with monofilament cords, each light fixture illuminated a pair of three-meter-tall cylinders filled with a clear, viscous fluid boiling with air bubbles. Michael gripped the piece of rebar, but the stiff iron suddenly felt inadequate.

Michael took three slow steps to be faced by a frail little man wearing a grey lab coat stained with greasy food residue. Blocking his path, the skeleton of a man had appeared with deceptive silence. A perfectly bald head, bloodshot eyes with dilated pupils, black like a servant of Lucifer. The man patted Michael's chest with a bony hand and checked him up and down. He stepped back and tapped his chin with a single finger and appraised Michael as if he wore a dress designed for scrutinization in a Paris fashion show.

"I have been expecting you," the little man said. "My Lord said you would want to witness the birthing day."

Michael looked past the man. A single human body resided in each vat, naked, fetal, and floating among a garble of feeding tubes and suspension wires. The rush of rising air bubbles shrouded their faces, their sex, their purpose. Michael tapped one of the clear cylinders with the pointed tip of the steel rod.

Thirty yards down the corridor, an eruption of liquid sprayed across the floor, expelling fluid like a placenta. A naked body slid across the polished floor. What monstrosity had the vat contained? Another mutated animal like he had battled in the arena above, or a monstrous abomination like those that had attacked the Moonie enclave, or something even more sinister? Samuel's corruption knew no bounds. Five yards away, another vat split to spew fluid and flesh.

"Yes. Yes. Beautiful. This will please him. But you are incomplete. We just need to insert a port." The man eyed Michael's neck as he reached into the breast pocket on his black smock. He retrieved a medical scalpel and removed the thin paper sheath. The man reached the scalpel towards Michael's neck.

Michael snatched the man's wrist in a tight grip. The old man winced, his bones close to snapping like dry twigs.

Michael flicked his chin down the corridor. "What is all this?"

The man yanked on his hand, attempting to get free. "You need a port. Samuel commands his legionnaires wear a port."

Another spew of liquid sounded down the shadowed corridor.

Michael's muscles tensed. "And if I receive the gift of a port?"

The old man widened his eyes and checked the corridor behind him. He pulled at Michael's restraint. "All new children need direction. Samuel's fallen angels are awakening."

Another vat spewed its contents.

He followed the odd man deeper into the endless lava tube. The crazy old man worked furiously at the neck of a birthed monstrosity. He placed a flesh-colored dermal patch near a short incision oozing blood, micro filaments whipped wildly until finding the blood, then it inserted itself beneath the skin and hid like a trapdoor spider, weaving its tentacles deeper until closing the wound to leave an oblong scar as a port.

He stared at a reflection of himself. His nose, lips, ears. The eternally white skin. A shell without a soul.

Michael lifted the old man's chin with his spear but withheld the death thrust. "What is this?"

The little man cackled. "It's you. Thousands of you. Thousands of Raphael. Gabriel and Uriel, too. And they're hatching just like he said they would."

"Is that what Samuel believes? His clone army will lead him to the throne of heaven?"

"Yes. No. No. You don't understand. My children are born with identical chromosomes of the originals. Their mitochondrial DNA will allow the surrogates to locate the prize—God's second son. They will flock to him like salmon returning to spawn. No, that isn't right. Like moths. Hardwired to return to the eternal light. Yes. Yes. All of them moths."

Was the old man demented? Perhaps, but Samuel wasn't. How did Lucifer know of Seth's arrival? Was this the reason Michael escaped prison and fled to the Craters of the Moon? Because of Seth?

Michael bared his teeth and stooped to squeeze the clone's slick throat. The windpipe cracked in his angry grip. It choked and gagged, its black eyes rolled back into its head. A piece of dead meat. He lifted his nostrils to smell the soul of the dead clone. Soulless.

"The Arkoff Ports. Why do you need to . . ."

The old man stepped back. "To provide the soulless a surrogate soul. For the fallen acolytes of Lucifer to inhabit. Azazel, Beelzebub. Thousands wait in consciousness transfer chairs across the planet to inhabit hundreds of Michaels. And Gabriels. And Raphaels. And with God's second son as a bargaining chip, Lucifer will walk into heaven."

An army of demons masquerading as righteous angels of God. The concept was almost ridiculous. Almost. The ramifications were profound. A plague of demons let loose on the world to suck the last whispers of hope from people surviving the coming apocalypse. His destruction approached from the star unimpeded, at the speed of light. The world would truly descend into a living hell, one ruled by Samuel. Another vat splashed open. Then another.

Michael looked at his meager weapon and squeezed the metal hard. He could spend eternity battling the clones and . . .

Another splash sounded.

Michael grabbed the old man by the arm and led him down the hall to a clone of a naked Gabriel writhing on the floor. The imitation rolled over to stretch its legs and flex its hands, its black eyes slowly filtered into a milky shade of grey. An Arkoff Port installed beneath its ear caused Michael to lean down and study the abomination. He frowned. Seth or Serah or even Cyd might never see the difference. Until too late. The clones would wreak chaos.

"It's getting accustomed to its new body," the old man said. "And look . . . the wings are emerging. They will be formidable soldiers in the War of Ascension."

A War of Ascension. The final battle. Samuel's gambit. A war Michael could not win against so many just like him.

Another vat splashed open. Raphael, Gabriel, and the others had not joined this battle. Had the Father ordered them to other lands? Why was he abandoned to fight alone against so many? Determined to slay Samuel, even Cyd would not arrive to help.

Currents. Michael found himself lost in a swirling back eddy of indecision. A slipstream of ignorance dragged on him. He had no other choice but to fight, with every ounce of his strength, every second of his life, until he was unable to lift his measly weapon.

The stone beneath his feet rumbled. Vats spewed their contents. The polished floor would run deep with blood. His own blood.

JURGENS RUSHED INTO SAMUEL'S OFFICE. He sucked in air until he caught his breath.

"Michael has found our rookery," he said.

Relaxed in the consciousness transfer recliner, Samuel continued to swipe at the holo screens flashing all about his face. "As he was destined to. But even the great Archangel will pause at the magnitude of the forces rising against him. I can see his face now. Shock and awe. His face whiter than white, impotence wrinkling his expression." Samuel chuckled and turned off the screens.

"The security AI hasn't located Cyd, but I'm sure it's only a matter of time."

Samuel plugged a tiny fiber-optic cord into his neck port. His eyes blinked rapidly as his head twitched to the side. "She's probably right outside that door. Debating whether to step over the threshold and face her dearest Daddy." The lighting dimmed. Cold air spewed from the vents. Samuel shimmied deeper into the consciousness transfer couch. "I'm going to take Rondo for a ride."

Jurgens loomed over Samuel. "Right now? On the eve of our victory."

Samuel gripped Jurgens wrist and squeezed, harder and harder until the man cringed, and his legs buckled. "There will be no victory unless Cyd is taken off the chessboard." He glanced at a holo-screen. "You have my instructions. Do not disobey them. No matter what." Samuel twitched his jaw then smirked. "I believe His white queen has arrived."

Samuel executed the preset commands to initiate transit of his consciousness into the wolf. He felt the muscles and nerves of his aged body relax. He smiled with the thrill of transcending untainted dimensions. The animal would soon be unworthy of the god he would become. Brief slivers of memory flashed, His endless realm, the power of turning thought to reality, the ultimate orgasm, out of his reach since before time, but only for a few more moments.

Samuel's acolytes would search the world and locate His second child hidden from him. And the boy would escort them to the Promised Land, prodded by the sharp point of his blade.

A cavalcade of scents bludgeoned his senses. Pine. Sulfur. Aspen. The nuanced mix was intoxicating. He shook his head to clear the buzzing of an insect flittering around his ear. He licked his dry paw. Samuel laughed. The odd effort caused him to cough and hack hair out of his dry throat. He stood and searched his surroundings. Exactly as planned. He trotted to a spring bubbling up in a grove of thick willows and lapped cold clear water as he watched insect larvae scurry from his long tongue.

Samuel jerked his head up with the yowling of a wolf pack miles away. He leered as best as his elongated jowls would allow. New acolytes.

He trotted across a lush meadow reeking of skunk and racoon scat, his nose held low and searching for the one scent that ensured victory. He scrambled over an escarpment of basalt crusted with deep orange lichen, up to a ridge overlooking a long narrow valley divided by a spring creek meandering across the grassy tundra. A huge herd of elk grazed on the tenderest of grass shoots.

A flash of movement caught his attention, and he narrowed his eyes. A newborn elk calf wobbled on unsteady legs as the mother grazed a few yards away. The aroma of placental fluid and blood summoned him to an easy kill.

Maybe he would partake in the blood of human children after dealing with Cyd. He licked his lips. Maybe he would partake in the blood of angel children. Yes, he would. He could taste the warm, tangy blood of his adopted daughter even now.

Saliva dripped from his jowls.

CYD STOOD OVER SAMUEL, HER silver blade twitching nervously inches above his throat. She would end the torment of Satan for an eternity. End the misery of billions with just a quick stroke. Reclined in the consciousness transfer chair, Samuel was helpless.

She pulled the blade back. Helpless and unafraid. Too easy. The serpent had escaped, abandoned his body. This was too easy for the trickster. Even pausing the tick of time, she might search for millennia before she found his trail. He was playing with her even now.

She screamed to vent her frustration.

Jurgens waited motionless inside the office wall filled with data monitors. She eased next to him and curled her lip. His perspiration reeked of 3Bz. She checked the screens one by one until finding one with biometric data frozen in time. Pushing her face closer, the data seemed to reflect two separate individuals.

She looked back at Samuel and smiled. High blood pressure and an erratic EKG suggested one was Samuel's. The other's rapid heart rate and higher body temperature suggested an animal. A predator. Samuel had escaped into Rondo. Just like the snake he was.

She took the blade and cut the Arkoff Port out of Jurgens neck. The stagnant blood flow reeked of 3Bz. She snapped her fingers as she pressed the blade's sharp point up into Jurgens' chin. "You really need to get a better security system."

Jurgens stuttered with a feeble response then slapped a hand onto his wound.

"Next time I'll cut something," Cyd threatened. "He's riding in Rondo, isn't he?"

"Well . . . well . . . that was his . . . plan," Jurgens stammered.

Cyd snapped her fingers. A plan to ride out the battle for heaven in the form of a wolf. Disguised as a snake, maybe, but not a wolf. She paced the large room, staring at Samuel's flabby jowls, his thin lips, the bulbous blossom of a nose spiderwebbed by deceit, a man unsentenced for crimes spanning thousands of years. She was missing something, but time was on her side. Time.

She snapped her fingers.

"Why don't I slit his throat and save us all the aggravation?" Cyd said.

Jurgens recoiled. "You can't . . . I mean, the AI protocols will automatically relay his consciousness to another body. He said you would miss your only chance for revenge." Jurgens pointed at a recliner chair pushed tight against the wall. "He said you'd want to find him. But you'll need an Arkoff Port."

"Nice. Stick my consciousness into a fucking mouse and let him eat me."

Jurgens snorted. "I hadn't thought of that. But he selected Sheba for you."

Cyd frowned. Even without a body, Samuel continued to manipulate and dictate the game. And yet she was compelled to play on. She turned her face up to the ceiling and closed her eyes, picturing herself standing on a bridge intending to jump, just as the old Fisherman must have seen her. His gentle words, His presence, calling her down.

I will hunt him down. If you're not okay with that, then . . .

The floor buckled beneath her feet. Not as an answer but a warning. The war for heaven raged beneath her feet and Michael was all alone. Time was but paused. She clicked her fingers. Jurgens arched his eyebrows, begging for an answer.

She sat in the recliner and waited as Jurgens approached her with a tiny scalpel. An impotent weapon against time. He extracted a bean-sized module from a clear package, a tiny device that had allowed Samuel to achieve the ultimate goal—dominion over man.

"What happens if Rondo dies?"

Jurgens chuckled. "He comes back to his body, I think. We haven't even considered that scenario."

She shuttered her eyes. Samuel's arrogance was appalling. Her foolishness was no less. And she was a fool, baited to be a hero. The answer waited with the snap of her fingers.

She rose from the chair and loomed over Samuel. She stared at an entity without a heartbeat, a face of stone, a false father, a usurper of heaven, a malevolent demon steps away from victory.

Cyd felt nothing as the tip of her knife slid easily through cartilage and ligaments and up into the man's brainstem.

CHAPTER TWENTY

THE ROAR OF SPLITTING VATS splashing clones over the floor soon mimicked the chaotic rush of a stream swollen with spring runoff. Embryonic fluid tinted red with blood washed Michael's feet as he found his way to the next hatchling.

The demons gained strength and awareness with every second of his hesitation. A freshly hatched clone sat slumped against the base of its vat and swiped at its pale face. Michael looked down at the easy kill and stabbed the steel rod into the clone's brain. A hundred, a thousand, the bloody hell of slaughter made Michael scream.

And advertised his presence to a multitude of demons who turned their scattered attention towards him. Naked angels leered with revenge.

The numbers of clones was overwhelming. The battle was futile. Retreat, and maybe find salvation with another course of action.

A burst of fresh air from a vent over his head cooled his angry thoughts. The Fisherman positioned his chess pieces intimately, moved each with omnipotent precision, and yet placed him inside this underground lava tube, at this exact time. To find defeat? Inconceivable.

The old man rushed past him to check another vat blaring an alarm to signal an oncoming birth a few yards away. Michael should simply kill the attendant, but the frail old man did little but check data on a holo screen floating near his face. His assistance to the demons was inconsequential, gathering useless information for Samuel to review. He wiped his nose and snarled at the blood staining the back of his hand. A lucky punch from a demon Raphael.

Why am I here? Precisely at the birth of demons designed to destroy You?

The old man swiped screens as he loomed over a facsimile of Uriel slapping embryonic fluid from its face. The sneakers and trousers worn by the old man had wicked copious bloody fluid from the floor. The man squeezed his legs together tightly, as if needing to use a toilet.

Michael stabbed his staff into the brain of a freshly spewed newborn and twisted, blending its brain matter with his disgust. An expression of horror on the man's face quickly softened with the splash of another birth far down the corridor. The man mumbled and aimed for the new birth. Michael used his weapon like a tollgate to stop the odd man.

"Why do you help Samuel?" Michael said.

The old man looked beyond the steel barrier, his eyes intent on finding the demon. "These are my children. I have been raising them for . . ." He gazed up at Michael. "For as long as you."

"You've been down here for fifteen years?"

"Of course. They grew like you did. Their muscles gained strength like yours did. Their brain activity spiked with your escape. They are you, Michael. Down to the last chromosome."

Currents.

The old man grabbed the blood-stained rebar to lift Michael's restriction on his movement. Fifty yards down the corridor, a crowd of demons huddled to conspire beneath an overhead light, signaling time was running out. The demons conspired to find their escape. Fresh air spewing from another vent above his head pollinated an idea. He pushed the old man back.

"You say your children are just like me?" Michael said. He grabbed the man and yanked him back towards the main door. "Show me how your children have lived. How did they breathe and eat? I find this chapter of my life fascinating."

The old man stuttered and stumbled as Michael checked the maze of spiral ductwork hanging from the stone overhead, then eyed the bubbles of lifegiving air swirling through countless vats of the unhatched. The old man quit resisting as he was pulled along. "You were six years old when you and the others were found. Mr. Arkoff spent trillions on farming children with DNA the others provided. I protested with the redundancy of so few. Gabriel and Uriel and the others provided an inadequate sampling for mass production. But your immunities opened the floodgates of knowledge to perfect all the clones."

"That is fascinating. Can you show me the equipment room and how you feed air and food into the birthing tubes?" Michael said.

The man's expression changed into utter joy, one of a small child showing off a living room fort, or an A-plus on a school exam, and he hurried to lead them around corner after corner in the shadowed cavern. The increasing frequency of vats cracking open to splash fluid and meat over the floor played like an odd, canned melody.

The man waved his hand in front of a tiny red biosensor embedded in the basalt, a concealed device Michael might have never found. A door whooshed open with fresh cold air. A warehouse-sized cavern occupied by air handlers equal to railcars hummed and buzzed with air flow. Tall control boards blinked with red and green diodes like Christmas trees. Michael pulled the old man inside and tilted his face, expecting an explanation. The door whooshed shut.

The old man stammered with air flow requirements, balanced nutrients, fluid consistency. Michael cocked his ear towards the deep rumbling of an unruly mob crowding the corridor outside the door. Time was up. Time was key. His staff pressed against the old man's chest to prevent the man's attempt to flee. Samuel's acolyte would serve a greater good. Michael kissed him square on the lips, pushing spittle into the man's mouth.

I kill myself with everything I say and do. And maybe these Raphaels' and Uriels' and Gabriels'.

The man drew back, his black eyes horrified and confused. His throat bobbed with spasms. Capillaries in the whites of his eyes exploded.

Michael gripped the man's shoulder. "May your soul find His eternal kingdom for your sacrifice."

The man dropped to the floor with epileptic convulsions, blood trickling from his nose. Michael tore loose a wide section of galvanized spiral duct. Fresh air scented in pine and freedom flooded the room. The breach of pressurized air flow went unnoticed by the gigantic air-handler.

He lifted the body and snapped brittle bones, shoving it to fit into the tight spiral ductwork. The violent rush of air quickened the man's death. Eyes dripping blood, the man reached out with a feeble hand. Michael held the hand and nodded as he used his staff to slice open the man's chest, then the femoral artery. Blood and fluids flew into the fan blades distributing the air.

Sucked into the massive metal blades, the body disappeared.

The incessant banging on the door a few feet away was haunting. Moloch's taunting voice called for him to come out and play. Michael's hand twitched, ready to open the door. He would be overwhelmed by their numbers. Defeated before the battle had begun.

Michael sat on an orange mop bucket and leaned his staff against the rock. Clones born with his DNA, his immune system, his physical prowess, his wings, and birthed to rip out his throat. Born with the same impeccable immunity to a myriad of diseases that had been injected into his arms, or that he'd been forced to inhale, then suffer, and survive, only to be introduced to another plague. One or two might be fought off, but a combination of over fifty deadly pathogens, all at once, should prove lethal—he hoped.

The door twisted and buckled in its frame with the clones' relentless assault. A rumble buckled the concrete beneath his feet. Pebbles and dust rained down from the rock ceiling, to be sucked into gaps torn from the duct. Michael looked up at the diffuser blowing cool air and sniffed. The aroma of demon souls fleeing back to Hell fouled the fresh air. Or they might rise, seek forgiveness from the Father. Finding none, each would roam the planet to infect others with their bitterness. Just as Samuel did.

The floor lifted in a violent heave of stone, sending Michael tumbling against the door. The concrete rumbled beneath his prone body like an approaching locomotive. The empty mop bucket rolled back into a dark corner as if to hide.

He stood and roared at heaven, "What are you telling me, Father?"

Let's go, son. We have line to mend.

Michael held on as a horrendous tremor lifted the floor, shattering ten inches of steel and concrete. The stone floor sank into a depression two feet deep. He eyed the door and thought of the murdered old demon wedged into the duct crumpled by the tremors.

Fight his way out, through thousands of cloned angels? Perhaps the old demon had been the fortunate one.

Michael picked up the staff, and with two fingers, he tweezed the blunted metal tip into a sharp point.

The floor surged beneath his feet again as pebbles and dirt showered him from above. He rolled his shoulders like a fighter then punched the air like a shadow boxer. His death would be glorious. His death rewarded by a treasured place at the Fisherman's side.

A silly death. Needless. A martyr's death claimed by—

The floor rolled again, snapping thick slabs of concrete, exposing rusty rebar to twist into teeth for a hungry maw. Scorching hot air flew up from the dark tube. Michael sidestepped the opening and pressed his body against the rock wall. Hell would devour him, and the clones.

Simple. And naïve.

CHAPTER TWENTY-ONE

THE NAUSEATING PERCEPTION OF CORKSCREWING through an infinite black hole caused Cyd to squeeze her eyes shut. She clenched her teeth and thought to snap her fingers to end the miserable sensation, but the sickening rollercoaster ride only quickened. The passing of time continued.

The immense darkness in her mind slowly gained a faint kaleidoscopic light, its intensity building until bludgeoning her senses as the fall eased. She dared a quick peek as the vertigo subsided. A cool cave steeped in dark shadows. A cavalcade of abhorrent stenches assaulted her—rotting animal bones, feces, burning urine, and an unfamiliar musk. The scuttle of a rodent made her cock her head towards a labyrinth of volcanic rock.

She yawned as if waking from a nap and stretched her legs. Four long legs covered in soft fur. Oh. My. Heck. She was truly inside Sheba. All her thoughts, emotions, and senses dwelled inside a mountain lion.

She bumped her head on the low rock ceiling as a wave of panic took her. She scrambled to the cave entrance on unsteady legs and leapt off a ledge into a thick bramble of scrub oak, then scrambled out of the brush like a house cat escaping a miscalculated fall into a fish-filled aquarium. She crouched and viewed the burnt remnants of a forest. Insects flittered over tall shoots of grass and aspen saplings.

A glint of sun knifed bright swords of light through the misty new growth. The beautiful gift of a benevolent God.

A crack of deadfall lifted her head, and she searched her surroundings with keen eyesight. She eyed a marmot attempting to lure a mate by dancing a funny jig atop an escarpment of volcanic rock.

Her memories gained traction as she tried to recall why she, Cyd, was here, in this strange body, in this exact moment. A moment in time she could have easily suspended. The consciousness transfer dropped its final load as Cyd realized what she was.

A four-legged animal. A cougar. A predator requiring stealth and lightning quickness to survive.

And at the mercy of Samuel's intentions.

The distant howls of wolves raised her head. Her body tensed. She cocked her ears and searched for danger, thankful Sheba's innate instincts of survival overrode her muddled response to potential danger. She wrinkled her nose at an odd stench oiled on her rear haunches then walked silently to a tree stump to rub off the pungent smell. She shimmied both sides of her rump against the rough bark. The sensation was glorious, a massage by magical hands.

A snorting snicker.

Cyd crouched and searched for the source. She wrinkled her nose at a familiar scent. Rondo beamed beady eyes from behind a garbled jam of deadfall. The wolf was at least fifty pounds heavier than her emaciated body. No doubt Samuel had starved Sheba in preparation for their encounter, though she couldn't remember reading of confrontations between cougars and wolves in the park.

Rondo stepped forward and lowered his head. The hackle on his neck rose, and he narrowed his eyes. A swelling of anger made her charge, sprinting ten yards with long leaps. She snarled and leapt, aiming her open jaws for the neck beneath Rondo's collar.

The wolf sidestepped the attack and circled back. She hissed and swiped her long claws at his face. Rondo's canine teeth drooled thick saliva. He lunged. She jumped over him with ease and swiped her claw across his hindquarters. Rondo yelped and turned to face her. He snarled.

Cyd retreated a few paces as they circled each other. Samuel wouldn't place himself in a gladiator's battle. Not risk his life in a one-on-one death match. His guile demanded better. Rondo feigned an attack, and she leapt back. The wolf made a deep, guttural noise. Was he laughing?

She charged, her quickness catching the dog flat-footed, sinking her teeth into its hindquarters as her claws raked the heavy fur on its midsection. Rondo howled and rolled across the grass to throw her off, then retreated a few yards. He barked and bared his fangs, then stepped back again and howled to the sky.

Her adrenaline kicked up a notch, stemming Sheba's visceral reaction to escape. She eyed the foothills with plenty of trees and heavy, dense brush in which to disappear. Rondo howled again.

Sorry, girl, but I need to finish this.

She stalked Rondo, looking for an opportunity, her hisses and snarls, a decent substitution for all the words she might have said. Blood stained the gray mat of fur along Rondo's flank. Her teeth would sink into his neck just beneath the collar with the next charge. End the miserable existence of the great Samuel Arkoff.

Rondo cocked his head then sat as if expecting a doggie treat. The dog smiled. Cyd froze with the yips and yowls of a pack of wolves cresting the grassy foothills behind him. A mix of black and gray and even several white subadults sprinted down the hillside, leaping charred logs, and aiming straight at them.

Reinforcements. Damn! She knew Samuel wasn't brave enough to fight her fairly. She thought to snap her fingers, then hissed with her own miscalculation. The ability to suspend time remained with her body back at the lodge. She turned and sprinted to the opposite hillside, eyeing low-hanging branches of pines and spruce capable of holding her weight.

Rondo raced just yards behind her, yipping loudly as if to lead the pack. She weaved between the huge trunks of Ponderosa pines and ignored the slender lodgepoles as the yipping of a hunting wolf pack gained volume. She spotted a tree that suited her needs twenty yards away.

An impulse, and she turned to charge Rondo. The dog squeaked its surprise and turned in cowardly retreat. Her teeth missed their mark, but a claw found Rondo's muzzle as she rolled past him. He leapt with the opportunity and clamped his teeth on her hindquarters. She snarled and raked his muzzle with her long vicious claws before he released his grip. Rondo withdrew a few yards.

Cyd bolted for the tree, the searing pain in her hip intensifying with each bound. Her claws dug deep into the thick tree bark as she scaled the old-growth pine with ease. Cyd fought off Sheba's innate instinct to find a limb higher up in the canopy, and instead chose a sturdy limb ten feet above the ground to watch Rondo as he sat atop a thick bed of pine needles and licked his wounds.

She licked her own wound. Samuel had suckered her into this farce. Goaded her right back into the suffocating mirage of childhood, trapped and helpless, his sphere of cronies arriving to play sick games, chiding her with an unearned pedigree, or disregarding her as much as they might an empty drink cup.

She growled. Her angelic ability to suspend time was rendered useless. The aid of Michael would never be delivered. Hunger and thirst would eventually force her to flee her perch. Weakened and outnumbered, she would be ripped apart by the wolf pack. Samuel had planned the ambush beautifully.

She hissed at two wolves joining Rondo below.

The wolf pack was large, at least thirty, unusual for a Yellowstone community. A skinny grey stood with its front paws high against the trunk and stared curiously at her. Others scurried beneath the tree sniffing her scent. She checked the higher branches then looked for the next available tree if she needed to flee.

Angry growls and yips of pain returned her attention. Ten wolves circled Rondo, yipping, and snipping at his hindquarters. Rondo turned and snarled at each intrusion, his hefty size failing to intimidate the pack.

A big black male charged in, baring its long canines, and found the fur on Rondo's neck. Others joined in, biting at his hindquarters and legs. Rondo shook off the black and spun on his hind legs, snarling at the attackers. The pack swarmed Rondo, trapping him within the umbra beneath the branches. Big males and subadults darted in and out to deliver a nasty nip.

Rondo's torture and approaching death sickened her. Samuel's life of torment precluded his soul from rising to face Michael's judgment. Rising on surefooted paws, Cyd offered a tiny mercy to her adopted father—a being that deserved none.

She snarled and roared malicious intent at the murderous gang.

The battle paused as the wolves stopped to stare up at their nemesis. She tensed and hissed again as if to attack.

Rondo barked at her, his lips stretching backwards. A smile, or a sneer? She could never be sure. He used the interruption to flee. His long legs hobbled by wounds, the dog was swift even with ten others chasing him like a wounded elk.

Cyd licked her wounds again as seven wolves circled the tree, barking as if taunting her to come down for a merciful death. She could wait them out. Time was on her side. Cyd chuckled mirthlessly at the ironic thought. The tree limbs shook violently with basso vibrations. Her claws stabbed into the branch as the trees all around swayed as if a gust of wind had blown through. She settled into the crook of the branch and squinted languidly at the wolf pack chasing Rondo up a grassy foothill. The pack would break off the chase at a territorial boundary, allowing Rondo a respite to lick his wounds and wander into the domain of another pack, to be rejected again. And again.

Samuel's transferred consciousness was now that of a pariah.

Cyd yawned and stretched her legs, then stood and hissed at the few dogs remaining, intent on a fight. She eyed a jumble of branches that offered a makeshift bed and walked a tightrope across flimsy dry branches.

Instinct caused her to extend her claws as the dry branch cracked, and she fell into the darkness.

CHAPTER TWENTY-TWO

HIS HANDS GRASPING AT AIR, a clone of Uriel lifted its body up through a crack in the concrete, his face contorted in anger. A violent tremor shifted the floor sideways. Uriel's bones and skull cracked and crumpled inward like a sheet of paper wadded for the wastebasket, to be sucked back down into the searing hell it had climbed out of. The gaping hole bubbled brilliant gold and blood-red magma. The deadly heat rippled the air. Angry fists pounded on the heavy door.

The rushing whoosh of the furnace slapped Michael from his fugue. The Fisherman wouldn't send him into battle just to die, not without a purpose, not without recourse. And he needed options.

Michael tore open the spiral duct. A rush of pine-scented air from the surface blew in his face. The gusts of cold air freshened his resolve. He stuck his head inside and looked up towards bright sunlight fifty meters away. His wings wiggled like puppies excited for a toss of the ball. He climbed into the duct and began shimmying up. His fingernails stabbed into the metal to hold his position as his toes found seams and rivets to cling to. A violent rumbling of the cavern sent dust and pine needles to fall into his face.

A sickening cackle just beneath him, the wet slithering of a clone glistening in embryonic fluid following. He refused to look down at the faces of those he once treasured. Gabriel. Uriel. Raphael. Sariel. Faces that had once inspired hope for humanity. Faces to offer a path forward in the eclipse of an apocalypse. Faces that would now deceive, spread Samuel's malignancy across the globe. Faces that could not be allowed to find their freedom on the surface.

Michael scoffed and climbed. The final battle was a myth, a misconception of religion and his own silly dogma. The ultimate battle against thousands of clones was never meant to be. Samuel's demons masquerading as emissaries of the Fisherman would spread like voracious flies to feed on the carcass of humanity. The misery and torment of billions might alone purchase entry for Samuel to negotiate a return to an ethereal kingdom. And with the Fisherman's second son as a hostage . . .

Michael climbed. The Fisherman needed him to keep the clones penned. A warning rumbled with each step higher. Keep the clones impounded. Then strike a massive fatal blow from deep beneath the caverns. The gambit was brilliant.

A strong, frigid hand snatched his ankle. Michael winced and glanced down to see Uriel smirking up at him. *Forgive me, brother.* He spread his wings and wedged his body tight inside the tube, then freed the steel rod hooked to his armor. He speared his metal rod down into the eyes of the abomination, jackhammering the steel into the sockets.

Slick white hands reached up past Uriel to replace him. The putrid stench of a demon soul rose into Michael's nostrils. He kicked free of the bloody hulk and scrambled up the tube. His pinched wings fluttered and protested the confinement of the metal tubing. He climbed higher as sunlight brightened his course.

A violent shake of the land sent the tube wobbling into a zigzag. The sunlight disappeared. Another rumble opened seams, popped rivets, and rained metal. A vicious aftershock reformed the tube into a passable portal.

Michael groaned. "I hear you, dear Father, I hear you." His wings trembled. "I hear you too. And if you have a suggestion, please enlighten me."

Twin spines of sinew and magic unfurled inside the tube, shoving Michael's cheek flat against the cold tin.

"I guess you do," Michael mumbled. "Go. Go. Go."

In a blur, Michael exploded up the duct. The wings shimmied and crawled, his cheek sliding against the smooth metal. He exploded through a mangled steel enclosure protecting the duct's inflow.

Another Uriel stretched out a long arm to grab at his foot, its cherubic face with red, bloodstained eyes contorted with a malicious grin. It bared sharp fangs only to be dragged back down into the shaft by a clone of Gabriel. The demons screamed like banshees, fighting themselves to exit.

Michael tore the metal cage from its foundation and slammed it into the gaping pipe. Blood and screams erupted as the tips of his wings pounded the metal down into the pipe like a cork. Demons pounded and scratched at the flimsy metal. The plug wouldn't hold long.

The dormant Old Faithful geyser erupted with plumes of white steam. Then morphed into a violent spew of burning rock and black ash, fouling the air with sulfur and ozone. Lesser geysers dotting the valley floor followed, shooting steam and ejecta high into the air.

A tremor rolled the surface of the parking area like a storm-churned ocean. The pole barns swayed, then collapsed like a house of metal cards. The lodge walls and roof buckled like fragile toothpicks. A demon found a gap for its hand to scratch at the metal blocking the tube.

Michael launched into the sky. He circled the hotel like a vulture, fighting the uplift of superheated thermals. The cedar shake siding on the Old Faithful Inn smoldered. Smoke billowed from the dormers and gabled roof. Hot rock and ash continued to fall like rain onto the dry roof shingles. Pine and spruce ignited in flames.

He flared his nostrils, searching for a familiar scent, then dove like a missile into a window on the second floor. Thick timber logs and Kevlar-reinforced glass shattered. Dust rained down. Shrill alarms pierced the air.

Folding his wings tight to his back, he frowned at the odd scene. Samuel. Cyd. Both appeared asleep on soft recliners, each connected to fiberoptic threads inserted into their necks. Arkoff Ports. A device Cyd had vowed to never wear. Wall monitors flickered and flashed numerical data. Beneath lay a crumpled old demon. The hilt of Cyd's knife protruded from the base of its neck.

A ferocious tremor sent the floor sliding sideways then buckled down into the floor below. Ancient timbers screeched with brutal splintering. Michael yanked the thin fiberoptic thread out of Cyd's neck port. He studied Samuel's response, and the fiberoptic connection. Michael's nostrils flared at the ugly stench of Samuel's soul. He lifted his staff to impale the Fallen one, a merciful reprieve for the beast tormenting the Fisherman's children. A final act denied him an eternity ago. A gesture of generosity and forgiveness only the Fisherman could offer.

Cyd grabbed his wrist. "Don't. Let him run."

Michael held the deathblow and frowned, confused. The ceiling buckled inward. A tremor rippled up the battered wall framing. The monitors went black. Dust and drywall rained from the upper floors. Cyd's raised two fingers as if to snap them but only checked the fiberoptic connection inserted in her father's neck.

"You will absolutely explain this." Michael picked her up and cradled her in his arms. His wings as a shield, he leapt out of the building. Burning roof trusses collapsed, splintering lumber and log timbers. Tons of burning timber collapsed into a pool of hot lava bubbling up from deep beneath the foundation.

Cyd placed her hand on his cheek. "A story for the campfire."

For the first time in almost a million years, an ancient super-volcano erupted, as if announcing Lucifer's demise. The shock wave with a blast zone of eight miles obliterated everything, natural and artificial, racing outwards another ten miles to topple large trees like blades of grass mown by a scythe. Rerouting the course of two mighty rivers in seconds. The sky darkened with plumes of roiling hot ash to trigger an angry storm of dry lightning. The incalculable volume magnified each second as Yellowstone exploded towards the heavens.

EPILOGUE

EVEN WITH THE NAKED EYE, a massive black spot fifty times larger than planet Earth could be seen on the surface of the sun. The angry star spewed geysers of plasma. Immeasurable solar storms of unparalleled magnitude flooded the planet with bursts of electromagnetic energy pulses. Computers, electric vehicles, drones, and most electronic equipment were rendered useless, including Arkoff Ports. Governments and civil order descended into chaos.

And yet the monsters had retained machinery insulated to protect their unholy torture of innocent souls.

Michael swooped down onto the flat oblong roof as flurries of hot, feathery ash fell from the sky. In the distance, Yellowstone continued to expel huge plumes of steel-gray ash, roiling up into the stratosphere to drift eastward. Bolts of dry lightning quickened in the dense clouds of ash and stone. A surreal light show unseen for eons. The incalculable volume of ash would cool the planet, fertilize barren fields, repair the scars of the monsters, and offer the planet a chance to slowly reclaim its glory.

Michael studied the mechanical equipment shielded behind wire netting and coated in a patina of ash. An assortment of rooftop backup generators purred and vibrated beneath his feet, their fan blades inhaling and exhaling air from the building. His nostrils flared with a familiar scent rising from an exhaust duct.

His wings folded on his back as he walked over to the roof parapet and looked down at Cyd waiting impatiently with her hands on her hips. Her ability to suppress time whittled at her patience to complete a task. A cord of wood needing to be chopped might reappear in the blink of an eye, stacked and ready for the campfire. Clothes, food, supplies often appeared inexplicably across the Moonie camp.

Cyd had expressed her desire for the Fisherman to return her to that special river, show her the nuances of fly fishing with all its subtle undercurrents requiring her patience, or offering metaphors, or teaching her lessons for life, difficult traits she strived to master. And with the memory of the Fisherman holding a special place in her heart, she followed Michael with blind faith, her goal singular: return to His kingdom.

She waved at Michael to return. She had promised Michael to let him enter his old prison first, but in Cyd's brusque style, warned all bets were off upon breaching the threshold of the front door. He dropped twenty feet without unfolding his wings and landed at her feet. He cocked his head and lifted his eyebrows, a warning for her to uphold the agreement.

"Yeah, yeah. I got it," Cyd grumbled. "But if . . . Oh, never mind. Let's go."

Michael leaned in and kissed her forehead. "Those last two words helped me escape this shithole."

Cyd frowned in confusion. Michael took quick strides, then pulled the front door free of its hinges and tossed the heavy glass into the parking lot. His memory sharp and his purpose determined, he entered the foyer to rip each door from its frame then proceed down a familiar corridor lined with Kevlar-reinforced glass windows. The empty pens of caged angels. The impregnable glass of each pen shattered as the sharp tips of his wings took their vengeance. Shards of composite glass coated the slick white floor. He turned to Cyd following close behind to offer a sly expression suggesting the petty revenge felt righteous.

She shrugged with a wry grin.

He lifted his face. The faint scent refocused his attention to increase his pace along the hallway. A slow, sickly cyborg stepped out from an alcove, its pincers whirring, its eyes aiming red lasers to guide its weapons. Michael blinked twice before the soulless man-machine fell to the floor with a fountain of pink fluid spouting from a small puncture in its neck. He glared at Cyd over his shoulder, who simply shrugged. Michael shook his head and snickered.

A familiar piece of glass made him stop and investigate the

oblong pen. Memories stirred from the white on white, the narrow bed mattress, the white desk, the toilet. He pressed his nose against the glass and tried to remember the blur of fifteen long years he spent inside. The monotony, the boredom, the futility, each day nurturing a growing madness like a sapling. He might've taken his own life a hundred times over had the opportunity presented itself. A revelation Cyd might want to hear, at the right opportunity.

Except the white room had served as the flame with which the Fisherman forged one of His greatest weapons, tempered with responsibility to the tribe of Moonies, and then honing His blade with Seth's kindness, exuberance, and purpose.

He turned to Cyd. "Leave this one."

The lights flickered. The hum of cool air flowing out of the ductwork sputtered and spat dust. He pursed his lips and frowned to accuse Cyd of a broken promise.

Cyd shrugged. "Well, I might've . . . Just go. She's waiting patiently, but not for long."

Michael blew out a breath and shook his head in exasperation. He moved quickly down the corridor, checking the empty enclosures on each side, until reaching a room identical to his own. A single white crib was bolted squarely beneath a bright white grow light. Tiny fingers wiggled and reached helplessly for the sterile overhead light.

A flutter in his chest made Michael swallow. Two cyborgs stepped out of alcoves inside the pen and . . . fell dead to the floor. Cyd stood over one, sporting a malicious grin and a bloody knife dangling in her hand. She beckoned him to hurry inside the cell.

Michael stood over the crib and stared at the pureness and innocence God bestowed on each newborn child, conferred with a soul tasked with finding a path through the currents, to be corrupted, or blessed, or maybe tossed aside, or endlessly swirl in the back eddies of life. Or find greatness. He picked up the child, inhaling the exquisite fragrance of a reborn soul.

A soul now free from the confines of monsters.

"We should go," Cyd whispered in his ear. "I'd race you but . . . C'mon, brother, lets go." She opened her cloak sewn from the softest pelts of dead demons to offer warmth for the child.

"Do you think she will accept it as her own?" Michael asked.

Cyd shrugged and held the child to her armored bosom.

Michael unfurled his wings, and with one mighty flap, the prison walls exploded out into a fenced exercise yard he had been forbidden to use. He took Cyd in his arm and shot up into a bleak grey sky. He soared like an eagle, the heat of a scorched earth lifting them higher and higher. He gazed down at the darkened husk of Idaho Falls.

A glint of spectral light hovered above a high school football stadium overwhelmed by refugees of the surrounding towns. He dove like a falcon towards the light until he circled like a buzzard above abandoned vehicles, murdered corpses of monsters and demons, the trainwreck of humanity. Rivers of people streamed towards the stadium from every direction, crowding the buildings and parking lot, and encircling the grandstands.

Michael swooped in close, then hovered above the source of the brilliant white light. A small angel walked carefully among the destitute, offering her hand, to comfort the wails of children, to silence the sobs of the displaced. A young angel sent down from Heaven, a beacon of hope, a mythical creature calling all to see that God had not forsaken them.

A scene that would play out around the world.

Michael screamed, the last angry remnants of imprisonment, a roar of pent-up rage lingering in his lungs. The ground shook. Thousands dropped to their knees, bowing their heads, frightened eyes afraid to look up at the grand spectacle of the great Archangel Michael soaring above their heads as if to judge their worthiness.

The young angel looked up at him and smiled. Josie. Gabriel's daughter, shimmering in white feathered armor, a slingshot hanging on her belt. She nodded an acknowledgment. Michael agreed.

"Show-off." Cyd punched his midsection. "Take me home."

Michael looked towards the White Cloud Mountains and shot up. "You gotta learn the nuances, little sister. That little stunt will be talked about for generations. Etched on stone tablets if that's all that remains."

Upwind of a radioactive bombsite and a close neighbor to an angry volcano, a bustling farming community labored in fields plowed from the backwoods of the angel's hideaway. Many raised their heads. Others waved long-handled hoes, shovels, and wide-brimmed hats as a greeting. The Moonies had abandoned their robes for the discarded clothing of Gabriel and the others.

The angels would not return, each given a new task by the Fisherman. Michael had searched for Raphael often, only to find a broad swath of dead demons buried in volcanic ash. He was left to wonder if Raphael had conquered, or been vanquished in the challenge set before him? Had Raphael wielding the Fisherman's mighty sword truly stemmed the tide of the demon horde?

Gabriel and the other great angels had toiled to lay the foundation for a new community, log homes, wells for fresh water, fruit trees, fields of grain. Zeke raised a long wooden pole in greeting. The range boss, now elected mayor, was a superior decision.

Michael dropped with a thunderous thud on a plot of churned dirt near Myra. She ignored his intrusion and kept chopping a shallow drainage channel in the hard soil with her hoe. Her sweat, or tears, indistinguishable. Mary leaned against her shovel and eyed him suspiciously. Cyd shoved the squeaky bundle into his arms and receded, then disappeared.

Michael stood tall, walking gallantly to offer his squirming gift to Myra. The child wailed a screeching noise. "The child is yours."

Myra craned her neck to see his offering then turned away to keep busy.

Michael swallowed a dry lump. "Then I will put the child to death. And its soul may only hope to find another mother."

Myra froze but gave the bundle a sideways glance.

Gritting his teeth, he said, "The Lord has commanded you take care of the child, or I return its soul to His kingdom."

Myra frowned at him with angry eyes that would simmer in resentment for eternity. She would never forgive him. And he would expect nothing less. The child cried. She took two steps and snatched the bundled child then stumbled across the churned soil to show the child to Mary. Their murmurs and cloaked smiles told Michael the child would be accepted.

Sometimes as sneaky as Cyd, Serah grabbed his arm and led him to an outcropping of basalt brilliant with flowering pumpkin lichen. She was muttering. Something about a sketch she needed. The voice in her head issued demands yet offered her fingers unmatched talent. She pushed Michael back to stand aside a hefty boulder upon which

Seth sat stroking the neck of a newborn lamb. She pointed at Michael and ordered him to wait then ran off to retrieve Cyd and pull her to stand on the opposite side of Seth. Seth giggled at Serah's command of the almighty angels.

For long minutes Serah posed hands and feet, feathers, fur, and hair, shushing the grumbling and giving Michael pause to reflect on the portrait she staged. He stared at a young boy with an infectious laugh, a disarming smile, an unbridled enthusiasm for life, and a healing touch. All the wisdom of a heavenly Father. Innocence and vulnerability.

And the purpose of Michael's birth crystallized in his thoughts. He was born to be an intricate cog in a kingdom the Fisherman had bequeathed to His second son. One for Seth to rule and heal. And Michael to serve as His protector. As His mentor. But above all else, as His friend.

Serah stood back and began sketching the portrait set before her, fingers and pencils working at a manic pace.

As if summoned, a skinny cougar eased in, its snout scarred, its legs ratty with foxtails and burrs. It circled once around Cyd's legs, taking in her scent, then lay at her feet. Cyd's usual dour expression transformed with a wide grin stretching across her face.

Unfazed by the predator's entrance, Serah talked to herself as her hand worked furiously. "That's it. You'll like this one."

Her scent rivaling fresh-cut sage, her dimpled cheeks cute, her plump lips moist, Serah sketched as Michael smiled thinly. And wondered if he was still human.

The lion and lamb resting at the feet of a new King. One to be protected by Heaven's army.

A second chance for humanity.

Held in the delicate hands of a child.

ACKNOWLEDGMENTS

THANK YOU FOR READING *GOD AND MONSTERS*. I hope you enjoyed this novel.

Keep exploring this world in *Rage of Angels*, the forthcoming sequel.

Please check out my other novels at rmgayler.com and join my mailing list for updates about this novel and others.

And if you have a moment, please review *God and Monsters* at the store where you bought it. Help other readers to discover this fantasy and tell them why you enjoyed the book. Thank you.

Thanks to Clara Abigail for superb editing and story enhancements.

Thanks to Michelle Argyle Park for an amazing cover design and interior formatting.

Thanks again, dear readers.

www.ingramcontent.com/pod-product-compliance
Lightning Source LLC
Chambersburg PA
CBHW020359120726
47904CB00002B/634